When you do things
13.50

Innocent things
13.51

For fun
13.52

But naive, frivolous things
13.53

There will be consequences
13.54

Especially if you keep doing them
15.45

The Lines Between Lies

Nigel Stewart

Published by Purple Parrot Publishing

Printed in the United Kingdom

First Printing, 2020

ISBN: Print: 978-1-912677-88-7

             Ebook: 978-1-912677-89-4

Purple Parrot Publishing

www.purpleparrotpublishing.co.uk

Edited by Viv Ainslie

Follow Nigel at:

  https://nigelstewart2017.wixsite.com/website

  Twitter: @menigestew

Acknowledgements

My old friend Chris Nebard and I had an inspiring, giggle-filled time roaming around Lancaster station one chilly evening in February 2020. Some of the photos that grace this book's cover are the result. As ever, Chris produced some astonishing images and it was incredibly difficult to pick the right ones – but that's a good problem. Thank you, Chris: it means a great deal to me that you're willing to work with me.

I'm blessed with many fabulous connections on Twitter, two of whom didn't hesitate to give me help when I asked for it. Thank you, Jules Swain and Lorna Atherton, for all you did.

Sometimes, any words of encouragement and enthusiasm are worth their weight in gold. Thank you:

Sarah Jamison

David Knaggs

Steve Morgan

AH

This is my second collaboration with Vivienne Ainslie at Purple Parrot Publishing. From the moment she saw the synopsis in 2017 her encouragement and love for this book never wavered. For making it what it is from what it was, thank you is not enough.

In memory of my brother, Charles
1953-2010

Prelude

Whenever I walk the streets of London I fall in love once or twice every twenty-five metres.

With the buildings, bustle and business.

All those shapes and sizes; old and new. Eras in stone, brick and concrete. Glassy, steely mirrors deflecting architectural critical disdain. Towers touching the clouds, wherein a formidable minority look down on this industry. Down here no-one ambles, waiting to see what happens. No-one takes time. There are no halts, with sudden smiles of recollection or bemused indecision. A default gait proves everyone is on it. There's stuff to get done; so much stuff.

And with the noisy grandeur of mobilised metal.

A sky full of planes, howling and straining. Helicopters flitting like wasps; spies, perhaps; or vertical taxis. And pricking the sky are the right angles of cranes, swinging to and fro as if conducting some mighty symphony. Roads crammed with boxes that seem linked to each other, all dashing to the next brake light and stop sign. Battling omnibuses bound for The City or maybe a Waterloo.

And yes, all right, with the endless stream of achingly smart, cool, gorgeous, unattainable women. They all seem perfect; as if their existence in this place has mystical significance; immutable and powerful.

If places can have a gender, perhaps London is the mother of all cities?

More than any of this, I fall in love with that sense of being at the centre of something Titanic: it's overwhelming. The knowledge that if I turn left at the next junction and keep walking, I would still be somewhere in London after two or three hours. It's a setting in which there are so many places to look that it's easy to conceal things. A round of hide and seek would last a lifetime, ready or not.

But listen to me. I'm supposed to despise this midden of power and glory and all it stands for. Me; a Northerner? I can't possibly like London or be in love with its coat of charms. I'm here on loan, with work as the sole motivation; here so that what I do can be consumed for a day or two before I'm put back in my box. I'm supposed to be desperate to get back on the train to Lancashire: to My North; my mills and chimneys; my back to backs; my new money enclaves. Where baths and cats get pronounced the same.

Where the women are just as unattainable, gorgeous, cool and smart.

Unless you ask the wrong questions.

Part One

Lines Drawn

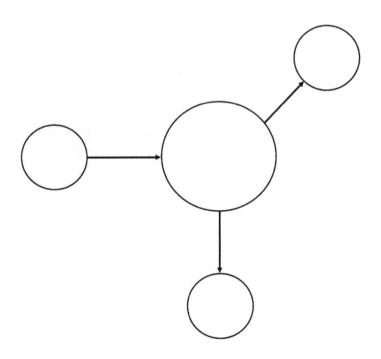

1

As I consider that left turn, my work phone's ringtone warbles in my headphones and I find my manager's face flashing at me.

'Annabel: hi.'

'Morning Ed. When will you be in the office? I expected you ages ago.'

'Less than five minutes. I'm just on London Wall now.'

'Right. We need to talk as soon as you get here. I'm leaving for Bucharest much earlier than expected so come straight up to my office. I'll fix some drinks.'

'No problem.'

Her tone softens a little. 'Can I get your usual?'

'Please.'

'Okay. See you shortly.'

Her voice had an edge, which usually means she has been handed a problem.

I'm still walking along the bustling pavements but I've stopped falling in love. Today's journey is almost over and this burst of mainly fresh air is all I will get for around twelve hours.

I travel to London every week and have been doing so for ten months. At first, the change in my routine was difficult but energising. I ran my trips like clockwork: preparation on Sunday evenings; early starts on Mondays. But familiarity turned the routine in to a process so now I enjoy more of my own time on Sundays, get up later on Monday mornings and travel much lighter on the same train I've always caught.

As I put my phone in a pocket and slide through the revolving doors at the office, I note that it's just after eight thirty-five. I'm slightly earlier than usual and feel a bit stressed by Annabel's comment about being late.

'Good morning Eduardo.'

Brandon, the morning shift security guy, is all smiles. Gemma, our receptionist, is less attentive.

'Hello Brandon. Hey Gemma. Good weekends?'

Brandon is full of football news. His teams won at the weekend: one in the FA cup; the other on a muddy pitch in Streatham. He has discolouration under one cheek and a vivid scratch on his neck. He pushes the internal visitor book across the counter.

'How about you Eduardo? How was your weekend?'

'I went walking near Wast Water. Listened to some music. Talked to my kids. The gym. Stared blankly at the next-to-nothing on TV. Same old same old.'

It prompts a discussion about the Lake District. Gemma has been and loved it. Brandon dismisses the notion of ever being that far from London. He's warming to this theme when a visitor ambles towards us, perky and pulling one of those wheeled laptop bags.

As I wait for the lift, I check my personal phone and browse through SocMed. I posted some photos late last night from my march along the shore of Wast Water and there are many Likes and several comments. Then I see that my university friend, Tina, has posted something impossibly rude about her failing marriage and I snigger at it. I don't know how she gets away with the things she says, especially since her husband seems to Like everything she ever posts. Once he commented on one of her posts and, in reply to him, she wrote: *Please stop stalking me you fucker.*

He Liked that too.

The lift cuts me off from the world for fifteen seconds of ascension to floor 5. The cabin smells stale, a smoker's unwashed shirt at the end of its second day worn. Just as I'm on the verge of a gag reflex, the doors open and I'm relieved no one is there to blame me for the aroma.

And anyway, I'm thinking about something I'm going to post; something I captured earlier on the train; it will raise smiles and laughter around the squad when I finally get the chance.

In the immediate vicinity of Annabel's office there are a couple of dozen hot desks, none with occupants. As I finish the last few steps to my chosen desk, I've trawled through a few dozen Peeps and liked everyone's photos on Postpix, most without even looking at them. She looks at me through her glass wall and I see she is talking into a wireless headset. A well-mimed series of gestures tells me to get settled at a desk and that she won't be long. I'm soon on the network and the emails I wrote on the train go skittering off around the globe. I see that my diary is unchanged since last night and I'm free until nine thirty.

'Ed - I didn't get time to grab our drinks. Let's go together now. I can tell you some of what you need to know.'

Annabel wears simple but very smart outfits and a subtle amount of something fragrant. Tall and slender, she has a firm handshake. She always shakes my hand when we meet. She also gives me a small hug whenever we part; but that's generally not so firm.

She seems to have forgotten any sense of my being late. 'Good trip?'

'Yes. Problem free, but man that train was busy after Preston. Full of civil servants getting their breakfast on the taxpayer.'

She laughs. 'Which leads neatly into something I need to tell you.'

We're in the lift now and she smiles across at me. There's been an occasional hint of flirtation in her smile ever since my divorce and we came very close to spending the night together in an hotel. She wasn't my boss then.

'Have I been busted for claiming too much wine with my evening meals?'

'Shit, no Ed. The world knows you're above reproach on that score. No: this is about you getting more expenses rather than increased scrutiny.'

This makes me frown at the back of her head as she strolls off to the coffee bar. Annabel orders her americano and my cappuccino with extra shot. I grab a chocolate muffin too. She pays and we head back to her office. By the time we get there, Annabel's outlined that she has been handed significant additional responsibilities without the luxury of a promotion. In turn, she needs me to pick up some of what she does.

We discuss the changes I need to embrace. I must provide leadership, direction and impetus for the team. It's the same deal for both of us.

'In effect you're making me a first among equals.'

'No. You're already that Ed. But I need you to step up to this pretty much with immediate effect.'

'Define *immediate effect* please.'

'You've got this week to close down whatever you can and get your head around what's needed. I'm in Bucharest from this evening, then all of tomorrow and Wednesday. Back Thursday; late morning. But it's business as usual despite that. I'll be in Sweden all next week working with this new client. I want you to be ready by close on Friday, okay?'

'I can be. How long am I doing this?'

'Until at least December - to all intents and purposes, a year.'

'Right. And you mentioned expenses?'

She reveals I will benefit from minor material things that I don't really care about.

'Do I get to piss in the executive toilets?'

She smiles widely. 'Don't be obtuse Edward. You know there is only sex and coke in there.'

We're both laughing now.

'Seriously: this isn't going to be easy for either of us, and I'm not going to offend your intelligence by pretending there'll be some higher reward at the end. We do what we have to do.'

'Do you still want me in London each week?'

'Absolutely. Yes. And plan to do three days instead of two; whatever fits your own needs. You need to be more visible up and down the food chain and especially with clients.'

I'm immediately thinking this through. It presents no obvious concerns aside from a slight change of routine. I'll need to switch some activities back in Lancaster. And it possibly opens doors.

'Do you need a definite answer today?'

'I need an answer now.'

'Okay: I'm fine with it.'

'Thank you Ed. I knew I could rely on you.'

She squints at me and seems to be hesitant about what to say next. 'There is one thing to think hard about, because it's a massive problem for both of us.'

I know what she's going to say, and it involves two words: Paul Wilson.

'Have you thought any more about Paul's behaviour last week?'

I need to be careful. Paul is my peer and reports to Annabel just the same as I do. On a conference call last Thursday, he flatly refused to do something she asked him to do, citing a greater than bearable workload then augmenting his refusal with a criticism of Annabel's management style.

He went too far and I can't defend him.

'Paul's attributes and experience are excellent. But it looks and feels like he's started to show signs that he can't cope.'

'Give me an example.'

'Project Andromeda: he lost weeks' worth of time and effort because he didn't properly update or maintain the project plans.'

'How do you know?'

I explain that the project's delivery director told me these problems, concluding that she will refuse to have Paul as lead on any of her projects.

Annabel looks troubled. 'Why didn't you tell me that?'

'I told her she should let you know her concerns.'

Annabel makes a short note on a writing pad. As she scribbles she tells me: 'You should have told me.'

'I'm sorry...'

She waves a hand dismissively. 'Paul thinks everyone is against him because he's over fifty-five.'

'Really? He doesn't look a day over fifty-two.'

'Let's keep it serious Ed. This will hit your desk after this week. He's a problem child: wants to disagree with everyone about everything; obsessed by whatever his job title and grade might be. He's living in the 1970s. So you better start thinking about how to deal with him.'

'That's really not fair Annabel.'

'Get used to it. Once next week comes around, you could be getting that kind of question from more important people than me. They will be coming to you about it.'

Am I being tested, or is this a friendly mentoring session? Nothing in Annabel's eyes suggests it's a half-baked challenge to pass the time of day. I'm required to slip on a pair of manager's shoes, even if I can't tie the laces.

'But you said I have no management responsibilities as part of this new world we're landing on.'

'Correct, but you will have to handle behavioural challenges from Paul and others.'

Whatever was causing her hesitant manner earlier has evaporated.

'Look at this.' She points at her laptop screen, where an email from HR summarises how Paul uses our internal messaging system to say some pretty abusive things about Annabel. She scrolls down to a transcript of a chat he had with a colleague. It's traditional worker whinging, at first. But then it descends in to pretty vile misogyny, bordering on libel. She scrolls down some more. I'm not surprised to see:

Paul W - and Ednatail is back again

Stewart H - he's here a lot

Paul W - if he got his tongue any further up BabyBel's 4rse he could lick her bowels

Stewart H - eeuuwww. LOL

Paul W - he's such a boring tw4t. A boring, thick, northern tw4t. I bet he voted for Brexit

Stewart H - why is he here so much?

Paul W - I have a serious concern that he is being groomed to take over from BabyBel

Stewart H - why?

Paul W - have you ever seen them together?

Stewart H - not really

Paul W - a total fkin mutual appreciation society mate. Birds of a feather, corporate bull5hitters

Stewart H - plenty like them around here mate

Paul W - I reckon they're sh4gging

'Should you be showing me this?'

My phone vibrates; it's fifteen minutes till my next meeting.

'I'm showing you in confidence because of the reference to you. It's a bloody good example of what anyone is up against managing this team.'

I try to soften the impact of what I've just seen. 'Well if I look at this objectively it's just gossip.'

'It is gossip; bar room banter; from the 1950s, as if that makes it nostalgic and cuddly - and therefore acceptable. But I'm not having it done on the company's time and on my watch. It's misuse of company systems too.'

'How did you know this sort of stuff was being said?'

She reaches over to her laptop and turns it away from me.

'Let's just say it came up in a conversation.'

I laugh: 'Are you checking my messenger conversations?'

'I am now Ed.'

'What do I need to do?'

'Nothing yet. But be careful dealing with Paul, especially once the shit hits the air-con about your elevated status.'

I nod. Annabel looks at me and there's something akin to sadness in her eyes, as if she doesn't want this burden. I thought it was her additional workload and travel commitments that had caused the edge in her voice earlier. But it's this: Paul Fucking Wilson and his one-man crusade against everyone and everything in his way.

'Paul will be on the weekly checkpoint later. Is there anything I need to do differently?'

Annabel shakes her head emphatically: 'I need you to move that call so it starts at eleven. I will announce the changes to our roles then run the call as usual. We still need the team's updates.' She sighs. 'I could definitely do without this trip to our favourite city.'

Her phone rings, she touches her headset and I make myself scarce as she starts talking.

Back at my desk I start all the admin needed to regularise this new order. A flurry of acceptance mails flashes up on my screen; Paul's is the first; the new eleven o'clock call is real.

On my personal phone I see I've also got a notification from the *matchmates* app: Gail from Leicester has Liked me. When I delve deeper into the details, I find that she has no photograph, describes herself as a Funlovinlass in the opening sentence of her profile and is looking for a man who can dance. That doesn't sound like *fun* or *lovin'* to me. She is of no interest whatsoever. I block her.

It's very interesting news that I will be spending more time in London. It creates a wider, deeper pool for my internet dating activities and, in less than two minutes, I've updated my profile to show that I spend plenty of time in the capital.

Word up, ladies.

Paul Wilson interrupts my dreams of nights in Maida Vale and Pimlico with a chat message: 'Ed – what's this additional meeting all about?'

I wait more than a minute before replying; the politics of dancing around handbags.

'Hi Paul. Annabel asked me to set it up. It's in lieu of the regular team call this afternoon.'

'Why didn't you just move this afternoon's call?'

I sigh, shake my head, tut and mentally call him a fuckwit. Within a few seconds, and with apologies to all, I've updated and corrected the schedule. Paul doesn't comment further.

I'm soon immersed in preparation for the team call. While I work through my updates, I'm constantly distracted by the knowledge that messaging and conversations might be tracked by the company. I've never used the tool for anything other than business communications with colleagues; low key and professional. Yet I feel guilty. It's troubling to be spied on, even when you've done nothing wrong.

Then I cheer up when I think that, in extremis, I've never used silly euphemisms and abbreviations instead of open swearing. Paul's quaint use of a 4 instead of an A is fundamentally naïve, or so it seems. The spyware isn't triggered because you might write *fucking hell* or call someone a bastard. You can type *far canal* or *bar-steward* all you like. Someone is watching and calculating; regardless.

By now I've finished the current status of my owned projects, so I call legal about the need for a Non-Disclosure Agreement on Project Martian.

Then Annabel messages me: 'Slight change of plan. I'm going to drop out once I've made the announcement. You can run the regular agenda for updates.'

With a few spare moments before the call, I go to BizSoc and change my role title to *Director of Project Management*. I love the illusions it's possible to create on there. You can be anything you like in the big wide world of corporate self-promotion and my branding is such an illusion, grown from all the seeds I've sown.

Annabel's announcement is met with silence. She ends it with the words: 'This is a challenging time for us all and requires adjustment and positive action. Give your full support to Ed, who has my and Peter's complete confidence and trust at all times.'

When she leaves, there are a few statements of support and congratulation then the call progresses smoothly towards its scheduled finish. Stewart Hatton, the other correspondent in the exchange Annabel showed me earlier, has the last word.

'I'm not sure the team can cope with the extra workload these changes are going to cause.'

Someone makes an assenting noise. 'If you're not running projects then that means everyone else gets more to do. We're just not resourced for that.'

'Like Annabel said, I will be running projects and nothing is being handed off to anyone else in the team.'

Paul picks up the baton. 'But you're not taking on any new work. Annabel made that clear: so inevitably we, and I mean all the rest of us, will be taking on more.'

'Only if there is more to do.'

He just wants to argue. I feel I'm not in control as Paul launches into a speech about his workload and how everyone is already working crazy long hours. It seems people are stretched beyond the tolerance of their elasticity. The call has overrun by more than ten minutes and I think about using the bluff about *taking this offline*. But even as I think it, I realise that will seem weak; a very early defeat in my tenure as make-believe leader.

Paul is still talking and, just as things seem bleak and complex, he throws me a lifeline by making a dumb remark about me being paid more to do the same job. Sometimes, people talk themselves out of a hole, then dig a deeper one and fall back into it.

'Paul, this isn't the place to discuss reward - for anyone - but for the record I am not being promoted as a result of this situation. Let's move on.'

And then another blessing drops from the sky and before I can refer to it, Georgi Mihaelescu does it for me.

'Paul; you need to look at Annabel's mail. It just arrived. First, she confirms what Ed said about promotion. Second, she mentions that she is getting two interns to support everyone. Third, she says Ed has accepted he has to do more work and we should all follow that lead. So that's what I'm going to do.'

The call ends fifteen minutes late. I message Georgi to thank her. She comes back shortly with: 'No problem. You always get my support and if you need anything while you have so much more to do, ask me for help. I will give it.'

Annabel's mail was timed to perfection and it means I'm smiling contentedly as I settle down to tasks and activities that take me through to the early afternoon and a pause for lunch.

The canteen at our office is a nice enough place to take a break and by one o'clock I'm in there with my iPad checking emails, but none of them is important. While I slurp my way through a bowl of soup, I get on to SocMed and post something that's been making me giggle since it happened on the train.

There was a smartly dressed man sitting in the seats ahead of me and, not long after he joined at Lichfield Trent Valley, he was busily engaged on his laptop and phone. Both machines were top of the range, and his MacBook had an hypnotic screen saver that kicked in after any short period of inactivity. Through the gap between the seats it was easy for me to see what he had typed in an email, as well as a series of exchanges on his messaging app.

The email was titled *Fixing Troublemakers* and its opening sentence indicated a complex, controversial message to follow. The messages were a stream of filth for which sexting was a wholly inadequate term. I had no business to look, and he had no business to be so indiscreet, especially about his company's workforce. But I was captivated by his toys and amused by the notion that he might mess up. I was willing him to mistakenly include a phrase like *I loved it when you slid that champagne bottle up my arse* in the email. I couldn't resist taking a couple of pictures between the seats.

Looking at the photos now, I'm giggling away to myself about the fact that expanded and enhanced, it's possible to see several details - including the email recipient's name. The text of his physiologically graphic chat with Foxy is less easy to read, and her small profile photo is blurred; perhaps that's a good thing.

I save versions of the photos that reveal some of this detail and, as I finish my soup and start crunching through an apple, I'm setting up a post on SocMed that includes the two photos.

'Look at the state of this lads!'

Before I've started tidying away my things, Likes are popping up. I knew Tina would be first, but others follow.

It gives me a buzz: doesn't everyone like Likes?

When I clear away my tray, I notice Annabel at a table talking with Kate Farmer, our Human Resources lead in the UK. They are smiling, somewhat severely, through whatever topic is in train but the smiles fade to dutiful solemnity when they are joined by Kalvinder Lal, our Security Director. It takes him no time at all to finish a sandwich, then the three of them stand and leave the canteen.

I look around to see if anyone else has noticed this alliance: all I see is people eating, talking and laughing in a room filled with the smells of food bought from the cheapest bidder.

The hot desk area has filled up with people and noise. On the room booking system I see that Devon is vacant, so I grab my laptop and move there for the rest of the afternoon. I always run my project calls in a private room, mainly so I'm not tied to a desk. I like to stand and walk around the room while I listen to the inputs of others via speakers or headset, perhaps making notes on a flip chart. Somehow, I think better when I can move and have a changing landscape, even one with four walls, a door and a triple-glazed window.

It's how I work best, and helps me run meetings effectively: facts first; details if essential; focus on timing; remove barriers; convert negative to positive; be clear and open about threats and how to counter them. There's no gossip or speculation. No unfounded optimism or pessimism. Just facts.

My afternoon disappears in this haze of lucidity. And there's somehow an added bounce in my style and demeanour: I'm not only in charge of these seven projects; I'm also in charge of the others in charge. *Le Grand Fromage*, picking up *BabyBel's* crumbs.

Then an email from Annabel drops into my inbox and it drizzles on my parade. She's at the airport and the few lines of text are clearly about venting.

'Have had a shit-storm of mails and complaints about your new status, none of which does anyone any credit. Sometimes I just don't need this. Be careful. Also, I'm back a day early: will be in the office on Wednesday so can you arrange to stay till then? Don't forget to upgrade. Also, London is full of people protesting the proposed visit by POTUS. Nightmare on the underground.'

I tell her I'll sort out the additional night and ignore the reminder about upgrades. I don't want any more snide remarks about favouritism.

My last meeting is with Alan from Legal. He hands me a draft contract and reels off a series of instructions and a statement that he thinks he's covered everything.

Like a rabbit caught in his headlights, I nod my agreement and he departs with a cheery farewell. I'm alone once more to complete the actions he outlined, whatever they mean.

When I leave the office at seven, I know that all my projects are on track: green lights all the way.

Gemma has gone, and Brandon's colleague Jarrod is outside having a cigarette. The vacant reception area could be in clear and present danger, but Jarrod needs that smoke. As I walk past his clouded ambience, I can't be bothered to do more than nod cordially at him. I've done my job today plus a whole new set of things I didn't know I'd be doing when I left home fourteen hours ago.

2

It takes five minutes to walk from our office to the hotel. But I want air, even air that is filled with exhaust fumes. So I go the long way round, via Cheapside and Prince's Street and plug myself in to some music. I need to zone out, avoid my work phone and, with a chanting soundtrack of monks, watch the commuting City simmer down from boiling point. Even at this time, past seven o'clock, the main streets are chaotically busy. Back home, any feeble pretence at a rush hour is done and dusted by six: yet this madness seems almost eternal.

The music dims briefly and a default ping indicates a text: it's Dave Ellis, checking that we are still having dinner.

I reply: 'Of course. Did you doubt me?'

'I know your busy. You executive typoes are hard to tie doqn. Are you sure you can spare th time for me?'

'Stop taking the piss. And sort out your typing.'

'Fuck mytyping. And I've takn the piss from you for twenty something years E and I'm not stoppping now. Wher are you?'

'I'll be at my hotel in five minutes.'

'We're still good for wight thirty?'

'We are.'

'Then I will heas to the station now. See you shorty. Looking forwad to it.'

'Likewise: and don't call me shorty.'

He sends no more messages.

As I walk the last couple of hundred metres to the hotel it feels that my working day is finally done and I can enjoy the coming evening. Dave and I have been friends since university but, in spite of my regular trips to London, it's been several weeks since we last saw one another. This will be the first time this year.

When travel to London first became an occasional feature of my working life, I used to stay with Dave and Ella more or less every trip. I loved having a home from home. But this was a routine that didn't become part of the process. Late finishes and early starts were a burden on my hosts. It had to be stopped and I learned that business travel cannot be blended with a social life. The trips to their home stopped, replaced by an occasional catch up with Dave.

We talk most Fridays as an end-of-week summary and a pre-cursor to the weekend. But that is all we have because of Dave's refusal to use social media. His texts, fumbling and inaccurate, are sparing and reserved for moments when he guesses it is inconvenient to call.

The hotel's over-familiar revolving door seems less lacklustre with the knowledge that Dave will walk through it later and we will enjoy a couple of hours together.

Check-in is smilingly, routinely quick and I'm soon in my room. It's the standard anodyne box within a box, lit subtly but soaked by dull colours. I put my keys, cash and work laptop in the safe, ready to be locked, and it's not long before I'm all set for some on-line catch up.

My priority is family.

Beth answers, only to say hello and she loves me but she's in a theatre group session till ten. We can chat later.

Joe's phone goes to voicemail. 'Joe, it's Dad. I'm in London so this is just my usual check in to let you know. Will try you by Vidicall later. Message me if you're not around. Love you son.'

He won't reply.

I've a new Chattabox follower, *&kirsteemay*, but no idea who she is. I use Chattabox for two things: to share small thoughts about literally nothing; and as a route to ask questions or get things done by errant retail service providers. I don't have any earth-shattering insight and I'm completely aware that I have no real reason to have an account. I don't have a voice that matters. I'm not selling anything. I don't have any need to tell the world what to think and feel, just because I think and feel it. *&kirsteemay* is most certainly not interested in me nor any of my stuff. Smiling happily from her profile picture, she is about twenty and it's a banker that her sole interest is in me as a number on her list of followers. If I follow back, it will be minutes before a DM lands, saying *hi*.

My SocMed post from lunch time has caused much hearty amusement: lots of Likes and Laughs; and some comments, ranging from:

what a rude man!

to

twat!

to

some people would be sacked for that

to

it's utterly indiscreet

to

he's a cockwomble.

As I'm scrolling through the post, one of my friends adds a comment saying, *I've messaged you.* Within seconds, two devices provide audible proof of that statement.

Jason Mason works for an IT outsourcing company and is incapable of saying anything in brief. This message is no exception, full of paranoid statements about online security. And it's so long that by the time I reach the end I've forgotten whatever point he was making.

I reply, 'Thanks Jason, but don't worry. No-one reads my drivel. Just friends. I doubt anyone even clicked on the photos to see any detail.'

His reply is instant. I sometimes think he's always online, always available, always in touch. Probably just the same as I am.

'Just make sure your settings are OK and you only post privately.'

I tell him I am a very private person, but he doesn't grasp the playful tone and ticks me off again for being too open on SocMed.

I'm soon on *matchmates* checking all my profile hits and Likes. There's an array of Smiles from faraway places, but just three are

27

close to Lancaster. I get quite excited about the two in London, but they are under thirty and that's not what I'm looking for.

Closer to home, Juliet (45) is in Richmond and has a labrador in every one of her photos. She has two kids still at home. Loves walking and is as happy in wellies as she is in a frock. Wants to travel to new places. Dislikes liars, cheats and snakes.

Snakes? What the actual fuck?

The other two are both on the Fylde Coast in Lytham St. Anne's. Sensing a challenge, I scroll through the content of Mimi's profile. Likes cocktails, cuddles, dining out and running her own business. Divorced, with a son just starting university. I look at her profile photo: a soft-focus shock of platinum blonde hair frames a perfectly shaped face with dazzling blue eyes and urinal-white teeth. Other shots include the ubiquitous selfie pout with lips pushed out: another shows her in that pose - hand on hip, slightly side-on, best foot forward, curves accentuated by stance. It's alluring, apparently, but in this case the affectation is ineffective. Mimi is forty but her photos suggest she still thinks she's nineteen and her words drip with the false, broken clichés of a hipster. By the time I've looked at her ninth photograph (there are thirteen) I've made up my mind that this is not a match I should strike. I'm soon completing her profile in my own words: *thinks an Art Gallery is where you keep the crayons; likes theatre and films but only if they have dancing and singing; dislikes poor people, immigrants and lefties (one and the same thing, of course); only puts out for blokes in Astons; looking for that certain special someone so they can dress up like a circus act and do coke together before heading into the glossy, leafy, downtown lights.*

Ignore.

Run.

But don't hide.

Then Karen looks nice. Two photos show an open, slightly shy smiling face. Her words suggest she is unsure about being on the site; an introvert perhaps, still smarting from wounds she thinks will never heal. No long list of likes, dislikes or demands. Just an implicit statement of frustrated loneliness and anxiety that there is no-one who can or will makes things better. I read through her words several times and review her photos repeatedly. There is a pained loveliness about Karen that I find irresistible.

I decide to send her a Smile - a trivial attempt to suggest she should be happier.

As I touch the smiley icon and my opening shot flies off into the London sky, a pop-up tells me that Carla from Bradford is viewing my profile. Then she starts Liking stuff: lots of stuff; all my stuff. Then she sends a Smile.

The rush I get from this attention is hard to quantify. It's like a definitive endorsement. Someone, somewhere has looked at my five photographs, read my truthful but restrained profile and is so besotted that she already has her hand down the front of her jeans. I feel loved and desired; fancied and required.

When I check further, Carla is almost certainly not the kind of woman to masturbate while looking at me on a phone or computer screen. But she is very interesting indeed: there is no string of platitudes; she loves places to see, not places to be seen in; she loves live jazz and art galleries; she loves to meander around towns and cities (*meander*: that is such a beguiling word; Carla is neither fussy nor judgmental). She's confident, perceptive, understanding and has great empathy. She likes to be in the woods, walking and thinking. I laugh aloud at several of her statements. There is an edgy humour at work here.

Her photo shows a raven haired, blue-eyed beauty. No pouting or strutting. She looks real, not painted.

This is someone I have to get to know.

It's insane isn't it? A virtual world of dating and romance which is in fact nothing of the sort. A marketplace more like. An invitation to treat. An exchange of hopes, wishes, desires and fibs. I've been using various dating sites on and off for nearly three years, and, despite some vague kick-starts, have achieved nothing whatsoever from it. Just a debit on my bank balance. It's like heroine (or maybe, these days, like gin): a hopeless addiction in which what is consumed delivers nothing more than a buzz or a hit, or a temporarily inflated ego.

Carla Likes me within the confines of the dating site process. She's sent every possible indicator of that and has reviewed my profile again and again. It has to be done. I return all the favours and, after a short break in which I drink from my free bottle of sparkling water, I send a short message: 'Hi Carla, thank you so much for getting in touch. Shall we dance? Teddy.'

While I wait for her reply I wonder if *Carla* is a code, synonym or alias. Technically forbidden on the site, it wouldn't be difficult to not be who or what you say. Carla probably really is Carla and might actually live in Bradford. But her name might just as easily be Chardonnay or Eupheme.

She's replied before I drain the bottle.

'Hi Teddy, this is so weird isn't it? Cx'.

I look at my watch. It's just after eight. Freedom fighters permitting, Dave's train from Wimbledon is probably rattling along the District line between Victoria and Embankment and I can't possibly keep him waiting when he gets here. He's always punctual. His semi-retirement means he has the time to be where he says he will be with no risk of external intervention. But I have to make sure Carla is hooked.

We begin the chat.

'It IS weird. But thank you for your smile. The virtual emoji was a real treat after a long day, but your actual smile is very lovely indeed.'

'Thank you, Teddy. I love that photo of you standing on the beach. Where is that?'

'Near La Rochelle. It's from last summer.'

'All my photos are less than a year old. How is Lancaster today? It's ages since I was there.'

'I'm in London! I come here every week on business. My company's UK head office is here. But when I left Lancaster this morning it was chilly, dark and a bit sinister.'

'LOL. I love London, but only in small doses.'

'I love it too. I think if I had unlimited funds, I'd want to live here.'

'If I had unlimited funds I still wouldn't live in London. But I'd go there every week to do something crazy xx'

'It's also ages since I was in Bradford. Used to go there to visit friends, who've since moved on.'

'I'm in Skipton, not Bradford. It's always been my home.'

Well there you go.

Carla is closer to me already.

'I've just been looking at your profile again. You like listening to Gregorian Chant!??! That must make you unique on a site like this. Or anywhere.'

'We need to tell the truth. And I love that music. It's so soothing. I drift off to sleep listening to it every evening. There is no rhythmic pulse, no words to sing along with or challenge or distract and no harmony to make you fall in love. There's just Latin; and echoes.'

'You're not selling it well – LOLZ.'

I'm not sure how to feel about that and there's a long gap that I don't know how to fill. My iPad screen shows me it's 20:21 and, right now, Dave will be marching up King William Street from Monument station. I need to close Carla down, but in a manner that isn't blunt or dismissive.

She helps me: 'It's been lovely chatting, but a friend has just called. Can we chat more later?'

'Of course, but it will be quite late. I'm meeting a friend for dinner and he hates me spending time on my phone while we're together.'

'That's fine: like my profile says, I'm a night owl. Message me on here when you're free: anytime up until 1am.'

'Perfect. Have a lovely evening.'

My iPad, with all the thoughts and revelations it contains or accesses, is locked down in the safe and soon I'm in the lift heading to the bar.

3

Dave is there chatting amiably to the guy serving drinks. Two pints of Stella are glistening drippily in front of him and he's holding a bottle of wine, glancing at it intermittently during his discussion. He hasn't seen me, and I tap him on the shoulder. Our hug of greeting is warm, beery and affectionate. We learned to do this as part of the catharsis I experienced during my separation and divorce, as if our years of friendship finally found a real reason to be overtly tactile.

31

'Jake here is telling me that this is the best red in the house. What do you think?'

He hands me the bottle. It's a Chilean Cabernet Sauvignon with a simple label.

'How much?'

'Expensive enough to keep its head above the usual suspects. Cheap enough to warrant a second bottle if we fancy it.'

I wince inside. Dave is a big drinker, with almost no reasons to refrain from alcohol on a school night.

'You decide Dave. I'm working tomorrow and need an early start. But I do need that lager.'

As he hands me my pint, he has a broad smile and, once I've taken a gulp, we finally shake hands. With a nod, we head to one of the tables and its neighbouring sofas.

'How was your trip this morning?'

'Hassle free: train loaded with suits and scary self-importance. Also, caught sight of a bloke sending threatening emails while sexting.'

'Those were the days.'

'Indeed. I was desperate for him to mix up the two recipients.'

I explain how I'd taken photos of the scene and revealed it to the world on SocMed.

'That sounds like a very silly thing to do.'

'It was fun. It made people laugh.'

Dave looks at me with a combination of disbelief and puzzlement.

'Not the action of a competent young executive though.'

'Exactly. Nothing wrong with stepping off my pedestal occasionally. All work and no play...'

'... makes Teddy indulge in silly games.'

He's smiling, but this is direct criticism. 'Was this some kind of holier-than-thou exercise? Naming and shaming?'

'No. Just a bit of harmless fun. I like making my friends laugh.'

'Mmmm. I'm sticking with it being a silly thing to do. Are you ever not on those pointless media? Seriously; you're forty-four in three months. Is it really essential for you to be so wired to the world?'

We're sitting on the plumped-up soft sofas which are comfortable but hopeless for any combination of drinking and conversation. I'm reclined so far back in mine that I can smell its inherent dustiness. It turns every attempt to reach for my pint into an ab-straining sit up. It also makes me feel intimidated by Dave's challenges. He's watching me closely over the top of his glass.

My fight back is somewhat meek. 'It isn't essential.'

'Yes it is. Ella often shows me your proclamations. It seems that some days you are constantly in broadcast mode.'

I wonder if Dave gives his wife this much stick about SocMed, where she and I are friends. She's more of an addict than I am, especially when it comes to posts about their daughter's progress at an American university. Dave distracts me from these thoughts by necking his pint to empty and nodding at my two-thirds-full glass.

'Same again? And shall I set up a tab? What's your room number?'

I take a half-hearted quaff, say yes to both and hand him my room card. He's soon back, taking a swallow of beer as he walks. I ask him about his plans for the rest of the week.

'Apart from tomorrow, not much. Ella is off to Madrid early afternoon for a conference. I will take her to Heathrow then head over to see Dad.'

'How is your father?'

'All things considered, he's pretty well. Still very affected by mum's death and I think he feels lonely, despite the regular attention from Charlotte and me. He loves it when C goes because he adores the kids.'

'Well give him my regards.'

'I will. He always asks after you, and whether you've ruined any more carpets.'

We laugh at this. Once, when a stridently drunk eighteen-year-old, I threw up all over Dave's parents' house in Witney.

'Carpets and me are old enemies. They are banned from my home.'

'Really?'

'If you ever ventured north of Silly Cunt Valley you might

know that my home is a temple to *hygge* and the delights of Scandi-style. No carpets and categorically no cushions.'

'It sounds ghastly. And wilfully masculine. But is this man-cave open to any womanly wiles?'

'I don't know what you mean.'

'I mean are you fucking anyone at the moment? Or is your exile from relationships a never-ending saga?'

'We speak every weekend Dave and you never enquire after my sexual welfare. When I'm reclined in submission on a badly maintained sofa in a public place, I get your unshakeable interest.'

'This is a conversation worthy of a face to face encounter.'

He's made me laugh but I still try a decoy.

'The two are mutually exclusive, aren't they? Fucking and relationships.'

'I suppose so. But seriously: don't you want to be part of a couple again? It's been a few years since yo-yo panties pissed off.'

Dave's reference to my ex has me giggling. He adored her all through our college days and beyond and occasionally travelled north to stay with us when Amy and I created our marital home in Lancaster. But when she decided to run to be part of better things, he became indignant with loathing for her. It was more than loyalty or friendship. Dave detested what she did to me, despite the full disclosure of what I did to her.

'Actually, I am seeing someone on and off. We met at a beer festival. It's conveniently and mutually uncommitted.'

'So, fucking and no relationship?'

'Yes.'

'It's not enough for you. You know it isn't. What's your plan? You're a good-looking guy with a lot to offer. You can't seriously tell me there's no-one out there.'

'I didn't say that.'

The guy from the bar interrupts to say our table is ready and he's loaded it with our bottle of wine. Dave swallows a half pint of lager in one go and we walk across the dividing line between the fading luxury of the bar's sofas and the restaurant's starchy linen. As we take our seats, I feel my personal phone vibrate a few times: single pulses, not a sustained tingle to indicate a call.

It will irritate Dave beyond words if I interrupt our evening by looking at either of my phones. My restraint is almost unbearable. I want to know the who, what and why of all this buzzing.

'I thought you were using a dating site. Have you had any luck?'

A waiter arrives and opens the wine for Dave to try. He also reels off a list of specials: a superfluous speech, for a blackboard advertises these options for all to see. But it has given Dave time to sniff at the wine, take a tiny sip and nod his acceptance.

'That would be lovely with some duck. Anything like that on the menu?'

'Yes sir. There is pan-fried duck with Girolle mushrooms and a Madeira jus.'

Dave nods again and looks down at his menu. The waiter slips away.

'I do use an internet dating site, yes. It's good and bad.'

'How do you mean?'

'Well it's all a process. There's no real engagement. You just look at a few photos, read a few lines of text and make a judgement.'

'A shop window?'

'Pretty much, yes.'

Dave is scanning the menu. 'I fancy the scallops, then the duck.'

I wish I shared his gift for looking at a list of dishes and deciding within minutes what to have. All that is easy on *matchmates* but with food I'm much less resolute. It takes me ages to choose because I get too embroiled in the detail and in the right combinations. Dave just instantly knows what he wants to eat. His decisive thrust makes me focus on the menu to catch up with him.

'Tell me about this bimbo you're seeing then.'

The waiter is back to enquire if we're ready to order. Dave raises an eyebrow at me, and I tell the waiter to give us five minutes. Dave shakes his head.

'Bit judgemental there, mate. She is categorically not a bimbo.'

'Yes, all right. But let's hear it.'

'She was at the beer festival with a bunch of friends and we ended up standing together at the bar, ordering the same beer. Small talk ensued about how her husband would hate the beer we'd chosen. A bit later, I'm back at the bar and she's alongside me suggesting we try a blonde rather than a pale. I'd just got a new phone, and she asked me to unlock it so she could have a look. I wasn't really paying attention, but it all seemed innocent – she looked at the screen and weighed up the handset. After that I didn't see her again but shortly after I got home, she replied to the message she'd sent herself from my phone. Flirting became a conversation. And it grew from there.'

'Her husband?'

'Yes, she's married.'

'You silly prick. That really isn't good, is it?'

I've decided to have beef carpaccio followed by the chargrilled tuna and make a gesture to the waiter that we're ready now. I make Dave shake his head again by asking for a bottle of sparkling water.

'I don't spend too much time fretting about the situation. And Jude doesn't spend time telling me her woes.'

'Jude the Detour then.' He makes a huffy, stuffy noise through his nose. 'It sounds like you're settling for something easy. How do you actually feel about her? Would you settle down if she was free?'

'I've never thought about it. The whole point of what we're doing is that it's a distraction for her from a bad decision, and a distraction for me from being celibate and lonely.'

'So you're using her?'

'We're using each other.'

My personal phone has vibrated five or six times since we sat down. I look around to see if there are toilets nearby - a sanctuary in which I might be safe to review all this incoming.

'Are you happy? Does having an on-tap hook-up and a virtual flirtation domain add up to the sum total of your desires?'

'For now, I think it probably does.'

'You told me once that, when Amy left, you thought it was a release and a good thing. That it provided an opportunity to adjust what you needed in your life and find someone right.'

'Yes. That's what I thought would happen. But with each month and year I've realised I can't define what *right* is. I don't know what I'm looking for.'

'But isn't there a number one priority? That the right person makes your heart skip a beat and your trouser front expand?'

'Well probably. But that second criterion was the whole sorry problem with Amy. Huge physical attraction, on both sides, but when the desire and passion dried up there was a gaping hole in the connection.'

Dave looks at me sadly.

'Sorry mate, I didn't mean to dredge all that up again. Let's change the subject.'

'No, there's no need to do that. It's fine. I know you mean well.'

Dave's gaze seems to combine great love for me with a confused concern. He is about to reply to me, but our starters arrive and are placed on the table with great finesse and showmanship by the waiters. We are the only people in the restaurant, so we get a waiter each. Over in the bar, an assembly of macho male business types is sitting behind their plates of club sandwiches, chips and sides. Some have wine or beer; most have water or a softie. Dotted around the bar area, isolated, imprisoned, these men are the embodiment of their respective companies' travel policies.

'I think you should stop farting around online and seriously consider ditching your adulterous wanderings with this Jude. Get out into the real world Teddy. Join a walking club or something. Or go and lurk in the pubs and bars in downtown Lancaster. Find a wingman and do some of what we used to do. Ah, those first-year nights.'

He's right. I know he's right. But all that was much, much easier when we were nineteen. He doesn't realise how hard I find it now, and how easy it is to fall back on the remoteness of sites like *matchmates*. Nothing ever feels like a failure on there, even if it never delivers success. I think about Carla's smile and want to look at it on my phone. I drain my remaining lager and try my beef. It's pretty good. Dave is also noiselessly sampling his food.

'Dave - this beer has gone straight through me. I just need to pop to the gents.'

He looks up, chewing. 'Leave your phone.'

'What?'

'Leave your phone. I can tell you're desperate to get away from reality and do some ShattaMed gratification. And I'm not letting you.'

Bang to rights.

I take out my work phone and place it screen down on the table. Dave moves it towards him, like a defending, guardian angel.

'And the other one.'

Double jeopardy. I pull out my personal phone and place it alongside the other.

'Right: off you fuck.'

Deprived of my fix in the gents, I'm soon heading back to the table and, as I approach, I see Dave examining one of the phones. The cheeky bugger.

'Couldn't resist a quick peek then?'

'If it wasn't for your password, I'd have added a flirty note telling you how much I admire a bitter man. But actually, the reason I looked is that while one phone vibrated constantly in short bursts, the other one suddenly erupted like an unfettered dildo. I felt like a fucking game show host. But more to the point you've missed a call. I suppose you better check it.

The missed call is from Costin in Bucharest and there's a voice message symbol too.

'Dave, I hate to interrupt but this is work and I need to see what's wrong.'

'You don't need my permission to deal with work: just do it.'

I plug in my headphones and listen to the message, memorising the key points: go-live on Project Shotgun is a week away; one of the lead suppliers won't agree to our standard terms; without their software, Shotgun is shafted; procurement aren't helping with any kind of plan; main stakeholder is doing her pieces about risk.

It's only a matter of five or six hours since Costin reported that Shotgun is on track. Someone has messed up or lied. Possibly both.

'Do you need to make any calls?'

'I'm not making calls at this time. My colleague is in Romania and it's almost midnight there. Nothing can be fixed this evening. But I need to send an email.'

Dave gets up and wanders over to the waiters. I see him indicating our table and nodding ensues. It takes me about ten minutes to complete two actions in which some colleagues are advised about the problem and others are given instructions. I log questions that need answers and schedule a meeting for the morning. As an aside, I tell Costin to stop working and get some sleep.

Dave asks me about the problem, and I give him a synopsis. I also mention my temporary elevation in status.

'I've always admired the way you can focus so quickly on things Ted. As for your new responsibilities, it sounds positive to me. You must be highly regarded.'

'Maybe. I'm definitely seen as a safe pair of hands but never sure how far up the chain that view exists. Annabel trusts me completely, especially with difficult things.'

I explain the dilemma caused by my colleagues and how I am inevitably going to get dragged into whatever happens next with Paul Wilson.

As I tell my tale, Dave is watching me while sipping from his wine glass. I've never, ever seen him sip alcohol before. He's a gulper; always. But then he takes a slug of wine that empties his glass. He refills it, then offers me a drop more and says: 'You must be seen as capable and trustworthy at least one level above your immediate manager. She can't make a decision like you've just outlined without some sort of sponsorship. And that means you will be well supported in whatever you do, or don't do, regarding this disruptive buffoon. We should celebrate your importance with a toast: to elevated status!'

He raises his glass with mock solemnity, and I can't stop myself clinking it with mine. For several moments we are chuckling contentedly at Dave's salutation. This leads to a longer spell of largely irrelevant chatter in which there is no controversy. He's stopped digging up the bones of my relationship status and we stick to the economy, politics, the state of the nation and the world. These aren't topics we ever avoid, but our hearts aren't in them. One of the reasons our friendship was formed so readily at university was this lack of commitment to an ideal. We swayed left then right. We wanted the capitalist dreams of comfortable wealth, then foamed at the mouth about the failing Major government. We saw bad in the good, and good in few things. There was perversity in the fact that Dave's education at a posh school in Cumnor had given him pink-tinged views. These amply countered the old-school toryism I hauled through my time at a Lancaster secondary modern. We jousted through a few encounters in the Guild during our first term at Birmingham and were soon such firm friends that I was invited to spend the coming New Year celebrations with Dave and his parents.

Once I'd spent Christmas at home with Mum and Dad, I jumped on a train to Oxford where Dave met me in the station concourse. Outside, his father smiled at us from a gleaming old MG 16/60 and we were soon laughing together, while slithering around on the leather upholstery for the short trip along the A40 to Witney. After several malt whiskies to celebrate a newly welcomed guest, I was allocated one of sundry spare rooms where I slept until a second was needed.

We were out drinking in the town every evening and I learned that Cotswold girls had a way with them. Dave's parents seemed oblivious to any level of wayward drunkenness. At home, I'd have been confronted by either a waiting mother at one in the morning, or a glowering father when I arose the next day. Both would give me a scripted lecture about self-control and risk.

Mr and Mrs Ellis were more likely to greet us with a glass of cognac.

And so it was that, in the very early hours of New Year's day 1992, I vomited copiously and noisily all over the bedroom and the landing. I was found in a shuddering, malodorous heap at the top of the stairs and removed, without judgement, to a different bedroom wherein I awoke with a shout of horror shortly after one pm.

In my tender adolescence, I had not learned that a Bloody Mary was a pre-requisite hangover cure. But after two, I felt remarkably well enough to cope with an adult party involving several dozen pairs of family friends. It also involved the arrival of Jess and her mother, Charlie. Dave had told me all about his teenage sweetheart. Still at school, embarking on her final year, Jess was beautiful beyond words yet brittle and insecure, like a frozen poppy would be. She smiled disinterestedly at me when Dave introduced us and took him away for the rest of the afternoon.

But Dave hadn't told me about Charlie. While her daughter was smartly dressed, reserved and restrained, this mother was in jeans, a tee shirt and an old waistcoat, her frizzed, auburn hair pulled up in to a carefully arranged mess. Mrs Ellis greeted her with screams of delight, and soon Dave's father was on the scene hugging and cajoling this arrival. All eyes were upon her, but at least half the glances were stares of unrestrained dismay.

'Did you keep in touch with Jessica?'

'Well you know she visited me at college a few times during our second year. And you know it was a passionate and unrestrained relationship.'

'Yes, but what became of her?'

Dave took the story through a segment that I knew (the slow dissolution of their relationship once Jess had gone to university) and an ending I'd only ever heard him hint at.

'We'd lost touch completely by the time we all left Birmingham. It was over. Forever. But then, Christmas 1994, the parents had another of their mind-blowing gatherings, and there she was: still at university and twice as staggeringly pretty and stunning. And with the most powerfully irritating fuckwit in tow, who she pulled around the room like an errant puppy, dazzling one and all with an engagement ring the size of an ashtray. I hadn't met Ella at that point and was standing there alone, like the proverbial. Stop laughing Edward. This is heart-rending stuff.'

'I know. Go on.' But I'm still laughing openly. Dave has a face that makes any anecdote hilarious, regardless of the subject matter. Having finished around three-quarters of the wine bottle, his delivery also has a tipsy comedic hesitancy.

'When the gallant pair reached my station, she brushed my shoulder and introduced her fiancé - I can't remember his name: Benedict Rectal-Thermometer or something. And then she introduced me as the boy who deflowered her in our school library. Poor Benny didn't know where to put himself but I stuck my chin out like Clark Gable and told her to go and fuck herself. And I never saw her again.'

'And what of her wonderful mother.'

Dave is looking across at the waiter, waving the empty wine bottle and mouthing *another of these please*.

'I knew that was your agenda Teddy. You didn't care about breaking my heart in recall of my first true love. You just wanted the low down on her wanton mama.'

Dave smiles cruelly at me. He knows the plot and all the stage directions of what happened that New Year's Day in Witney. Then his smile disappears, replaced by a sad, wistful pursing of his lips.

'We perhaps shouldn't joke too much about Charlie. Or at all.'

'What do you mean?'

'She was killed last summer: knocked down in Wantage; hit and run job.'

I'm stunned into silence. By the news itself, but also by the fact that Dave hadn't told me.

'Cat got your tongue?'

'That's so sad. Why didn't you tell me?'

'Bit selfish of you. All this was close to the time of Mum's illness and death. One was... preoccupied and in many ways Charlie's death barely registered.'

'Okay; sorry.'

'Don't be. You didn't know. Anyway; we found the time to go to Charlie's funeral.'

'You saw Jess then, right?'

'No. She didn't show up.'

'How come?'

He smiles again, with a hint of cruelty. 'Benny had been relocated by his company to Dubai and not long after they moved there, he was uncovered as a major-league fraudster. Insider trading. Creative accounting. Hands in tills. These were the days when corporate misdemeanours were punished, rather than encouraged. Jess fled but, as is often the case, found that his entire life had been built on shifting sands and she didn't have a pot to piss in.'

'But surely that didn't mean she'd miss her mother's funeral?'

'That didn't, no. But aimless gallivanting around the Med was her only priority.'

'Ah.'

The second bottle of wine has arrived, and Dave waves away the need to test it, signalling instead that the waiter should fill our glasses. I stop him when mine is half full.

'How come you know all this about Jess? And how come you haven't told me before?'

'You haven't asked.'

'True, but even so. Largely we've always shared the details of our histories.'

Dave shrugs with Gallic indifference.

'The details? No. You and I, while never actively avoiding any topic, have generally refrained from history, haven't we? And anyway, this wasn't a history I felt needed too much of an airing. If it had mattered to you to know of her, you'd have stayed in touch with Charlie independently. You didn't, so either consciously or otherwise, you were disconnected from her in spite of any history.'

He can be ruthless with his logic sometimes. I'm left feeling a little hurt.

'And, to your other question, I know all this because I grew up in a small town in Oxfordshire where everyone knows everyone's business.'

And now Dave looks saddened, as if relating this subject has affected him very deeply.

'Are you okay?'

He looks at me with great affection.

'I am. Thinking of Mum and Charlie: such great friends all through school and life; kindred spirits who chose fun always. Neither saw the other's end. Mum was in palliative care at the time Charlie was killed and was fading quickly away. Charlie had been there every day, sometimes twice a day. But Mum was too poorly to realise that her oldest friend had stopped calling in to hold her hand, sing songs and make her wear massive floral hats. It was like the clock that had been running all through their friendship suddenly stopped: no one had the keys to wind it up. After being friends for nearly seventy years, they died within a few days of each other.'

Dave is staring at his wine glass as if it contains the answers to every question but, deep down, he knows that each mouthful makes the knowledge disappear.

I top it up for him. 'Here, finish this. I shouldn't really encourage you to drink this much, but you can enjoy it more than I can. I can't afford a hangover.'

'Underneath your shallow, corporate slave, money-talks-bullshit-walks persona, there's a real person isn't there?'

'Sometimes. But a desperately dull one.'

'You're never dull Ted.'

It's close to eleven fifty when I get back to my room. Dave has gone, with a farewell hug, a final word of wisdom and a slight stagger. I always worry about anyone travelling alone across London and out to the burbs. He always tells me he feels safer in this city than anywhere in the world.

As if our evening has never happened, I'm quickly back in the clouds raining messages and thoughts down on friends and family. And briefly on Jude.

'Can you chat?'

'I can, but not for long.'

'I'm missing you. Like always.'

'Same. You all finished with Dave? How is he?'

'Wonderful. We had a good time.'

'Meal ok?'

'Decent. He drank loads.'

'Are you pissed?'

'No. He is.'

'Sweetheart, let's leave it there. I'm tired.'

'OK. But let me know if you get horny in the night.'

'You'll be first to know. Night lover boy.' She sends a horned devil emoji.

All this is Enid Blyton-esque compared to the stuff matey and Foxy were up to earlier on the train. I look on SocMed again to remind myself how my post has been received. There's no new reaction. It's nearly twelve hours old and around half that time since any Likes or comment. That makes it pre-historic in social media terms.

I Vidicall Beth but she doesn't answer. A moment later she messages me to say I woke her up and she's pissed off with me for calling so late. Feeling fed up with her, I start a reply to apologise, but when I'm halfway through the message she calls me back by phone.

'I'm sorry Dad. I shouldn't have snapped at you. It was me who couldn't talk earlier so wrong of me to cut you off.'

The daughter/father thing kicks in. I can never resist my baby girl.

'It is late and perhaps I should have messaged first. So, let's not talk long.'

'Okay.'

She does sound sleepy.

'How was your theatre group.'

'Excellent but tiring. We didn't finish till nearly ten.'

'What are you working on?'

'It's a piece written by one of the tutors here. I've a big part.'

'Good. Are you still coming to me at Easter?'

'That's the current plan. Is Joey going to be around too?'

'I don't know what he's thinking, but you know what he's like.'

'I'll find out. He told me he might be staying in Leicester for the Easter vac.'

'Yes, now you mention it, he did say that to me.'

I hear Beth stifling a yawn.

'Let's leave it there Beth. I can tell you're tired.'

'Thanks Dad. Call me when you get back tomorrow evening.'

'It will be Wednesday. I'm going to be staying two nights a week for the foreseeable future.'

'Oh. Is that ok with you?'

'Yes, it's fine. Go on: get yourself back to bed and we'll talk later in the week.'

'You rest too okay? No silly late-night mating calls.'

'Night Beth. Sleep tight.'

Expecting he won't answer, I text Joe to wish him goodnight and suggesting we talk tomorrow. I am astonished to receive his reply a few minutes later:

'Hey old man Dad. Love you too. Sleep well. Let's Vidicall tomorrow, early evening.'

Then I get a message from Beth saying she forgot to tell me her friend Kirstie is following me on Chattabox and thinks I'm funny. Knowing that @kirsteemay is a friend of the family makes her less problematic and I follow her back, then Peep something inane about how I love London.

I've missed a message from Ella. 'David is safely home. It looks and smells like you had fun.'

'We did. Glad he got back ok. How come you're still up? Thought you had a big few days coming up.'

'I do, but it's not an early start and I like to make sure my man is safe. Is it true you stopped him having a cognac?'

'I did.'

'Harsh. He's very resentful.'

'He had most of two bottles of red and two pints of wifebeater. Possibly three.'

'Then a cognac won't come amiss.'

I send a LOL emoji.

'Come for dinner soon. It's been ages. Are you still in town each week?'

'Yes. And that would be lovely.'

'Next week looks good, but after that I'm toast socially.'

The chat peters out with an agreement that I might stay with them one night the following week.

I'm kind of envious about Dave and Ella. She's beautiful, talented, a successful entrepreneur and funny in a way most people can only fantasise about. By any measure you might dream up, they are a perfect couple; perfectly matched; perfectly anchored in one another with a depth and strength to their love that seems to defy any cliché. It makes me proud to be part of their lives, both as a couple and as individuals. It gives me hope that the truth is out there for me.

But it may or may not be on *matchmates*. Once I've got my ablutions done and, reeking of minty goodness, have climbed into the undeniably comfortable bed, I start trawling through the app on my iPad. I'm told about new matches I might want to discover. I read through the messages shared earlier with Carla, then work through her profile and photos again. Perhaps this time the algorithms have aligned properly and she is the one?

I message her: 'Hi Carla, it's not too late so checking in with you to see if you're still around?'

She doesn't reply and maybe I've already uncovered the One Great Lie that all dating site profiles are said to contain: Carla clearly is not a night owl.

With scepticism pricking my curiosity, I drift off to sleep.

4

It's Wednesday, but the day of the week makes no difference: Moorgate tube is bedlam when I descend to its concourse and start my voyage. It always seems as if something catastrophic is about to happen there, such is the randomised sense of panic and lack of direction in the looming faces. Races are run, to take their competitors somewhere unattainable in the fastest possible time. Chaos is not a theory here.

But we find our escalators and finally there is calm: order comes in to play; we filter into the right lines to be interred in the tubes below. I jostle my way to Platform 7 where I'm blended into the black line towards Euston. After the crushing madness above, in which it seemed impossible that any journey could begin, I am heading inexorably North. Standing on the platform, thick with silent hopeful people, I begin a tranquil countdown that should end at a place called Home.

I'm thinking...

Some of what happened in the last two days might be called achievement. Yesterday's Project Shotgun meeting ran from:

escalations

to resistance

to defensive push back

to begrudging acceptance

and finally to a result.

In the end, the procurement leader said I'd done a Great Job.
And I had.

The tube is packed so I stand and sweat, with my bag held up
close to my chest. I never feel fear on the Underground, but I'm
rarely far from panic even when it's not busy. Ever since the
2005 attacks I've found it impossible not to think about what
would actually happen if someone detonated a bomb in my
carriage. I don't mean in the sense of looking around at the
faces, wondering which one belongs to the mass murderer-in-
waiting and then attacking them pre-emptively. I just mean in
the sense of what the explosives would do, what agony and hurt
I would feel and which bits of me I wouldn't miss, in priority
order, if they got blown off.

Probably it's as horrible and painful and humiliating a way to
get injured as any statistically more likely one: being flattened
by a truck while cycling in the city centre perhaps; or drowning
while swimming in the public baths; or being injected with
the wrong dose of pain relief in hospital. Statistically, yes,
more likely to happen. But our newspapers tell me every day -
scream at me every day - that I am in danger in all public places
because of a threat that invokes hatred of everyone in its path.
There are no headlines in the dailies telling me to be scared of
contempt-filled truck drivers; or poorly motivated lifeguards;
or negligent medics: but those people exist. So, my fear and
panic are carefully managed, directed and controlled by media
which, I'm sure, care deeply about us all. Especially while under
ground.

The train rattles on towards Angel.

I'm still thinking...

> Tuesday had small satellites of other activity, mundanities
> for the most part. My way of working involves fluidity and
> changing outlooks, but most days it is consumed by routine.
> There's bureaucracy, calls, meetings, the occasional decision,
> then more bureaucracy. There's the constant shuffling
> forward of programmes through processes and checkpoints

in which multiple fingers are thrust into the pie. The fingers are attached to hands and arms that exist solely to create diversion and doubt and to justify the existence of managers around the company who aren't needed, but whose pay packets are justified by ownership of something.

If only the company had a head and a heart, two arms, two hands and ten fingers: work would get done; things would get completed; productivity would grow; objectives would be surpassed; revenue would flow. Instead, like a blue-suited hydra, the whole chain of command is multi-layered and malignant. Cut out something that's broken, and two new more dreadful things grow back in its place, breathing ice and acid instead of fire.

But I get on with things and keep my head above the water by being assertive and honest. I wrap the humdrum in sparkly paper, so it looks inviting and special; I smile frequently and avoid the pitfalls of being a good old British workplace moaner. It's the right thing to do - the only thing to do - even if it's a glossy façade, projected internally at meetings and externally on my CV and BizSoc. All for the sake of uniformity and loyalty, but it's not the image I see when I look in the mirror.

I work hard to fulfil a destiny beyond an imaginary horizon. A fruitless ambition, like running on a treadmill. Success is whatever result I want it to be. No-one is listening.

And on Tuesday it seemed that things got worse for Paul Wilson. He was bullish during our daily project review call but also quite friendly towards me, as if he had accepted my new status.

I was surprised when he arrived in the office just after four pm and immediately closeted himself in one of the private rooms.

Surprised, but disinterested.

I had too much to do.

He was still there, sitting in darkness, when I returned from meetings. He hadn't removed his coat and his laptop bag was still on the chair where he'd thrown it earlier. His face seemed to show a kind of resigned concern, as if he was searching for something on his screen that he knew, deep down, was lost.

He was still there when I left for my hotel at seven thirty.

I'd set myself a curfew of ten forty-five. I ate and spent some time perusing my media. When I logged in at work at nine, Paul was still online at the office. With half an eye on his messaging status and location tag, I chatted with friends, talked with family and probed into more detail with Carla. Paul's green light finally turned grey at just after ten - very late for him to start his journey home to Sittingbourne. I felt a pang of sorrow: he was leaving to travel to an empty home. For him, as for me, living alone and having nothing to greet you when you've been working away is terribly dispiriting. Even if you've nothing to say, having no-one to say it to feels like you truly have no reason to go home.

I'm squirted out on to Euston's busy Northern Line platform and push my way directly towards the tunnel's arching wall. I need this break from the constant proximity and endless blind enslavement to the dungeon's regulations. I make two short journeys on the Underground each week and it's about all I can handle. I'm sure it's much worse doing it infrequently than doing it every day. When the train departs, I begin the walk towards the *Way-Out* signs and now I'm smiling because phase one of the journey is over. It's the shortest but worst segment and I feel the same release I always feel as I rise up to the main concourse at Euston. This station is part of the North, much like Gibraltar is part of Britain. I feel, whenever I'm there, that Euston is a dislocated extension of Lancashire. Home from home. Light at the end of a tunnel.

I'm less anxious now, and it takes me around ten seconds to locate the column headed *19:30 - Glasgow Central*. It's *Being Prepared*. I know I'm in Coach C, seat 27 but I still check my phone for the ticket details. It's just past seven-ten, so there's time for me to grab a drink and perhaps a snack. I roam the retail outlets wondering what to get. The agony of choice defeats me and I return, empty handed, to the mass of humanity waiting for a train. I wish I'd nipped out to the Euston Tap for a pint of ale, but I'd want at least two pints and that would have me pissing like a stallion for the entire trip.

I find faces that all look worried; some are even contorted in rage; but all are staring up at the giant black screen with its illuminated orange text. The board controls all our lives during whatever time we are captured by its reports. Euston is a secretive place, dispensing its knowledge to we travellers in carefully packaged lots. You can't even see the platforms and trains. You just have these words and they orchestrate lurches of anticipation via several key pieces of information.

First comes the initial appearance of the service on the display board. This is crucial because it means your train is probably in the building and might leave as scheduled; but it might still be broken in some way; so it's a worrying time lasting up to fifty minutes; any more than that and your train is possibly fucked so you look along the column headers for the next option going your way; you wonder if Liverpool Lime Street trains are worth catching; maybe change at Crewe?

Second, when the words *Being Prepared* are displayed. This is progress; the crew is doing something - it could be anything - to make your train look nice; you don't actually care; you're going home and you'd travel on a high powered skateboard with a giant bulldog clip holding you in place just to get out of London and on your way; but those words still galvanise the audience; a murmur of expectation becomes a babble.

Third, and finally, when the words *Boarding, Platform Z* are displayed. It's a lottery, and part of the game, to understand or guess which platform it might be and then stand nearer to that end of the concourse. But it causes a bellow of joy and a migration of dozens, from all around the concourse, towards Euston's sloping access ramps where staff may be waiting to check tickets and cause a pulsating log jam at the gate.

Looking around me I can see an almost religious fervour in the faces, even in the ones stuffing pasties or sucking on coffee cartons. These are factions; cliques. Their existence here might notionally make them consumers, but they are followers. The ones bound for Northampton are radically different to the ones headed to Stafford or Runcorn. They have different needs and they group together as close as they can to their chosen column hoping their intimacy makes them safe from the influence of non-believers.

And now I'm over-thinking...

Today had begun with a noisy notification of a text from Annabel.

'Ed, I got back to LHR just after midnight, and to Ascot a little before 2. I didn't explain why I'm back early because I can't tell you. Things will be clear soon. Don't worry.'

And she'd sent me an email, titled *Urgent - Please Action ASAP This Morning.*

She told me to cancel the scheduled checkpoint call as she was going to organise a session for later this afternoon and doesn't need two team calls.

The email was timed at 05:20, so maybe Annabel hadn't even gone to bed.

I'd done as I was told, taking less than five minutes. By 06:35 I'd strode out for the office, arriving a little after seven. While walking I'd done a mental mind map to understand what is happening. In the end all I have is a wall, and the biggest brick in the wall has *Paul Wilson* written on it. This was not going to be a normal Wednesday, and not just because I was still in London.

Annabel's meeting invitation showed that she'd scheduled thirty minutes starting at three, and she'd called it *Team Call - New Agenda* which seemed slightly bland.

But I had loads to do and had got on with it. No-one else from my team was in the office but by nine, I could see that everyone except Paul Wilson was online.

Annabel had arrived looking shattered; something more than just tired. We'd chatted about inconsequentialities for a moment before she'd excused herself and headed to her office where she'd closed her blinds.

It had taken a couple of minutes for everyone to join, and there was no small talk. I'd switched my messaging status to Do Not Disturb.

Annabel had been unfussy in her opening few words but I had the sense of an impending bombshell. It all seemed theatrical. Then it got serious.

'Unfortunately, Paul Wilson has had to take leave of absence. This comes at a difficult time given the announcement on Monday about my and Ed's new roles.'

The word *fuck* had zapped through my head.

'I'm afraid Paul could be away for some time – weeks rather than days.'

Someone had tried to say something, but Annabel demanded no interruptions.

'I will be working with Ed to find the ways to prevent this from causing any additional strain on our team and I'm confident that in the short term we can cope with Paul's absence. I also realise that you will have concerns and may even be worried about this news. That's understandable, but please try to carry on with business as usual. This isn't anything to worry about but I urge you not to indulge in speculation or gossip.'

No one spoke until a shaking voice had said, 'Is Paul okay?'

'He needs time out of the business and away from work. But please don't worry. Let's focus on working together.'

I'd thought, as she said those words, that something must have happened unbelievably quickly. On Monday, Paul was part of the team, irascible and difficult. But that was nothing new. Now, something smelled funny.

The call had ended, and it hadn't taken long for Stewart to hit me with, 'WTF?????'

Dubious, I had replied with, 'Indeed.'

'Did you know about this?'

'Nope.' I'd desperately wanted to speculate.

'What would happen if I get in touch with Paul?'

'I don't think it's worth finding out.'

'You're no fun,' smiley face.

Then I'd sensed movement behind me and swivelled to find Kate Farmer gazing at me.

'Ed, could I have a word please?'

I'd shut my laptop with a creeping guilt rising in my gut.

Kate had been calmly neutral. 'Kal and I need to interview you formally. It's very short notice but you need to join us now please.'

We'd walked in silence to the lift, my mind devoid of thoughts. The sense of guilt had reached my chest.

In the room, formalities had been brief: thanks; assurances; impartially stern faces; a blast of cologne.

'Ed, this is a formal meeting related to an investigation into an alleged serious misconduct. Kal and I will be asking you questions and we're recording everything to save note taking. You'll get a copy and a transcript. Is it okay to proceed on that basis?'

'Yes. No problem at all.'

A voice had made statements in my head: *Ask what this is all about. Tell them you want a third-party present. Say you are innocent. Innocent of nothing.*

'Thanks Ed. Then let's begin. We are investigating allegations that you and Annabel James have been involved in a sexual relationship for some time, and that you have benefited from favouritism on her part. We will be asking you questions relating to those allegations. Do you have any questions before we start?'

A great wave of relief had crashed over me. This was going to be easy.

'No. I'm good.'

Kate: 'Great. Have you ever had a sexual relationship with Annabel James?'

'No.'

Kal: 'Has there ever been any form of intimacy between you?'

'Yes.'

'What was it?'

'We once kissed.'

They had alternated question by question; good cop/good cop.

'When and where was that?'

'In early 2015. January. In Bucharest.'

'What led to that situation?'

'We were visiting the Romania team. A long day ended with a meal and a couple of drinks in the hotel. At the end of the evening, we were in the lift together and... we just kissed.'

'Who instigated it?'

'It was mutual.'

'Had you been publicly flirting during the evening?'

'Kind of.'

'What kind of flirting?'

'The kind that a single woman and a divorced man might do.'

'Can you be more specific?'

I'd been flummoxed; that question seemed tangential. Perhaps they were just after titillation.

'I can't.'

'Okay. What happened after the kiss?'

'We reached my floor, and after another brief kiss, we said goodnight and I left the lift to go to my room.'

'Did either of you suggest that you'd like to take the kiss further?'

'Not really. From memory, she said something like: *this isn't a good idea is it?* and I replied something like: *it's a nice idea, but a bad place to put ourselves in.*'

'What happened to Annabel?'

'I've no idea. I left her in the lift.'

'Did you kiss again at any time?'

'No.'

'In January 2015, what was your work relationship with Annabel?'

'We were peers, both reporting to Steph Woolston.'

'Have you ever exchanged intimate or candid written communications with Annabel?'

'No. Never.'

'Would you like to have a relationship outside of work with Annabel?'

'No.'

'Do you think Annabel has ever given you the benefit of favouritism?'

'Such as?'

'Such as a more positive appraisal?'

'In December 2015, Steph gave me a better rating than Annabel gave me two months ago.'

'Annabel marked you down?'

'No, she gave me the rating HR said everyone should get.'

Kate's eyes had registered this with a sudden darkened squint.

'Did you do or say anything to obtain the additional duties and temporary promotion that you've been given?'

'No. It was a complete surprise.'

'How would you describe your working relationship with Annabel?'

'Focused. Professional. Open. Honest. Diligent.'

Kal and Kate had looked at one another. It seemed that was it.

'Thank you, Ed; there are currently no further questions but during the investigation we may need to talk with you again.'

'Understood.'

'This meeting was confidential, and you must not discuss it with anyone. Do you have any questions?'

I'd said I didn't.

Before I'd left the office, Kate returned to hand me an envelope with a small lump in it. 'Ed, as promised here's a copy of the recording we made earlier along with a letter explaining the outcome of our discussion. You'll have a soft copy by email within a few minutes. Are you heading home soon?'

'In about an hour. Train's not till seven-thirty so no rush.'

'Doesn't that make for a late finish?'

'I'll be home just after ten.'

'Make sure you get a lie-in tomorrow. Speak soon.'

When I'd opened the envelope, I found a flash drive and a piece of paper headed *Personal. Confidential. Not to be copied.*

It continued with details that were self-evident: Dear Edward; here's a recording and transcript in duplicate; retain both securely; we will too; digest; sign both copies, or tell us why not; we're still investigating; you're not off the hook; yours sincerely.

I'd read it with a heightened sense of theatre and drawn a small mind map on a notebook with a question: *if Paul W is the source of these allegations, why is he now absent? Has he been suspended?* Then a short line from that to another question: *allegations about Annabel and me can't be the reason he's absent. Either he's done something else, or he's ill. And if it was that, we'd be told.* I'd scribbled more notes with assorted conspiracy theories then, in large capitals, *SMOKESCREEN.*

My train was shown as Boarding at Platform 13. The rush began and I strolled along behind it to join the queue at the gate, giggling to myself at the indignant huffs and puffs of passengers who had to find their tickets for inspection. I flashed my phone and its e-ticket at the guys, who nodded and smiled. Euston's cavernous featureless space opened up in front of me. The train was there, and a snaking line of people marched alongside it, occasionally sloughing off an individual into a carriage. When I reached Coach C, I stepped up into it and through the electronic sliding door. The interior already stank of food, sweat, alcohol and deodorant. Voices were raised on phone calls. But it wasn't too busy and when I found seat 27, I slumped down into it and waited to see if it would get more hectic.

It didn't.

As the dumbed down announcements began, explaining how

to travel on a train and where to get endless food and drinks, I was the only occupant in any of the surrounding seats.

Silently, the journey began again.

5

The carriage is cold and, so far as I can see, everyone is sitting in their coats. As the train blasts through Watford Junction a voice jabbers something over the PA about electrical problems affecting the heating in all coaches. He offers the insincere apologies of someone who can't stop the problem, isn't really to blame but knows he will still get harangued. I make a mental note that there'll be no ticket inspections.

My laptop stays in its bag, but I do a quick scroll through new work emails on my phone. I reply to a couple, mark several for action tomorrow and leave the rest. Nothing from Annabel about anything, and nothing from anyone about Paul Wilson. I'm still certain this can't be personal and must be a disciplinary matter. It can only be something bad, and I conclude that I might never see the man again, which causes no feelings of sorrow. More than five years ago, I stopped having any sense of being a pack animal at work. You're on your own in business and having friends - real or made up friends - that are also co-workers is a gamble I prefer not to take. What's the point?

I won't miss Paul when he's gone – for now I've decided he will be gone. We've worked together for several years and I've grown to know him as someone who does his job well. He has faults, just the same as everyone, and he can have moments of quite brilliant insight. Yet being in a team with him has never made us a team. I see him as a diminishing star with very different views about how we should do our, notionally identical, jobs. Being ten years older than me should make no difference whatsoever to our working relationship, but we are poles apart on almost every aspect of the role and how to deliver it. Of course, like everyone in the company, we have to pretend this fissure doesn't exist; that we are jointly focused and committed to excellence and making the whole team a unit; frictionless; clean; unsullied by dissonance. That's not the truth though. Working today isn't about mutual benefit or the kind of camaraderie that might once have made Britain Great. Paul was what he was, I am what I am.

There is no Team in I.

And now I realise I'm thinking of Paul in the past tense. He is History.

Another announcement bursts from the speakers, this time from the on-board catering team. It seems there are Elysian levels of snacks and drinks available from the buffet, but you need cash as the card system isn't working. I almost fall from my seat when the announcement concludes a long list of items available by pronouncing the penultimate syllable of *Orangina* the same as it would be in *Vagina*.

I get my iPad out and start flicking through my Chattabox feed. There's not much to excite although I double check a Peep from *@kirsteemay* about the production Beth is in. There's an amazing piece of footage showing a dance routine; Beth hadn't mentioned dancing, but she's always been a natural and my mouth drops open watching her. It makes me Like the Peep, then I Repeep it, saying 'Look at my super-talented Beth in action.'

I find the usual array of emails from sources I don't know; marketeers, retailers, suppliers, people asking me to complete surveys. I send it all to junk, where it joins several other new mails, a couple of which show lascivious women in their underwear who might be potential brides. There's nothing from friends or anyone close. Email is almost dead as a communication tool. Joe and Beth tell me they only have accounts because it helps to identify and tag them, making them more easily tracked by corporations and government agencies.

Maybe one day there will be no more email? Just like there are no more telegrams, hand-written letters, faxes and post cards. Yet it remains ubiquitous in the world of work. In the time I've taken to look at my personal mailboxes more than a dozen mails have dropped into my work account. It fulfils something in the psyche of middle-aged people who can't be arsed to pick up the phone and actually talk to colleagues; it's traditional and formal; it puts things in writing; it covers your arse and avoids confrontation. Points are scored via an unblinking, first-strike stare across desks, borders or oceans.

But maybe one day, who knows?

Another announcement is made about the heating: apparently an engineer has been alerted and will meet the train at Warrington Bank Quay, in about an hour's time. There are rumblings of discontent down the carriage, but these are smoothed over when the announcement goes on to mention that free hot drinks will be brought through the train for the rest of the journey. There is a loud burst of crackling static and then silence, which appears to be the end of the matter.

My nearest travelling companions are five rows away: two women, about thirty, who looked pretty drunk when they got on, and who have pulled out bottles of vodka and Cointreau plus a carton of cranberry juice. They are musing on whether the train shop will have any ice and one of them staggers off to check. She soon returns with four paper cups, causing those whoops people do and a little dance from the ice hunter-gatherer. This is going to get ugly, and sooner than anyone in earshot would wish.

I grab my headphones and select a playlist.

On SocMed nothing much is new. Tina has told everyone she's away at the weekend and would anyone be willing to pop round to feed her pussy? Someone has posted: 'I'm free Mrs Slocombe!' and that is followed by a barrage of gags rooted in the one-liners of 1970s' sitcoms. I post that I'm homeward bound but might not see Lancaster again due to the onset of frostbite. I also observe how all the stations on my journey appear to have three words in them: That London Euston; Lichfield Trent Valley; Warrington Bank Quay; Wigan North Western; Once Proud Preston. I quickly get thumbs, hearts and smiley faces.

My game on social media is about engagement: keeping in touch; banter; laughter; friends near and far in a corral of shared understanding. About closing a circle around me to distract me from my loneliness. No controversy between the players, even if content is vexing. It's all very simple: I say what I say in the hope that people join in with the spirit and letter. Probably, somewhere out there, friends look in on my posts and think I am a total cock some days. Overindulgence in self, underestimation of effect. But, broadly, my rationale is this: if you don't like the cut and thrust, steer clear of the content.

Is it just me that plays the game with these rules? Probably not: I think we're all the same. There is no disagreement or offence between contacts on Planet SocMed. The whole point of the medium and its baby brothers and sisters is that it has no depth or breadth of emotion in which friends and acquaintances actually say what they think or feel. It neatly epitomises today's obsession with projecting the perfect. Nothing is allowed to be wrong or off the rails.

Like one of those parties, where everyone wears outrageous masks and disguises, we express feelings by posting memes or reposting the one-liners of unknown others or celebrities or newspaper columns. That is the confrontation; indirect and impersonal; pointing at a big picture; correcting the direction of whatever one's small thoughts might be. Dissent or disappointment exist yet must be expressed privately or by stony silence. This give and take means there is no ill-feeling, so relationships and opinions remain intact and uncontroversial.

The ultimate sanctions, unfollowing and unfriending, are the stealth option; used instead of the truth.

Not much is going on with *matchmates* and I don't feel that concerned. The last few chats with Carla have been increasingly knowing and she posted something to me earlier in the day saying she's out with friends for the evening and I shouldn't worry about her not being in touch.

I've looked at her profile perhaps fifty times, but I do it again now and see she's added a new photo. She is standing with her back to a five-bar gate - wintry fields, hedges and hills stretching out behind her to infinity. I blink, besotted by this new image. She's gorgeous. Fit as fuck.

The Hot Drinks Team has worked its way through the carriage and arrives at my row. I'm offered tea, coffee or hot chocolate. I shouldn't do it, but I ask if there's any Earl Grey tea. The man with the coffee pot stares at me in a way that suggests I would get a good kicking if he had a chance. But his companion smiles and says the tea is just the usual rubbish. I choose the coffee.

During this happy banter, a surprisingly accurate text has popped in from Dave: 'Teddy it was lovely to see you th other evening. You look well and I could have sat chatting all bight. It's been too long. E says shes invited you to stay next week.

That was prematre of her as she didn't know that we will be away from Sunday afternoo. Taking a surprise short break in Brusels. Sorry.'

'That's no problem at all Dave. Maybe the following week?'

'Yes, that could work so I will check with E. Are you in transit?'

'Yep. Somewhere between Nuneaton and Lichfield I think.'

I look out into the darkness and see nothing.

'How log to Lancster?'

'Another ninety minutes or so.'

'Lon day and late fnish. You really do ave my admiration.'

'Of course!'

'Will call you on Fri. Saf-e onward trvels.'

'Love to Ella. Get some lessons about using telephone keypads.'

I'm smiling at Dave's old-world charm. He'd never dream of writing: 'Respect to you dude.' Even ironically.

The smile fades when I try the coffee. How can anything that is supposed to be coffee not smell like coffee? It's insipid and tasteless and I pour both sachets of sugar in to turn it into something vaguely worthwhile. But all it does is make the drink insipid, tasteless and too sweet.

I drink it anyway to ward off hypothermia, then I get up and after safely storing away all my stuff take a walk along the carriage. The movement makes me realise the extent to which I've become chilled and I ask the two drunk women to keep an eye on my bag for me. They agree with gushing sincerity.

Freed, albeit briefly, from my allocated space, I walk the entire length of the train back to the first-class carriages. These are also cold, possibly colder, and in the three coaches there are less than ten people. From next week, I will be able to join this comfortably numb élite, and won't I deserve to be all alone like this lot? The discreet lights cast pools of white on to the tables. The wider, more padded seats look inviting, but I dismiss the idea of upgrading now. Patience is virtuous, even in a world that has eradicated patience and virtue as valued characteristics.

The train suddenly pitches violently to left and right and I'm forced to grab a table with both hands to stay on my feet. Then it happens again and I'm wondering if something disastrous is happening. But normal silent running resumes and I head back to coach C. The guardians of my property are now pretty much legless, but they smile amiably, and one raises a cup to me.

I smile back. 'Cheers, thanks again for keeping an eye on my things. Where are you two headed?'

'Are you flirting with us? I think he's flirting Caz.'

This causes a laugh, then hiccup from Caz who says, 'Take no notice of my friend Mr Nice Guy. She is, and I am, very very drunk. That is because we are headed to Carlisle which, if you've ever been there, you will know requires it's best to be drunk before you arrive.' They both wail with laughter at this.

I know Carlisle well, but can't imagine what they mean.

'Thanks again you two.'

I walk back up the carriage to my seat and just about feel I'm far enough away to be safe. I really don't like drunks when I'm sober. I don't much like them when I'm drunk.

Memories invoked...

Amy was an appalling drunk. Not rude or violent or suddenly prejudicial. She just became incapable; as if a switch in her head got turned off. At university, this had been fun, because it just happened to make Amy incredibly horny. But once the kids were born and during their toddler years, that had all evaporated.

Except - it turned out that it hadn't.

After fifteen or so years of socialising as a unit, Amy began to crave Girls' Nights Out; and that was fine by me. Our careers were busy and successful. I was often far away from home and by Friday was more than happy with an evening of childcare, music and films. Her new social aspirations weren't an issue; I smiled on it.

These nights out were clearly unrestrained and joyous, for Amy sometimes arrived home needing help from amused friends; help getting to our door; help finding her shoes or handbag in the taxi. Her behaviour went unchallenged, by everyone. It only happened monthly. Where was the harm? And the mornings after, she always seemed sweetly oblivious.

The monthly event soon became weekly, and on one occasion I was still up watching TV when Amy arrived home. Through the window, I saw that it wasn't a taxi that dropped her off. The next day she brushed aside my questions about who she knew with an Audi Q7, eventually claiming one of the Girls' husbands had picked up and dropped off the whole gang.

I started to stay awake to see Amy's return and, for the next few weeks a regular Lancaster taxi pulled up outside. Except now, she hardly seemed drunk at all.

Something about this made me feel uneasy and I soon developed a disquieted internal debate about what might be happening. It could be innocent; it probably was; yet I couldn't shake the sense of this being wrong.

Then, one night, she didn't come home.

My unease became a full-scale derailment. We'd been a bit distant but, until that night, I'd never felt there was anything terminal in play. Once more, she brushed aside my questions – this time with the excuse that it had been a really late finish at a club, and easier for her to stay with Wendy than come home and disturb me.

Now I felt indecisive around Amy and couldn't challenge her with further questions or any kind of confrontation. At first, I just curled up and withdrew. But soon I found the resolve to take an action that ended up being conclusive.

Weeks passed and overnight stays became a pre-announced default.

This was no longer a surprise; I knew why they were happening.

Things came to a head in the spring of 2013. After a week or so of increasingly silent sadness, Amy sat down with me at the kitchen table and told me she was unhappy; she wanted us to separate.

I asked why.

She repeated that she wasn't happy, so I asked her why; again. She said she couldn't explain. This was strange. Amy was eloquent and intelligent, yet now her words had dried up. She shed crocodile tears and reached out a hand to touch mine. I withdrew it.

'Is there someone else?'

Her reply was emphatic and rapid: 'No Teddy. It isn't about that. It's just not working between us.'

'Are you sure there isn't someone else?'

She stared at me and repeated her denial with added emphasis. I told her to wait and when I returned to the table handed her a brown A4 envelope. She slit it open with a fingernail and pulled out the contents; sheets of typed paper; some photographs.

Amy was aghast. 'You had me followed?'

'I had you investigated.'

'That's outrageous. How dare you?'

'I think it's a bad time for you to take the moral high ground.'

'How could you DO this Teddy? What did it cost?'

'I think the going rate is one marriage.'

Now her tears were real. 'I'm staggered that you've done this.'

'And I'm staggered that you've destroyed a marriage, crushed our family and damaged, beyond repair, our relationships with our children.'

More tears and some baying sobs.

I left her to it. I booked the day off and went to my solicitor to have particulars drawn up.

I returned late that afternoon to find Amy had despatched Joe and Beth to visit friends for convenient sleepovers. It meant she could be belligerent.

'I'm going to fight you all the way on this, you bastard. I may not have been blameless, but I will contest whatever you throw at me. I will shred your integrity, lay bare your lack of commitment and have your use of an investigator turned in to an infringement of my rights and a betrayal of trust.'

I replied, 'Talk to your solicitor.'

She went berserk. All this came out in what sounded like one long scream: I was boring; I had no life in me; I ignored her needs for a more compellingly aspirational social life; I hadn't made her come properly since before the kids were born; I treated her like an idiot; I wasted money on all sorts of shit; I dressed like a tramp; I drove an embarrassing, boring car; I smelled; I snored so badly it hurt her ears; she'd never really liked me and definitely didn't love me. And then she walked towards me and punched me in the face.

I just told her to tell her solicitor.

She hit me again then picked up a case I hadn't spotted and ran from the house to her car.

I didn't see her again for two days.

The children returned and didn't question the story that Amy had gone, at short notice, to visit their grandparents in Derby. It was Amy's suggestion, by text: *Tell J&B I've gone to see M&D.*

It seemed like any other weekend; the kids scattered around the house wired up to their friends online; me doing bits of work, for self and company; shared meals; a walk along the riverbank.

Another text landed that Sunday morning, this time telling me we needed to meet on neutral ground. Soon after, we sat down at a table in the southbound buildings of a motorway services to have the most grown up discussion we'd ever had.

When I got home from work the next day, Amy's car was parked outside. Inside, everyone was crying. Joe was fifteen, Beth nearly seventeen. They were bright, witty, open, happy people embarking on important academic adventures. Without being told anything, they knew what was wrong.

Amy took the lead: 'Your father has found out that I have been stupid and, in so doing, I have stepped over a line. I can't turn around and make a return crossing. It means that your mum and dad must separate, and eventually get divorced.' She had rediscovered her intelligent eloquence.

'But none of this is ever going to affect you two. Daddy and I may have hit the buffers but neither of you must believe it's the end of us being your parents.'

She'd turned and looked at me for back up, which I gave

in full. We'd agreed not to mention investigations and new partners.

Our honesty didn't stop the children spewing out a torrent of grief and questions: where would we live? would we still go on holiday? will we have to change schools? why did you do it Mummy? why couldn't you stop her Daddy? couldn't you try to forgive each other and stay together?

We answered, turn and turn about.

Amy said she would be moving out but living close to the family home.

I said we would need to re-think our planned holiday.

There was no question of changing schools.

This would remain our home and we would all meet there whenever we needed to.

Then, after they were at university, wherever Mummy and Daddy lived, that would also be their home, singly and collectively.

Amy said she couldn't explain why she did it, but they were to blame her and not me for what had happened.

Beth had gone to her at that point and hugged her mother. And then she hugged me.

Their last question proved most difficult. I'd stammered: 'I'm really sorry - Joe, and Beth - but what has happened makes any kind of reconciliation...'

And before I could say it myself, Amy said: '...impossible.'

This was devastating for our children. They had grown up in a home in which their parents never squabbled, never had rows, never contradicted or countermanded each other and never did anything other than project affectionate love for each other and for the family. All meals were shared. Help with homework or feelings or change was never withheld. Time was always made for laughter, music, food, debate, ideas, fun, cuddles, tears or curiosity.

These amazing, perfect children were old enough and wise enough to know that relationships fail. Yet they had received no signals of anything being wrong.

For the rest of the week, Amy stayed at the house and the children saw what we had set out to show them. That we intended to be civil and maintain our joint responsibilities to them as our children. That we couldn't be a couple, but we were still their parents. That, in spite of everything, we remained a family.

Amy left the house for good that Friday morning and when the children returned from school all three of us sat down and cried as if we'd never stop.

My work phone rings. It's my contact at everyone's favourite supplier; she sounds breathless and a little scared. 'Ed, we might have a problem supplying the temporary keys.'

It isn't a very long call and when it ends I am focused, compelled by the need to fix things. A long-ish email and then calls to Annabel and the project director. One is still working, the other reading to her son at bedtime; both of them swear profoundly.

This supplier was taking the piss with their silly demands and counter-demands.

But we have right on our side and, as the train hisses forever northwards, I join up the dots to prove it to them. The carriage is now my office. I'm in control.

The train stops at then leaves Warrington Bank Quay. No warm air pumps through the pipes and, sure enough, an announcement follows that, sadly, no engineer has been able to join the service. However, the free hot drinks are now being offered with a complimentary soft or alcoholic drink.

Emails are flying around the globe creating activity and affirming our power over this situation.

As the train slows into Preston, a withheld number pops up on my work phone. I hate that and I rarely accept. But, given the events of the last thirty minutes or so, I reckon I need to answer a caller who introduces herself as Fiona Wilson, UK operations director from our favourite supplier. She offers apologies and expresses her dismay that a misunderstanding has arisen. She keeps calling me Edward. And she keeps side-stepping any blame.

The train has begun to accelerate out of Preston. Lancaster is less than twenty minutes away and I have time to send a short email to my colleagues: 'Problem solved. Keys delivered.'

Memories interred...

When Amy smacked me in the mouth that day in 2013, it seemed like the start of a fight that would never end. Her silence over forty-eight hours had made me predict a tidal wave of disagreement, disrepute and dismay.

Yet our meeting over a grubby service station table revealed a change of heart. By now, Amy knew that no matter how much she might want to punch me and dispute what I'd done, she was in love with someone who had no intention of being dragged through the courts as part of her battle with me. That man's interest in Amy didn't come at the cost of his reputation.

She set out what was proposed: no contest that she had committed adultery; agreement to a divorce on those grounds; she would move out of the family home, if we formally agreed she still had title to it; we'd continue to pay half of everything until the family home was sold; we'd split the proceeds 50:50; we'd share all the costs, equally and in perpetuity, related to Joe's and Beth's education; there was no need for access rights so the kids could be wherever they liked, whenever they liked.

I told her I wouldn't accept any of that unless she agreed to pay off the mortgage and cover all the costs of selling our home out of her share of the proceeds.

Her glare had been like Medusa's. She thought her magnanimity would be non-negotiable. I looked at her hands, expecting to see them clenching into fists. She'd removed her wedding and engagement rings.

I'd already valued mine for scrap.

Then she sighed, shook her head, and agreed she would accept that. She just wanted agreement. Something mutual that avoided exorbitant solicitors' fees. When I said I needed to think it through, despite it being mainly civil and equitable, she slapped the table hard and told me to get real. I had the evidence I needed. She was bang to rights, and while she would love to fight me, she needed to keep Phil out of the equation and courts.

I watched her saying this with a feeling of disgust wrapped in a layer of distrust. I didn't want to know about the man who had taken her from me.

As we stood to leave, I told her there was one last thing we needed to agree.

'No Teddy: play time is over. You've got your pound of flesh.'

'No Amy. I don't know and don't care where you're going now, but your choice of this service station means I have to drive to fucking Preston and back in my boring car - 35 or so miles. So the least you can do is buy me another coffee to go.'

She'd burst out laughing and brushed her hand on my upper arm. 'Oh; is that all?'

Then tears: 'Shit Teddy; what have I done?'

I step off the train.

It is cold and misty in Lancaster, but I am close to my house. Back to being Edward Granville Clayton, resident of this city for most of the last forty-four years. My stamping ground; the place where it all began.

Journey's end.

Interlude

Marcus Mapplewick was rarely outwardly happy. He was too consumed by the need to convey the contempt and scorn for which he was renowned and by the need to be the big, brash business bruiser he knew and loved.

On a good day, he might smile discreetly as he slid into his Maybach – a smug contentment from the knowledge that none of his peers had such a car and he'd outdone them all. If the day went well and he did a deal that saved him money and increased his wealth or reduced his overheads, he might smile again as he opened that daily bottle of champagne to toast his own brilliance. And if his beautiful wife was uncharacteristically willing to treat him, his smile might even be converted to a grin as he lay between her thighs.

But today was not a good day, and Kriss Jarvis braced himself for the fusillade of invective he'd been expecting since their brief phone call the previous evening.

'Tell me again, Mister Jarvis, why you were typing emails that some peasant could easily read in a public place.' MM had stressed the word *Mister*.

In the five years they'd been working together, MM had called him *Christopher* no more than ten times. He never, ever called him *Kriss*. Or *Chris*. Forenames were like foreign words to Marcus – difficult to say with confidence or certainty. Instead, MM fell back on what he saw as old-world formality, keeping employees, suppliers and clients at arm's length. It wasn't out of the question that he did the same with his wife and children.

'From the photo on SocMed it's clear that what I was doing was visible through the gap in the seats. But this bloke must have spent time looking. It couldn't have been chance.'

'You're saying he was deliberately spying on me?'

'No, I'm not. But he didn't just take a peek then look away. He saw what he saw and decided to record it. But the way he's posted it on SocMed suggests a coincidental encounter and nothing more than a prank.'

'A fucking costly one, by any number of measures, Mister Jarvis.'

Kriss paused. The actual cost of his professional indiscretion was almost certainly next to nothing. He'd been careless that day, rushing after being distracted by Kat's early morning bout of Foxy misdemeanours. That email should have been written and sent the previous evening while he was still at the office. But his priorities were destroyed by Kat's unexpected announcement that she was back in Lichfield and free all night. It meant that he had had to work, in a rush, on the train to London.

But Kriss' instincts were that the whole situation was a minor inconvenience: messy, but manageable. And it was his fault, so no point denying it or trying to deflect blame to a third party.

'I'm sorry Marcus. It wasn't appropriate for me to work on the train and I regret it. But I'm not sure there is a serious cost to either MarMap or you.'

MM sucked through his front teeth, creating a hissing snarl.

'No serious cost? That photo on SocMed shows your email address and by association the name *MarMap*. It also shows my email address, the names of at least two of the scum protestors and the reference you made to *alternative deterrents*; plus all the filth you were parping about with your slut. Who is she by the way?'

Kriss lied his way through an explanation that Kat was a one-night stand he'd picked up in Birmingham and brought home to Lichfield for a hook-up. He guessed, and hoped, that MM wouldn't recognise Kathryn Tasker; the photo was blurred and inconclusive. If MM had known who it was there would be cause for a very swift exit: from MarMap; Lichfield; and probably from Britain. But his instincts were right; MM paid no attention to detail unless there was a pound sign at the start of the equation.

As Kriss spoke, Marcus watched him closely reflecting that he was lucky to have this trusty chief of staff: he rarely messed up and always fell in line with what was needed. They'd resolved many problems together, usually because Kriss was a clever, streetwise individual able to cover almost any eventuality with an apparently limitless set of resources and contacts. In this case, though, Marcus disagreed with his fixer's view about the seriousness of the present situation. In the hands of the scum protestors, and any of their liberal, tree-hugger, Flat Earth allies, that SocMed post was the proof they needed to implicate MarMap in dirty tricks and illegal actions.

'Do we know who this peasant is?'

'We're learning. So far, he seems to be a regular nobody. Works for a multi-national telecoms company. Lives in the north-west but seems to be travelling a lot. We've got someone following him on social media and soon, thanks to him telling so much of himself on SocMed, there'll be a connection on the dating site he uses.'

'Any reaction from the scum?'

'Nothing. And they've had a couple of days to have latched on to the post. That's why I'm not so sure we've a problem.'

'We've a problem for as long as the fucking post is in the public domain. Does anything we know link him to the scum protestors or to any of their local chums?'

'Nothing yet, but gut feel there isn't a link. If he'd been from their camp, he'd surely have posted the photo with a fanfare of righteous indignation? And a hashtag or two. It all points to a completely innocent, albeit harmful piece of mischief.'

Marcus nodded. 'True. Remind me how you got to hear about the SocMed post.'

Kriss explained how friends, and friends of friends, had created a chain of links from the post to his door.

'This all sounds fucking precarious to me.'

'It's hugely tenuous. Which is good. I am, and you are, many steps away from the originator. It's all about my networking and information sharing. A favour with no expectation of anything in return.'

'For fuck's sake. I don't like this at all. It's been through the hands of so many people.'

'No Marcus. The photograph has names in it, we can't escape that fact. But the way I found out about the post all happened away from SocMed. No-one can look at the post, and all its Likes and comments, then find me. I don't exist. Especially on any social media.'

'Medium. You idiot.'

Kriss sighed within. It was always tough when MM pretended to be academic.

'Since he posted it on Monday, he hasn't commented further and there's been no activity on it since then. Days have passed, and it's forgotten.'

Marcus looked at his colleague and did his snarling thing again.

'I wish I shared your confidence that this can be just swept under a carpet. Can't we just get SocMed to take it down on grounds that it's offensive or libellous?'

'We shouldn't do that Marcus because it draws attention to the content, and we'd have to justify why we want it removed. If we just ignore it, it is consigned to history. People who use SocMed are so shallow that the chances of Matey or any of his chums going back through their posts to reflect on what they contain are very small indeed.'

MM wasn't backing down. 'That might be true Mister Jarvis, but from what I know about SocMed it's entirely possible that one of this peasant's friends might see the post days or weeks after he posted it and comment on it. That pushes it back to the top of the agenda on the timelines of everyone involved.'

Kriss was impressed. Sometimes, MM knew more than he let on. He must have been talking to one of his kids again.

'And worse, in a year the peasant could get a tidy little reminder that it's the anniversary of the post. So, he takes a look and then realises that in the year that has passed, MarMap has become a name to be reckoned with.'

Kriss could only nod.

'I want that post removed. I don't care how, but we need to get it taken down and I suggest, Mister Jarvis, that your best course is to get Matey to do it himself. He needs to be convinced with some subtle negotiation techniques.'

Kriss knew what MM was hinting at but he was alarmed by the proposal. His instinct was absolute: drawing attention to the post would only make things worse. The risk of leaving it alone was much smaller. But MM wasn't finished.

'Anyway: if you learned about the post via some flimsy set of lucky connections, who's to say that one of the scum can't also find out via a similar set of circumstances?'

Kriss hadn't thought of that and could only nod sheepishly.

'Get it sorted Mister Jarvis. I don't care what you do or how you do it, just get that post removed from SocMed and make sure the peasant is under no illusions about the consequences of fucking with MarMap.'

Kriss didn't like this at all. He was certain that threatening this man, this Teddy Clayton from Lancaster, might get out of control. But MM was packing away the things on his desk and their meeting was over. He couldn't stand in the way of MM's will and after a few moments reflection he closed down his concerns. He was well paid by MarMap and solving problems was his key performance indicator. Not doing what MM demanded would mean being outcast, and eventual dismissal. Then the cash would quickly dry up: no more coke; no more weekends at Cap Ferrat; no more Kat; no new car twice a year. Instead he'd be back into the hopeless corporate vacuum that

Clayton probably lived in - where any number of illusions couldn't mask the sheer awful tedium. He wasn't going to be dumped into that, and even if his fears were realised and MM blamed him for an even bigger mess, Kriss would still have a kind of power.

MM soon departed leaving Kriss to open the safe and take out the old mobile phone handset and stash of pay-as-you-go SIM cards he needed to get things moving. After making a single call, Kriss removed the SIM card and placed it in an envelope with its holder and documents. This small package of evidence was soon fed through the shredder.

He was still unconvinced that MM's instructions were the right way forward, but a pop up on his phone diverted his attention and anxieties away from MarMap.

The text from Kat - his erstwhile Foxy - was brief. She'd used her secret phone. 'There is no way we can see each other again. You've really fucked up my life.'

He shook his head in disbelief, sent a two letter reply then deleted her as a contact. He would miss some of her charms and all of her orifices. But this was no time to be sentimental. Kat wasn't the sort to send messages like that if there was a way back. This wasn't the idle threat of a pissed-off wife berating an errant husband.

It was over. It would have been good for her to have remained on tap, as she had been for several months. He narrowed his eyes and looked at Teddy Clayton's photograph. Perhaps the twat did need a lesson after all.

Kathryn Tasker had been beside herself with terror ever since Kriss told her about the stuff on SocMed. Within minutes, she'd deleted her own accounts and everything on her regular phone that might link her to Kriss. If her husband discovered the messages she'd shared with Kriss, or any messages involving another man, it would be the end of everything she'd worked for. All those nights in and around Birmingham chasing the men with money; the capture and seduction of Jeff Tasker, divorced millionaire, entrepreneur and much older man; their overtly ostentatious courtship and engagement; the new home near Lichfield and dazzling purchases that filled it; the wedding in Antigua and honeymoon all over the Caribbean.

She had it all, but after eight years Kat was trapped by Jeff's personality and cloying affection. He was an aggressive violent man, and even though that was never directed at her, she knew he was thoroughly unpleasant in all his other relationships. Kat had slowly been able to join up the words *organised* and *crime* when reviewing Jeff's business activities. Notwithstanding that alarming knowledge, Kat still needed the colossal allowance and occasional ad hoc payments with which he showered her. She still needed to have the luxury of her apartment in central Birmingham and to show Jeff it was the right place for her to be – close to her family - when he was out of town. She still needed to conceal the reality that it was a place used to entertain men closer to, and often younger than, her own age. Above all she knew that if Jeff ever discovered the extent of her infidelity there was nothing to stand between her and a messy post-script. He was a face, connected to other faces. He would use those to close down anything requiring rapid resolution. His adoring love for her, which she saw had refused to abate after years together, would be unerringly replaced by the scowling retribution she had no doubt was dished out to double crossers.

Kat needed to wipe a lot of slates. Her conscience needed cleansing of encounters.

She'd met Kriss one evening in Tamworth at a charity fund raiser. Jeff was busily starring in the show, so she was instructed to mingle and get people to empty their pockets. She quickly targeted the table funded by MarMap. They were easy pickings, renowned for unscrupulous business behaviour, especially where money was concerned. Owner and Managing Director, Marcus Mapplewick, was also a legendary show-off when it came to flashing his wallet at events like this. With a dazzling smile, Kat had dropped onto a seat between Tracy Mapplewick and a tall, hench man who looked bored, but attentive. Kat's demand that they cough up for some raffle tickets - all in a good cause - made Mrs Mapplewick smile at her with condescending dismissal. If only she knew how small she and her husband really were alongside the grown-up money. But the fit guy, who introduced himself as Kriss Jarvis, was clearly unable to resist either her smile or her well-scaffolded bosom. He'd pulled out two hundred quid to pay for ten tickets, half for him the other five for the Mapplewicks. Kat rewarded his generosity with a squeezed thigh but didn't linger and floated off to other tables with no backward glance.

Kriss had watched her go, expecting they would never meet again. He knew something of Jeff Tasker's exploits and assumed that the lovely Mrs Tasker would be an impenetrable fortress, despite her flirty selling skills. It was a significant shock, therefore, when he looked at his five tickets to find a scribbled note suggesting a meeting, a mobile number and a X. He didn't know whether to be excited or terrified.

A few weeks later, Kriss realised he wasn't the only man in her life but that suited him. It was simple and efficient for him to have the benefit of a situation that was going nowhere. The encounters with Kat involved sex and a hefty coke habit, both of which they enjoyed to the fullest extent possible. They could never project their relationship publicly and all their meetings were midweek trysts at either her Birmingham love nest, or his cottage in the countryside north of Lichfield. But the secrecy and terror of being discovered made it somehow frightening, dangerous and doubly passionate, making Kriss understand why things like erotic asphyxiation might be a turn-on. They'd agreed from the start they would keep written communications, by text or messaging, to a controllably innocent minimum. But something had been switched on in both their heads and during the Christmas just past they'd found themselves massively aroused by explicit, uncensored sexting. Like addicts, they were incapable of stopping themselves writing filth to and about each other and supplemented their scribbling with frequent photographs of inventive and enticing poses.

When Teddy's SocMed post had been discovered by its victims, Kriss' primary concern was the impact on MarMap and how to explain his poor security to Marcus. But he'd very quickly realised that the short passage of sexting captured in the photograph was more cosmic in its potential consequences than anything in his email to MM. Kat's face was there alongside her lewd suggestions; it wasn't easily identifiable as her; someone glancing casually at it would not easily discern her features; but someone with decent enhancing skills might easily draw out Kat's portrait from the tiny blurred image.

Kat hadn't needed to see it. The very existence of something so public was a dagger through her mind. After cutting all ties with Kriss and all her other fuck buddies, she decided to head for the hills and pray that Jeff was too preoccupied, and everyone around him too habitually scared, to find out about Teddy Clayton's post. Jeff was always telling her to get away during the winter, so she got his PA to arrange for her to be at their alpine retreat until further notice.

6

It's ten fifteen when I get to the apartment. Within just a few seconds I know Jude has been and it must have been recently, perhaps within the last half hour. A large amount of post is neatly stacked on the shelf inside my front door and there's a quite powerful reminiscence of the Issey Miyake perfume she often wears. I follow the fragrance along the hall to the living room and kitchen then back to my bedroom. She's left a pair of her knickers on my pillow alongside a post-it note saying: *Smell these and weep.*

At least, I assume they're her knickers.

Jude forgot to set the alarm when she left, but I've given up trying to get her to be more careful with my security. And my happiness.

Although... it's not true that I'm unhappy here. It is a simple abode filled with baubles, framed joy and almost none of the material things Amy and I had accrued. My life has been enhanced in many ways since I moved in just over six months ago. I sometimes call it my home but really this place has simply become the base camp from which I set out: working, eating, sleeping, communicating, administering, fornicating. Perhaps sometimes I drink beer or wine, then dance or sing along to music. An occasional guest adds to the illusion that these various walls, floors and ceilings are an Englishman's castle, and perhaps the children add to that romantic notion when they come to stay.

This is all a mirage. Like an imagined oasis in the desert it promises hope and succour for the journey ahead; but that is quickly crushed by the truth; that neither is there.

The poorly heated train and short walk from the station have made me cold and I'm tempted by bottles of scotch and brandy, even though it's a school night. But rules are rules, and anyway I'd had more than enough alcohol with Dave two nights past. Instead I make hot chocolate and add some squirty cream, creating a mound of gooey joy that slowly dwindles into the drink. It tastes richly comforting and I soon make a second mugful.

Despite my long-standing routine of travel, the journey always makes me wired and pacey and prevents me from sleep. It's only after the homeward trips, as if somehow a drug is released on the West Coast Mainline that builds me up to be shot at and jumpy. Do I dissolve when I get home? Become a vapour, held in a suspension until Monday comes and I'm sprayed out from my front door, substantial once more? Is my life just travel to and from a place where it is governed by a corporate faith in all things? Maybe not; maybe so; maybe maybe. Perhaps this hyper-tension is nothing more than a reaction to the numbed tedium of rail travel? Or to the certainty that work is all I have; the centre of my existence, and when it ends, I am feverish from the reality of having nothing else to do.

Enriched by the two hot drinks, I fire up my iMac to sync everything from the days away. I get Joe on Vidicall to let him know I'm in Lancaster. He's a bit drunk and doesn't talk for long but he's funny when he's had a few beers and seems slightly more talkative than usual, albeit about nothing. Beth is offline but she replies to my text saying she's glad I'm back safely.

Jude sends me a text: 'I've put something in the microwave: 4 mins on Nuke Setting.'

'Thanks honey.'

'Make sure you eat it.'

'I will. You're a star.'

'Nearly asleep so can't chat now. I'll drop round for lunch tomorrow. Make me a cheesy toastie xx.'

I find an Indian ready meal in two plastic boxes; rice and a chicken korma. On the worktop nearby, there's a packet of mini naans alongside cardboard instructions for cooking the meals. Four minutes later, a bell sounds and the contents of one box are hissing and bubbling like a geyser. I fork the food on to a large plate then grab and take this unexpected treat to the dining table.

'Just what the doctor ordered. My turn to treat you soon. No need to reply - see you tomorrow. Sleep well babe x.'

Having taken four minutes to heat up the food, it's almost twice that long before it's safe to eat. While I wait, I check two new followers on Chattabox, neither of whom is known to me. Dave (*&dpdevs*) has a profile that tells me no more than mine would tell a stranger. He has a nondescript face, is based in London and his recent activity is a couple of Repeeped news items about uncontroversial subjects. He has one follower and follows five. I assume he's a new starter, a Chattabox novice who won't last the pace and will soon be gone.

I am a test case.

I don't want to be a test case.

The other is Tina Thomas (*&teena8shu*). No photo or header; nine followers; following seventy-seven. It could be anyone or anything and I don't follow back. The lack of a photo might suggest a bot, or someone with something to hide. But, in both cases, I dip into their retinues to look for names that connect them to me or to each other. I find none.

I should probably block them, but I never really know if that helps. And anyway, I lack the mettle to use blocking and unfollowing as a weapon, the way I see others do. It suits me to just amble on, without the courage to have an opinion or standpoint; something I could endlessly recycle, like a bot, to be met either with the faint echoes of agreement or with the battering ram of dissent. My politics are unfashionable, and I have no faith. I see the world through my own eyes, not something granted to me by a credo or hand-me-down. It means I'm not told what to think and feel and, in turn, I don't get pulled to pieces by a sense of inadequacy and cowed submission.

So, instead, I Peep away to the world with banal indecision about walks at Helvellyn or the Madness of Kings Cross. It's meaningless bloggerel but I'm made comfortable by that translucent suit of no colours, woven from threads of grey.

The chicken is soft and tender.

A message from Carla makes me smile and drops me back into reality. She's home from her evening out and feels like a catch up. In our three days of chat, she hasn't once asked the default questions, like what I do, why my marriage ended or whether we should plan a holiday in the Maldives. She also doesn't pepper her written words with smiley faces or emojis. It's been a grown-up discussion that dances around the handbags of our respective enquiries and it's got me thinking it could soon be a good time to suggest we meet.

I reply that I'm back safely and eating a hasty supper.

'Doesn't all the travelling get you down?'

'It's a means to an end. The alternative would be to move south, which I'm not sure I could handle. I tried it for a while and became very homesick, which is ironic because Lancaster doesn't always feel like home anymore. And I believe - I think I believe - that it's not the kind of loyalty I would receive in return.'

'But you said you could live in London.'

'I did. But only with the back-up of several million quid and no day job. I wouldn't live within fifty miles of it doing and earning what I do today.'

She doesn't reply for several minutes and I am distracted by new matches. The extended reach of my search means that London and the South East are becoming the main focus of what the site offers me. But the smiles and stories are no different in Guildford or Barnet than in Gildersome or Barrow. None of the latest cohort of opportunities draws me in, and none of them has checked me out.

Carla is rapping on my door again.

'Do you have other women contacting you on here? I am getting inundated by messages and smiles. It's very distracting. Some of these men are a bit gross.'

It's no time to tell lies.

'I'm not chatting to anyone else, but I do always try to thank people if they send me a smile and reply politely to anyone who messages me.'

'You must be a very kind man. I'm much more abrupt. Some of these blokes are clearly just players. I suspect many of them are probably married. I wonder how many women fall for it?'

'And how many are perfectly happy to go along with it.'

'Yes. I suppose that might also be true. But not me. Although the reason I stopped just now was because there is this guy who's been very persistent. Paul from Morley.'

I wonder if this is building up to something and am tempted to back off. She proves me wrong.

'But I've told him to leave me alone as I'm interested in you. I didn't tell him your name, obvs. LOL.'

'That's very nice of you,' and then, boom...! 'Maybe we should arrange to meet soon?'

'What do you have in mind?'

Result: she didn't say *no*.

But it's possible that there is no question more loaded with significance than the one she just asked. The photos and the words in people's profiles are a jumble of truth, public relations and temptation. They suck you in and you make a play, reviewing the profile time and time again - looking for clues, loopholes or escape routes. If you remain sucked in, what follows adds to the attraction because the chat messaging enhances the allure. There can be bumps and scrapes but assuming your correspondent isn't evidently psychotic, you learn to see that there is a straight road ahead with green lights for go-go-go. The words you use, both of you, create a bond. It's not a conversation you want to leave, but you're not speaking so you never need to stop to breathe. You can be pen pals forever if you're not careful, so meeting in person has to be the objective with anyone who's retained your interest for a few days. But there's a small sub-routine that sits meekly between chat on the site and any initial exploratory meeting. It's an important next stage and I walk on to it, lines learned.

'Why don't we catch up by phone first? I'm more than happy to give you my number, but there is no pressure at all for you to give me yours.'

'It's a great idea. But I'm tired now, and I expect you are too so perhaps we wouldn't be at our best. Then I'm visiting my parents' tomorrow evening. What about Friday after work? I generally get home between six and six thirty on Fridays.'

'That would be lovely.' I tell her my mobile.

'Okay, thanks.'

Within a couple of seconds, a text pops up: 'Hi Teddy. It's Carla. Maybe we can chat on here instead of on the site?'

'Seems we're all joined up. That's good news.'

'I'm tired, but I'm glad you want to talk. It's silly to just keep messaging.'

'Yep. Agreed. Let me call you Friday. Shall we say six forty-five?'

'Perfect. Gives me time to get in, get changed and pour a glass of gin or two.'

'K.'

'Will look forward to it.'

'Night Carla xx.'

'Night Teddy. Sleep well. Xxxx'

Who has snared who? The fact that we're going to talk is inconclusive, but it's a big step up from mere chat. Sharing phone numbers is something you're advised not to do without being really clear about the risks. Suddenly you're no longer within the confines of a site that notionally governs what you can say and do. Now you're up to where you might be after an evening chatting someone up in a bar: numbers exchanged with a view to progression and a whiff of something magical to come. Except: it's nothing like being in a bar; I have no idea if Carla is real; I've simply taken it on trust.

I feel like I need some help and advice and wonder about asking Beth or Joe. It took me ages to get over a sense of guilt that I was using a dating site, and that my kids would neither want nor need to know. But when I hinted at it, Beth said it was completely normal and Joe told me it was time I got back in the saddle. It led to some interesting conversations but they didn't last long, and these days the subject doesn't come up.

It's close to midnight, but I decide to quickly go online to check up on progress from the licencing and other problems. Nothing has changed; I can rest assured, but I send a final email confirming we are in calm waters.

While I'm finishing the last few words of that message, I see a pop-up on my iMac screen showing that I have a *matchmates* message. It's from Mimi in Lytham St. Anne's.

'Hi there Teddy. I've been looking at your profile and think you're really interesting and stand out from the crowd. I admire that in anyone, but especially in a man. Would love to know more about you. Like what you do and where you work. Can we chat on here?'

It reminds me that three nights earlier I'd smiled benignly at Karen from that same neck of the woods and have heard nothing back. When I check Karen's profile, the small traffic light system alongside her name is shaded grey, and when I hover over that it says she has not been online since Tuesday. She's also never visited my profile. A loss to the system and to each other. She looks so kind in her photos. Why did she start up on a dating site and then back off so soon? I sometimes wonder if some people get drunk with their mates who encourage them to find love on-line. Gripped by the intoxicating power of virtual possibilities, they concoct a profile and photo collage - an irresistible on-line entity. Less than two days later it all seems horribly wrong and they back off, terrified of the consequences. Or, perhaps, terrified of the costs.

Karen has gone. We will never be matched mates.

I reply to Mimi: 'Hi. Right now, I'm sort of focused on someone I've met on the site and don't want to waste your or her time. Hope you find what you're looking for.'

Within a few minutes, her message has disappeared from my in-box. I am deleted. I never existed in her world, and that's a considerable relief.

I have a hot shower and, once dry, slide naked into bed and set up my music streaming system to play the Benedictine Monks of Clervaux chanting their liturgical Latin. I set the sleep mode to give me forty-five minutes, by when it will be past two am.

I didn't think I would sleep well, but it's almost eight when I wake. I lie there, listening to faint noises all of which are an invasion from outside the building. Birds, trains, muted voices, traffic, dogs. These are almost nebulous. I am in a peaceful place. My apartment is in a massive Edwardian house, converted in to four dwellings with a large common entrance hall: mine is on the ground floor; Johnnie and Joanne are upstairs; Amber is on the second floor, with a bedroom and bathroom in the loft (the developer called it the duplex flat but she calls it the penthouse); and Barrie has the basement. We mainly keep ourselves to ourselves and there is very little noise up or down the floors.

For most of the last ten months I've woken on a Wednesday morning after my trips to London; not Thursday. While I throw on a tee shirt and some joggers, then make porridge, I rewire my head to adjust. I'd woken up with one schedule ticking through my brain like a telex. A different schedule now confronts me, and it isn't long before I'm engulfed by the work needed to re-assign Paul Wilson's projects.

I have exactly the same adjustment the following morning. I crank start my day slowly and informally and the space I'm afforded pretty much continues into the next couple of hours. I have no meetings and very few emails, so I make myself busy with Martian and Lighthouse. I don't abuse the freedom, but sometimes abuse the people responsible for giving our projects such abject codenames.

Carla sends me a couple of texts and is clearly looking forward to talking later in the day. I respond in kind. But she also wards off further chat with news that she will be in a client meeting all morning and early afternoon.

At ten thirty, I run my end of week team call. It's usually little more than a summary from everyone to close down five days of effort but, this Friday, there is a frisson of the unspoken. I'm not interested in that and have no intention of being drawn into anything other than business as usual. I don't even run the meeting sitting down at my laptop. I've things to do so I roam the apartment listening on my Bluetooth headset while I do bits and pieces of housework: clothes loaded in to the washer; a mound of unsolicited mail and fliers cast out in to the recycling bin; bedding stripped in my bedroom; four unfeasibly thick slices parted from a loaf of wholemeal bread; cheddar cheese grated; tomatoes sliced, chives snipped. I interject with bland platitudes every once in a while, but this is pretence and I have no guilt about it. I still manage to finish the call on time at midday and immediately set myself as Do Not Disturb. The toastie machine is soon heating up and when Jude's key rattles in the door, her two-inch thick sandwich is a one-inch thick grilled sensation.

We kiss just inside the door. It's a passionate, searching thing. Time was when we just used to fuck right there in the hall, but today is about food and chat. Soon we're seated at the bar in the kitchen, each with a plate of food and a glass of water. My work laptop is adjacent to my plate so I can deal with or track any potential intervention.

'Did you enjoy your supper?'

'I did. Thank you.' I reach over and kiss her on the neck below her ear. She tilts her head, so I do it for longer before whispering: 'How's your sandwich?'

'It's delicious Teddy. Revoltingly bad for me but so are you, and you're less fattening. I'm going to miss our workout tonight.' She licks crumbs from her mouth and makes a disgusting slurpy noise.

'Remind me why you've ditched me this evening?'

Jude sighs bitterly. 'I have to join the husband on this trip to see his brother.' She breathes in deeply and her next words form part of a long exhalation. 'I shouldn't be so callous; Lewis is very poorly. Craig, in a last-minute switch from his recent routine, is flying back to Manchester so I can join him in Scotland. It could be the last opportunity for us all to be together as it seems likely Lewis won't see Easter. He's become increasingly drowsy, interspersed with spells of delirium and agitation. We'll be driving up more or less as soon as Craig gets dropped off this afternoon and return home on Sunday evening. Sorry Teddy; you know how much our Fridays mean to me. But family is family; even the husband's band of intolerable goons.'

Since mid-November Jude and I have enjoyed almost every Friday night together. For years, Craig has been constantly away, either at his company's head office in Rotterdam or travelling the world. But in response to his brother's increasingly fragile health, Craig started a new routine: weekdays away; end of week in Scotland; Saturday to Monday at home with Jude.

She didn't take long to create her own routine with me, safe in the knowledge that Craig never calls her.

It's all too good to be true and, best of all, Jude covers up her Friday absences with that wonderful old alibi, *the Girls' Night Out* (and isn't that irony heaped on fucking irony). I double check all this regularly with Jude, but it seems Craig has totally bought the story that she visits her friends, Paula and Gill, in Ulverston and usually stays over so she has company. Paula and Gill are models of discretion, and Craig doesn't know their numbers. So, Jude heads out of their house in sparkling clothes, a trolley case bumping along behind her with next to nothing in it. A taxi collects her and heads for the town centre and Lancaster station where I pick her up.

We never go out. These Friday nights are just about food, a few drinks, a lot of talking, cuddles, a bath together and sometimes a long, sensual massage. And then whatever those aperitifs encourage for the main course.

Once, I asked Jude why she kept up the whole charade with her clothes and bags. She replied that it was a bizarre question from a man who had spent hundreds having his shameless wife investigated. But she also said that the pretence was part of the game for her. Part of ramming her husband's lack of care and attention right down his gullet, without him ever knowing.

She sighs again. 'At least it means I won't have to sit in the house with him for yet another of his interminable Saturday evenings: cooking; drinking; saying fuck all; listening to his shitty music; watching him chatting happily to his friends on chat groups; resisting his urges.'

I watch her say all this and feel a small lurch of dismay. 'I'll miss you too. It's been a funny week.'

Jude finishes off her sandwich and I watch her tidy away our things. In the time since we started seeing each other she has changed her hair colour so many times I've lost track. Today it's a sort of ash colour, but it looks as if there's a kind of violet thing going on too. It depends on the light. She has pale blue eyes and always tells me to beware should they turn to an arctic ocean colour. They never do. She's wearing quite nondescript clothes: *my out and about doing-good-deeds garb* she calls them; flat shoes; black tights; a knee-length woolly grey skirt; a pale blue jumper. She looks sensational. But now she's caught me gazing at her and we're soon entwined in kisses and silent tactile wonder.

'Tell me about your funny week babe. There's something bugging you.'

There's plenty to tell her, but some of it I ought not say. She's wiping away crumbs from my chin and I find, like I always find, that her face and eyes are so easy to look at and speak to. So I tell her all about my new responsibilities, dinner with Dave, the extra nights away and, without a care for any potential breach of confidence, about the Paul Wilson imbroglio.

'That sounds like he's some sort of nemesis for you.'

'He's not that, but Paul is certainly not my kind of colleague. And I'm pretty sure he's been suspended.'

'What do you think he's done?'

'I really don't know. He's been the team's problem child for months but in an irritating, whining, muttering way.'

'That wouldn't get him suspended though.'

'It wouldn't even get him a slapped wrist.'

She's looking at me with concern.

'There's something else, isn't there. Are you in trouble too? Tell me.'

'I'm not in trouble. But I have been interviewed by HR and Security about an allegation of misconduct.'

Jude pulls her face away and puts her hands either side of my face.

'I knew something was wrong.'

'Nothing's wrong.'

'What are you alleged to have done?'

I tell her about the interview and questions.

'Such invasive questioning.'

Now she's gently massaging my head with her fingertips.

'It's just about establishing the facts. Misconduct, real or false, has to be investigated.'

'Didn't you feel abused?'

'No, because there was nothing to worry about. Nothing to confess.'

'Could you have had a third party in the room with you?'

'Funnily enough, that went through my head when I was asked to attend the meeting. It all happened ridiculously quickly.'

'But nemesis Paul and this investigation are linked. They must be.'

'Change the subject. I'm not in trouble. And I'm not guilty.'

Jude still has my head in her hands. I feel comforted by it as if something is being replenished through her fingers.

'There is no point speculating. The only certainties are that he's on leave of absence, and I have been interviewed about alleged misconduct. It's easy to tie the two together, but that's inconclusive.'

'Aren't you linking the two?'

'Of course I am. The third certainty is that it's easy to get rid of a problem. If he's done something bad it might be something relatively trivial, innocent even, that gets him kicked out.'

'Which is when it starts to look and feel sinister.'

'It isn't sinister. It's just how the machine works.'

'And screw the labour laws. That's how Craig sees it.'

'It's how everyone sees it. Our rights as employees are a contemptible nuisance in the eyes of most business leaders.'

'There's still something behind your eyes that looks like worry Teddy. Talk to me.'

I smile at her and she smiles back. We have nothing together except this kind of open discussion, as much curious impetuous sex as we can fit in and a vaguely loving affection for one another. There's no conflict: no responsibilities; no arguments about unresolved repairs or failed gardening experiments; no broken promises.

'There is something bugging me.'

'I knew it.'

'Two things actually and both are about confusion and turmoil.'

Jude pulls herself closer to me. I'm still sitting on a bar stool and she's wedged between my legs with her hands down the back of my joggers.

'The questions about Annabel made me feel as if I'm missing out on something – on her perhaps. She isn't what I want – I've got you. But what do I want?'

Jude's hands have moved up my back and are kneading my deltoids. 'And the other thing?'

There's the other problem we never have to resolve. There are no defensive over-reactions to worries or concerns. I suppose it's because what we're doing is wrong on rather too many levels.

'I'm a fool because I invest all this time chasing people on dating sites. It's like an addiction. Why do I do it? Why do I need that when I have you?'

Jude laughs.

'But you don't have me. We're not an item. We will never live together, need a mortgage, go to each other's family funerals, have a pet, become swingers, announce that we're in a relationship on SocMed, walk at loggerheads around Sainsbury's looking for the right coffee beans or take a holiday on Santorini. We fill the holes in our respective lives. That is all.' She accompanies those three words with scratches down my back; one-two-three.

'I know. But sometimes I feel like I'm being unfaithful to you.'

She laughs again.

'You dozy prick. How can you be unfaithful to an adulteress?'

That really is quite a good point, but I persevere.

'Dave told me I should ditch you, because you're married, and get out on the town to pick up a full-time bird.'

'I have never met Dave, but I am prepared to bet he never used the word - the wholly offensive word, I might add - *bird*.'

'Actually, he referred to you as a *bimbo* which I hastily corrected.'

'My hero.'

'He also said I should join clubs to meet like-minded women. And I should stop using internet dating.'

'He's right. Look, we've agreed all along that this is just about fun and being with someone because we want to be with them, not because of some ancient list of ritual vows. What we have won't last forever but if you want to see other people, it won't stop me wanting to see you. Just keep Friday nights free, don't ever make them toasties, and above all don't do that thing you do with your tongue.'

'Which particular oral delight do you mean?'

'The talking. You cannot begin to imagine how wonderful it is to sit in a room with you and talk as equals. I honestly can't put a price on it.'

Craig is his company's finance director with a reward package that could keep some countries afloat. He is much older than her and, notwithstanding a romantic courtship and happy early years together, most of their marriage has been a toxic waste. So far as I can tell, he treats Jude like a child; a servant; a handmaiden; a dumb waitress with neither brains, culture nor class. In fact, she has all three in abundance. He never discusses work with her, dismissing any offer of help with an arrogant shake of his head. Yet, to compound all those crimes of dispassion, Craig revels in showing the world that he has Jude; sensuous Jude; beautiful Jude; voluptuous Jude; MaxMara-clad Jude; bejewelled Jude: the veritable trophy wife.

Very early on in our relationship I asked why she stays with Craig. Her reply, that she couldn't do better, was a shock; and she went on to say that, in spite of everything he does and says, she stays because she needs the freedom his money and time away allow her. Which was nothing to do with me: I was just icing on the cake. She said she didn't need to work but did her voluntary and charity work to keep her from being (in her words) another sad, middle-aged woman addicted to doing coffee, lunch and shopping. She also did it to remind Craig that they were childless, due to his non-functioning innards. She'd desperately wanted children with Craig; she couldn't deny it. But his inability to deliver ended up being a mighty relief.

So, they rattle along in this rusting charabanc, with signs on the front saying *All is Well* and luggage packed carefully away on the roof; bound for the seaside, frolics and all. A destination that doesn't exist.

Jude is never concerned that Craig might learn of her misdemeanours despite the fact that, underneath his suave business persona lurks a menacing alter-ego that craves *shoot 'em up* and other more bloodthirsty forms of virtual slaughter. Which makes me doubt her confidence that he won't find out. Jude always calms me by saying he'd never know because he's impervious to other people's feelings, wants and needs. All she has to do is stay.

'And now, my sweetest of hearts, despite the fact that I would love to make use of this persistently flattering boner, I am going to have to get back to work. Why don't you go out tomorrow evening? Give Luke Lively a call and have a stag event. You never know; you might find a nice younger model from the uni.'

7

It's murky and raw outside so it's easy to immerse myself in work. A small bow wave of mails has built up during the time spent with Jude, but it doesn't take long to clear them. Then it's a typical corporate Friday afternoon: no-one is rocking boats; no major escalations; no disquiet following the bombshell about Paul.

But then the boat does rock ever so slightly.

Annabel and I aren't connected on SocMed and, to the best of my knowledge she doesn't use it much. It's almost dark outside when my iPad pings an alert from messaging. It's her, asking that we connect. I'm initially sceptical: she can easily contact me over our corporate network.

I use that to ask her: 'Is that definitely you?' And she confirms that it is, so we link up.

'Hey, sorry about the cloak and dagger, but recent events got me thinking it made more sense this way.'

'Sure. What's up? I'm a bit rattled.'

'Don't be. But I am worried about something.'

'OK.'

'I really shouldn't have shown you that email on Monday. The Wilson/Hatton convo. With hindsight it was stupid of me.'

'I don't see why.'

'No. It really was a bad thing to do.'

'Is your office bugged? Does your laptop webcam record what you do?'

'I guess not.'

'Then no one knows except us. And I won't tell anyone.'

'Keep it that way. Please.'

'Have you been interviewed about our alleged affair?'

'We must not and cannot discuss that.'

I'm wondering what to say next, but she sends more.

'Have a good weekend. I'm not in London Monday so we should talk early. I'll stick something in our diaries.'

'I won't be there. New schedule. There Tues-Thu.'

'Makes sense. But it doesn't stop us talking.'

'Are you ok?'

There's a long gap until the dots start dancing in the messaging window. Then they stop and, soon, her status changes briefly to *Active 1m ago*.

'I'm fine.'

I feel overwhelmed by the sense that she's hiding something from me, and her change of tack doesn't help. 'At least you won't have PW to deal with.'

'True. Got plans for the weekend?'

'Packing. Airport shizzle. Hotel bed. You?'

My list of plans doesn't elicit much enthusiasm and Annabel soon closes the conversation. The exchange of messages, in the stark light of my iPad screen, troubles me. It isn't like Annabel to be fluffy or touchy/feely but, even for an online chat, her messages are coldly blunt. As I work hard through the afternoon and into the early evening, I find suspicions bubbling to the surface and popping around my head like the thought bubbles in a cartoon.

Is she in trouble for something above and beyond the misconduct charge?

Is her temporary status uplift a step too far, and she knew it?

Is there something between her and Paul Wilson?

Is her concern about showing me that transcript just an excuse to get in touch on a personal basis?

But it can't be that. It's so long since that briefest of kisses in Bucharest. How can it be important now; to anyone, but especially to me?

Nor is it her style to be fragile but the curt, disinterested way she'd messaged me is a very sudden, polar, uncharacteristic change. I want to message her and renew the discussion with direct questions about what is going on and her motives for contacting me via a social messaging tool. I suppress that but the bubbles keep popping up, especially since my eventual conclusion is that her problem might simply be her enduring, unending loneliness.

It's been more than ten years since tragedy altered the course of her life. Weeks before she was due to marry Philip, the man she'd been with since they were teens, he was shot dead in Chicago while there on a business trip. A random act of armed robbery became lethal in a busy street just a block away from his hotel. It left Annabel eternally bereft; sometimes she refers to Philip in the present tense, as if he will be there when she gets home and their plans are all on track. But, like Miss Havisham's wedding cake, that life and those plans are coated in dust, cobwebs and the bitter aroma of loss.

While we were still peers at work, and especially after Amy left, she often surprised me with stories about her affairs: sticky dates with dead end opportunities. She told me I was a safe pair of ears because I didn't challenge or judge what she saw as her spiralling wantonness and plummeting reputation. It was after one of those discussions, that evening in a Bucharest hotel bar with beer and wine as stimulants, that I nearly became another dead end.

Her promotion to director and leader of our team meant our discussions and any hint of intimacy stopped happening. Last summer Annabel became the real deal as a leader. Everyone noticed, and no one was surprised when, around Christmas time, the office grapevine trembled with news of a further promotion to a European role. In the two months since those rumours began, she's been strong and confident, driving the team hard and displaying a level of assertive strength that seemed to grow exponentially.

But none of that explained what we'd just shared.

I don't stop working on a Friday if there is anything outstanding with my name against it. Methodically, rhythmically, thoroughly, I am industrious to an extent that few would rival on a Friday afternoon. But it leaves my mind free and gives me the confidence that, when I eventually close my laptop, no-one can say *Ed hasn't delivered this week*.

SocMed is ramping up to its usual weekend start. Increasing levels of posts and chat; plans for the evening, excitement mounting about cocktails, the food people will be eating, and which bistros and bars will prevail. My ageing hippy friend, Nick Sumner, has chosen The Who's *Who Are You?* as his chosen groove tune – a musical kick start for the evening and weekend to come. Our mutual friends respond in kind with other toe-tapping sweetmeats. One or two of my friends have culture on their agendas; the theatre; a film; a concert - mainly pop or rock. Sitting in and around all that is the endless recycling of memes, humour and headlines. It feels good to be part of it. My life is improved by this cavalcade of shared love. The electronic connection is unbreakable and impervious to jealousy or the vagaries of body language. I don't have much to say but I hit a few likes to show I haven't left the building. I heartily endorse Nick's choice of song.

As five pm comes and goes, my on-line contacts list shrinks and shrinks until only Georgi, Annabel and I are online: green for Available.

I send Georgi a message telling her it's late on a Friday and she should be in a bar to start the weekend with her husband. She sends a smiley and says she has to join a call with The Americans at eight her time.

Dave calls, and we spend fifteen minutes reviewing events since Monday evening. It's a calming discussion about nothing much, but it's good to hear a friendly voice.

By six I'm feeling low because, usually, Jude is on her way by now. Instead, she's in a car with her husband making small talk about his week and trying to avoid the subject of a dying brother. We'd agreed no messages, but I'm tempted to break that promise. I feel a growing sadness about her absence and keep looking at an unwashed glass with her lipstick marks. I won't see her again for a week, yet possibly she will come and go from my apartment at least once in that time.

Annabel drops offline just after six fifteen and I'm still thinking I should get in touch to check what's going on. As I pick up my personal phone, it bleeps and shows me a text from Carla: 'Hi Teddy, I'm home and just getting changed and sorting my first drinkie. Are we still on for our chat?'

'Hi Carla - of course! I'm looking forward to it.'

'Me too. Laters. xxx' There's a cocktail glass emoji after those kisses.

With time to spare before Carla, I tap in the digits of another contact. Luke Crossthwaite and I met in primary school and remained fellow pupils until, at eighteen, we set off on separate academic voyages. Mine ended at Birmingham, Luke's at

London where his first in English seemed a good reason to stay in the capital forever; a success in all things.

His phone goes to voicemail. 'Hello mate, it's Ted. Hope your week has been okay. Just wondering if you feel like hitting town tomorrow evening for a few beers and a bite to eat. There's a handful of places with live music if you fancy it. I'm in all evening, so give me a call.'

Within just a few moments of my call with Carla, I realise something is indefinably wrong. We greet each other enthusiastically and it seems we are relaxed and calm, like this is reacquaintance rather than a new dawn. Slowly, we reassemble all the pieces of the online jigsaw because now we have the real person on the line and can properly assess things: like how our profiles fit together; questions about specific comments; laughter about the throwaway lines. It's going well, except I still can't put my finger on the thing that's bugging me.

Maybe it's a lack of spontaneity?

I'm still in this dither, but manfully keeping up the chat, when I see a mail land in my work inbox. It's titled: *Shotgun - We Are Live* and explains that the client's new system has been successfully rolled out. It's a confident message and ends with: *Many people have contributed to the success of Shotgun and they are all in cc. They have my thanks for a job well done. However, I have to call out two people: Costin Iordache has managed this project with great skill, keeping everyone (including me) on track with his usual quiet efficiency. And Ed Clayton, who in the last few days stepped in to support Costin and resolve a last-minute drama that was in danger of becoming a crisis.*

While Carla is talking into my headphones about her son's lack of effort in the build-up to his A levels, I write back to the project director: *It was my pleasure to help out on Shotgun. Am delighted it has finally been implemented and hope it keeps the client happy for years to come. Costin deserves the kudos. He did all the real work.*

Within just a few minutes, Annabel is back online and adds her own praise for our team's efforts in a mail that she has copied to her boss, Peter Dixon. The hierarchical backslapping has begun, and I decide it's time to log off and end my working week. I've laboured hard, and without complaint, despite increased workload and responsibilities. I'm a model corporate citizen, supportive of my team and my manager, setting the right tone in all that I've done and said. I reacted positively and openly to the worrying allegations about my conduct; I fell in line and complied. My kids are doing well and enjoying life and we've told each other that our love is always in place. The evening with Dave, a cherished old friend, was timely and joyful. There's been fun and banter on SocMed and I might have found someone on *matchmates* who might be The Answer. Jude isn't with me this evening, but our forty-five minutes together earlier today were enough to make us one after almost a week of nothing but e-chat and a couple of quick phone calls. I've a long walk, some shopping and an evening out planned for tomorrow. Things are joined up properly and ticking quietly along as they should.

Time for a small celebration.

As I look across at the collection of beer bottles on my kitchen unit I realise what is troubling me about Carla. At the start of our call, now in its twentieth minute, she mentioned she had already poured herself a large gin and tonic. This asserts itself audibly with the ringing of ice cubes on crystal and noisy swallowing. She has mentioned drinking and referred to getting drunk on several occasions. Then I hear the sounds of a bottle top unscrewing, fresh cubes in an empty tumbler, the sibilant pop of a can being opened.

Two gin and tonics in less than thirty minutes.

I hate that: solitary drinking to get drunk.

I'm not a prude about alcohol and I happily get drunk when the occasion merits it. But the role of being Dad's taxi and realisation that work makes every night a school night mean I never drink at home when there is so much I might have to do that requires sobriety. As it's Friday, I might drink a couple of those dozen beer bottles but don't see it as an obligation. Carla, it seems, is a bit of a lush. That isn't good for her. And she won't be good for me. When I hear her making a third drink, just on forty-five minutes into our call, I make a hasty withdrawal citing the arrival of a takeaway and my hunger. She doesn't seem too bothered that the call ended and there's no *it was lovely talking* follow up message. I'm so disappointed by the realisation that, as is so often the case, someone who looks good has a flaw that is fatal in my eyes. Her beauty and smile and fine words set her aside; but she is just another sham, with an online persona that doesn't exist in reality; a shambling dipso not worthy of my time or pursuit. Another false start.

But the disappointment doesn't last. I talk to Beth for nearly forty minutes and am laughing and smiling throughout the conversation. Joe isn't available to talk, but we exchange brief written words of happiness that the weekend is here. There are other faces on *matchmates* now and that means I can start again. I'm happily bantering with friends on SocMed and Peeping about my walking plans. Luke Lively has messaged that he definitely fancies a night out and will call me tomorrow to firm up. There's a fifties jazz playlist tinkering away in the background. I print off the very basic map of the walk I will do tomorrow and pull together the small array of accessories I will need for the short trip and route. I cook and eat a supermarket pizza then settle down in the living room to continue reading the autobiography of an ageing rock star who used to float my boat but, from his own words, now seems riddled with self-pity. Perhaps he wishes, behind the lines, that he had snuffed it with all the other celebrities in 2016.

This happy time is accompanied by just two beers that I savour with a kind of love. Another kind of love, unhurried and calm, full of gratitude for the brewer's efforts.

Much later, Jude messages me to say she is safely in Scotland.

8

I'm out of the door by seven fifteen. It's still dark as I trundle the car out into the avenue then cruise quietly away. The city is mute, slowly waking up, and I'm soon accelerating onto the M6 for the short hop to Carnforth, then on to Arnside. It's longer that way, but I can drive much faster on the motorway.

Despite being on my doorstep, I've never done any walking at Arnside. I usually speed on to Coniston or Keswick and the sexier Lakeland walking routes.

The town is still asleep despite the automated announcements at the railway station, loud enough for me to hear as I drive past it. The railway line snakes out from the station and over the river on a sturdy viaduct that looks suspiciously like it's built on shifting sands. Past closed pubs, cafés and cake shops I drop down to the pier and promenade and revel in the solitude that confronts me. In the murk of a wintry early morning, the tide is ebbing away, leaving a horizon filled by rippled sandy mud and I can just make out the northern shore. Away to the west, some lights are sparkling; I check the map on my phone and conclude that it must be Grange over Sands, about three miles yonder: a league apart.

Mine is the only car parked in the bays facing the estuary and I'm not surprised, for when I slip from my front seat, the air is cold, and a teasing chilly wind is ripping along the shoreline from the north west. The same gusts keep many flags, and perhaps the whole nation, aloft: I've never seen so many houses flying the Union Jack.

Dave's assertion that I should join a walking club was a reasonable enough thing for him to think, but it isn't for me. Being in such groups is too cosily enclosed; too bound by inside knowledge and rules. I want to walk on my own terms, without being governed. Walking is a pastime that needs no encumbrance; I can't be doing with rucksacks, maps and flasks of beverage. I need my boots and warm socks, a hat, a light waterproof over a fleecy top and layers. Under my old track suit trousers, my legs are encased in thin lycra leggings. Today I'll wear gloves too but even in all that, I still feel cold as I finish my preparations.

My phone is fully charged, and its walking app primed to track progress. I stuff a spare battery charger and cable into my jacket breast pocket, some cash and my wallet in the other. The final accessory is my digital SLR, carried in case there is some sight, view or wonder worth recording. I gulp down a final mouthful of tea from my travel mug, then throw away the slops.

And I'm all set for this route that I've only seen on a cartoon map from a website and which, if I get my timings wrong, could see me swept away into the bubbling polluted depths of the Irish Sea. Care is needed but it doesn't occur to me that I should have at least one companion to mind my back over the coming three hours or so. The only person who knows I'm doing this is

Jude, and she's probably still slumbering uneasily at her in-laws'.

It's light enough now, so I check in at Arnside on SocMed. It's around eight am and no one responds. Despite my slumbering buddies, the confirmation of my location helps me feel that I'm not alone; I'm secure; watched over.

The tide has left the beaches too slippery, muddy and sucky to enjoy so I stick to the pathways and pebbly nearshore, occasionally stopping to read the memorial plaques on benches facing the water. A couple of anglers are set up near the water's edge - rods and nets set in geometric certainty that fish will bite. There is a constant echoing counterpoint of birdsong, calls I can't tie down to any species. The grey wet sands smell of the sea, salty and somehow dirty. Small rocky crops are coated with foamy yellow flotsam. It's drearily unattractive.

After I've made a couple of hundred metres progress, a noisy rumble makes me look back towards Arnside where a train is crawling across the viaduct away from the town. Once it reaches the far shore, the silence is briefly overwhelming as if all the birds are scared and have taken flight. It's several minutes before the whistles and screeches resume.

I turn to find a collie looking amiably up at me.

'Hello pal. Here.'

I stretch my gloved hand towards him. He wags his tail enthusiastically and does that dog-thing that looks like a smile, until a shout of rage ahead of us makes him cower and retreat. In the distance, I can see a man and hear him shrieking: 'Fenton: Jesus Christ Fenton. Come ON.' My new pal rushes away to his master.

I sometimes feel I'd love to get a dog, but I know I can't. My scattered working life would make it impossible, or prohibitively expensive. Even so, I always feel my existence, especially on walks like this, would be fuller with an excited furry friend alongside me: and I'd give it a proper name, befitting a dog rather than a haulage company.

I'm not warmed up yet and realise the slow pace walking on pebbles and mud isn't helping. Ahead I can see a rockier landscape, but the seaward side is still characterless mud that sweeps around in curves, marking the places where the outlets of small streams dribble into the estuary. To my left, leafless tree trunks and stumps are growing twisted from the rocks and there is no noise, not even from the waters flowing away to the west. The silence is eery and slightly threatening, not helped by signs warning of constant danger from hidden channels, quicksand and rapidly rising tides. I'm fine; untroubled. But I could imagine this environment making some people struggle with the implicit danger and peril.

I need a piss, so I head behind a crumbling wall above the beach and relieve that need. There are small clumps of snowdrop and bluebell making their mark on the ground here. I hope I haven't killed them.

A few hundred metres more walking and I turn south. The wider expanse of Morecambe Bay is suddenly pervasive. I still have angled cliffy rocks to my left but, although Grange sits as a reminder of a certain civilisation on the opposite shore, the overwhelming sense is of a grey, neutral, empty void.

I stand and look at this nothingness. It seems to encapsulate all I have: eroded, sinking, crumbling rocks behind me; swampy mud to suck me in if I put a foot wrong; an engulfing roaring noise, unseen on the horizon; not a soul in sight; no rescuer should I stumble and fall. It's still early on a Saturday morning in late February 2017. The whole world is, apparently, in tatters and I can easily generate a scenario in which I strip off my clothes and leave them to be found by a puzzled dog-walker in a couple of hours. A mystery disappearance.

What would be the outcome? An easily filled vacancy at work. A new squeeze for Jude. My children faced with an imposed, acceptable, accepted father figure. Empty spaces in the already devoid world of my social medium. A few lines in the local papers, perhaps words from the north west's finest newscasters. Yet who knows? It might all be a subtle ruse; I might not have committed myself to the deep; I could be hermetically sealed in a cave, warmed by driftwood fires and living on cockles and samphire. A simple life - presumed dead.

I look at my phone, seeking solace and guidance. There is no signal.

Forty-five minutes later I pass signs telling me I'm in Lancashire and Silverdale. I'd been aiming for the latter but had no idea I'd left the former. Someone has scrawled *bust* above the county name: that's mildly curious, but graffiti isn't what it used to be.

Once away from the beach I'd picked up the pace, even on the quite narrow cliff-top paths. My frequent halts to take photos and to breathe in the atmosphere mean I've been walking for nearly ninety minutes and, as I drop down into the village, I can't make my mind up about whether to find a café for tea and toast or to press on. The homeward leg involves some moderately steep climbs and I decide the challenge is more important than fuel. But not before I've taken advantage of a rare signal on my phone, and the opportunity to upload some photos to Postpix. They soon attract the attention I crave and I rest for a while responding to comments, and checking posts by other contacts.

I hear the sound before I see the car. It's unmistakeable; the low throb of a Jaguar V12; I know it well; too well. The strange beauty of the car rolls towards me on the other side of the road. As it heads past and out of the village, the engine suddenly roars, and it rushes off into the distance.

Shortly after retiring in 2010, my dad spent some of his hard-earned savings on a 1973 E-Type roadster. It was only just roadworthy and in need of the tender loving care dad gave it over the next couple of years. A few months after proudly unveiling the glitteringly modified and rebuilt car, dad swerved to avoid a dog that had run in to the road. He didn't regain control and, when the car raced on towards and then under the trailer of a parked articulated truck, mum and dad were killed by the collision.

I was their only child.

In less than a year, Amy left me.

Alone.

I head up into Eaves Wood and the steady climb to the Jubilee Monument above Silverdale; its signs refer to it as *Pepperpot*, which seems harsh on Queen Victoria's memory. When I reach it, I find a sturdy little obelisk with yellow lichen dotted around its stonework, like dried snot from a giant uncontrolled sneeze. This small doff of the cap must have seemed consequential and relevant in 1887. Now, on its barren plateau overlooking the monochrome wastes of Morecambe Bay, it is as distant and neglected as any part of VR's empire must have been.

The woods are naked and cold, as if they will never be leafy or shady again. The chilly morning isn't warming up and no sunshine provides light and heat. I've turned around on the return trip and soon feel my lower back, thighs, knees and calves straining from some relatively steep climbs. The exertion is enough to raise my heart rate and cause a light sweat.

This is why I walk: work; effort; achievement; focus. A sense of movement towards, and then back again.

It's late morning when I reach Arnside Knott and I stand there wondering what the scene might be on a fine day. I can just make out the north shore of the estuary; the bridge out of Arnside looks like it belongs in a model railway set. Beyond it, the view vaporises. I slowly turn through 360 degrees and find myself thinking that without these cloudy barriers I might be able to see some of the dales to the north east, Cartmel Fell to the northwest, perhaps even the Old Man of Coniston. To the south, I suppose Morecambe and Heysham are there if you're interested.

This is the beauty of walking alone: I can imagine a whole geography without being corrected.

As I stand debating all this absent scenery, a couple comes running up the well-worn path from the east. They are clad in colourful branded clothing and footwear; lithe; moving with that wonderful efficient silence that serious runners achieve. They don't appear to be breathing heavily or sweating. It's very impressive. We exchange cordial nods and a muffled few words, but they don't stop to join my reverie. It turns out that these two, assorted pedestrians, fishermen's friends, Fenton and Fenton's owner are the only creatures I see during my walk. And the sole smile was Fenton's.

It's rare these days, but in the time between the divorce and his departure for university, Joe and I walked together almost every weekend. It was sublime to have my son alongside me as we trekked over hill and dale. I felt proud that he would give up his time, sometimes a whole day, when he could have been doing teenage things: working; music; gaming; sport; time with mates; aimless loitering in the streets. The walking underpinned and accelerated our transition from Father/Son to Man/Man, providing as it did the opportunity to talk without always needing eye contact. I still wonder if, without that activity, we might never have moved so far so quickly. Joe, by watching and listening, learned why I loved the time away from familiar haunts and routines. I learned that Joe, after a resentful hissing adolescence, had become a compassionate analytical young man with carefully constructed ambitions to succeed as a hedge fund manager. We fed each other with ideas and plans and, while sometimes Joe still resisted my clumsy paternal mentoring, there was at least a cessation of the daily flashpoint whenever I asked a seemingly innocent question.

Now our walks are restricted to just a few weekends a year, but it is Joe who always contacts me to say: 'I'm looking forward to this weekend at yours - where are we walking?'

When I reach the upper outskirts of Arnside, my knees and shins are aching from the strain of a rapid descent. I've also got a sore hip as a result of a tumble on the matted dewy grass.

Back at the car, I grab the electrolyte drink I'd prepared the previous evening and gulp it down as I walk along the promenade to find a coffee and some cake. The walk has been a perfect start to my weekend. I want to get home to sustain that feel good factor, but some irresponsible calories will help.

The café is warm, all vanilla and coffee and chocolate smells, and while I'm waiting for my latte and cake, I turn to see someone struggling up the steps outside. In a couple of paces, I'm at the door, have opened it and am helping a woman into the café. White haired, quite tall, a blue and grey checked woollen coat topped with a royal blue Pashmina, she seems the very epitome of enduring elegance. Not even an imperceptible stoop spoils her youthful image.

'That's very kind of you. Thank you. I don't know why these places make it so difficult to get in.'

'It's my pleasure. Can I help you to a table?'

She looks around as if lost and I wonder if perhaps she is waiting for a friend or family member. Then she nods and says 'Yes please my dear. That one there, so I'm not in a draft from the door. Maybe you could ask them to come and take my order?'

It makes me smile.

Back at the serving counter, my order is ready and as I walk into the café to consume it, my new best buddy asks me to join her, saying she'd welcome the company. I sit with her, nervously sipping my coffee and nibbling my cake. It's a bomb of sugary, sweet, sticky pleasure.

'Your cake looks lovely. What is it?'

'Salted Caramel Chocolate cake.'

'My, my. That sounds wickedly good.'

I confirm that it is and offer for her to taste it. She chuckles.

'No need my dear: I'm going to order some, even if I won't be able to eat it all. I'm sure they can put whatever I don't eat into a box for me to take away. My name is Constance, by the way. And you may not call me Connie.'

'Well I'm Edward. Edward Clayton. And you may call me Teddy, which all the best people do. And it looks like they are a bit too busy to come for your order so why don't I go and order it for you?'

Soon we both have a plate in front of us and, opposite my still steaming mug, she has a pot of tea for one. She takes her tea black and tops up the pot regularly with hot water.

'Tea must never be too strong: all that acid. What brings you to Arnside, Edward?'

'I've been walking.'

'Good for you. How far did you go?'

I explain the route, and some of the sights seen.

'Don't expect you saw much from the Knott this morning. It's a horrible day. Did you have a fall?'

She's caught me out.

'Well yes, but how can you tell.'

'You've mud all down your left trouser leg and on the back of your hand. Nothing broken I hope.'

I hadn't even noticed these tell-tale signs. 'Just injured pride; thankfully no-one was around to see my embarrassment.'

She is having a proper go at her cake as if she has no intention of leaving any. When she finishes one substantial mouthful, she resumes her questions.

'Walking on your own isn't everyone's idea of fun. No significant other, or band of brothers to do it with?'

'My son joins me when he's home from university. He's the only person I feel like walking with. We can walk for miles without talking. Neither of us likes to combine exercise with a social event.'

She looks at me over the brim of her cup.

'And where is home? Not too far from here, if I hear your accent correctly?'

Her curiosity is rather compelling. Perhaps she is missing someone to talk to and share thoughts or feelings.

I tell her I live in Lancaster and often work in London. And I have two wonderful children who make me proud every day. And I have a simple home and a great car. And I am lucky to have a job I like, and I do it well.

It's very easy to be this open and she listens patiently.

'You're a parent with no ring on your finger.'

'True. My marriage ended some time ago.'

'Maybe for the best Edward. Not many women would hang around very long with someone who likes to walk for miles without talking. Being a loner does not a good marriage make.' It feels like a starkly conclusive judgement, until she adds: 'All the more reason to find one who will. She'll be the one.'

Her smile is knowing and warming.

'Does your daughter ever join your walks?'

'She doesn't. And now you mention it, I don't really know why that is.'

'Perhaps you have a more cerebral connection with her? That's sometimes how it is between father and daughter.'

I watch her take a final mouthful of cake. 'And what brings Constance to Arnside on a chilly February day?'

'My daughter lives here and I'm visiting her. She's gone off to watch my grandson's football match in Carnforth. He plays right mid; whatever that means.'

There is a wry playfulness about her that is easy to join. I feel glad that she isn't lonely.

'So instead of sitting around her house on my own, I asked her to drop me in the town to have some fun. I grew up near here, and it's where my late husband and I raised our family. But when George died, I moved up the road to Kendal. Bit of an odd one that isn't it? Usually it's the kids that fly the nest. Perhaps I'm a cuckoo.'

We talk on, the way that strangers sometimes can: with neither an agenda nor the grinding of axes. An hour later, as I join the

M6, I am still smiling at the memory of a lovely encounter. I'd give anything for a date with someone my own age that was as open and charming as my brief encounter during that café time.

And I'd give anything to still have my own mother around; she was always full of chat; the same kind of chat that I shared with Constance. Inquisitive, perceptive and heart-warming.

I miss her so much.

9

Later, mid-afternoon, I'm in the city doing frivolous shopping. I don't really need anything but feel that my night out requires an accessory or two. My home town has the usual amalgam of shops you find all over England. It doesn't make it a special place, but it's still special in its way.

I buy things here and there: a pair of shoes; tee shirts; a smart shirt; some jeans; a glossy grooming set.

While I'm paying for one of these fripperies, Luke calls and we exchange ideas about our evening together.

'Shall I come by yours for pre-drinks?'

The guy behind the counter is bagging up my things with that look used to condemn customers who aren't concentrating.

'Pretending to be teenagers isn't what I was planning.'

I punch my pin into the card reader and nod when the guy asks me if I want a receipt.

'But we are going on the piss and on the pull, aren't we?'

'Yes; and maybe not.' I'm unwilling to commit to anything involving Luke's fantasies.

'Then we need pre-drinks.'

All done with my transactions, I thank the guy with another nodding head and smile. He is already greeting his next patron.

'No, we don't. That whole idea is pathetic and I'm not doing it.'

We're both laughing. We have this unwritten, unspoken sense of togetherness.

'You don't change Teddy. So puritanical.'

By now I'm in the street getting drizzled on. It's turned cold and I'm gazing at the sky wondering if it might snow.

'Don't talk bollocks Mr C. Neither of us needs to go out drunk. We've got more than enough money between us to spend on the requisite amount of beer and shots when we are out. Pre-drinks are for paupers and saddos, and we've been neither of those things since our respective divorces.'

'Very forthright Mr C. Okay then, where shall we meet?'

I propose either/or venues convenient for me. Luke has to travel into the city, and I know he won't object to these suggestions. And so it proves.

Shortly, with our plans set in stone, we've moved on; laughing with an escalating mania at various subjects that start and end in verbal cul-de-sacs; dead-end babble with no purpose other than to make ourselves laugh. It's a good overture to the coming evening. There will be limited thinking, purposeful flirtation and significant drinking. Long before the call ends, I've passed my bus stop and keep walking all the way home.

In the vestibule, I find Amber from upstairs knocking on my door. She jumps with a start when I greet her.

'Teddy, I was sure you were in. I'm sorry to trouble you but I have a bit of a problem.'

'It's no trouble. How can I help? Cup of sugar?'

She giggles as I unlock my door. 'I'm wondering if you've had any mail for me. Something quite important has gone missing. I've checked with the Wallaces and Barrie, but no joy.'

'Come in. I'll check.'

We've been residents in the same building for several months, but Amber has never been in my apartment. She follows me in and stands expectantly by the door as I deactivate the alarm.

'My sister sent it regular first-class mail. It's a... it's very important.'

I head to my study and grab the week's mail. So little of what I receive by post has any real significance and I clear it all on Sunday afternoons. Close to the bottom of this week's pile is a cheap white C5 envelope addressed to Amber Goodall. When I show her, she grabs the envelope, starts to pick at the corner and then seems to decide it's better not to open it.

She's staring around my small hallway then says, 'You had an early start this morning.'

Is she watching over me or did I make too much noise and annoy my neighbours?

I explain I went walking.

She makes a final excuse and turns to go. I stand at my door and hear her footfall on the stairs, then the sound of her door being slammed; it's almost like a warning. The vestibule seems to be silent, but then I hear the tinkling of music and Barrie's singing. I suddenly feel insecure, as if a rare encounter with one neighbour and the tuneless braying of another are a threat. I close and bolt my door and stand near it, listening intently for louder singing, footsteps down the stairs or a banjo duet. I'm rewarded with well-insulated silence.

Amber's intervention means I've missed a call from Carla, but she's left a voicemail: 'Hi Teddy, it's Carla. It was really amazing to talk with you last night. You do have a very sexy voice. Maybe you're already out and about and I've missed you. But let's talk soon? It would be nice. Bye then.'

During my walk I'd made up my mind that I wouldn't take things further with Carla. I'd stopped to look one last time at her profile pictures and check the words to see if they mention drunkenness as a way of life. Of course they don't; why would they? No-one mentions their faults on *matchmates*; that's a given. I don't tell anyone I'm having an affair with a married woman, nor that my wife left me because I'm boring. It's an easy decision. She is gorgeous; really quite astonishingly beautiful, in a knowing and bountiful way. But that's just photographs. A camera might never lie, but the photographs in her profile no longer have the same appeal.

Now I need a kiss-off. As I soak in the bath, warming up from a chilly walk home and relaxing the residual aches from my hike, I create a mental message. I'm still immersed in lavender and can't decide whether to message her or call. Neither will make what I want to say particularly palatable, and I'm torn between a bland *not sure* or a blunt *you're a drunken disgrace*.

It has to be done by phone. Once I'm cooled down from my bath, I pick up the phone. It goes straight to voicemail without ringing. Somehow it feels much worse telling the machinery and I stumble into my speech.

'Er... hi Carla. Sorry I missed you earlier. Oh... it's Teddy Clayton by the way. I think it might be better if we don't take things further. Something didn't feel quite right when we spoke so it's best not to prolong any contact. Erm... sorry. Good luck with your search. Bye.'

I wish I could hear it back and perhaps correct all the *ums* and *aahs*. But I console myself with the knowledge that I've been honest, if somewhat evasive. And that is the polar opposite of what I feel Carla has done in our exchanges and in her profile. I delete her from my contacts list on *matchmates*, then block her on my phone. We aren't linked by any other medium. Carla and her drinking will not be my problem. She is no more.

10

Luke Crossthwaite and I started school together at the age of five in amongst an excited chattering of infant uncertainty. But it was only when we'd risen out of the infants into the giddy heights of junior school that we finally connected. In fact, the moment of truth arose during a mass football match in the playground. He was quite a footballer and slotted a perfect pass to me. In on goal, with just Melissa Chadderton to beat, I placed it wide of the left-hand jumper. As I fell to the ground, wounded and in tears, a cacophony of cruel laughter engulfed me. Luke sauntered over and picked me up, but it didn't seem comforting given he was still laughing, almost hysterically.

As we shake hands in our chosen rendezvous, I ask him if he remembers that first ever meeting.

'Of course, Mr C. You completely failed to score against a girl. Completely unforgettable.'

I tell him he's a wanker and we clink our pint glasses together and drink awhile. The pub isn't rammed but it's filling up. Luke and I chatter away about work: business as usual. We always get that stuff out of the way early doors, leaving the less fundamental nonsense for later. Luke is constantly distracted by passing women. Perhaps I am too, but I hide it by checking my phone for SocMed updates, Peeps and new activity on *matchmates*. I've had dozens of likes for all my Postpix photos today.

'So you've been promoted Mr C? Congratulations. I salute you.'

'Thank you, Mr C. It's a privilege. I'm proud.'

'You should be proud. You're working in a sector that has delivered one of the most perfect pieces of brain-washed consumerism, like... ever.'

'What the fuck do you mean?'

He points to his top of the range handset and kicks off about how controlling they are, feeding and bolstering human insecurity and the terror of being ignored.

I tell him it's just progress.

'Curing cancer is progress. Developing and sustaining healthy clean water sources is progress.'

I shake my head dismissively.

But Luke's on a roll. 'It's a stroke of sheer fucking brilliance. Convincing people they need to talk to or message people while they're in Asda, standing at a bus stop or watching fireworks. Sell them a phone and they can communicate about fuck all for hours on end instead of reading a book or playing bridge or enjoying a massage. Same again Mr C?'

While he orders two more pints of Lancaster Blonde, I tell him there's nothing wrong with talking on a phone while you're in a supermarket.

'You're shopping Mr C. Shopping. Focus on one thing at a time. Get your cereals, your vegetables, your bathroom accessories, your doggie poo bags, your chicken stock cubes without discussing Our Nina's Haemorrhoids.'

'Multi-tasking is a great skill...'

'... it's a heroic load of old bullshit Mr C. In my company, almost everything that goes wrong is caused by people trying to do everything at once, instead of managing priorities.'

Luke is Operations Director at a company with a small chain of prosperous garden centres in the north west. He will soon be made managing director.

I persevere. 'Are you saying people used to read books while shopping?'

He admits no one did and hands me my second pint.

'And what about you Luke? Did you used to sit around reading Camus, and learning how to formulate a pre-emptive bid while weak in diamonds? And did all your friends and colleagues? I think not. Smart phones most definitely have not quashed cultural engagement. If anything, they've created the opportunity for people to be better. It's up to them if they grab the chance.'

'I doubt anyone is a better human being for having a mobile phone Mr C. We've become slaves, especially in the eyes of anyone demanding our attention.'

'That's plain lunacy Mr C.'

'A generation is growing up that is so controlled by these fuckers...' he waves his handset at me again, '... that it's an employer's dream, sitting nicely alongside this headlong rush to automate jobs.'

I shake my head. Luke and I have always disagreed about everything and rarely succeed in finishing a cogent structured debate, possibly because we never really start one.

He clinks my glass again. 'This Blonde is awesome beer Ted. One more in here and on to Mephisto's, where we will get laid in no time.'

Our discussion moves on to sport, Luke's holiday plans, my lack of them, and whether we want Indian, Chinese or Italian food later. I'm making my case for neither, and my preference for a Thai, when Luke straightens up, pulls in his gut and fixes a dazzling smile to his gob. Ship ahoy, is the evident signal.

He deploys a skill I have never learned: the art of the unsolicited cheesy chat up. 'Good evening ladies. Care to join me and my handsome friend Edward in a bottle of prosecco?'

Some bite, others laugh and politely decline, most tell him to go and fuck himself; and rightly so. Luke simply doesn't care. His opening gambit is a shot in the dark, and he feels no shame or loss if it misses the target. I suspect he feels no particular elation if it hits the target either. It's a means to an end.

The women he's harassing decline his invitation with smiles, one of them saying: 'We don't like prosecco. Try champagne next time.'

I shrivel at this put-down, but Luke shrugs and tells me to get another pair of Blondes.

He was divorced a couple of years before me. The guilty party, he was hammered in a settlement that seemed both harsh and fair. He quickly moved on and picked up the pieces to create a life well lived. A series of false start partners was found, with no commitment by him.

As we walk the half mile or so to our next destination, Luke has conveniently turned the Prosecco Rejection into a failing on my part.

'You're a rubbish wing man Mr C. Why didn't you come straight back with an offer to buy the Lanson, or whatever passes for champagne in these Europhobic times. You've done us out of a rollover there, bud.'

'Seriously Mr C, we will be much better placed in Mephisto's where we both know that the offer of prosecco, and not even a whole bottle of it, will be a compelling one.'

'You better be right Mr C. Those two back there were my bread and butter.'

Luke has always been like this. Converting a smile across the room into the conviction that every possibility is a certainty. All through our teens, Luke got girls just by showing up. He had neither style, nor grace, nor charm; he was forward, direct and handsome and those seemed to be winning ways. As he chalked off success after success, and lost count of the notches on his bedpost, he became impervious to rejection and immune to any tumult he might cause in the hearts or minds of his conquests.

It's just after nine and the noise inside Mephisto's is a mélange of high-tone place and low-level intentions. The bar is full, with more women than men. A small number of regretful-looking couples stands tentatively in groups as if unsure of their right to be here. If single, you just have to show up, look good, spend more than enough money and exude the right demeanour. It isn't about longevity or fidelity: this place is where you make tonight's dreams.

I wait at the bar to order. Luke is already distracted by the sights and sounds; he's in his element.

But we are out of our depth.

Here, surrounded by a cohort young enough to be our children, it quickly strikes home that we are like an Olde Curiosity Shoppe: there, but of limited value; potentially attractive in a certain light; but not the real thing; full of fake artefacts and humbug.

'We might as well be at home watching Netflix, Mr C.'

Luke looks at me as he sucks his second julep down in one through a straw. 'Nonsense Mr C. We might be being ignored. But at least we are out.'

'I thought your champagne socialism forbade you this kind of leering tyranny.'

Luke shakes his head contemptuously. 'Really Mr C; you're still playing these ancient party-political games.'

When we were thirteen, Luke became frantic about the possibility that Neil Kinnock's Labour Party would crush the ruling Tories with a renewed sense of righteous endeavour. He had no debate in him, just a glowering resentment that it was time for renewal. When I wasn't listening to his zealous yaps, I heard my father's dispassionate reality: we've come this far; we've transformed and corrected many things; it's no time to switch tracks; it never will be. This is a blue yonder. Forever and ever, amen.

'Maybe so Mr C, but old or new, your politics are riddled with anomalies.'

'Such as?'

I make a shortlist, including his income, status as a company director, his car and house, a resolute lack of equality where women are concerned, his private healthcare scheme and his company's ban on any trades union.

'These things don't stack up alongside any number of the main principles in Das Kapital.'

He blinks slowly a couple of times. 'That's just nit-picking, Mr C.'

I shake my head at him. 'You're a card-carrying anathema. Your fake socialism exists solely to counter your dread of being middle class and how well you've succeeded.'

He tells me his success doesn't prevent him being caring, compassionate and working class. I tell him not to be ridiculous.

'Okay, then what about you Ted? With your tame Toryism and idealistic, individualist self-preservation.'

'My politics are consistent, Mr C. As are my questions about some of the party's principles.'

'Fuck you're bold; expressing doubts is a distinctly un-Conservative characteristic. So, I demand retraction of your anathema jibe.'

I shake my head vigorously, but he hasn't finished. 'This hesitancy about your party places you massively out of step with the wider vision. While you're tottering towards the centre, and possibly beyond, everyone else has bolted to the killing fields on the right.'

'There are plenty of decent people....'

'Where are they? In the cabinet? In industry? Where? Your bygone ideology, with patronage graciously handed down the orders so they knew their place and honour their obligations to a community is gone forever.'

'Bullshit Luke.'

He looks at me with a slight snarl and I brace myself for a more vicious attack. Instead he makes a drink up gesture and turns to signal the bar staff.

'I tell you what else is bullshit. Me; the charlatan; about to be made CEO and I don't know why. Well educated, but essentially ignorant. Haven't read a book for years. Theatre, cinema, music - all occasional ventures, but with no curiosity about the alternative or provocative. Just conventional, same-old tat. We should move on after this one.'

'Agreed Mr C. Let's go and eat.'

In the time between our ninth and thirteenth birthdays, Luke and I had obsessed about the A Team. Whatever heady metaphor was intended about good's triumph over evil and injustice, our sole focus was on the behaviour, words and hairstyle of Bosco Baracus. We loved the show, but worshipped B.A. and, with a surprising level of irony for two such young lads, we decided to call ourselves Mr C. Thirty years on, it's stuck to us like fly paper, to the mystery and confusion of anyone listening in.

As we walk away from the bar, I ask Luke why he thinks he's a charlatan.'

He slows our pace to a dawdle. 'Life's so fake. Work. Success. I go to the office every weekday, then spend every Friday and Saturday visiting stores handing out bon mots and incentives to the teams. I say and do nothing controversial or revolutionary. I simply spout the same things I've spouted day in/day out for the last five years. No-one notices Mr C. No-one challenges.'

I'm not sure I care and say nothing. Today's default is that you succeed by being in charge while doing nothing and keeping a distance between you and any cause of failure. Luke knows that and his apathy is troubling. But I give him some support.

'Most people would say that it's a measure of success, not failure, if you deliver results by repeatedly doing what works.'

'I'm sure they would Mr C. But once in a while I'd just love it if someone walked into my office with their cock hanging out and asked me if I know I good tailor.'

That makes me giggle. 'A nice idea Luke, but you know it won't happen. Craving the absurd is pointless. Business is too dominated by the bland shaping of American corporate culture.'

'I know. But that doesn't mean we can't discuss football or sculpture or theatre. Yet no-one does.'

'Not even us Mr C.'

'I know. Why is that? It's not like we're idiots.'

'No, we're not idiots. But we're part of a machine in which we earn, feather a nest with needless makeovers and wear the badges of material gain. Work, play a bit of sport, eat out by way of a sole, sham sophistication, ignore anything anyone can call an issue. It's the cycle of life, and for fuck's sake don't fall off or get a puncture.'

He tells me I sound like a whinging leftie, but it isn't that. I am completely clear that corporate life means culture is an either/ or option, and most of us take the convenient, conventional low road:

be an employee

don't think - it makes the whole house of cards collapse

conform, because rebellion is plain evil

repeat - don't think

just do.

My phone chirps from its nest in my jacket. The tone means it's a message from Jude.

We've reached the restaurant and, while Luke haggles for a table, I check Jude's message.

'Hi babe. Back early, Craig still there. Long story. Where are you? Has Luke found you someone to fuck?'

'I don't need someone to fuck.'

'Sweetheart: you complete me.'

'We're at the Beau Thai.'

'Where next?'

'It depends. Luke's a bit pissed and weird.'

'Oh dear.'

'Are you OK??'

'Yes. I thought there'd be no Teddy-Love this weekend, and now there will be. If Teddy feels like giving it.'

'He does.'

Luke and I take our seats to continue the journey across the unscripted void of our friendship.

When we leave at just past ten forty-five, the streets are thronged with a kind of mobile partying. It's good-natured, but there's an occasional spike of aggression or abuse.

'You know what I discovered the other day, Ted?' He stops walking and grabs my arm, turning me inwards to look at him. A worm crawls into my head with a tiny voice: Luke is going to die.

'I've learned something in the last few days that changes my outlook on everything.'

He squeezes my bicep and I don't know what to do. He turns and walks away. I'm soon alongside.

'What is it?'

'Well, it seems... it seems that the name Crossthwaite is the 354th most popular surname in Lancashire.'

The total, utter and irretrievably obtuse prick.

He's smiling at my discomfort. 'What's up Mr C?'

'I thought you were about to tell me you are ill; it would have explained your twattish behaviour this evening.'

'Your name, Clayton, isn't even in the top one thousand.'

I almost walk off to go home. I think about my kids, far from a home that doesn't exist; about Paul Wilson; and Annabel's worries; about the possibility that one day Jude's husband might find out about me. Luke's pathetic attempt at comedy is the worst possible end to an already wrecked evening.

We've arrived at the cocktail bar and I don't want to go in.

But Luke insists, and finesses it by insisting he will buy all the drinks.

This bar has the usual ambient amorality but now the hubbub is augmented by the sniffs and sneezes of cocaine users. You can be refused entry because your shoelaces aren't properly tied, but a powder-encrusted nose is a fast-track.

I grab a table and focus on a quick internet search.

Luke joins me with a tray. There are two champagne saucers and two taller glasses. The latter are filled with something sparkling. The former contains a pleasant muddy yellow liquid that seems to have bloody phlegm floating in it.

Luke knows I have an uptight attitude to silly, fussy drinks. 'Porn Star Martinis Mr C, just what the doctor ordered.'

We sit and look at the grotesque combination. I'm puzzled. 'What do we do?'

'I've no idea Mr C.' He looks around the bar for clues but we are alone in our cocktail confusion.

'I tell you what Mr C: you mix yours together and neck it; I'll neck mine then neck the fizz plonk as a side shot.'

'Okay. I'm going in.'

Whatever the sparkling wine is, it turns the main drink a slightly unpleasant shade of diarrhoea and tastes similar.

Luke seems to enjoy the main drink but winces at his sparkly shot.

'It tastes like toilet cleaner Mr C. You could clear away any amount of errant pubes with it.'

'Go and get something less ridiculous Mr C; something using rum.'

'I know just the thing Mr C.'

He returns shortly with zombies. These taste much better.

'Anyway, Luke Lively, I have more news on the surname front.'

'Don't tell me you've found an opposing poll in which Clayton is right up there.'

'It's not about my name. It's more news about yours, specifically the suffix Thwaite. Seems it's very common in North West England.'

'Of course; contributing to Crossthwaite being the 354th most common surname in Lancashire.'

'Yes. But did you also know that the suffix is from Old Norse? It meant a clearing or meadow. It has a Norman off shoot too.'

'You see Ted? I am a cross-cultural icon.'

'Indeed you are Luke Crossthwaite. And the Orkney and Shetland version is Twatt. You're so cross-cultural that, up there, you'd be a Crosstwatt. That really is iconic.'

He raises his half-empty glass: 'To the Thwaites and Twatts in all their forms.'

We clatter our glasses together. We're laughing again; the evening has been not been wasted. I'm still chortling away when I go to the gents and, while there, another message from Jude announces itself.

'Where you up to hon?'

'Gents. Just shook off the drips and tucked myself in.'

'LOL.'

'We're in the Herbalist. Bit pissed.'

'I'm at yours. Where are your spare keys, I'll come for you?'

I tell her how to find them.

'See you in ten.'

I feel a drunken surge of affection for Jude. I wonder if I love her.

When I get back to him, Luke is standing with two women near the bar. He's getting another round.

'I'm going to bail Mr C. Footie tomorrow and need to do some work.'

He looks at me with a smile, then hugs me.

But he's more interested in them than me and I head for the exit. I'm pretty pissed and try not to clatter into anyone. The Neanderthals on the door look at me with contempt but they aren't distracted for long. I'm safely well-dressed and old. Not a risk.

My car growls up to the kerb and Jude smiles insanely at me when I climb in.

'Oh Teddy - you smell revolting. Garlic and alcohol. You're going to be no use to me tonight.'

11

Jude unlocks my front door and, perhaps because I'm drunk, it makes me feel as if this is the place where we live together. There is no sense of her being a guest or visitor. It's like she is the heart of my home.

But it's not because I'm drunk. It's because she finds time to be with me that might otherwise be filled with nothing. Here we are, safe from harm; she is flawless in Converse, joggers and a tee shirt under a denim jacket. All evening, I've been gazing on a cavalcade of glamour that seemed worthwhile, after a fashion. But Jude is a sight for sore eyes.

'You look perfect. Can we kiss?'

'I'm not putting my mouth anywhere near yours, stinky.'

'Well a cuddle then. Here.'

We stand in each other's arms, silent and calm. It's the kind of embrace that would follow weeks or months apart and, as I stroke her back, I sense her frame loosening. But she disengages, gets out her phone and shares some music. It's jazzy; Jude Loves Jazz.

She's brought an array of nibbles, some basic, some more posh. I pour myself a large glass of sparkling water and it perks me up; my mind isn't as pissed as my legs and hips.

'How was Luke?'

'A bit dismantled. Something has got him picking holes in himself.' I relate Mr C's concerns.

Jude looks up and frowns, her work making sticks of carrot suspended. 'Is he having a mid-life crisis?'

'Not sure. Do you have those at forty-three?'

'These days it seems you can have them at any age. When is yours due?'

'The day you leave me.'

She's busy arranging things on a baking tray. 'Let's not go around that whole discussion again. One sad day, one of us will walk away and never come back. It won't hurt. It will just be over.'

'I know.'

She dips a stick of carrot in the hummus tub and extracts a dollop the size of a golf ball. 'What else was bugging Luke?'

As Jude crunches an accompaniment, I explain Mr C's silliness about his surname.

'It sounds like you didn't really enjoy yourself this evening babe.'

I guzzle down more water and, belching quietly, help myself to more. 'It was ok. We had a few laughs. I want a kiss.'

Jude takes me in her arms and kisses me tentatively. When she breaks off, she licks her lips extravagantly and strokes her chin.

'You're still quite...' she makes a wafting gesture. 'Come here.' I'm pulled towards her but, instead of another kiss, she sniffs and licks my neck and on down to the top of my shoulder.

'It's not so bad on your skin. What's that cologne?'

I tell her it's a sample I picked up during my shopping trip. She tells me to buy a bottle.

My phone pings; a text from Luke bragging about an impending threesome. When I show Jude, she shakes her head and tells me my friend is an arsehole. 'Are you jealous of his wicked ways?'

'Not even slightly. You should have seen these two. And the earlier couple: exactly conforming to the type Luke has always won: unmistakably and irredeemably available; eyes on the size of his wallet, the cut of his jacket, the bulge in his jeans.'

'Sometimes, your stereotyping of women is pretty offensive.'

'I know.'

'Do you care?'

'Are you offended?'

'Not even slightly. You're talking to a woman who stays with a man because he earns a couple of million pounds a year, rather than because of his romantic gestures and sparkling emotional intelligence.'

'Am I a cure or a disease?'

'You cure me Teddy. Every time I see you and hear your voice.'

'Shame on you.'

We kiss, deeply and beautifully.

'Let's go and sit in the comfy zone; bring the wine. Are you going to have any?'

I shake my head.

Jude drinks sparingly: quality over quantity. When we cuddle up on the sofa, conversation and food are neglected for several moments. The water has made my drunkenness recede and I recover some curiosity. Jude shakes her head when I ask why she's come back alone. I turn her face to mine, and she looks indescribably sad.

'Lewis is terribly unwell. It was quite shocking to see him. Their parents are beside themselves and Freya is like a ghost. The onslaught of seeing the man she loves dying, while trying to hold it together for their kids, is killing her. Craig's being very brave and unemotional, but I think he's hurting really deeply. It's all so sad. I can't help feeling great waves of despair, especially for Freya and the kids.'

She looks close to tears. I've never seen Jude like this and hug her, whispering into her hair: 'Shouldn't you have stayed too?'

Jude holds me tightly. 'I offered. But Craig has decided to stay up there to supervise. He's going to work at their Edinburgh office until after the weekend. I'm driving back tomorrow evening with loads of his stuff. Then I'll stay for as long as needed.'

'That's a lot of driving for you. How come you got sent home?'

She unravels from me to focus on a miniature chicken Kiev. 'It wasn't quite like that. I kept telling Craig we should travel with a plan, but he knew best. We went with like an overnight bag and his *trust me, I'm a senior exec* bullshit. As soon as we got there, I knew the lack of preparation was going to cause problems.'

'Maybe he didn't want to assume the worst?'

'The worst was already in play; it's why he dragged me up there. I'm pissed off with Craig for not knowing - or maybe not accepting - how bad Lewis' condition is. And for being immune to any challenge. But that sums him up.'

'But why didn't you just stay?'

There is something akin to despair in her expression. 'I felt like none of them wanted me there. When Craig and I finally got time together last night, he revealed his plan to work in and commute to and from Edinburgh. No discussion or check with me. Just another decisive moment that affects me without involving me. I jumped at the chance to come home. And I got the very real sense he was happy for me to leave and so...' Jude starts to sing *I drove all night, to be with you.*

'So is this another evening with the girls in Ulverston?'

'It is! I can't wait to wake up in your bed on a Sunday and you're going to pamper me, in the most vigorous and extreme senses of the word, all night and morning. You've got me until about noon tomorrow, so let's go and be creative.'

12

This relationship is built on talking. There are no stormy silences or sulks and the talking can be about anything. But when we're in bed, naked and aroused, the talking is focused: what we need; why we need it; how it could be different; what it feels like; when to explore; when to wait.

Tonight, our passion is more intense than usual. Perhaps Saturday nights are more innately sexual than Fridays?

We don't get much sleep and it seems like no time until it's light outside.

'What pampering did you have in mind?'

She smiles at me dopily. 'You did the vigorous extreme stuff brilliantly so, right now, I want a cup of tea and some toast and marmalade. Can you sort that?'

'Coming up. Don't go away.'

She giggles but her eyes are fluttering back in to sleep.

I feel all right as I make breakfast. I gulp down what's left in the bottle of fizzy water. Even though its effervescence is waning, it cuts through the dregs of my dehydration. And I'm still finding it strange that I'm not alone on a Sunday morning. What will that mean?

When I get back to the bedroom Jude is lying face down on the crumpled duvet, asleep I presume. I examine how she looks: the ash-grey-purple hair is a tousled mess; her broad, swimmer's shoulders are nicely toned and the tattoo on her left shoulder blade is a sole blemish on her back; the curved mound of her arse seems to just blend onwards in to thighs that go on forever. But then she starts to clench and unclench her bum and mutters an obscenity at me before getting up on to her hands and knees, yapping.

By the time we've finished, the tea is cold and the toast is limp.

This time Jude follows me to the kitchen, enveloped in a large towel. As I operate all the machines, she hugs me constantly from behind.

'Let's have a bath after we've eaten.'

'That would be perfect. What time did you say you're leaving?'

She smiles broadly. 'My train from Ulverston gets into Lancaster at about twelve fifteen. We have three hours. Can you drop me at the station?'

'Of course. That fits nicely with my football later; one pm at the uni.'

'Will I get to see you in your jock strap?'

'I've never worn one. Horrible things. Will you get some rest before you drive back to Edinburgh?'

'Loads. In my vast, icy, marital bed.'

'Please make sure you do. We didn't sleep much and that road from Carlisle through the Borders is terrible in the dark.'

She brushes a hand through my hair. 'I never go that way babe. So please don't worry. I'm going to run a bath.'

My bath is large enough for us to lie comfortably top to tail. And we talk. Jude has added something foamy to the water, and there's a perfume I can't place. She tells me it's a combination of ylang-ylang and jasmine oils which, she assures me, are noted for their ability to generate female arousal.

We bathe together often, and one of our rituals is to dry each other afterwards; slowly; tenderly; with great care and attention to detail. Usually, it's on a Friday evening, before heading to bed, but it's no less precious and equally sensational during the course of a Sunday morning, even though the next stop is elsewhere.

Back in the kitchen, Jude's full of questions about the age of food items and about where my friends are at weekends.

She finds what's safe to eat but keeps nudging me about my social status. She doesn't get why my friends shuffled off after the divorce; nor why my closest friends are distant and only engage on SocMed; or why so few friends from Lancaster are connected now. It doesn't help that I can't explain my home town isolation.

She makes a frittata vibrant with vegetables and Mexican flavours. While we're eating, Jude digs some more about Luke and why I see him so infrequently.

'Is he hard work? Does he get on your tits?'

'Almost always.'

'I'm being serious Teddy. Either he's your friend or just a has-been. And from what you said last night it sounds like he's a whole box full of problems. Did you try to help? Or was it strictly come bantering?'

'The latter. His problems are just a performance. He's too grounded to have self-doubts and too innately cocky to be weak. He's also too inherently awful to be the socialist he so desperately wants to be. But he keeps up the charade.'

Jude is watching me intently, and I know a challenge is coming. 'Do you ever look at what he's achieved and wish you had it too?'

I tell her that I never do. I'm good at my job, I do it well and I'm well rewarded. But I lack the entrepreneurial side that Luke has; Dave Ellis has it too. And I never feel like I have a dark side. That ruthless streak. That whole thing about being feared rather than loved. The willingness to go outside the acceptable.

'To do illegal things?'

'Possibly.'

Jude laughs.

'I wouldn't be surprised if Craig has broken the law.'

'Nor would I, but there'll be many layers between him and culpability.'

Jude tilts her head to one side and asks if I find it hard to keep going at a company where that might be happening. And I reply that, if I ignore it, I can't be paralysed by sentiment. Taking a stand means replacement. The company always wins.

'And is this a universal lack of morals?'

'I think so. No-one quits on principle anymore.'

'But you don't have to like it.'

'I didn't say I do. But if you choose what you do and don't like in this insane model, you get twisted out of shape. It...'

'What do you mean by *it*? And don't say *capitalism*.'

'It isn't capitalism anymore. I mean the culture of corporate power. The all-consuming engine that owns everything; politics; people; ideas; philosophy; and perhaps even religion. It exists to make money no one sees.'

'And to create wealth.'

'It doesn't do that anymore, at least not for most of us. Business doesn't reward people with a slice of the pie. That's gone. Forever.'

'But you get well paid.'

'For now. But a salary isn't wealth creation. I just keep my head down, ignore that shitty stuff and take my pay packet.'

'Fuck Teddy. That sounds like the sort of thing a guard at Auschwitz might have said.'

'I suppose it does.'

'And I suppose Craig controls that shitty stuff.'

'Yes. He runs the money and delivers non-stop benefits to shareholders and investors; or he's out on his arse.'

'And to customers, surely?'

'No. That's just lip service. Customers are only marginally, fractionally more important than workforce. But both are an irrelevance to the markets.'

'And I thought your attitude to work was about professionalism and rectitude.'

'It is about those things.'

'But not about caring.'

'I get paid if my company makes enough. That's all I'm there for; a month-by-month circle of self-interest. Caring isn't a factor.'

Jude shrugs. 'And what about Luke? Where does he sit in this hall of shame?'

'He's the same as me, but wrapped in a different coloured flag, spouting wanky ideas that he could never be governed by. Often quite hurtful things.'

Jude looks baffled. She tells me it's ridiculous for friends to cause each other pain.

'What has Luke done to hurt you?'

I say it's how he makes me feel. That I'm a monster; uncaring; unfeeling and cold. That I don't contribute, and lack empathy with causes.

Jude shakes her head. 'You've contributed massively; don't let him bully you. You put in and take very little out. I can't believe you let him demonise you for being what you are, especially given his bonkers stance on Brexit.'

Luke voted Leave because it was what Tony Benn wanted.

That kind of bonkers.

Jude's warming up. 'Craig was and is livid about Brexit. It's hilarious. He says it's no one's decision other than business, and especially not the celebrity politicians and their flocks.'

'Let the money decide.'

Jude nods.

I sigh. 'Except the money itself was and is hopelessly split on the question, and therefore no different to the politicians. A collective rabble of self-interest standing on the far side of the river beside their burning bridges.'

Jude giggles. 'The men in our lives are full of shit, aren't they? Notionally opposite but with the same basic argument: we know best; everyone else is thick. But you're different, aren't you? A rose between two cocks.'

It's quaint that she's lined me up alongside those two. Luke and I share a past but probably no future. And I'll never meet Craig in any time zone.

'You're the really dangerous one, aren't you? With your wicked lack of loyalty to the cause.'

Jude knows I'm torn but she always doubts my doubts.

Pay more tax for a better health service? Why would anyone do that?

Divest from fossil fuels? What about that gas guzzling car?

Re-nationalise the railways? That I only ever use if someone else pays?

Really? Really?

'You're an anomaly just like those two; three cocks in a row, but you're the only one drooping.'

I know she's right. Agreement across the barricades is treachery.

'I can't believe we're discussing my fucking husband and the massive mistake he represents.'

'Then stop.'

'I can't stop. I'm stuck. I have to stay because of his insecure loneliness. He'd fall apart without me. I smile for the camera and play along with the brittle sham. And I get all he has forever. And he gets all of my fiction.'

'Is he really that dumb?'

'He is really that complacent. About his allure, wealth and power.'

'Even though I know it so well - my beautiful friend - that really is a very sad story.'

'Am I your friend sweetie?'

'Of course. Sometimes, I think you're my only friend.'

Jude looks at her watch, then her phone. 'I can't be. Or is this about us being friends with benefits?'

'I hate that phrase.'

'I do too. I'm sorry.' She strokes my face to reinforce the apology.

'Maybe *friend* was the wrong word. But I do think of you as an equal, walking alongside me neither leading nor following.' She starts shaking her head emphatically. 'Yes, I know what you're going to say; we aren't a couple; we never will be; we can only be this. But in my mind, a big part of this is that equality. It is friendship. Companionship. Like-mindedness.'

'Surely all this adds up to is secret, closed, doomed reality. Ill-fated and ill-conceived. Right but very wrong.'

'It's an intimate reality. These twelve months have made us much more than fuck buddies.'

Jude laughs. 'Another horrible term. You're such a romantic.'

'I'm not. But, for the record, last night I thought for the first time that I might be in love with you.'

'I've been in love with you for weeks: since before Christmas.'

'Then we'd better be careful.'

'I think it's rather wonderful.' She looks at her watch again. 'I need to start getting ready to leave.'

'When did you say you're back from Scotland? Thursday?'

'Yes. But there's a small possibility - a very small one - that Craig will also come back.'

'No Judy-Love then, potentially for more than ten days.'

'That won't do, will it?'

13

I am on top form in the football, brimming with non-stop energy. I score two goals and create a couple more, albeit in a friendly match between my team - RedRoseRovers - and some lads from the university. They are younger and slightly fitter, but we edge it thanks to middle-aged guile and our work as a unit. After the game I let the team know that, until further notice, my availability for Wednesday night league matches will be zero due to work commitments. It's not well received: one or two of them ask why I bothered showing up today knowing I wouldn't be around in future. When I say it's because I still want to be part of the team, the blunt response is that I'm not.

As the others head off to their cars, bound for the pub where they always meet for a few post-match beers, I drive in the opposite direction and get an hour in at the gym. It's quiet, with no waiting for any of the machines or weights. Towards the end of my routine of bench presses, I finally start to feel the fatigue I've been expecting since earlier.

I head back to the apartment and go straight to bed where I sleep for thirty minutes. It's the noise of a message from Jude that wakes me: 'I had a wonderful time my love. Thank you. You were really on top form last night.' There's a dog emoji at the end of the sentence.

'You make me good.'

'True.'

'You're amazing xx'

'How was footie?'

'OK. We won. They're pissed off about me not being available.'

'Find another team. Play at weekends.'

'Yep. I think that's the right plan.'

'I've been asleep since I got back. It's helped, but I don't feel like driving.'

'I think it's crazy that you're driving back so soon. Stay tonight and go first thing.'

'No sweetheart. It has to be this evening. I'm just getting ready to go.'

'Call me when you're close to getting there. And no messaging while driving.'

'xxx'

When I get to the hospice, I can tell something bad has happened. The place feels sombre, and before I speak to any of the staff, I know someone has passed away.

One of the staff soon greets me in the reception area and tells me the sad news that Mrs Weir has died. It wasn't expected this soon.

'Would it be better if I don't hang around?'

'Definitely not. We can always use you, especially on days like this when we need to focus on a family.'

'Good. Then where shall I start?'

'Can you make some drinks? We will need a steady supply. Then guest room two needs cleaning please. First, let me quickly introduce you to Mr Hodgson. He's waiting for his family to arrive and I'm sure he'd love a brew.'

She takes me through to one of the conservatories and I see a man sitting upright in a wheelchair. He has a book open on his lap, but his attention is elsewhere; out through the windows and an open door to his left.

'Mark? This is Edward, one of our regular volunteers.'

'Hello Edward. Mark Hodgson.' His voice is calm and unbroken, and he holds my gaze as we shake hands.

'Hello Mark. Ted Clayton. Are you warm enough next to that open door?' He nods and gestures at the blanket covering his legs.

'I've a hat somewhere too. Don't worry about me Ted.'

'I'm about to make some drinks. What would you like?'

'Tea please. Black, with a spoonful of sugar – but don't stir it please. And don't leave the spoon in.'

I head off to the kitchen and make myself busy. Through the hatchway I can see Mark nodding as the staff nurse talks to him. He keeps looking at his book and, once alone, he lifts it to read.

Once the tea is ready, I pour a mugful, then add the sugar and take it to Mark. As I put it down next to him he looks expectantly over my shoulder, then shakes his head.

'Good win for Morecambe yesterday. Bit up and down though, aren't they? Did you go?'

'I didn't. Haven't been for a long time.'

He laughs, but his laugh turns to a cough.

'No, me neither. Last proper game I saw was at Deepdale. Must be five years ago. Always see a decent level of football there: ball to feet. Who do you support?'

I tell him I'm more a fan of playing than watching.

Mark picks up his tea and takes a sip, his eyes registering approval. 'Just right Ted. Thank you.'

I tell him I need to carry on with my duties. 'Quite right. I'll be fine. My boy and his wife will be here soon.'

'I'll bring them drinks when they get here.'

He looks over at the door again.

Once I've distributed drinks and made another pot of tea, I take a quick look in the guest room to see how messy it is. The bed doesn't look slept in. A crumpled towel on the bathroom floor is the only sign that someone had stayed over. I head to the utility room to grab a laundry bag and vacuum cleaner.

Mark is still alone in the conservatory. I wash my hands then go to ask him if he'd like more tea. He says he'd love some.

'What's the book you're reading?'

'Dickens: A Tale of Two Cities.'

'Enjoying it?'

'Yes, and no. It's a bit bloody late for me to start appraising English literature.' His laugh morphs into another cough, then a bout of croaking and wheezing. When he recovers, he holds up the book. 'It's a grand story, this. I keep going back to that opening. *It was the best of times; it was the worst of times.*'

He looks like he's in his late sixties but could be older. He has a military bearing.

'I've read a couple of Dickens, including that one. It is a remarkable prologue isn't it?'

'People my age keep talking longingly about the good old days, while all others want is progress. He wrote that book more than a hundred years ago, and it refers to life in the century before he wrote it. And here we are today, still torn between belief and incredulity. Aren't we?'

'I think maybe we are Mark. Let me sort that tea for you.'

Now he tuts and looks at his watch. 'I thought William and Deborah would be here by now. What's kept them?'

'I'm sure they'll be here soon, Mark. Why don't you keep reading? I'll make more tea then go and see if anyone knows where your family has got to.'

'I don't know why I'm reading it. It's too late to finish it.' He seems agitated so I go and let one of the staff know. She's quickly at his side and, as I make his drink, I see her talking quietly to him. His shoulders droop and the book falls from his lap.

'Here's Edward with your tea Mark.'

I hand him the mug, then pick up his book. 'Here you go Mark. I think you should keep going. Try to finish it.'

I wonder if I should tell him how Dickens ended it: new oppressors, rising from the ashes of the old; struggles for freedom revealing an evil that constantly reinvents itself. Rest like he has never known.

He lifts his right hand and I clutch his hand in mine. 'You're right lad. I'll crack on with it. Will you be back soon?'

'I'm here most weekends Mark.'

'Good. You make the best tea I've had.'

I'm still derailed about my new routine. It's well past six and usually, by now, I'd be relaxing in front of the telly or listening to music, prior to an early night. But now, my Sunday routine is changed so I decide to fill the time with a bit of work then some catch up with the kids.

I'm all done with work by seven and ask Beth and Joe if we can have a three-way conference. Joe says yes, Beth says no.

A shame. I phone Joe who is in great spirits thanks to strong feedback about some work he's done. After a troubled couple of weeks at the start of his course last September, Joe has grown into his subject - Economics.

'It's good to hear you so positive. Is this about the Employability segment?'

'Yes. Part of the assessment for that module is to create a personal development plan and my tutor said what I'd done was the best he's seen. For like five years.'

'That's brilliant Joe. Can I see it?'

'I can send it or, if you can wait, I'll show you at Easter.'

'Do you know your plans for Easter yet? We need to celebrate your birthday too. It's not long now.'

'Beth and I will be at yours at some point during the holidays. But we need to get to Mum's as well.'

'If I know your plans, I can help with travel arrangements. I can also take some time off work and/or make sure I'm working here instead of London. But I don't want to have plans dumped on me at the last minute. This is why I wanted to talk to you both at once.'

'I know Dad.'

'Beth said you might be staying with Lucy.'

'We talked about that, but she also has family pressures.'

'Joe, there's no pressure from me about this. Don't think that.'

He laughs. 'I don't. But Lucy definitely has pressure. Her mum thinks she's doing no work because of me.'

'Is that true?'

'She's unbelievably hard-working Dad. I'm definitely not in the way of anything.'

'That's good. Make sure you keep it like that.'

'Well term ends on the seventh of April and I was planning to get some time with Lucy in the last week before we go back to Uni. So basically, there's two weeks to divide between you and Mum. I need to talk to Beth.'

I can hear it in his voice: the sadness he feels about our fractured family. It affected Joe more deeply, and for longer, than any of us. He had loved the togetherness of mum, sister, brother, dad. On holidays, during mealtimes, at family weddings and baptisms, or just walking in the park. The big and the small.

Joe would love it if his parents reunited and recreated a single home for him to go to.

'I'll be talking to Beth once we're finished. What's your preference for coming here?'

'What works best for you, Dad?'

'Joe, what works best for me is getting some quality time with you and Beth. It can be three hours, three days or the whole three weeks.'

'It just felt so bad at Christmas. I felt like I'd rather stay somewhere on my own than feel like I'm just on loan at several places.' There's a shake in his voice.

'Hey. Are you okay? How come you're upset like this?'

There's a long pause. I wonder if he's crying.

'I'm fine Dad. I just wish I could feel like I have a place I can call home.'

'This is your home whenever, and for as long as you need it.'

He sighs deeply. 'It's not really is it? It's just the place you've bought to help you move on. It has no history for me, no anchor, no memories, and arguably no future. And nor does Mum's place. It's like you've both set up a place in which your children are marginal.'

'Joe, you have everything you need here. Your own space, storage, belongings; everything. Are you saying you'd have preferred to stay at the old house?'

'No. Maybe. I don't know. Beth and I both realise you couldn't stay there. I get that you don't want the memories to be in the way. But sometimes I wish my memories hadn't been taken away from me.'

'I feel that too. And, for what it's worth, this place where I live… it really isn't that special to me either. But what does makes it special is when you and Beth are here, together or on your own. And that your things are here.'

'Now you sound upset.'

'I'm not upset but I am determined to stop you having such negative feelings. All I do - the work and travelling and long days and early starts and being the best I can be - is to make our family strong and keep us all together, wherever we are.'

Joe laughs. 'Thanks, old man Dad. I know you do. And I love you for it. So why don't you suggest to Beth that we come to you for the first week of the holidays, and head to mum's over the Easter weekend? You and I can get some walking in.'

'We can. And that works for me. I'll message you when I know what Beth thinks.'

Much later, I finally get Beth who tells me we have fifteen minutes. She explains she's been very busy with course work and needed no interruption. We talk about that, and about the coming storm of finals. She's unbelievably strong and level-headed. I've never known Beth express anything close to the notion of being stressed. She once told me that I am the best influence she's known when it comes to handling pressure and working through what needs to be done in a structured way without panic or haste.

We have the discussion about Easter and Beth seems happy with the plan, although she wonders aloud if Amy will be all right about missing Joe on his birthday. We don't properly conclude that discussion but I tell her I feel it's my turn to share – to really share - one of their birthdays.

Then I repeat all I said to Joe about my apartment being their home, and she gives a similar reaction to Joe; except she also says I shouldn't beat myself up about it. I ask her to keep checking in on Joe, which is pointless because I know they talk every day.

As the conversation seems to be drawing to its close, she says: 'Daddy?'

When she calls me *Daddy* it means she wants to say something that makes her uncomfortable.

'Mum called me last week.'

'How is she?'

'I'm not sure she's so happy at the moment.'

I say nothing. I agreed with Beth and Joe some time ago that I would happily discuss Amy with them insofar as it affected logistics or pay and rations. But part of the deal was that I wanted no part of any conversation about their mother's life and times.

'She suggested she's perhaps going to lose her job.'

'Redundancy?'

'Yes, I think so.'

'That's tough.'

'She also said she's on her own again.'

That *again* has an imperceptible emphasis.

'Beth, we...'

'Daddy: I know what you're going to say. I just felt that you should know. I don't expect you to care or do anything. But if she's going to lose her job as well as her relationship, it will be tough for me and Joe.'

'I understand that; you need to be supportive, and I know you will be.'

'Even if it means spending most of the Easter vac with her and not you?'

'Yes. Even if it means that.'

Beth goes quiet, and after several seconds I look at my phone to see if the connection is lost. 'Beth?'

'I'm here. Just thinking about what to do.'

'Talk to Joe and talk to your mother. I can't make this decision for you. If it's looking likely that you need to be in Shropshire for the holidays, then I'll fit in with it.'

'That's just not fair on you.'

'Don't think like that. If Amy needs you there, it's important you both go and give your mother your love. The only thing I'd like to have is a bit of notice about what is happening. Make a decision soon and let me know what it is, okay? Change the subject: when is the play you're in? That clip your friend put on Chattabox is amazing and I'd love to come and see it.'

The call goes on and fifteen minutes ends up being forty; Beth ticks me off for distracting her, then laughs lovingly and says she loves wasting time talking to me. About ten minutes after the call ends, a message pops up filled with emojis; hearts, flowers, sad and smiley faces. And three words: 'You're my hero.'

I message Joe to let him know Beth's feelings about the plans for Easter, but also tell him to call his mother.

It's time to eat and with a 90s playlist in the background I prepare and cook my dinner; simple stuff, but I jazz it up with unexpected complementary things. I look at the bottle of wine Jude opened last night; there's more than half of it left but I don't want any.

Jude starts a chain of messages:

'Am at Gretna Services and thinking of how we love each other - LOL.'

'Don't worry. I'm not driving.'

'Sat Nav says another hour and 50.'

'Can we talk when I'm back in the car?'

'Want to hear your voice.'

I reply: 'I'll call you in 20. Just about to eat.'

'That works.'

In the end, we don't talk for long. Jude says the motorway is too scary in the rain, wind and darkness and she can't cope with the distraction. There's a sense that we both feel low about the fact that it could be more than a week till we see each other again. Opportunities to talk will also be scant. But we have a pragmatic approach, always, and agree that the worst thing we can do is take risks. So, all our thoughts must dive, down into our souls.

As I tidy away pots and pans to the dishwasher, and put away jars and tins, I find myself reflecting on conversations and encounters over the last two days. Family, friends, team-mates, neighbours, strangers, a lover, a dying man. Am I lucky? Should there be more or less going on?

In search of answers, I fall back in to the simple, comforting mundanity of SocMed, Chattabox, Postpix and *matchmates*, where I find several new matches and two new likes. Liz from Cumbria has a funny profile full of smart one-liners and wisdom. She is slightly older than me, blonde and tall. There is a challenge in her profile, that potential suitors must carefully check her wish lists before contacting her. Neat. Then Sue from Macclesfield: fifty; divorced; a profile dripping with references to travel; photos show her posing in various locations; the Golden Gate bridge; the Great Wall of China; the Burj Al Arab; the Amber Fort of Jaipur. It's intimidating beyond words. If you want me, it says, then have bottomless funds for our lifestyle.

I Like Liz and Hide Sue.

On Chattabox I post something about Arnside being a lovely place, then copy the URL for the site where I found the walk I did yesterday. Then I finish with *#cumbria #arnside #walking*. A flurry of likes ensues, eventually including one each from *&dpdevs* and *&teena8shu*, so I decide to follow them back for a few days to see if I learn something.

Yesterday's photos on Postpix are still getting a trail of likes and comments. There are also several new followers: a restaurant on Kos; a fitness coach from Des Moines; two personal bloggers whose photos are all of food. There's also an advert from a distant designer outlet near Chester. It's sometimes a hopeless, futile medium, but I persevere with my efforts to use it as a kind of online postcard system.

SocMed is the usual mash up of happy family news, pointless recycled memes, funny one-liners and tit for tat political barbs. The capacity of some of my connections to say nothing of themselves while they hoist up the flags of others is sometimes unbearable. It feels so preachy sometimes; fingers pointed; we are friends but might easily be enemies - so here's a reminder of how horrible the world can be in the wrong hands. But I ignore all that and upload a dozen photos from my walk. The post soon gets a nice trickle of Likes and feedback.

There's a post from Ella, checking in at St. Pancras International bound for Brussels. I wish them safe travels. She doesn't reply.

With nothing much going on among my following I decide I want some attention and post: 'This will lighten a cold rainy night. Add one word to a film title to make it giggly. My starter for ten: *Saving Private Ryan Air.*'

I throw these challenges into the mix quite often; it's usually a laugh and sometimes my friends are quite brilliantly clever with their answers. Perhaps I am too. Within less than two minutes, Tim Morgan - I knew it would be Tim - is in with his starter for ten: *A Hard Day's Night Gown.* Not bad; 6/10. There will be dozens more comments on the post over the course of the next couple of hours.

I can hear rain spattering hard against the windows and start to worry about Jude. She should probably be there by now and I wonder about messaging her to check. Then I decide not to in case she is still driving. Instead, I go around the cycle of social media again; reviewing profiles on matchmates; exploring Peeps; scrolling through SM posts and comments. I don't learn or say much. Over here is a friend sharing posts about a hate crime in Milwaukee. And there's another calling out their fears and judgements, as if they have friends they don't trust or really know. Oh, and now someone's advertising their new book, scratching the surface of a potential readership.

This is an existence two steps back from reality. With nothing else to do, no people to see or talk to, these places I visit are like a magic carpet ride on which I float over oceans of narcissism and islands of conviction. It might be false and deeply insincere; a mental medication. But it does me no harm. I'm safe within these walls; placated and calm.

It's just after nine when Jude messages me: 'I'm here. Horrible journey. Radio silence now babe. Might chat tomorrow. xx'

I send a single x that is converted into luscious red lips by my phone's all-conquering message software.

Our love is a clanging symbol.

It's strange to go to bed late on a Sunday evening. A week has come and gone, yet the coming week will somehow be different; scenery will change on a new day; routines will switch tracks; locations will be adapted. But for now, with the smell of Jude and our lovemaking lingering on my bedding, I have reached the final box in last week's flow chart.

The next process step says: *Advance to Go - Yes or No?* If I follow the *Yes* arrow on to next week's chart it will be more of the same; the ordinary life of a modern day nobody; conventional and bourgeois; who does nothing wrong, but nothing of value; who is bland, uncommitted and trapped.

If I take the *No* path, do I just have to hope I throw a double six and land somewhere further away?

Part Two

Lines Crossed

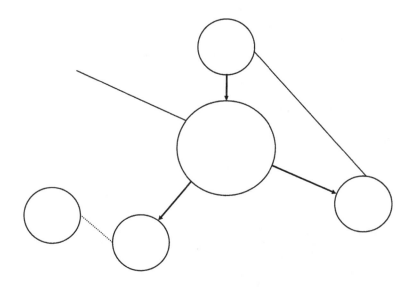

14

It's also utterly strange to have a Monday filled with amended stages. Like getting up late, at six, to go to the gym. Like eating breakfast at home; nice tea and a bowl of scrambled eggs. Like being online at work by seven forty-five and finding that shortly after that I'm fully in the thick of it. Yet somehow, I still feel I'm on a train, decelerating into Euston watching people preparing to disembark and wondering why they are also here. It seems ten months of that process have made it a default in my head.

It takes me most of the morning to shake the belief that I'm somewhere else. The day seems to amble by, doing things in my study that would normally be at a hot desk in London. I exchange greetings virtually with people I normally see face to face. The schedule is the same, and I'm still in control of all the processes. Yet the place is wrong and it's stopping Monday from being Monday.

As planned, I have a meeting with Annabel about the coming week and a presentation I'm creating. She guides me through some changes to the content and format of what I've already done so it will please its audience. She says it's good work and I should be confident about presenting it.

Then we chat for a while and she tells me it's amazing in Stockholm: cold and snowy; yet unruffled. When I say I've never visited any Scandinavian countries she says she will need help soon and I should have a case packed with warm clothes, scarves and gloves.

I want to ask if she's all right following our discussion on Friday afternoon; to dig deeper in and resolve the questions I didn't ask; to burst those bubbles of trouble. But she's busy and we soon disconnect; I'm left with the same sense of doubt she gave me last week.

By lunch time my head is straight. While I'm nibbling some carrots and hummus, I go to the health club's web page and get details of current standings in my squash league. Half an hour later I've fixed two matches for this evening.

Liz from Cumbria has been looking at my profile again, but no reaction. The post about film titles now has more than 210 comments, including several in which people are arguing about the rules or taking offence at being copied. My favourite is from Damon Hay: *The French Connection Pullover*.

My project meetings come and go and so does this working day. By four, I haven't heard from Annabel, so I check in: 'Hi, everything okay?'

She's shown as active, but I don't get a reply for several minutes.

'Hi. All good.'

'Great. What's your hotel like?'

'Very pleasant; lovely location near Gamla Stan.'

'Sounds like a market town betting shop.'

'LOL. It's what they call the old town. I might have a stroll later if it's not too cold.'

'I'll google it.'

'I meant it earlier. Pretty sure we will need someone like you to run projects for this client. Perhaps before the end of March. Would you be interested?'

'In principle yes. But would need a lot more detail.'

'Hold that thought. I need to stop chatting. Got stuff to do before I leave office.'

'K. Enjoy your evening.'

'U2.'

Annabel is in her element. Efficient, intuitive, perceptive. In less than a day on site with a new client, she has this clarity about them needing a project manager. She finds root causes with ease and is strong at selling too. It means I have to take her seriously; the opportunity to work in Sweden is real. It gets me thinking about being based in another country and how my life would be structured if my loaned-out base was there.

Part of me doesn't want to be further away from Joe and Beth.

Where would their home be then?

The health club is quiet, and I change in isolation. My first opponent is five places above me in the ladder and, if I beat her, I will be third in the league. I don't know Victoria Wright and, when she joins me on court, she shakes my hand and tells me she's warmed up the ball on another court. After a short knock up I win the right to serve first.

She takes the first game 9-3. I can't adjust to her being left-handed, nor to her pace around the court so I stop trying to power my way past her and focus on placing my shots on her backhand, which is weaker. I also stop trying drop shots.

The second game ends 9-1 to me and I feel like I'm warmed up now. Victoria taps me on the shoulder with her racquet and mutters that I'd played a great game.

We match each other winner for winner in the final game but, when I grab a 7-4 lead, I'm sure I've won the match. Then she wins back service before smashing five unplayable serves over my left shoulder leaving me stranded in my half of the court. On the back foot, I play poor returns and lose the game to seven. She's beaten me with my own tactic.

'That's as good a match as I've had. You're a class act.'

'Thank you. Those last serves were unplayable: I couldn't deal with them.'

'Let's go for a drink some time. Be nice to get to know you better.'

Before I can stop myself, I reply, 'that would be lovely.'

She delves into her bag then hands me a business card, shakes my hand, smiles broadly and without another word heads for the changing rooms.

'Victoria Wright - Owner - Maroon Creative Services'

There are also an email address and two phone numbers. The reverse of the card is all symbols and colours and shades of maroon. Some might be violet.

'Teddy Clayton. How the devil are you?'

Arif is walking towards me looking lean and mean. He's a seriously good squash player. I wonder why I've challenged him. We shake hands, then embrace briefly.

'Good to see you Arif, it's been a while. How are Ferzana and the kids?'

'They are missing you, and Beth and Joe. We must fix that.'

'Yes, we must.'

'How did you fare at the hands of Ms Wright?'

'Lost 2-1. She's an outstanding player.'

'She whitewashed me the other week.'

'You're joking. You scored no points at all?'

'It is only because I let her win. Left handers might all be bastards, but they sometimes need a boost. Are you ready?'

We have a hard-fought match and I win.

Arif is on a losing streak, despite being league champion in 2016. As we shower and change, he tells me he can explain his loss of form. I know him well enough to realise he might want to talk.

We became friends watching our sons in their formidable bowling partnership for the school's cricket teams. Joe was a year older but Shaqir was so good that he played at the higher age group for their whole six years together at the school. So Arif and I got to know each other, standing on the perimeter of assorted cricket squares around the county. Like a lot of school parent match ups, it snowballed into a family affair. Dinner or barbecues, or whatever, with Ferzana and Amy and all the kids. Then more of the same, without Amy.

'Let's have a drink. Come on. My shout.'

He looks on the verge of declining, but then agrees.

The small bar area is quiet: there's a guy pumping money into a fruit machine; two Lycra-clad women are drinking at the bar; a bored looking barman nods a welcome. Arif asks for a sparkling apple juice. I have water.

'You seem distracted. Is everything all right?'

'I'm not used to losing. I was top of the league three weeks ago; been overtaken by six players since then. I don't like it.'

'But you said you let Victoria Wright win.'

'Yes. That was a gift from me for something.'

I watch him say this and it doesn't sound like he's being creepy. But it's an odd thing to say. I press the point that I'm willing to listen if he wants to unload.

'There's some heavy shit going down; family and work.'

'How heavy?'

He explains that his daughter Alisha is being bullied and abused. Arif and Ferzana are beyond the end of their wits trying to cope with it.

'It's systematic Teddy. She's fourteen for fuck's sake. Some of the stuff she's endured on social media is hideous: threats of rape; of death; of torture; of disfigurement.'

'Has she been physically attacked?'

'Low key stuff only. Taunting. Name calling. Pushes and shoves. The kids doing this are mainly girls and always cowards. And they are led by one individual at the school.'

'You're joking? What's the school doing about it?'

'They are being helpful, to an extent. It's a quality school, we both know this. But they are confronted by a conflict they can't control. The daughter of a wealthy fee-paying parent being torn to shreds emotionally by the daughter of another wealthy fee-paying parent.'

'But it's bullying.'

'And it's also denied by the bully, despite the evidence on assorted media.'

'Maybe you should take it to the police?'

'Why? To get whatever their latest version of sympathy looks like?' He downs his drink. 'Rhetorical question.'

After checking with me, Arif goes to get a second round.

'When did it start?'

'It seems it originally started during Ramadan last year. The habitual hatred, made worse because Alisha might be weak from fasting.'

Arif's eyes are filled with a perplexing mix: despair; and defiance.

'What about Shaq. Is he getting similar treatment?'

Unexpectedly, Arif laughs loudly. 'Fuck me Teddy - when did you last see him? The boy is a beast. He works out twice a day. Eats nothing but protein. And he hangs out with a group of lads who most people would think twice about attacking in any context.'

He pauses to drink.

'Alisha is an athlete, beautiful and focused. She is part of many other groups and societies; dance; drama; music. She just wants to be part of as many opportunities as possible and be accepted. Like all kids do. Mainly, and thankfully, she is. But there seems to be an element on the periphery who want a piece of her.'

I'm astonished. Joe and Beth each spent seven happy years at the same school. There was no suggestion by either of them that another pupil might cause this kind of destructive pressure and be supported in it by parents.

'Have you made a formal complaint to the school?'

'Yes. I met the headmaster last week, along with Ali's form tutor. They made profound apologies but told me that the other party has made counter claims. That Ali supports terrorism. That she has made fun of the victims of attacks. I asked for evidence, which they said they don't have. But they say they are investigating. I was asked to see their problem and they didn't like it when I said I couldn't.'

Arif goes on to explain that he offered to make Alisha's phone and laptop available for investigation and for her to provide access to all her social media accounts, if necessary, for examination by an expert third party. He also offered to have a meeting with the other girl's parents and even for Alisha to be suspended while the investigation is concluded. The school's officials said none of that is needed and that a meeting with the other parents was not possible.

'Later, I found the reason why the head is so defensive. It seems this girl's parents are making significant donations to fund the school's netball tour to South Africa this summer.'

We both sit there shaking our heads. It seems that by paying for our kids to be kept away from supposedly hostile problems, we simply expose them to equally malignant horrors. With cheque books and, in extremis, barristers.

'How is Alisha coping? Has it affected her work or her running?'

'She's been fine, very strong. But it's like the loss of innocence. She is a loving, kind kid, growing up quickly. And all this has made her see other people as a constant threat; as a potential killer or rapist; as someone who would take her to Morecambe Bay and throw her in to the sea.'

The two women at the bar burst out laughing. One of them has a braying laugh, a bit like Sybil Fawlty. It makes Arif look at me with a chuckle and smile, but I'm not smiling back. The two women get up to leave.

'And what about work? What's the script there?'

Arif is a senior partner at a local accountancy firm. He looks around, furtive and anxious, at the slowly filling bar.

'I've been accused of sexual harassment. I'm suspended on full pay while this is investigated.'

He says it in such a matter of fact way that I almost do a double take.

'Why didn't you tell me till now? Can I help in any way?'

'I shouldn't really have told you this much. I have a confidentiality agreement in place.'

He looks around the bar again, as if there might be spies. 'Better if I leave it there.'

'Have you got legal support? You'll get the accusation dismissed right?'

'Of course. Don't worry about that. I will, because the allegation is a lie and a smear. It can't be evidenced. I didn't do it.'

'And it involves an employee of yours?'

He looks around again and lowers his voice slightly. 'Yes. Her accusation came out of nowhere in January. She claims I touched her breasts at the company Christmas party. She joined us in 2003, has brought in clients and revenue, has been promoted several times and was employee of the year three times.'

I am stunned.

'Is there anything more sinister going on?'

'Such as?'

'Such as racism.'

Arif sighs. 'That is at the core of why Alisha is being bullied. As for my accuser, who knows? But she will lose, whatever underpins her behaviour.'

'Is it worse since June?'

He shakes his head sadly. 'No. The referendum result changed nothing. It never went away; it's been there, like a chained, rabid dog, snarling and snapping at its victims. Forever. But you must stop this dialogue about Brexit being a choice driven by hatred. I voted to leave and there is no hate in my heart. I simply support our party's stance on self-governance and relinquishing membership of something we don't control.'

I side-step his lecture. 'Is there anything I can do? For Alisha or for you?'

'Nothing; but thank you. One snowflake can land, but it makes no difference.'

'Snowflake? That's insulting. Really insulting.'

He's looking at me again like I'm naïve; an innocent. And he sighs once more. 'You're a kind, loyal friend Teddy. Our families have been close for years. I know you're compassionate and thoughtful, but this is weakness.'

'So you just turn on me with an intimidatory insult?'

'It really isn't intimidation.'

'It is. Dismissive contempt and name-calling disguised as debate. The general tendency to use these terms – Snowflake, Liberal, Remoaner – is feeding the kind of mindset that's attacking Alisha. They believe they have right on their side, because anyone in authority has lost all contact with decency and gravitas.'

Arif reaches across to touch my hand. 'No Ted. You're wrong. Your despair about prejudice is virtue signalling. It literally means nothing.'

I'm slack-jawed. Arif's hand still covers mine.

'Your friendship means a great deal to me. It was good of you to care enough to talk this evening.' And then he claps his hands, as if summoning a servant. 'Come round for dinner soon. Bring your amazing children. We would all love to see you - it's been too long.'

I still feel broken by the disdain, verging on frivolity, of his manner.

Arif is looking at his phone. 'I need to go. Thanks for listening, and thanks for the match. Next time, you won't get a point.'

I'm home by just after nine and eat a distracted meal of leftover bits. I check in to work emails and find nothing needs my attention.

SocMed is light, but as I scroll through the detritus of shares and recycling, Arif posts: 'I am very lucky to have Teddy Clayton as a friend. We all are.' Within minutes, a flurry of Likes and Loves crops up on the post then comments endorse his praise.

I boil over and can't stop myself replying: 'You treated me like a fucking child earlier Arif. Not my idea of friendship.'

Inexplicably, someone Likes my comment.

Arif's reply is like a red rag. 'Have you been drinking Edward?' The ensuing emoji compounds my rage. I start typing out more of my pent-up fury but when I hit send, there's a message telling me the post no longer exists. I re-type it as a direct message, but it sits there unopened for ages.

There's no solace on *matchmates* where Liz from Cumbria has deleted me. I'm a bit hurt, but really this should probably be seen as an equaliser for my own treatment of Carla. It's simple for everyone like this; Liz doesn't have to tell me why I'm not her type; why she's upset or offended by me liking her; why she in turn also hit Like, then changed her mind; why I just won't do. The site provides an arm's length defence mechanism; you can walk away from a smile just by pressing a button.

There are bars in town where walking away from a smile is cause for actual bodily harm.

I pack away the accoutrements of work, ready for tomorrow's early start. Some simple clothing is massaged into the same bag and I wonder briefly if my extra night means I need a bigger case.

But I feel troubled and unhappy and end up sighing my way through another review of all that has happened today.

15

I'd forgotten about the pictures I posted last Monday. But it seems someone else has not. As I clear up to leave the office on Tuesday evening, a pop up on my phone tells me I have a Chattabox direct message from *&dpdevs*. Before I have a chance to open the app and read it, another pop up says there's a message from *&teena8shu*.

Both say the same thing, word for word: 'Your post last week with those photos from the train was a big mistake. Take it down or you'll get hurt. Badly hurt.'

Then a second message is duplicated from the same two sources: 'Don't ignore this message. Do as it says and do it *this evening*.'

I start to sit down, blinking at my phone's screen, and almost miss the chair. Someone says goodnight as they walk past my desk and I wave a hand at them without looking up. My disbelief becomes mingled with indignation and apprehension. Then I feel a wave of aggression and start to type in a furious retort: *who do you think you are; go and fuck yourselves right up the arse; this isn't a police state; I can say and do what I like in private.*

Some greater sense of perspective kicks in. I don't send anything and listen instead to the small voice in my head mumbling about vengeance and cold dishes. Then another small voice starts telling me to be afraid. I put my phone away and finish my packing, then hit the streets.

I walk the shortest route and it still seems to take forever, each pace like a step in to the unknown. What have I done wrong? How could such harmless fun be taken seriously? How did these people find me? Am I actually in danger? How can someone message me on Chattabox when I'm not following them?

In fact, I know the answer to most of the questions wriggling between my ears. And that makes things even more scary.

Then I remember that I made the decision to follow those fuckers.

All the while I can feel and hear my phones pulsing away in my pockets; stabs of dismay; pricks of concern. Or perhaps nothing so relevant. I should be checking for work issues but don't dare risk seeing more ultimata.

I feel like I've been physically attacked.

But now I'm thinking about how Jason Mason ticked me off; be careful; check your settings; think about your actions.

And then Dave's words about silly games. They were real; offline. But on message.

I took no notice but, in any event, they were too late.

When I get to my room I search online about messaging on Chattabox and quickly realise my fears are founded. Anyone can send and receive messages from someone they follow. I begin an initially calm but increasingly frantic search on my phone's Chattabox app, fumbling with the buttons and selecting wrong options. Eventually I manage to hit the link to *Privacy and Safety* and it's all clear. I have actually ticked a box that means anyone can message me whether I'm following them or not. I untick it, then for some reason tick it again. Maybe I might need evidence if complete strangers start sending me threatening messages in future. Better to give them the rope and hope they hang themselves.

Looking at the plethora of settings and rules I suddenly feel overwhelmed by the fact that anything I say on social media is never just between me and a chosen audience. This process is designed to make you a public entity unless you take very precise, very cautious actions to lock yourself down. In this malfunctioning state, I sign out of Chattabox, Postpix and SocMed and sit staring at my iPad for ages, hoping its silent screen means safety.

matchmates breaks the hush when it bleeps a notification that Mandy from London has liked my profile. A small wave of relief courses through me; a distraction; just what I need to quell the worry and anxiety. I look at Mandy's profile and find a gorgeous face in each of three photographs including the ubiquitous one holding a fluted glass, fizzing with content. Then standard stuff in her story: not sure about being on here; friends told her to give it a go; looking for Mr Right; sure he is out there.

She has messaged me too: 'Hi there Teddy. Wanted to get in touch with you to let you know you need to remove your SocMed post from last Monday. You know the one. Do it quickly and that will be the end of the matter.'

My worry and anxiety are rapidly burgeoning in to fear. Is this blackmail? Am I being given more than a warning? Is anyone in my family at risk? Unlike the Chattabox messages, this one suggests no further consequences, but I can't stop believing that if someone or something has begun this process, the threat isn't idle or finite. This is orchestrated and direct.

This time I decide to reply: 'Mandy, who are you? Why are you doing this and who for?'

It feels reassuring to ask questions but almost as I hit send, I'm overwhelmed by nausea and rush to the bathroom to be sick. It's all over in one heave, and I'm left shaken and drained. As I clean up and drink some tap water, I catch my reflection in the mirror; mouth hung open; eyes strained wide; pale; aghast. I wipe away a line of yellow from my chin.

The message dialogue with Mandy has gone from my *matchmates* inbox and I can't see her profile. I snatch up my phone to look at Chattabox and, before I've signed into the app, I already know that the messages and those accounts will also be gone. What were their names? Tina something. And Dave Deverham; or was it Deverson? I do an online search for both versions of the name then realise I'm pissing into the wind. There are dozens of Dave Deverhams and Deversons and they could be real or false, but my ability to link them to *&dpdevs* is non-existent.

It's too late for me to realise that I should have screen shot the messages, even though they might never have been believed. I've nothing to prove what happened. I'm in a mess of indecision.

The warning said I must not ignore it. So, I really mustn't. But what if I do? What if I just leave the post and see what they do next? Logic over threat, right?

Except: what did the training always say? Use threat only if you mean it.

So they meant it.

Jason Mason and Dave were right. I was careless and stupid. And all anyone will say to me if I ask for advice is that I was dumb to post it. All the likes, and hearts and laughing faces that people replied with; all the one-liners giggling along with my chortles; all those people failed to point out the single most obvious and important thing. I, Teddy Clayton, behaved like an attention seeking crowd-pleaser when I posted those photos.

Annabel is offline. Jude is incommunicado. The two people I feel able and willing to ask for advice about this intervention are distant and closed off.

I dare not ask my kids.

On my iPad I log back into SocMed. I click on my face and name in the top right and flick a finger up the screen sending my most recent posts flying upwards. It goes on forever, this morass of immature irrelevance. I find I recall all the words and photos I've posted as they scroll upwards, like the credits at the end of a soap opera. And I realise I've gone past the post and need to flick the screen in the opposite direction. Then it's there on my timeline. I touch the dots, top right.

Everything in this process seems to be top right.

The dots reveal a white square, with symbols about posting, editing and hiding.

Hiding. That's the one I should select isn't it? Make the post go away, but secretly lift a finger at these crazies because I have defied them and not obeyed their commands.

More symbols about deletions and turning off replies. I touch *Delete*. Pale writing tells me the post will be deleted but I can edit it if I just want to change it.

Bad things are written in red text; good things in blue.

I touch the red. A tiny roulette wheel mesmerises me. Maybe I've won big.

And then the post has gone.

Now I'm frantic again, poking my index finger at the *More* menu to find *Settings*. I poke *Settings* and then *Activity Log*. It doesn't log the fact that I've deleted a post. I stroke my finger up the screen again, then back and forth a bit until I find the date I originally posted the words and photos. The post isn't there but the items originally sitting either side of it are there, relieved of the thorn they once shielded.

Offence removed.

I've done as I'm told, deferential and obliging despite my tough shell.

I know my place.

155

All my reactions have dissipated: worry; anxiety; fear; anger; retaliation; disbelief - all gone. Or hidden. Now, I feel resignation and a growing calm.

On balance, I've done the right thing.

On balance, I've fallen in line.

On balance, this was a decision that needed no advice or validation. I've run and can hide.

On balance, I've over-reacted to an astonishing level.

I look around the room as if hoping it might reflect some gratitude back at me. In the mirror, I'm there again. Mouth shut; eyes squinting; a realisation dawning. Why did I delete the post without looking down the list of people who'd liked and/or commented on it? Every clue I might ever have needed about the source of all this heartache was probably lurking in amongst all that.

Suddenly my phones and iPad are lighting up with alerts from the assorted news apps I subscribe to.

'Brussels locked down after gun and bomb outrage.'

'Many dead in Belgian capital after terror rampage.'

'Police shoot dead two attackers: at least six thought to remain at large.'

Filled once again with the hopeless rage that these things are never ending, I begin reading the first reports. It's the usual horror. Lives snuffed out, murdered by people whose acts will be sunk into a silo and given a warped legitimacy by being called Terrorism.

It creates perspective for my own little earthquake earlier in the evening. Then, a mental click and whirr make me shout out loud: 'Fucking hell: no.'

I'm suddenly more frantic and manic than at any point I can remember, ever. On to my phone, calling Dave and Ella's numbers. No reply. Voicemail. I call Tina. She's heard nothing. We're both beside ourselves with alarm and fear for our friends' lives. Neither of us knows which hotel they were staying at, or their plans and itinerary during the visit. Tina says she'll call the Foreign Office hotline. I say I'll keep calling around friends and looking for clues on SocMed and news media sites. I check Ella's company website and go to her timeline, but she's posted nothing since earlier in the day when she was looking forward to their visit to the Magritte Museum. I go on Messenger and send an error ridden sentence asking her to get in touch. I message Harriet Ellis, but she's shown as inactive for days and it's clear from her SocMed pages that she isn't a frequent user.

I message Beth and Joe to tell them to call me if they're worried. They reply that they're fine and I mustn't worry about them. We exchange messages of love and regret. Neither of them has ever met her, but I still ask them if they know Harriet's phone number. They don't.

Tina keeps messaging me with names of mutual friends from uni who've heard nothing. I start to feel agitated that Tina's doing all the work. I wonder who I can contact and find myself drawn to the idea that I could call Mr Ellis in Witney, or Dave's sister Charlotte. I start scrolling through contacts looking for phone numbers. But as I reach the card for Phillip and Muriel Ellis, I realise I can't possibly call a recent widower to ask if he has news about a potentially murdered son. I don't have Charlotte's number, but it would be no less insensitive and traumatising for her.

What am I thinking?

Back on SocMed, mutual friends are exchanging updates about who they've called for news. It seems outwardly desperate, but this is positive and life-affirming. It seems we're all pulling out all the stops for Dave and Ella. They'd be doing the same. Wouldn't they?

Then Tina messages me, and shortly afterwards posts to our friends, that the FO has let her know they have no news of Dave and Ella's whereabouts: but no report of them being casualties. There's no way of reading that in a happy light. This cycle of reporting goes through several loops and it starts to feel like we're just repeating ourselves in order to validate that we care. After many too many minutes, it is starting to feel like defeat.

Then, like a sudden erupting firework, Ella's SocMed timeline lights up with a report that she has marked herself safe. A few moments later, she replies to my message from earlier: 'Teddy we're both fine. It's very frightening indeed, but we were nowhere near the station and have been safely back at hotel for some time now. Police everywhere. Lots of guns. Dave says your typing is a fucking disgrace. No chance of calling. But speak soon.'

I laugh out loud, and then my laughter turns to tears. I go to SocMed and, through watery eyes, watch myself post that I've heard from Ella and Dave and our wonderful friends are alive and kicking. Everyone knows, but I tell them anyway.

This good news is soon engulfed by wider reaction to the attack and by the rising death toll. The latest news is of a further gun fight near Charleroi where police have cornered suspects following a pursuit. News also of a second pursuit, into southern Belgium and the border with Luxembourg. In the time it takes me to read these summary headlines, the reported death toll has risen from 37 to 61. I go back into SocMed and type: 'I'm sick of these fucking cowards.' I look at it on screen for several moments. And then I don't want to say it after all. A lingering fear from earlier is tightening its grip on my stomach and temples. The news about Dave and Ella had made me feel calm and reassured. Now I just want to get off any medium that might expose what I think and feel to the wrong people. I discard the post and sign out of SocMed, then delete all its apps from my devices. I even log out of *matchmates*.

In contravention of our embargo on communications, I text Jude: 'Thinking of you.' She replies quite quickly: 'And me you. Be safe sweetheart xx.'

All the while, texts are dropping into me: from Luke; from colleagues at our office in Preston; from Annabel; and from Arif. The message is mostly the same: *'Are you in London? Hope all is ok and you're safe. Stay in your hotel. Be alert.'*

I give the requisite reassurances; bland; short; and sweet.

But I follow on with Arif with an apology for my outburst yesterday. He doesn't reply. I can't work out why things feel so negative between us.

I snap out of it and take a look at the television and its grisly news. Confirmed deaths now 79, including several police officers. It's also reported that seven of the eleven people believed to have carried out the atrocities have also been shot dead.

I mutter: 'Good. Bastards.'

There's footage from the main station in Brussels; a mass of flashing blue neon; emergency vehicles and personnel; walking wounded, shocked, tearful, disbelieving; blood stained pavements; morbid mounds swathed in blankets. Then of the suburb in Charleroi and of locked down border crossings.

Back to the studio for reaction and comment. The defiant, pre-scripted sound bites from world leaders are always the same except for the recently elected leader of the free world, whose deranged Peeps seem no different to the crowing vanity of the murderers and their adherents. Slogans. Final solutions.

I switch off the television in disgust and lie back on the bed, desperate to sleep. Soon I feel my eyes fluttering and that magnificent narcotic calm that indicates sleep is mercifully close.

But too close for comfort. It isn't long before I'm wide awake again, staring at the ceiling; knowing I should be thinking about dead people in Belgium; but, instead, obsessing about my own tiny distresses.

Within a few moments, I've struck up a frenzied internal debate about going to the police and then reporting all that has happened to the virtual authorities running the social media used to attack me. This sense of victimhood is dimmed when I realise how dumb that is. Two of my closest friends could easily have been gunned down today, maimed or murdered. I should man up.

But did I deserve to be treated as I have been?

And who has done it?

There's no-one around to answer this rhetoric. It's nearly two in the morning and I'm on my iPad looking at the three photos I took that day on the train.

What can I see?

The guy's MacBook Pro is resting precariously on the fold-down table. The email he's typing is addressed to *Marcus Mapplewick*. Funny name, but probably not a joke. No-one is in CC, and the subject is *Fixing our Troublemakers*. The mail is shown as from *Kriss - cjarvis@marmap.com*. The opening sentence reads: 'Marcus, you wanted an update on where we're up to with alternatives and deterrents. I think we...'

In the second photo he's holding up his iPhone 7 plus and is chatting with *Foxy*. I can see two bubbles of filth, his in green and hers in white. The circular image alongside her name is grainy and unclear. When I zoom in and enhance it, it looks worse; I can make out the thickness of eyebrows and lashes, and of lips and cheekbones. Dark hair pulled away from forehead.

The only real change in the third image is some additional text in the email that clarifies that, after all, this isn't about workforce. He's mentioned tactics being used to discredit protest groups and a conversation with the police about turning a blind eye to assaults by security guards. I hadn't taken that in before.

Why on earth would he risk expressing all that so openly? It's like there's vanity at work. Conformance to something outdated and old-school; put it in writing; provide a sitrep.

I'm still wary about being online but decide I can risk internet searches using my work laptop. If I'm being tracked somehow, nothing I do on there will be visible. So I write down a list of search criteria: *Marcus Mapplewick; marmap.com; Kriss Jarvis; Christopher Jarvis; Chris Jarvis.*

The internet is very slow, but the very first hit on *Marcus Mapplewick* is a link to the website for MarMap Logistics, where he is owner and managing director. It's a small town, small impact internet site but it's well presented and neatly packaged. Whatever customers it seeks to attract can be in no doubt about MarMap's ambition: to be logistics provider of choice for Midlands businesses. The verbiage is limited to simple, quite well-written paragraphs that draw me in to what they say. MarMap seems like an honest proposition with quality and value at its core. But it focuses on what MarMap does, not on how it delivers or why one might choose them over a competitor. This is a site conveying information, not garnering engagement.

Photographs of trucks and vans abound and very few of the images omit the main man, or a MarMap sign and logo. The signage is simple and striking using bold serif fonts in white on a blue background. A faint red border encloses each sign wherever it appears. The logo is two capital letter Ms, crushed together so they share a central pillar. The same font and colour scheme is used, and atop each point of the two Ms is a small image of a well cut gemstone, making the two letters look like a ducal crown.

Marcus is tall and slender, looks striking in well-tailored suits and has a quite genuinely warm smile. Overall-clad people share his smiles or whatever joke he's just told. He is tactile towards his team: shaking hands; arms around shoulders and waists.

One page is devoted to him and his good deeds in the community: charitable works; advocate of schools, in particular one specialising in physical and sensory needs; supporter and benefactor of local golf clubs and the RUFC; local business champion and entrepreneur; a champion for diversity; a paternal figurehead to MarMap's workforce, impelled by the need to assure their safety and welfare, especially while on the road. One section is devoted to a description of the local equestrian centre run by his wife, Tracy, which seeks to provide horsey fun for local schools and communities.

In the thirty minutes or so it takes me to complete my review of the MarMap site, I've written down several new search criteria: *Logistics firms Staffs; Cannock chamber of commerce; Tracy Mapplewick; Lichfield chamber of commerce; TMap equestrian centre; protest groups Cannock; protest groups Staffs.* I open a tab for each of these searches, then open a blank tab and type *Christopher Jarvis* into the search field. It returns myriad hits, so I add Lichfield to the name and touch enter. It's still throwing up dozens and dozens of hits and none on the first page looks right. I change the name to use *Kriss*, and while the hits change, it still isn't linking me to the person I saw that day.

I don't linger on this problem.

I cross out *marmap.com* from my list of searches and scribble a note on my pad: 'Check MarMap financials and company officials on Co-Stats tomorrow. Then BizSoc and perhaps Chattabox.'

It's past 4am now, and I get up to pace the room. I'm going to do more on the internet and know that I won't sleep at all. But these steps of mine are needed to work my mind around a dilemma - about going onto SocMed to look at whatever is there about these people. I am almost scared to look but I want to know if any of them is there; to know that I can hit back at them somehow; scare them like I've been scared.

Inter Alia

'Marcus, it's Kriss.'

MM always pauses before replying, sometimes for ten or more seconds. In person, by phone, even using video conferencing. He'd heard somewhere that it is a sign of power and indicates control in a conversation or negotiation. Kriss was used to it and always made use of the respite to do something worthwhile: like feeling his cock.

'Mister Jarvis. To what do I owe this pleasure?'

Kriss relayed the news that the Clayton post had been deleted from SocMed.

There was a massive exhalation of triumph.

'That's great news Christopher. Well done. When did this happen?'

'Within less than two hours of him being told to do it.'

'And has there been any reaction? Has the peasant made any further nuisance of himself?'

'None.'

MM made a vague whooping sound. 'We must celebrate. How soon can you get here? I'll crack open a special bottle or two. Bring your tart too.'

Kriss thought about Kat. In the days since this saucer full of storms had broken, she hadn't contacted him in any way. The people he used to spy on social media said she had disappeared from every one of the accounts she used. He felt a tiny prick of sorrow that she was gone.

'That was a one-off Marcus; literally nothing to me.'

'That's the best way with women Mister Jarvis. Keep it simple, and arm's length.'

Kriss was less and less disconcerted by the possibility that anyone could recognise Kat from the Clayton photo. But he didn't want MM digging too deeply into her identity.

'Give me twenty minutes to finish up here at the office and I'll be with you.'

'Get a taxi. Let's have a proper drink.'

Kriss didn't want a lot of time with Marcus because he would be crowing and vainglorious about this pyrrhic victory. Kriss was a bad loser, at everything, but could be gracious in defeat if he felt his opponent had earned it. MM's way of winning made the worst loser in the world seem chivalrous. On the other hand, MM's notion of a proper drink meant an evening of vintage champagne and XO cognac and that could make any bluster from his host seem tolerable.

He was shown in by the Mapplewick's maid who took his jacket and the bottle of Margaux he'd picked up en route. He watched the wine disappear and wondered if Sylvie actually handed it over to MM or Tracy. If not, she'd have several thousand pounds worth of vintage wine and rare perfume stashed away somewhere.

He stood in the entrance hall, silent and subservient; an employee, here to report on an errand. Kriss wasn't quite in the category of servant like Sylvie, and Tim the chauffeur, but in this counterfeit mansion he was furniture. A whispered aside. In abeyance.

MM's voice boomed out at him, then a wafted arm beckoned: 'Mister Jarvis. Welcome. Come through.' Kriss did as instructed. On the threshold of his study, MM shook Kriss' hand warmly. There was music quietly playing; glossy pop, almost certainly some dire eighties band. MM couldn't abide music from any other era.

'Tracy is out until later with Clarry and Benj. We can relax in here and have a few schooners of P-J. Sylvie is doing some bits to eat. And thank you for the claret.'

The small chill of disappointment Kriss felt about Sylvie's lack of larceny was swept away by the sight of a large black glass ice bucket swathed in condensation with a gold foil bottle top peeking from it. There was also an unopened bottle of VSOP Grande Champagne XO cognac and two good sized balloons.

'We'll start with the '85 if that's all right with you. Then try the '82.'

After extracting the bottle of Belle Epoque, deftly draping it in a napkin and removing the foil top, Marcus expertly uncorked the wine. Almost immediately Kriss could smell that smell; the

163

immense vintage champagne aroma; biscuits; apples; yeast. But with the Perrier-Jouët there was more; flowers; citrus; minerals.

When it came to top-notch fizz, Kriss knew his onions.

Marcus handed him a large flute, three-quarters full of champagne and immediately touched his glass against Kriss': 'To Victory!'

Kriss played along: 'Victory.'

They remained standing.

'We did it, Christopher, and well done. Another problem solved. Another thorn extracted.'

Kriss looked at MM; he actually did see the simple act of intimidation that had quashed a minor nuisance as a crushing triumph for his own good.

'Tell me again what happened.'

Kriss took a suck on his flute. The champagne was celestial nectar. As always, he found himself quickly dismissing any doubts about MM's churlish boyhood fantasia. He'd do anything if it meant he got to drink at this table.

'The troops hooked Clayton last week on Chattabox. Easy on there. But we also got someone to link on his dating site.'

'Dating site? I thought only married men used those, to pursue... opportunities.'

'Not in this case. Seems our man is quite the lothario on his chosen medium.'

'Sometimes, Mr Jarvis, you are too clever for me. Use smaller words and shorter sentences.'

He winked, and with a gesture, MM showed he was ready to top up Kriss' glass so he drained it. They'd each consumed around fifty quid's worth of bubbly in less than five minutes. Kriss chuckled to himself. Some people don't drink that much in a lifetime.

'They kept it brutal Marcus. Take down the post. Or face more consequences.'

'That's good. When was this?'

'Yesterday.'

'And he took it down quickly?'

MM poured another slug of champagne into their glasses.

'It seems so. Our requests...'

'Requests. Excellent. That's funny. You've a way with words.'

'...got sent late afternoon, then our dating-site babe hit him a bit later.'

'Babe? Someone recognisable?'

'Mandy. Real name Kevin McLean from Bermondsey.'

MM burst out laughing. 'That's fucking priceless Mister Jarvis.'

Kriss nodded and smiled before concluding: 'Anyway, the messages did the job.'

'Good. But no ripples caused by that?'

'He's gone pretty quiet.'

'Message received loud and clear then.'

'I think so. But last night's events have probably killed a lot of anyone's enthusiasm.'

MM sneered into his glass, then paced off around the room, fulminating against the instigators of attacks like the one in Belgium. Kriss instantly regretted that he'd mentioned it. MM's capacity for prejudicial hatred was ill-concealed at the best of times. But in the aftermath of attacks it boiled over and here he was again, spitting rage against the machinery over-running his land.

Kriss tried to get them back on to the winning ways they were toasting.

'We will keep an eye on Clayton in case he steps out of line. But my gut feel, Marcus, is that he got the message loud and clear. He won't be back.'

MM was back from his xenophobic circumnavigation.

'He better fucking not be. And you better remember that it was your crass negligence that got me in to this mess.'

Kriss blinked slowly at his boss. A turn for the worse was in play.

'Marcus, I've apologised for that and taken steps to resolve it. No-one knows about his post. No-one in the protest camp registered its existence. Let's track it over the next day or two. But, seriously, I don't believe anyone that matters will ever know his post existed.'

'Anyone that matters? Like me you mean?'

'No. Like the protestors.'

MM took an especially large suck on his front teeth. Then snorted. 'Those tree-hugging bastards.'

Again, MM gestured that Kriss should drink up and drained the bottle into their glasses. Before he could say more, he was distracted by a knock on the door. He bawled: 'Come!', and Sylvie appeared at the door pushing a small trolley towards them.

It was canapés and nibbles; finger food par excellence. Kriss was hungry and grabbed at bits and pieces while Marcus merely pecked around the edges. Then another bottle of champagne got opened and they moved to sit on the leather Chesterfield sofas. Sylvie soon re-appeared to remove the trolley and was instructed to bring coffee in half an hour.

'Now the '82 Christopher. A great year. I got my first job straight from school - a wet-behind-the-ears sixteen-year-old - in an old light engineering workshop in Cannock. Hard work, alongside real men; hard men. And the Falklands War. We ruled the world then.'

Kriss was born three years later in 1985. His father had been part of the Task Force, serving in the Second Battalion, Parachute Regiment. Kriss grew up hearing his father's tales of the landings at San Carlos Water, the battles at Goose Green and Wireless Ridge and then the final victory when Port Stanley was recaptured. His father said he had hated the Argentine troops who he viewed as amateurs. But his hatred for them soon dissipated, replaced by a seething loathing for politicians. The goose-stepping clowns in Buenos Aires who'd sent largely unwilling novices to fight professional troops. And the side-stepping clowns in Westminster who preached their fake patriotism and fervent national pride while slowly dissolving the Greatest Army in the World, all for the sake of cooking the books. He saw their love of country as profoundly insulting, especially to an injured mate who had been cast aside with neither support nor gratitude.

Before he was sixteen, Kriss was bored by all his father's stories and posturing; they had fallen out. When he left for university, Kriss also left home. The bad blood between father and son was never made good and, by the time he graduated, Kriss' obsessions with the pursuit of money, drugs and sex had made his father see him as a worthless, feckless ne'er-do-well. The kind who were making the country rotten to the core. Kriss didn't care and in return saw his father's pride in country, job, regiment and honour as wasted working class sentiment. He was long dead but, had he lived, Mr Jarvis Senior would have detested Kriss, all he had become and all that he was involved with. He would especially have despised Marcus Mapplewick and his memories of ruling the world.

'So, Mister Jarvis: we've eradicated this jumped up Northern Nuisance, and his pathetic childish intervention. What next? Where are we up to against the tiny waves of red leftism?'

Kriss chewed on the last morsel of food he'd been able to snatch before the feast was removed. A flaky pastry parcel, filled with olives, herbs and some sort of cheese. Stunning food, redolent of sun and sin. His mind wandered towards Sylvie. She was lovely, in a patently gallic sense. Maybe he should...

'Cat got your tongue Mister Jarvis?'

'Kat? No. I...'

'Fuck me Christopher, you look like you've eaten something disagreeable. Do you need some water or something?'

Kriss recovered quickly.

'No, I'm fine Marcus.'

'Well come on. What's happening at the construction sites? Are we still being blocked by the scum?'

'The police are helping.'

'That makes a change. Those fuckers are quick enough to hand Tracy a speeding fine for doing forty-two in a thirty, despite my constant support for them and their work. Yet when a few dozen beatniks descend on the county to disrupt honest industry, approved by the government, I hear the Chief Constable bleating about policing fairly.'

'Well she might be saying that in the interests of balance. And political expediency.'

'Political expediency is the fucking problem.'

'Maybe. But the plods on the ground have arrested quite a few people recently, making use of any old trumped up charge. They're loving it: all that overtime. Also, they've turned a blind eye to the security guards whenever they stick a steel toe cap in.'

MM was looking sourly at Kriss. 'One lot of worthless scroungers versus another.'

'Easy Marcus. We need to retain our public view that the police are doing a wonderful job and that the protestors have a right to their views...'

'...their pointless, flat earth views...'

'...indeed. But we do like free speech and have no problem with peaceful protest.'

'Well you know I completely disapprove of that stance Mister Jarvis but, as you keep reminding me, it costs nothing. What's happening on the social media front?'

'Every MarMap employee has a presence now on the pro road group. I think your speech at the local traders' dinner the other evening also caused a spike of new joiners. We've got a nice mix of respectable business leaders; good, honest, mainly local working folk; and a smattering of knuckle-dragging enforcers.'

Marcus smiled. He'd had a quick look at the *No Overtaking - Roads Matter* page the other evening and enjoyed some of the threats being poured down on the scum who dared to challenge. There was a strange beauty in the conflict, and he loved the way the pro-camp was so blindly in favour of something as irrelevant as a new bypass. Not one of them would benefit from it, yet they happily smashed into the protest camp, destroying every argument with either competing science, pure economics or street-fighting bombast.

'We've also got dozens and dozens of fake Chattabox accounts chasing down any protest groups or individuals on there.'

Marcus poured out the last of the second bottle of champagne. Kriss acknowledged his share with thanks for something special.

'You've earned it Christopher, and not just in the last few days. Take a day out tomorrow.'

'Thank you, Marcus, but there's a lot to do. We've that press release to get out and I don't like what the team has done.'

'What's wrong with it?'

'It's too much about the construction sites, and not enough about MarMap. I don't feel our guys have grasped the problem.'

MM drained his glass and signalled that Kriss should do the same. As he emptied the last dregs of champagne, Kriss heard the squeak of a cork being withdrawn from a bottle and watched MM pour two mega-shots of cognac into the balloons.

'Sylvie will be here shortly with coffee. Shall I ask her to bring anything else? Are you still hungry?'

Kriss could have eaten a three-course dinner but declined. Marcus had a strange detachment where food was concerned. He'd often seen his boss sit in a restaurant issuing orders to staff, demanding explanations from the chef or asking that the party at the next table be removed; all the while leaving most of his meal untouched in favour of simply being seen.

'I'm fine, thank you. Coffee will be good though.'

'Grasping the problem is the whole problem Mister Jarvis.'

Kriss only just stopped himself from laughing. He could and would never bite the hand that feeds, but sometimes he couldn't believe how much of an arsehole Marcus could be.

'How do you mean?'

MM swirled his XO cognac around in his glass then took a huge snort of its aroma.

'Our battle here isn't about whether or not the fucking stupid road gets built. I don't give a shit about something built for the benefit of a few salesmen in Vauxhalls and this pathetic nonsense about Northern Powerhouses. It's like the fucking rail link: why do we need to link our country with Europe anyway? Especially for the horrible shower of shite living in the North and beyond.'

Kriss nodded dutifully and was about to offer a vaguely contrary stance when the door opened. Sylvie was there again, pushing a small trolley with a cafetière, cups and saucers together with assorted bowls and jugs and a small mound of what looked like chocolate truffles. She was also wearing an apron.

Just an apron.

Kriss watched in unaccustomed astonishment as Sylvie escorted her cargo across the room and parked it in front of Marcus. Nothing he'd ever seen or heard from his monster of a boss had ever signalled this. Dutiful husband, with adoring wife and family, was the constant depiction. Solid upholder of values. A stalwart of rectitude.

And here he was smiling vacuously at his fixer as he lecherously stroked his servant's arse, and beyond, while she asked Kriss if he wanted black or white, cream or milk, and sugar or unsweetened. Through his blinks of astonishment, Kriss just about coped with giving his order of black coffee with sugar. Sylvie unhooked herself from MM's digital attention to pour this beverage and brought him the cognac bottle too. Kriss poured himself another cognac while he watched Sylvie pouring coffee for MM while she ground out a rhythmic tuneless groove in front of her Lord and Master, who appeared to be hypnotised and mute.

Then like some bit part player in a pantomime, Sylvie gave final gyrations of her gluteus maxima, one for the benefit of both men, and took back the cognac from Kriss. He tried to maintain eye-contact with her but failed. Within a few seconds she'd gone, with two pairs of eyes glued to the door after she closed it. The sound of the departing slap MM had given her arse still hung on the air, like a belly flop would on a swimming pool in the nave of a church.

'It's all perfectly simple Mister Jarvis. I need the money from supplying services into the construction sites. It's convenient for now but I will place my hat in any ring that makes me money.'

'And money for MarMap.'

Marcus sighed. 'Yes and no. I can make money anywhere I choose, and one major project is like any other. For now, this bypass thing is my cash cow and you benefit from it, like all my underlings. But you know I don't actually care about the workforce at MarMap: I'm not a charity. People can cling on to their nostalgic slush in the hope I'll take care of them. That's fine and if things go well and they do their jobs, then we fly together. Any turbulence though and I'm first out with my parachute.'

Kriss drained his cognac. It didn't taste as good as he wanted. 'Should I be looking for another employer?'

MM looked up at the ceiling then closed his eyes with a more protracted, theatrical sigh.

'No Christopher. I need you around. Just don't get sentimental about being part of something like a team. You're not. You exist to do what needs to be done for me to make more money. But don't dream about things being nice. That's what they do: the scum protestors who block roads that stop my deliveries; that spray abuse on my property; that think they own the right to make decisions for people. They don't, any more than the politicians. Decisions about what does or doesn't get built, does or doesn't get made, does or doesn't get drilled or flown or sailed or driven or burned or... fucking... anything: these are too important to leave to anyone other than the wealthy. We are in charge; we at the top table with right on our side. The rich and influential and powerful Mister Jarvis. And not just any rich people: we can't leave it to the also-rans in their half-million-pound town houses who think they're successful. Puppies, with their tongues lolling out, hoping they get their tummy rubbed and a chewy treat or two.' Marcus mimed his words, then panted like an eager dog; Kriss only just retained his composure.

'Too many of them have ideas above their station about being in control and being part of my world when, in reality, they are only a small step away from failure, redundancy, loserhood.'

Now Kriss nodded, but he wasn't aligned with his boss on this subject. It was virulent horseshit. He tried a minor intervention.

'The politicians are needed though, aren't they? We need our MP in the camp, and his influence in Westminster. Don't we?'

MM sighed again, like a parent frustrated by a child's poor exam results.

'Christopher, I sometimes wonder whether your university education has made you blind to reality.'

His stare of contempt was quite chilling.

'The direction of travel is simple. Politicians come and go, doing and saying nothing without consent. We put the right ones in place to assure all they do and say.'

He gulped a mouthful of brandy.

'The next target is the fucking civil service because they still think they are in charge. I don't mean the ones working in offices, dishing out money to tramps or whatever. I mean the top dogs; mandarins; Whitehall's wankers. When all that's been swept away, then real change will have happened. And complete power will be ours.'

There was a commotion somewhere outside the room; a returning family, stamping and voluble. Tracy Mapplewick's face and perfume soon appeared at the door.

'Hello Kriss, is Marcus looking after you?'

Before he could reply, Marcus had bounded across to his wife, wrapped her in an embrace and swamped her in platitudes.

'Come and have a cognac with us my love.'

'No, thank you. I will leave you to whatever conclusion the evening brings. I'm tired. Our children never fail to make me happy, but nor do they ever leave me feeling rested. I'm going to get Sylvie to run me a bath then have a long soak in it.'

Kriss couldn't prevent the dreamy vision of a naked Sylvie leaning over a bath, thrashing the water into ever increasing mounds of voluptuous foamy joy. He was hugely distracted.

His hosts exchanged a final spousal indulgence and Tracy departed, her good wishes ringing in Kriss' ears. As if their arrival had never happened, the sounds of family were gone. The house was silent.

'Join me in a final glass of this cognac Christopher. Tonight has been a celebration for us both and you deserve an equal share of these wonderful drinks.'

What Kriss desperately wanted was at least two lines of coke. And a night with Kat.

But she was an hour ahead of him, cuddled up in the arms of her husband who had arrived with his retinue at very short notice earlier in the day. He'd brought her a series of gifts, and she'd thanked him with a meal she cooked herself and then more fundamental recipes at bedtime. Now he was asleep, breathing quietly into the nape of her neck.

Kat was wide awake, troubled by why he'd arrived and what had prompted the lavish set of offerings that he bore. Kriss was history, a stranger to her already. Yet somehow, she was linking Jeff's arrival with the time she'd spent in her affair with Kriss. There was nothing in her possession, either at home, at her Birmingham apartment or here in Gstaad that joined up the dots between her and Kriss - or anyone. But it all felt very disturbing; above all because Jeff was never spontaneous; not even when he had people killed.

Kat was scared. Very scared indeed.

Before he fell asleep, full of pasta carbonara and Barolo, Jeff Tasker had snuggled up to Kat in a fake post-coital haze. He was composed and focused. This woman he'd married had been a decent enough addition to his stable, but the latest intel from the guys was compellingly comprehensive. Something would have to be done. But maybe, first, some fun with the good Mr Mappleprick and his vaulting ambitions.

16

The information I've been able to amass by the time I leave for the office defies belief; and I haven't finished. Somehow, I need to switch off all of that to get on with my job and the series of calls and meetings scheduled for this morning.

I find time to jump on to a tool we use to review the financial performance of companies, usually suppliers or clients. MarMap's report is soon on screen and I request a download to be mailed to me. I can print and analyse it over lunch. With five minutes to spare before my eight am conference call, I also go to the Department for Transport's site to get details of the link being built between the M6 toll road near Shenstone and the M42 near Appleby Magna.

And then I concentrate on work. The things that have pulled me out of shape over the last sixteen hours are consigned to the back of my mind. Today's objectives are simple:

stay awake

do my job

be 100% focused on the presentation later in the afternoon

support and direct my team in all they do

stay late to cover off anything I might want to do about my personal situation behind the safety of the company's firewall

and think.

The horror of Brussels is in our corporate conscience and all my meetings and phone calls seem to start with an assessment of what has happened. But it's generally a cold evaluation of wrongdoing; compassionate, but lacking passion. Like the Midwich Cuckoos, there is a single mind at work - a shared cell of opinion. No one steps off message into murky waters with submerged root causes.

The perpetrators have all been declared killed, but the groups claiming responsibility also insist some of their jackals escaped unharmed and are in France. The Belgian capital is still locked down and the fear is spreading out from the country like a virus, mutating into new more deadly forms as security services around Europe reveal significant evidence that more attacks are imminent. The media and politicians fan the flames; but that's their job and they excel at it.

I still haven't dared look on Chattabox or SocMed.

When I get a spare half hour, I move to a private room and begin rehearsing the presentation I'm doing later for Josh Niesmann. Annabel's helped me to craft the messages and design of the PowerPoint so it's punchy and simple and I'm soon word perfect. I've taken a look at Josh's BizSoc details for clues about his background, but his profile is bland. Aside from a basic work history and that he lives in Richmond, Virginia, I'm none the wiser about who he is and how he might behave.

As the day progresses, another topic closer to home seeps into the collective working mind: Paul Wilson. I join one of my calls a couple of minutes late and hear a few seconds of conjecture: a word is on the streets, it seems, but the conversation stops abruptly when it's clear I've joined.

> While the team runs through its updates, a message pops up from Stewart Hatton. 'You won't believe what I've just been told.'
>
> I'm watching the bottom of the screen where it says *Stewart Hatton is typing*, and my curiosity makes me forget my lines.

Someone says, 'Could you say that again please Ed? I didn't understand you.'

I shake my head, appalled by my lack of concentration. I don't even know who was just speaking. I apologise and make the flimsy excuse that something distracted me. There is laughter and Oana asks if I drank too much beer last night.

'Something like that,' I say. 'But please, could we go from the top again? What is the hold up from Operations?'

I listen harder now as Oana explains the assorted mixed up communications and ownership, and the resulting chaos.

'Everyone is saying that Paul has been sacked.'

He's underlined the last three words.

'Above all Ed, what really concerns me is that no-one from Operations ever attends meetings or calls. It's like they've become the only authority for this.'

'Can someone ping Karl Hopkins please and ask him to join?'

Stewart is typing again. 'Apparently, Paul breached his compromise agreement.'

'How?'

'Seems he contacted Annabel and gave her a load of abuse.'

'When?'

'Karl says he's joining now. In fact, here he is.'

Karl's face appears on screen, a broad side-on smile.

'Friday afternoon.'

'Morning everyone. How can I help?' Karl has a smooth, cultured voice. It makes his greeting and question appear unruffled and authoritative, yet contemptuous and patronising.

I've opened a chat conversation with Annabel.

Oana is talking to Karl about the lack of engagement by Operations. Karl interrupts her mid-flow and dismisses the notion there is any kind of problem. I open my mouth to tell Karl he needs to show some respect but he's still talking, in a tone that shows he objects to being challenged.

I shut my mouth, until it's clear I have to say something. 'Okay Karl, let's keep things simple. No-one would be challenging Operations if someone from your team had been on the last few project calls.'

Annabel answers my greeting with a mystifying, 'God Morgon.'

'I told my team to stop attending. The project team isn't running this delivery. I am.'

> Oana is messaging me now: 'How can he be so rude?'
>
> I reply that she needs to stay calm and we need to get this back on track. She sends a red-faced angry emoji.

'You are running the delivery Karl - one hundred per cent. But everyone on this call is part of that, and we can't provide our support and guidance if we don't know what you're planning and doing.'

Oana backs me up, but she doesn't seem to be as relaxed as I suggested she should be. This is going to turn ugly.

> 'Is God Morgon some sort of bizarre religion?'
>
> 'It's Swedish for Good Morning. Try to keep up Edward.' She adds a ROFL emoji.

Karl's smoothness is ruffled now.

'Look Oana, I didn't say I don't need your help. I just said we can't always get hold of people in Bucharest when we need them.'

'Ed, this isn't a problem for other teams is it? And everyone here in Romania is available during the UK working hours. So I don't see why Karl is being so dismissive.'

> I know I need to step in but I'm busy typing to Annabel: 'There seems to be incoming about Paul W.'
>
> She replies quickly with a single question mark; infuriating beyond words. It makes me sigh loudly.

> Oana messages me: 'Say something. You're supposed to be our manager.'

> Stewart is typing again. It seems to take him ages.

'Oana is right. No-one in Bucharest is ever unavailable. Can we focus instead on the programme and why it's ground to a halt please?'

Karl launches into another speech. He's slightly less patronising, but his passive/aggressive demeanour is infecting the call.

'Anyway, word is that PW has been very naughty indeed. Some sort of dodgy dealings with a supplier.'

Oana isn't happy with Karl and her voice is rising in tone and temperature. She's also starting to get personal.

I cut across both of them. 'Karl, all of this could have been avoided if there had been some engagement and communication from your team. Oana, I realise you're frustrated but let's focus on the problem, not the personalities.'

There is, briefly, silence. I continue. 'Karl, you said you have a new version of the Gantt chart showing latest timeline and milestones. I need you to share that please. I've made you a presenter.'

Annabel repeats: '?'

I almost swear aloud. I truly hate those solitary, lazy punctuation marks. No-one just types a colon; why type a fucking question mark?

It's taking ages for the presentation to build on my screen. Someone else in the call asks if he's sharing and there's a general hubbub of complaint that time is being wasted.

'When I joined my Project Ruby call just now, people were talking about Paul being sacked. And Stewart H has been messaging me about it too.'

'What are they saying?'

Karl's screen is now shared but the project plan is barely visible. People are asking him to increase the scale to see more detail. Voices are becoming impatient.

'Just that Paul has been sacked. SH is saying it's something to do with a supplier.'

'When can you talk?'

I look at my calendar. It's full for almost the whole day.

'This plan is not new. It's two versions out of date. This is ridiculous.'

Oana and Karl are bickering now. I've lost control.

'Diary is full. And current call a nightmare.'

Stewart has typed more: 'I've been told he's colluded with someone in purchasing to create orders for a company owned by his sister and brother-in-law.'

I've had enough of the call about Ruby. 'Guys? This is going nowhere.' I'm running and hiding again. Someone on the call makes an assenting noise. And then I clutch at a straw of potency.

'Karl and Oana, we need a call together ASAP and we're going to use that time to get this back on track and to prevent further finger-pointing. Let's stop this call now, take a deep breath and get back together when everyone is in a more positive frame of mind.'

'Thanks Ed, I completely agree.' Karl is no longer patronising. He's been found out and needs allies.

Oana messages me: 'You're right Ed. Thank you.' And then she apologises to Karl on the call before we finish it.

I look at my screen and the squares of information if contains. The recently ended call fills one corner; the open conversations with Annabel, Stewart and Oana are overlapped. I close the chat with Oana after sending her a final message of support.

'I'm free now.'

After checking if I'm in a private room, Annabel calls me.

'Morning. And that's plain English.' She sounds annoyed.

As she starts to talk a new message pops up from Stewart: 'You there?'

'In calls. Chat later.'

I close him down and switch my status to Do Not Disturb. The chaotic exchanges of the last fifteen minutes have left me feeling snapped and discarded, like an over-used rubber band.

'Hi Annabel. What's up?'

'Nothing. We've got thirty minutes before I need to be with the client. Tell me what was being said by the Ruby team please.'

I reiterate that I'd heard multiple voices discussing rumours that Paul Wilson has been sacked. Annabel tuts several times.

'Did any of them say where they'd heard this?'

'No. Once I joined the call they stopped, and I didn't ask for a synopsis.'

'Right. And what did Stewart say?'

I give her the details.

'This fucking company is hopeless.' She rarely swears but now embarks on a foul-mouthed tirade that lasts more than a minute. It shocks me in to telling her to stop swearing. There's silence, briefly.

'I can't tell you the details Ed. But the rumours are true.'

'Then don't tell me. I don't need to know.'

'That's technically true but given what Paul did I think you should have an overview.'

'Why? Because he implicated me in something?'

'That was the straw that broke the camel's back.'

I'm confused and stare at Annabel's face, framed within a frame on the messaging application's desktop view.

'Annabel: I'd rather not know.'

'Well that's all very gallant of you...' her tone is strained and sarcastic but before she continues, she tells me she has to go because her boss is messaging her.

She calls me back within five minutes.

'I don't believe this. It seems someone in HR has been blabbing openly about Paul. It's already at White's level.'

Pat White is our UK managing director. You don't want to be around her when she hears bad news.

'I wasn't being gallant and I'm a bit pissed off with you for being so sarcastic.'

'You can be as pissed off as you like. This is a total and utter fuck up and, until someone sorts it out, anyone that gets in my way gets a hard time. And you need to think the same way. Be a leader; think of the impact of this kind of news on your team.'

'What kind of news? I don't have any details.'

Annabel pauses and I hear her tip-tapping away on a keyboard.

'I'm just checking with Kate now about what I can tell you. Oh, for fuck's sake.'

'What? Why are you so wound up?'

'Kate says you can be told everything, but you'll have to sign an NDA.' There's more typing, and it sounds like she's hitting her keyboard with considerable prejudice.

'Kate is mailing you an electronic form. When you get it, just hit sign using the e-signature process and we're good. Call me back when you've done it.'

I feel crushed by Annabel's manner. I feel blamed. In just a few days she's gone from close to distant. I've never heard her like this. I have around twenty minutes till my next call and I lose five of those just staring at my laptop in a kind of catatonic daze. Then I realise I'm still set to Do Not Disturb and as soon as I remove it, Stewart is on with more gossip. I'm about to indulge in questions and answers with him; to understand what's being said and by whom. But then I think about the transcript I was shown of his conversation with Paul and stop typing. I delete what I'd started and tell him it's best to stop discussing it. He asks me if that's an order. I tell him it's a bad time to be indiscreet.

By the time I have e-signed and returned the NDA there's only around two minutes to go before my next meeting. But Annabel tells me to postpone it and talk to her instead. When I hear her voice, I feel as if I'm on trial. She says she now has fifteen minutes and that I should listen without interrupting. I'm also instructed not to reveal the details I'm about to be told and, if anyone asks me about the rumours, to tell them nothing until the company makes a formal announcement.

In ten minutes, Annabel sets out what happened, concluding that Paul has been sacked for gross misconduct. I barely hear the details. I'm astonished by what she tells me, and the lack of emotion in Annabel's voice. I only absorb the headlines. It seems that Paul has: influenced the use of a company as a supplier; made it look legitimate; hasn't declared that his brother and sister-in-law are the owners; started small, stayed under the radar; then they got greedy and dishonest; committed fraud.

I jump when I hear that word. This is crime; proper crime.

More headlines: Paul had a helper in purchasing; they manufactured things to benefit themselves; a discovery was made, completely by chance; wheels turned; a trend was established, and Paul's helper was the common denominator.

'She was interviewed, ostensibly to assess the need for training and development needs, but soon caved in. She's been suspended, a situation publicly packaged as long-term sickness. Then Paul was investigated.'

'How much money was he making from this?'

'No-one knows.'

Annabel finishes the revelations. Security, HR and Legal got involved, so did the top of the office; Paul's general conduct was investigated but uncovered nothing more than a tendency for acrid messages and emails; he was formally interviewed about that and given a warning.

'At which point Paul blurted out a string of counter accusations: of our alleged affair; of my poor management style and favouritism for you and others; of made up business trips with no justification, especially your constant trips to London; of poor performance by our colleagues in Romania.'

After that, everything was easy. Paul agreed to take leave of absence while his allegations were investigated. Full of righteous delusion he signed an agreement in which he was required to refrain from contact with colleagues. Then he left the office, unaware that his fraud had been exposed: he was just having his behaviour and allegations processed.

'We don't know how it happened, but someone must have tipped him off, because on Friday evening he called me. He was drunk; very, very drunk. But lucid enough to give me some vile abuse, which went on and on until I cut him off. I guessed he'd call back and I recorded the second call.'

'What did he say?'

'In between the swearing and graphically personal insults, he basically admitted the whole thing.'

I'm stunned in to silence as Annabel finishes the tale. Late on Friday evening she shared the audio from Paul's call with HR. He'd violated his compromise agreement. He'd committed fraud and breached multiple conditions of employment. He was guilty of gross misconduct and could be dismissed without recourse.

'Kate called him early yesterday. Paul's reaction and response are, as yet, unknown.'

'He doesn't have a leg to stand on, does he?'

'I'm not sure this is over, but we're going to defend our position. He won't get a fucking penny from the company, and if I had my way, we'd have him and his family in court.'

'It's almost beyond belief that he would be so stupid.'

'It is, but it's also been made much worse by the fact that someone has gossiped. It's forced a quicker than hoped-for announcement. But look - that's not our problem. What we have to do now, effectively and confidentially, is fill the hole left by his departure and manage any concerns the team has about what's happened. It will make people jumpy, so your job is to keep the focus on delivering what we do without being distracted or fearful.'

She soon ends our call, leaving me frowning at my laptop screen. Her manner throughout that ten minutes was cold and calculating. I don't understand why.

17

The financial report about MarMap is next to useless. There's virtually no accounting information and all it tells me is the names of directors, past and present. The company has a number of subsidiaries, including the riding school, and I can see it's heavily mortgaged: around five million of debt is shown.

When I look online for news items about MarMap, it's almost all in media local to that part of Staffordshire, and mainly in the newspapers. The reports are generally social - news of Marcus running a marathon for charity, is a good example - but there are also plenty of upbeat items about MarMap's fortunes as a company. It's all a bit bland but a couple of things make me perk up.

One is a report that the Mapplewick's home was burgled recently, resulting in cash and valuables being taken. The family was away for a few days and the colossally expensive protection system guarding the house had simply failed to work, allowing a forced entry through a patio door. The police and the security firm declared themselves mystified by the ease with which the alarms, sensors and cameras had been bypassed.

The next is an article about an accident involving a MarMap truck. The driver and a cyclist were killed and a brake failure, caused by poor maintenance, was cited as the cause. The bereaved families claimed to have evidence from within MarMap that its fleet of lorries and vans was un-serviced; evidence fiercely disputed by the company. Legal action was threatened by both sides and the press seemed to be enjoying an increasingly acrimonious bun fight. Then after much toing and froing, an article suddenly appeared with revelations that the truck's driver was a serious gambler with significant debts. Cynical opportunism had cashed in on a tragedy but now the credibility of any evidence about maintenance was crushed. The story soon petered out.

The final eye-catching item is about vandalism at the MarMap head office. There had been several weeks of minor damage, mainly graffiti and flyposting, but a much more serious attack took place in the holiday period between Christmas and New Year. Vehicle windscreens were smashed; some had their tyres punctured; and excrement was smeared liberally around the handles of the office doors. MarMap, the police and media were quick to blame groups opposing the construction of the new link road. The respectable majority in those groups denounced the vandalism but accepted that the actions of a small minority of radical activists had set back their cause. My eyes kept being drawn back to the statesmanlike comments by Marcus Mapplewick: 'We know the majority of those in the protest groups are decent people and while we don't agree with their opposition to the Tamworth bypass, we do respect their right to peaceful protest. It truly is a shame that a mindless minority have let down the rest. MarMap is open and ready for business. We will continue to work with the police to identify the people who attacked us and our property, but they have not and will not stop MarMap from doing what we do and supporting this much needed bypass.'

As I'm tidying away my lunch things, my phone rings. It's Dave Ellis. The call quality isn't great; he occasionally sounds robotic; and there's a constant hiss.

'Hello Ted. Thought I'd give you a quick call.'

'David; believe me, it's incredibly good to hear you.'

'You had a bit of a wobble yesterday. Admit it.' He's trying to be bluff, but I sense a tiny shake in his voice.

'Are you both all right?'

'Yes, we're being well looked after. Had people from the embassy at our hotel earlier handing out advice and clichés. The hotel people have been sensational. Very caring indeed.'

'Are you going to stay in Brussels?'

'Not a great deal of point really. The place is teeming with heavily armed police and troops. It's not easy to have a relaxing love-in with your significant other against a backdrop like that. So, we're booked on a flight early this evening. We should be back home by around nine. Assuming we can get to the airport.'

'Well be safe travelling.'

'We will. How is everything there? Are you in London?'

Something clicks in my head. I should tell Dave about the things that happened to me yesterday. He'd have a view, even though it's probably one I wouldn't want to hear.

'Yes, I'm at the office. London feels edgy, but probably no more than usual. A lot of people working from home. The office is quiet.'

He erupts into laughter. 'Pussies. Cowards.'

I laugh at his name-calling. And I don't want him to sneer at my own cowardice, so I say nothing about threats and consequences.

'Ella says hi. And she also says we must eat, so I need to cut you off. Thank you for all your concern last night mate. It was touching. And no less than I'd expect of you. We both appreciated it.'

I'm soon looking at Dave's photo on my phone's screen and feeling lucky. It gives me an enormous sense of being all right and having nothing wrong in my life. My friend could have died. But he didn't.

The thirty or so minutes over lunch were focused and structured. But now I can't think straight about the things I'm paid to do. In the end, I re-arrange several calls and mark myself as Do Not Disturb. After an hour like that, working through low level tasks and replying to inconsequential emails, I feel settled and capable.

Ten minutes before it's due to start, I move myself in to a meeting room to conduct the meeting with Josh Niesmann. When I switch my status to Available, Annabel sends me a message almost straight away.

'Are you all set for this meeting?'

'Yes; have prepared well and rehearsed the pitch a few times.'

'Good. I'll back you up if I sense you need it, but I'm sure you'll be fine.'

'Thanks.'

The meeting runs to plan, and my presentation is faultless. The main man asks a couple of predictable questions, then thanks me for an excellent piece of work. He gets it. Annabel is messaging me almost immediately, full of praise and compliments. After a few minutes of this, her boss joins in too, letting me know that Josh was impressed.

It isn't long before Annabel contacts me privately asking why I've been ignoring her messages.

'I logged out to focus on work.'

'I thought you were always on SocMed.'

'Who told you that?'

'You did!' A laughing out loud emoji pops up next. 'Well look, I'm sorry I was blunt earlier. You and I have been accused of some shitty things by Paul and it's made me annoyed and jumpy.'

'Don't you trust me?'

'Of course I do. But your manner this morning made me feel like you're trying to make this my problem. And I didn't like that.'

'It wasn't my intention.'

'I know. Forgive me. It's been a difficult few days.'

It doesn't make complete sense to me. But instead of allowing any creeping sense of insecurity to take over, I close down the conversation with her by suggesting we have a call tomorrow and make sure we're aligned. On everything. When she accepts the meeting invitation, her reply says: 'Great idea. Thanks.'

Then I'm back to the disarray, so I stay in the meeting room and stare at my laptop wondering how it is in effect the embodiment of a job: those hinged rectangles of plastic and metal; its liquid crystals; its compacted mass of miniature components. Without it I'm nothing: unable to think; or see; or listen; or learn. Or even to interact. My boss is in another country and I won't see her for weeks. The people I'm managing are scattered across Western and Central Europe; the last of them that I met face to face was Paul Wilson, just over a week ago; and I'll never see him again. I just received second-hand praise from a man nearly four thousand miles away, who I will never meet yet who holds power over my existence as an employee for our company. Today he knew my name and loved my work; but that doesn't change the reality that I am simply a number with a dollar sign on a spreadsheet, and that number can be reduced to nothing to save money and keep him afloat for another year.

I set myself as Do Not Disturb again and take out a notepad and pen. In capitals, I write at the top of the page: 'What have I learned about MarMap?' Then I scratch through it and write: 'Things still to do and look at' then add a short list:

> Look at the link road pro and con pages on SocMed etc
> Consider joining them?
> Dig deeper for stuff about Jarvis and the named company directors for MarMap
> What's the big picture on this road - who's in charge?
> And what is MarMap actually doing as part of the construction?
> Check the other group companies - where does he make his money?

As I begin a seventh bullet point, Jude sends me a text: 'Sweetheart, are we still going to the beer festival this Friday?'

This had slipped my mind. We'd agreed we must go again this year, even though we can't go as a couple or be seen together.

But I affirm it now. 'Yes. It's essential xx.'

'Good. I will stare longingly at you across the room as you sup your ale.'

'When are you back from Scotland?'

'Tomorrow evening. Without Craig. He's staying indefinitely.'

'OK. How's Lewis?'

'Comfortable. But he won't make it to the end of the month.'

I look at my laptop screen to remind myself it's March the first. White rabbits.

'I'm sorry.'

'Me too. It's awful.'

'Are you sure you want to go on Friday?'

'Super sure. When are you back from London?'

'Late tomorrow.'

'Can I stay tomorrow night? Instead of Friday?'

'You don't need to ask. I'll be home around ten.'

'I'll grab some bits.'

'Don't. I've stuff in the freezer.'

She sends a series of emojis; hearts & flowers.

As my working day draws to a close at just after seven pm, I log off our systems and apps, then open up the internet to continue my search for answers. It's nearly eleven when I pack up and walk cautiously back to the hotel.

18

Thursday passes quickly, too quickly, and I'm left with work to do on the train. It's a good distraction from my drama but I spend the afternoon getting increasingly edgy and wondering whether to stay another night.

But I can't.

I need a change of clothes and I especially need the powerful intimacy of an evening and night with Jude.

I pack up and head through the Underground, and as the Glasgow train pulls out of Euston I'm back online completing documents, arranging meetings and replying to emails. I make good progress, assisted by the relative calm in first class. There are just five people in the same carriage and, when the train leaves Preston, I'm the only one so I pack up my things and move to a seat nearer the crew.

As the train pulls into Lancaster, I message Jude to find out where she is.

'I am running a bath at yours xx.'

'Perfect. Did you bring those exciting oils?'

'Of course.'

'Will be wet with you in about 15.'

As I unlock my front door, I smell the ylang-ylang and jasmine and quickly realise it is powerfully stimulating for men too. Within minutes, and without saying a word to one another, we are making a proper mess of the bathroom. Assorted stresses and strains scream out of us in a slithering, pumping splash-fest that runs in to a second then third round and we still haven't said hello.

'My God Teddy, I can hardly breathe.'

All I can do is smile and nod.

'I've been in this water too long. Why don't you fill up the bath with some more hot water and soak for a bit while I finish warming up your supper.'

I'm still nodding and smiling, like a cartoon puppy. Jude gives me a long sloppy kiss and glides away across the treacherous tiled floor. I lie there with my eyes closed, breathing hard. I call out to her to come back and do it all again but when she appears, she's wearing a robe over pyjamas.

'We've got all night sweetheart, don't be so needy.'

'But look at this.' I nod down towards a foam topped hard-on.

'It will keep. You know it will. Come on: supper's ready.'

It's late to eat, but the trays of supermarket Chinese food are welcome, even if they're not entirely authentic. We slurp down some chilled beer too.

'What's up? I can see in your face that something is wrong.'

I tell her about how worried I'd been about Ella and Dave being in Brussels. She shakes her head and tells me that's not it. I give her edited highlights of the Paul Wilson denouement and as she listens to it, her eyebrows slowly raise in to arches of disbelief.

'He could be banged up for that couldn't he?'

'Not sure. It probably depends on the lawyers and how they decide to take it forward.'

'But that's not it either, is it? There's something more personal.'

'How do you know?'

'Your eyes are filled, deep down, with sadness. It's like fear. Tell me what's wrong. Please.'

I'd made up my mind to just keep quiet about the MarMap and SocMed thing. And I'd started to build a defence mechanism broadly on the basis that this didn't matter to anyone but me; I needed to deal with it. But Jude is compelling and before I can stop myself I start telling her about the post, and how everyone laughed, and how it was history inside a day or two, and how eight days after I posted it someone demanded I take it down or face violence and harm.

'Is that all? Really?'

'It wasn't nice.'

'But it's nothing. Playground politics in response to infantile behaviour; by you.'

'I realise that.'

'Do you really take fucking social media so seriously?'

'I felt threatened and exposed.'

'But you didn't seek out a sane view from someone less obsessed by how they look to the virtual world.' She removes her hand from mine and is sitting upright, staring at me with a kind of contempt.

'We were on radio silence.'

'All the time I've known you I've never heard you so weak. It's nothing. Nothing at all. People were murdered that night; my brother-in-law is next to dead.'

She gets up and tidies away our dishes.

'I took it seriously. And I still do it. It's derailed me.'

'Fucking hell Teddy. How many more times: it's ridiculous for you to go into a trough about this. Change the subject or I'm going home.'

She stays and, as we fall asleep in the early hours, she tells me: 'You're better than what you have done. Take a step back and look at yourself. Then take more steps to move away from what's happened. Don't make me stop wanting you.'

The beer festival is heaving when I arrive at eight and a band of middle-aged musicians is bumbling around on the stage as if in a dentist's waiting room. I wish there was no live music to spoil the ambience of talking and comparing notes about ale. But it seems that even a beer festival has to feed the need for the lowest common denominator.

It isn't long before the music starts, a loud rendition of *Sledgehammer* that the singer simply can't handle. No one else seems to have noticed how crap it is.

As I grab a second half of beer, Jude is ordering about eight taps to my right. She's exchanging laughter with the server and gives me a sideways glance as she hands a glass to another woman standing behind her. My phone soon vibrates.

'You here on your own?'

'No, I'm with this woman I love.'

'I don't see her.'

'She's around somewhere. Who's your friend?'

'Abi. And I need to talk to her. Come and stand close where I can smell you.'

It takes me a while to get to where Jude and Abi are standing. They're both dressed in skirts and boots with smart-looking jackets. Jude's is leather.

My beer is from one of the Lake District breweries and it's gorgeous.

It's strange to be within touching distance of Jude yet unable to talk. Her conversation with Abi seems animated but the music means I can't hear it. Every once in a while, one of them throws back their head in laughter. Passing men stop to flirt but get nowhere. Something passes between them and Jude turns to look at me, as if for the first time. She turns back shaking her head, and Abi suddenly smiles at me as she walks away to the bar. My phone buzzes again.

'Abigail thinks you're rather gorgeous. What do you think of her?'

'Stop playing games.'

'She's shameless. I've only got you. She's totally sleeping around.'

'I'm not interested. You're more than enough for me.'

'When she gets back, I'm going to the loo. Follow me, otherwise Abi will hit on you.'

I look around the hall and then up at the balcony that runs around three sides of the building. One end is curtained off, reason unclear. There are people up there, enjoying the chance to look down haughtily on all the rest of us. It's as if the same beer somehow tastes better up there.

Abi soon returns with fresh samples to taste, and after a quick sup of hers, Jude says something and hands her glass to her friend before heading off toward the exit. I head back to the bar, then cross the hall diagonally towards the stairs and toilets.

'I'm not in the toilets. Make your way up to the mezzanine.'

The area around the stairwell is crowded with people. I take the wrong stairs and soon reach locked double doors.

'Where are you?'

'Lost.'

'Hurry. It's quiet up here.'

Five minutes later I am up on the balcony and see Jude standing away to my right in front of the heavy-looking curtains. There are people along to the left of me who seem not to have noticed us. Jude is more or less isolated. We embrace and she whispers in my ear that Abi has made her want me to fuck her and she starts unbuttoning my jeans. Then we're behind the curtain and at it. Jude seems manic; her eyes are staring in to mine with such intensity; and then she comes really quickly; noiselessly; her head suddenly flops backwards. I wonder if she's blacked out and stop moving, but she tells me to keep going.

'It could be a long time till we can do this again. But don't hang around. Abi will be wondering where I've got to and oh.... mmmmm. No. Keep it in me.'

'Why will it be a long time?'

'I could be in Scotland again soon, and I'm not expecting to be here next weekend. Tomorrow and Sunday I'll be tied up at the house with some visitors and Monday I have a work meeting with the county council. Is your boner coming back?'

'Seems like it.'

'No time. Get it out now.' She's laughing. 'I'm expecting to go back to Colinton on Thursday evening, long before you get back from London.'

'What about the following week?'

'Come on, I need to get back to Abi. She's messaged me.'

Jude walks off without me then sends a message.

'I just have a feeling I will be in Scotland for at least two weeks from next Thursday. This lovely wet feeling is going to be it for a while. What will you do?'

'What's Abi's number?'

'If you dare go near her, I will never talk to you again and I might get my husband to have you killed.'

Then she adds a ROFL emoji.

'Noted.'

I stay up on the balcony until I see Jude reunited with her friend who seems untroubled by how long Jude was gone. They laugh and I can tell from their gestures that Abi drank Jude's beer some time back. They embrace and head to the bar.

Jude glances up at me and smiles.

The anaesthesia of a few pints of beer, combined with the almost total lack of sleep since Monday evening causes me to sleep deeply and it's past eight when I wake. As I turn over to bury my face in the pillow bearing Jude's lingering jasmine aroma, I expect to fall straight back to sleep. Then shards of information start pricking my brain and memory. It's only a matter of minutes before I'm at my desk opening internet sites, documents and notes. I'm sucked into the task and become absorbed by information gathering. I've begun to feel that I need to know everything about MarMap and its associations.

After ten, I start getting messages from Jude asking me if I'm all right. We chat briefly but happily until she tells me she needs to get ready for the arrival of friends.

I take a short break to check my phone, make tea and have a shower but I'm soon back in the groove, working away in silence and focusing on my list of questions from Wednesday. My tea goes cold, so I microwave it while I eat a bowl of cereal. It's nearly one thirty when I decide I need to get some exercise.

That ninety minutes at the gym is the only break I have. A whole day spent, some would say wasted, digging into the dirt and intrigue of a contest; of a battle; of a series of mind-games that have already scarred my brain.

The following morning, I start all over again except today I target a stop time so I can go back to the hospice to do my volunteer work. But my morning gets interrupted: the squash club contacts me to see if I can play a match tomorrow so I say I will; Beth Vidicalls me, wondering why I've not been in touch in any way since Tuesday. When I give a bland, unconvincing reply she gets mad at me and tells me I'm a waste of space, then shuts down the call.

Jude messages me with a barrage of smutty thoughts and I get drawn into reciprocal filth.

Joe phones me and asks what I've done to upset Beth; I tell him I've just been forgetful and hopeless. He ticks me off half-heartedly, but we end the call laughing. Then the hospice calls to say they don't need me today. I ask after Mark Hodgson and am told he's as well as can be expected. I want to know if he finished the book but realise it will seem a silly question if I ask it.

So now I have time to spare and head to the gym for another workout. As I grind a rhythm on the cross-trainer I try to summarise in my head what I've learned so far and, as I do that, I set my mind to spend the rest of the afternoon looking at the assorted social media sites associated with the link road construction in Staffordshire. On the muted TV screens all around me there is footage of the fallout from the killings in Brussels. There's also some sort of anti-austerity protest in London. In the absence of sound and narrative, I can't work out which is more important.

It's the first weekend I can remember, certainly since my divorce, that I have not at some point spent time working on company business. I reflect on that as I stir fry some vegetables and I'm struck by the realisation that it won't have made any difference. If I use my own time to do my company's work, no-one notices or cares. I get no extra reward and deliver no additional spark of quality. My time isn't replaced. When I work on my own time, all it does is trigger a feeling that I'm visible; I'm going the extra mile; killing myself, to make rich people richer. I open my work emails on my phone, perhaps expecting to find things I could have been doing. There are none. No gushed outpouring of gratitude either.

What if I don't do any work tomorrow?

What if I log in first thing, clear some emails, attend conference calls and react to whatever the day brings?

Do nothing else and fill the eight till six with my own needs.

Take back some pay for all those weekends when I gave for free.

When I open last weekend's half empty bottle of white wine, it smells all right but I'm sure that its true quality has been lost over those seven days. The stir fry tastes great though and for the first time since Tuesday I feel relaxed and safe from harm. Perhaps I need to ignore people more and put myself down less.

19

But I do work hard all Monday and I finish the day feeling proud of myself; for being good and ignoring those dangerous disloyal thoughts about doing no work; and for ignoring my impulses about the haters, and how I should hate back.

I play my squash match at six and easily win against an ordinary player who declines to play a third game after I win the match two-nil. As I'm changing, I find Victoria Wright's business card stuffed into a side pocket on my bag. While I'm showering I make up my mind to send her a message so we're linked up.

'Hi Victoria, it's Teddy Clayton. Hope you're well? We played squash last week. If you feel like another match some time, let me know. It doesn't need to be in the league.'

Packing distracts me so I miss her response and, when I get to it, I can't decide whether it's negative. And deep down I know I've no right to want it to be positive. I've got Jude; even though that is a conditional arrangement.

She's written: 'Good to hear from you. I'm away on business until late Wednesday. Will get back to you then.'

The way I do my job - amassing information, collating it, recycling it, making it make sense, putting things in order so they work, putting people in order so they do the right things - has a resonance with what I'm confronted by when I review what I've accrued about MarMap and its satellites of love and hate. There's a single infuriating gap in my analysis. Otherwise I'm clear about what I've learned.

MarMap is a haulage and logistics company with a fleet exceeding two hundred assorted vehicles, operating primarily in Britain and Ireland. It has a single major client contract, otherwise its business appears reactive and essentially transactional. There if you need them; on the doorstep. But MarMap is also some sort of parent or holding company for a wider organisation. The equestrian centre is the main subsidiary, but the group has its arms around a string of real ale micro-pubs, a complex of music rehearsal studios that includes a small venue for live music and a company managing waste from building sites. The company's officials appear to consist of Marcus and Tracy Mapplewick, plus three other named individuals; one wears a finance hat; another does fleet operations; and the other seems to be a kind of Chief of Staff.

Working in a large corporation, with its multi-tiered management structure filtering down from an executive board through regional, country and functional leaders, with someone somewhere in charge of something, I find MarMap's simple structure difficult to understand. How do they ever make decisions that look outwards?

There is plenty to suggest that MarMap sees itself as a major player in the link road construction, but I've found no clear statement that they have a specific contract to do specific services. So, while MarMap's web and SocMed pages have several statements that they are *Proud to Serve* the lead construction contractor, that isn't reciprocal. Mainly, it looks like all MarMap does is low level fetching and carrying; with a healthy dose of free advertising for the constructor and its role as lead contractor. There's also nothing connecting any of MarMap's subsidiaries to the bypass.

Marcus Mapplewick is wealthy: new money; old school. It didn't need many clicks online to pull together his back story. MarMap's site contained much of the detail; and an effusive article from 2015 in one of Staffordshire's newspapers provided the rest. Born to middle class parents in Wolverhampton, Marcus was left to fend for himself when parental drinking and then divorce drove him away. He left school at sixteen and drifted through eighteen months of labouring and dogsbody abuse until he passed his driving test and landed a job at a small courier company in Coleshill. Some of his drops took him to Birmingham Airport where a major redevelopment was underway. He realised there were many opportunities there to do off-contract work and was soon pocketing under the counter payments for early morning and late evening runs. He didn't ask what might be in those loads. Within a year, he had his own van and became a voracious gatherer and consumer of work; he undercut anyone to get contracts; and he drove himself into the ground working and driving up to eighteen hours a day. Growth fed growth, and within ten years he had stepped out of the cab and into the office. The dreams kept being realised: contracts with local councils; an expanding fleet; the step up from vans and three tonne trucks to articulated lorries; some therapy from retail contracts; marriage to Atherstone socialite Tracy Hardwicke; riding the global crash in 2008; kids; houses; cars; schools; investments; sponsorship.

Politically, Marcus was something of a surprise. Those early days on the shop floor had exposed him to the workplace politics of staunch Tory supporters who despised unionised labour. He became and remained a reliable Conservative advocate and donor with no desire to follow his former shop-floor pals into UKIP and beyond.

I looked and looked for something to contradict it. But Marcus Mapplewick seems to have no doubts about his loyalties. He's a Tory; in business to do business; driven to succeed.

He's just like me.

Isn't he?

And loyalties are the unwavering order of the day on the SocMed pages and in Peeps that oppose and support the new link road. Aligned behind their causes, the people speak and have spoken at length of the passion they all feel about the road building programme. Whatever arguments, whatever logic, whatever facts and science might exist they are submerged beneath righteousness and philodoxical conviction.

The core emotions seem to be simple:

we need this because it makes life easier;

we don't need this because it is an affront to decency.

The core arguments also seem to be simple:

you're wrong;

we're right;

so you can fuck off.

At the extremes are genuinely vile insults: name-calling; vilification; threats. But even at the centre ground there is no debate. This is a battleground which, even though the road is being built and will be finished to plan within ten years, creates a victor that seems incapable of walking away with the spoils of war. Instead, they keep stalking the battlefield, bayonetting the losers; with great joy and derision; with no honour or chivalry.

In exchange, a posse fights on, enhanced and engorged by wider interests. Causes, indirect and tangential are in play but at the centre of their reasoning is an ill-concealed hatred. They say they don't want the road because of pollution; abuse of public funds in the hands of private gangsters; safety risks and threats; disrupted, dismembered wildlife; ruined communities; rules being bent out of shape with no remedy; noise; smells; a conspiracy of interests that draws in multiple despised industries. But there is an overwhelming sense that this is class warfare: we don't like this road, for sure; but above all we don't like you - in your aspirational homes, clothes and jobs; you're all stupid and incapable of seeing the big picture. Or any picture.

You just don't care.

You're conventional, and that's a crime.

I've joined the main SocMed groups in a look-and-learn mode and, so far as I can tell, with no check on my credentials by the page owners. I asked to join, and my wish was granted.

I've also begun to look at tangential posts and threads. After three days working through this morass of moral indignation, I'm left unsure who might have a case.

Instinctively, I don't object to a road being built.

Instinctively, I can't side with the contempt of people who won't accept a concerted opposition and seem to feel an obligation to convert the people in that opposition into demons.

Instinctively, I disagree with the emotional illogic of those opposing the road.

Instinctively, I feel someone ought to dig in their heels instead of rolling over and dying under a we-know-best juggernaut.

So: there is a project that is opposed and supported; the project was imposed and is governed centrally, regardless of local feelings and needs; there is a minor player in the project who arrogantly assumed the mantle of flag-bearer; there is a very loud silent majority, on both sides of the argument; the establishment - police, civil servants, local councils - dances on a fine line between provocation and appeasement; and there is a government run by my party that seems to have imposed a top-down mandate to overrule local government, acting like some sort of supreme Soviet.

I want to pick a side, like everyone else has. Be in the camp that is right and nod my head with smug certainty that I'm backing the winner. But the winner has already won and, whether it's right or wrong, the road is being built; unstoppable; remorseless; cheered on by a crowd, like a phalanx of unreconstructed football hooligans, whose sense of being a winner makes them intolerant and intolerable; who square up to another firm whose martyrdom reeks from the embers of a burned out stake.

What a mess.

Yet it's a mess I'm drawn towards, like a fly to a freshly splattered cowpat.

My working week becomes entangled with extra-curricular events and news. I'm not out of touch with the things that pay my wages, but I'm constantly distracted and pulled towards what should be irrelevant yet has become my modus vivendi.

After an hour on the train to London, rolling through the barren wildernesses of Cheshire, I take a short break to look again for the missing piece. Neither Kriss, nor Chris, nor Christopher Jarvis exist in the ether. The names are invisible in anything aligned with MarMap, the construction project and the associated chattering in social media. Sitting here on the train, I can see his face as he approached the seat that day: I barely gave him a second glance, but recall a distracted, rushed expression. He was slim, fair haired, a bit haggard - but immaculately dressed. Once he'd finished with those messages that I partially captured and shared, he packed everything away and fell asleep. When I stood to leave the train at Euston, he was still asleep.

I know from the photos that Jarvis has a MarMap email address, but does that make him an employee? What if I send him a mail from one of the more remote personal addresses I use for internet shopping and engagement with officialdom? Would I learn anything? Would he reply?

The train slows then stops, followed by an announcement that another train has broken down ahead, then by a discordant mumbling of unhappy travellers. It makes me look at the SocMed page for the main anti-road group, *White Lines - Won't Do It*. I scroll through a few posts, avoiding any detailed review as I'm not in a mood for the vitriol. Going back several weeks there's an occasional picture and, at one point, I realise I've flashed past a reproduction of the MarMap logo. I work back to it and see that it's part of a post about companies supporting pollution and the destruction of wildlife: and everything else that is wrong in the world, apparently. Several other small companies are being pilloried in the same post. Clearly the campaigners have knives out for any business trying to eke out a living from all this evil and it gets personal; photos of people driving vans or providing security are shown under banners declaiming them as criminals. It takes me a while, but eventually I find a post with a photo showing Marcus Mapplewick, and others, with the words: *Happy to keep horses while killing all other animals in his path - if you see any of this lot around town, cross the street: they might kill you.* I shake my head, but as I read the names listed as *The MarMap Murderers*, I realise that one of them is the person named as MarMap's Business Development consultant in the online blurb. The Chief of Staff. He's called Graham Holton, but the face in the photo - the one gazing out from behind Marcus Mapplewick - is the man I'd seen that day on the train.

Graham Holton is there on BizSoc, with his MarMap job title and a short summary of his experience as a business development consultant, but his work history isn't shown. He has less than fifty connections and none of them is a MarMap colleague. I'm tempted to look deeper into his network but decide it's probably an irrelevance, and potentially a fiction.

I find thirteen hits on Chattabox when I search using his name, and SocMed shows me seven Graham Holtons one of whom has no photograph. None of the others is my man and when I look at the faceless one, I find he has sixty-seven friends almost all of whom are American. It isn't going to be him.

I laugh aloud; this is just plain bonkers. What possible reason can a minor company, not far from the back of beyond, have for creating an alias to hide the credentials of one of its people? For all the bluster of its marketing and PR, this is not a player; it has limited scope and ambition; MarMap is simply an apparatus for its owner to make money. So why the forgery? And which one is real? Kriss? Or Graham?

It's nearly 0945 when I get to the office. The train driver did his best to make up time, but that delay near Crewe added more than seventy minutes to my journey. I've been able to remain productive and run some of my meetings. I've also been able to make space in my diary for a personal call.

'Mr C; this is a surprise. What's up?'

'Hi Luke. Nothing's up. Just wanted to pick your brains. Got a mo?'

'For you, I've got five.'

'Have you ever known a company have a named employee who doesn't exist?'

'No. Never.'

'Okay. Then have you ever come across a company who employs someone using an alias?'

'What the fuck are you on about Mr C?'

Without reference to MarMap or any of its players, I summarise the evidence I've found.

'It's the most ridiculous thing I've ever heard Mr C. Where are you going with this shit?'

'It's a real situation but the context isn't important. So, humour me. Can you think why a company would do it?'

'I don't have the time for this. Sorry mate. Too busy.'

'Fancy a pint on Friday.'

'Absolutely Mr C. Message me. But no more fairy stories.'

When I call Dave Ellis, and ask him the same questions, he is less sceptical.

'Your corporate career means you don't see some of the esoteric things in small companies. But the scenario you've described could happen in a business that likes to play games.'

'What sort of games?'

'Your real man is probably some sort of fixer, who doesn't exist if the shit hits the fan.'

'Fixing what?'

'Competition. Critics. Supporters. Media. Suppliers. Employees.'

'A rule breaker.'

'And a rule maker. Perhaps intimidating employees. Or creating news. Or bullying suppliers.'

Sitting in the hotel bar that Wednesday evening, I do a bit of work and keep half an eye on the storm gathering around the Budget, and its proposed changes to National Insurance. After a couple of beers, I'm almost done with email but the insurrection is revving up. Someone in the Treasury has made a proper fuck up, and the Chancellor is getting mugged by his own back bench. How anyone, especially a superstar politician bound for a tasty role on the board of a company somewhere, could believe he'd get away with hitting the self-employed is a mystery.

Two emails require reflection, and I've left them till last.

One tells me I have no case to answer re. my alleged affair with and favouritism from Annabel. I'm thanked for taking part, for my integrity and honesty. I'm valued for my contribution.

In the other, Annabel tells me to make plans to be in Stockholm. Our new client needs concerted project and programme management and only I can do it. I'm instructed to make plans to travel next Monday evening and stay most of the week; and again the following week. Her boss, Peter Dixon, has approved the costs.

I begin a search for flights and realise I'm back in a simple place; consumed by my work; doing it as well as I can. Somehow, all that nonsense about roads, and threats and silly little companies with mystery agents of fortune has fallen behind me and maybe the best thing for me to do is just leave it there.

The following evening, I sit listening to music on the usual train out of Euston and looking at the two messages that arrived while I was in the Underground.

'Lewis has lapsed into a coma. He hasn't got long. I'm heading to Scotland later.'

I read this without emotion and can't decide what to say to Jude.

The other message is from Victoria Wright. 'Hi Teddy, it was good to hear from you at the weekend. I'm sorry I didn't reply sooner but been snowed under with work.'

I switch out of messaging to check new emails on my work phone. It's some time before I go back to Jude's message to reply: 'I'm so sorry.'

'It's awful, but it's been inevitable for a while.'

'Driving or train?'

'Car. It's quicker.'

'Drive safe.'

There's a long pause. Then Jude replies: 'Seems like something is wrong with us.'

'Why?'

'Not one of those messages has a x.'

Now I pause before replying. 'But it's a sad lot of messages. It's not about us.'

'It IS about us. I might not see you for ages.'

'xxx.'

'Too late.'

I decide to call her, as there is something deeply troubling about the second half of that exchange. But Jude doesn't reply. I leave a voicemail: 'Hi babe. Thought we should speak. Worried about those messages. Call me if you can, although I'm on a train so keep it clean.' And then we get cut off; I never have a signal through Milton Keynes.

It's several more minutes before Jude picks up the thread. 'Just leaving now sweetheart. Got your voicemail but really not up to speaking xx.'

'OK xx'

'Kisses reinstated xx'

'Yep xx.'

'Don't worry babe. I'm just really upset about what the next few days will bring. It's so sad. If I could share this sadness with anyone, I'd prefer it was with you xx.'

I don't know what to write in reply. There's a lump in my throat.

'I'll message you when I get to Colinton xx.'

'Be strong. Love you xxx.'

I've grazed my way through the complimentary food and a bottle of Estrella Damm. When I'm offered coffee and cake, I ask for another beer instead and it's soon on my table.

'Hi Victoria. No problem. I've been busy too.'

'Are you in Lancaster now?'

'No. Heading back from London.'

'Ah, ok. Was going to suggest a game of squash this evening.'

'That would have been great. But I'm not scheduled back until 10.'

'Wow - long day.'

'Been in London since Tuesday. It's my usual schedule.'

'Right.'

I take a mouthful of beer, unsure what to say next. Then I see she's typing.

'Why don't we grab that drink some time?'

I am still undecided about what to say. Then I type: 'Maybe.'

She is quick to reply: 'Sounds like a but is coming my way.'

'Well I'd like to get to know you, and a quiet drink or a coffee would be lovely. But I am involved with someone at the moment. And I'm not sure if that precludes me from seeing you, or anyone? Hmm.'

'Hmm indeed.'

I assume I've put her off, but then she's typing again: 'I'd like to get to know you too and, since you've drawn some very clear boundaries, I'm sure we can meet safely and without crossing any lines.'

It makes me smile, in spite of my involvement.

'Then a drink at some point would be good. Tomorrow? Or Saturday?'

'Saturday best for me. Let's catch up by phone to finalise. I'll call you Saturday.'

'Great. See you soon.'

'Safe trip x.'

After a few seconds she sends another message: 'Oops. Sorry about the x. Bad habit.'

'Don't worry. I often do it without thinking.'

'Me too. Put one on an email to my bank once. Ha-ha.'

My phone rings and I'm absorbed by an unexpected, complex work issue that keeps me busy for more than an hour.

20

Luke and I arrange to meet at The Pilgrim's Bar as usual, and I've already had a pint when he arrives more than forty minutes late. He compounds that poor form by arriving with a woman who he introduces as Pippa. They met the previous weekend. It seems what they have has escalated rapidly and they are an item, besotted and tactile. Luke's demeanour is unusually other-worldly and I wonder if he's taken drugs. I get a round in, and we have an hour of chat and revelation in which there is no offer of a return round. When Luke indicates they want to eat and asks where I'd like to go, I tell them I'd like to go home. I'm not asked why.

Victoria calls me just before lunch and suggests a drink out of town. Assuming she means a trip out to a country pub near Lancaster, I offer to drive and pick her up. But she has other ideas and suggests we jump on a train and head down to Preston, away from prying eyes.

We meet at the station with time to spare before our train. At first, I only vaguely recognise her from our squash match, but her smile is a give-away. She looks cool, relaxed, effortless and as I'm wondering whether an embrace is appropriate, she reaches out for a handshake.

'It's good to see you again Teddy.'

'Same. And good idea about going to Preston. Haven't been down there for ages.'

Victoria arches an eyebrow at me. 'Really? I go often; and sometimes on to Lytham and Poulton le Fylde. Some nice places - bars, eateries - around there. It's a goldmine for networking too.'

We sit side by side on the train and she tells me about her company and its recent successes and future plans. Then I take my turn explaining what I do and who I do it for. The polite small talk drifts on, predictable and unchallenging. When we arrive at the bar near Winckley Square, I've started to regret the marker I put down about being involved with someone. It seems to have created a bashful reluctance.

'What can I get you?'

'Gin and Tonic please. Unless you fancy wine.'

'No, a gin sounds great. Double?'

'A man after my own heart. Yes please.'

'Any particular gin or tonic combination?'

That smile is wider still. 'I'm old school. Gin tasting of gin and tonic tasting of tonic please. A slice of lime too.'

And now I'm smiling.

Our discussion remains on safe territory during that first drink, but when Victoria returns from the bar with a second round, she is primed with a challenge.

'Tell me all about this involvement you have. Or is it taboo?'

Her grey-green eyes are enquiring and curious rather than judgemental.

I tell her some things about Jude.

'Well that isn't what I expected. What made you want to be with a married woman?'

'It isn't a default criterion. It just happened.'

The bar is noisy enough for our discussion to be discreet, but quiet enough not to require shouting.

'Will she leave her husband?'

'No, and I'd never ask her to.'

'All spectacularly convenient then.'

'For both of us.'

She takes a drink.

'My husband left me when he found out I was having an affair. I didn't expect that either.' She laughs triumphantly. 'I hope your lady's husband remains ignorant.'

'Me too. How long have you been divorced?'

'Since 2014. Then my go-to affair petered out once my boyfriend realised he was potentially stuck with a very high maintenance woman who no longer had a lovely home and car. I've been unlucky in love ever since, which in part is why I'm such a shit-hot squash player, and why my company is thriving.'

We move on to safer ground for a while; houses and their locations; cars; pastimes; holiday memories. She lives down by the riverbank, on New Quay Road. I went running there earlier. Kismet?

'Shall we have another here or move on? Do you feel like dancing?'

'How about both?'

I'm rewarded with a dazzling smile as I take her empty glass away. As I stand for an eternity waiting for service at the bar, I feel a vibration in my pocket. I'm ignoring it stoically, but more buzzes ensue. I take out my phone to find messages from Victoria. She's found details of a pub a few streets away where a live band is playing.

'Let's go there and have some beer and a bop.'

When I turn away from the bar, she's beckoning to me; beguiling; a siren.

During the short walk to the pub, Victoria asks me more about my job and why I put up with the weekly travel. She seems unimpressed by my stock answer that I do what the company requires of me.

'Doesn't it make you too nomadic? Don't you want to feel grounded somewhere?'

'I'm not sure I could cope with working from my apartment every day. My base office is actually just up the road from here, in Fulwood. I did that commute for a while back in the day and hated it. Some days it took ages to get down the M6 and on to the business park.'

Victoria says, 'Back in the day: yuk. But isn't Lancaster your home? Doesn't it tug on your heart when you leave.'

'Not really. It's just become the place where I live. I'm kind of stateless.'

'And did you say you're off to Stockholm?'

'Yes. Next week, and the week after.'

We arrive at the pub where a combination of smoke and vapour forms a guard of honour to our arrival, enveloping us in fragrantly fetid clouds. The security chaps wave us through with a smile. It's bedlam inside but there's a brilliant atmosphere. The band is ripping through golden oldies and the place is bouncing.

Victoria yells that she wants lager, as cold as possible. We're soon supping pints and filling in more gaps, questions and answers in the brief moments between songs. When the band's guitarist begins the introduction to *Long Train Runnin'*, Victoria grabs my arm and shouts: 'Let's dance. Come on.' Whatever is left of our pints is abandoned.

She dances maniacally, all arms and legs and a shaking head. Her hair flies around and across her face reminding me of old pop festival footage, a memory aided by the amazing array of songs pumped out by the band. We just keep on dancing. It isn't necessary to be cool or reserved here. It's a proper pub and everyone is moving however they hear the music. At one point she pulls me towards her and tells me I'm an amazing dancer. Before I can respond in kind she's back in her own space, filling it with motion.

We get to Preston station for the last train to Lancaster and the night air has chilled our sweaty clothing. Victoria links arms with me and moves up close to my side while we stand on Platform 3 waiting for the train. As it slows and edges towards us, she starts singing: *Down around the corner, half a mile from here, see them long trains run, and you watch them disappear.* It makes us both laugh and then she's bumping her hip against mine and we begin a sort of dance in time to her singing.

Without love, where would you be now?

The train's busy so she leads me through to first class.

'They never check tickets this late. And anyway, we deserve these eighteen minutes of luxury, don't we?'

We sit opposite each other in the empty carriage.

'Was your divorce messy?'

'Is there any other kind?'

'Not in my experience, but I was the guilty party.'

'Perhaps if a marriage fails, no matter why, both parties are guilty.'

'My husband didn't deserve what I did to him.'

'So why did you do it?'

'Sex. Passion. Something that wasn't him. All very shallow and contrived. But I needed it more than I needed his heartfelt romantic love.'

'My wife also had an affair. And like you, her affair - her affairs - have not replaced a marriage. They simply caused its end.'

'What happened?'

'She fucked people behind my back.'

'Ouch Teddy. I'll consider my face slapped in her place.'

'No, don't. Every end is different; my ex had begun to see me as intolerably boring and physically repellent. So, she replaced me with an exciting alternative, who had money and property and, as it turned out, a long string of other unhappy married women at his beck and call.'

The train is picking up speed and Victoria looks at the occasional streetlights flashing past as we snake up past unseen places: Broughton, Barton, Bilsborrow.

'How did you find out about your wife's infidelity?'

'There were signs that, for a while, I ignored. But then I had her tailed by a detective.'

She sits back with a shocked expression. 'You're joking?'

'No.'

'What made you do that?'

'I knew she'd keep lying about it; keep pretending to protect herself when it came to a dispute. I made sure I had facts and evidence. For all of our sakes.'

Victoria nods. Then she shakes her head sadly.

'That must have been quite a difficult revelation for her.'

'It was neither better nor worse than the revelation I was given when I first saw the photos of her laughing and smiling, besotted by this man.'

Victoria squints her eyes at me slightly. 'That must have hurt you a very great deal.'

'Yes. But what hurt most were the left hooks she landed on me after I showed her the photos and investigator's report. They weren't great shots and caused no real pain. But it showed that underneath years of love, of building a life, home and family she could simply revert to violent, uncontrolled hatred channelled into punches.'

'Provoked by your act, surely? By your breach of trust?'

'If we go down the provocation and trust routes it just gets messy, doesn't it? When she didn't come home, time and time again, I suppose I could have slapped her about - as a sign of my hatred. But I didn't.'

'No. I see that.'

'It meant, in my mind, that she had never really loved me.'

She's holding my gaze and reaches out a hand to touch mine. 'Let's change the subject. We're in danger of ruining a wonderful evening. Tell me about your trip to Stockholm.'

When I get home, I feel confused and slightly overwhelmed. In spite of my need to remain faithful to Jude, I'm drawn to Victoria. She's lithe, physically powerful and quick witted. We've laughed together for an entire evening. Our parting at Lancaster station was low key; a dispassionate embrace and brushed cheeks; an unconvincing suggestion that we should do it again soon. Yet the events of the last five hours were, to all intents and purposes, a date; and as such it's the first I've had since I was in my second year at university.

Two dates in a quarter of a century; my, I'm a catch.

Everything with Jude is under the covers, between the sheets, in a vacuum. It's wonderful, it's powerful and it's special. But it's closed. I'd forgotten how it feels to meet, travel, talk, drink and laugh with a woman; like a couple; in the open; with no fear of being uncovered; or of reprisal. Not even the rare face-to-face encounters I've had with someone met online could be called a date; they were more like job interviews.

I spend Sunday double checking my travel plans for the next few days, then I work solidly from around nine thirty until early afternoon. I need to be at Manchester Airport for an early evening flight to Stockholm, so I won't get much work done after Monday lunch. I speak with Joe, and Vidicall Beth to make peace with her, and it isn't difficult mainly because there is a much bigger problem to resolve.

'Mummy says she is definitely being made redundant. She's really messed up.'

'Hold on. This has happened pretty quickly; it's not that long since you told me she might have that problem. Has she actually left the company, or is she at risk of redundancy?'

'What's the difference?'

I explain the process that should be used.

'I don't know dad; why do you have to dissect everything like this? Mummy is badly affected by what's happening.'

I count to ten before replying. I don't want another week of being in Beth's bad books.

'I'm sure she is upset but if she's still part of a process, it may not mean she will leave the company. Let's keep to the facts Beth, and then I can help you worry about the right things in the right order.'

She sighs crossly, but I see her face soften.

'Mummy hasn't said. She just said she's being made redundant. I better check, hadn't I?'

'Find out what she's been told. And like we said the other day, you and Joe better make plans to be with her over Easter. I'll...'

I don't know what I'll do. I want my share of the kids being with me, but I also want them to do the right thing for their mother. I will need to adjust my sails.

'I'll try to find a hotel somewhere near Much Wenlock to coincide with Joe's birthday. The three of us can do something then. But get arrangements resolved with your mum okay?'

Beth is looking at me with great sadness. 'It's not really fair on you Daddy.'

'It isn't a question of fairness. She'll be having a hard time, so you help in whatever way you can, right?'

'I know. And we will. I just...'

'What?'

'I just don't think she'd do the same for you.'

'No comment.'

Beth shakes her head. She wants me to be a guide but knows I don't want to be.

An hour later Beth messages me, saying that Amy has told her she is in a pool of eight people who are at risk of redundancy.

I reply: 'Then she should hope for the best and prepare for the worst.'

'Is she being a drama queen.'

'That's not in her nature. But just keep in touch with her.'

The gym is busy, so I do cardio for an hour then head over to the hospice for another few hours of help and support. I don't get to see Mark but ask how he is and learn he's increasingly poorly. His son and daughter-in-law still haven't visited. However, when he finds out I'm there he demands another of my brews and passes on the news that he's still planning to finish the Dickens.

When I finish for the evening, I write a short note to Mark telling him I hope his tea was up to standard and that I'm sure he'll finish the book soon. Then I add that Morecambe won yesterday.

When I get to my car, I make a note in my diary to make sure I always know Morecambe's results each time I go to the hospice.

As I work on through my calendar, I see the note for April 7th that Beth and Joe's Easter holiday begins and the marker that April 10th is Joe's birthday. It's not the end of the world that they won't be home during their college vacation, but it's not the best news. I decide the only thing I can do is take time off in that week before Easter and plan to be in Shropshire to share Joe's 19th birthday with him somehow.

Victoria sends a message: 'I had a wonderful evening. Thank you. x.'

Jude is in Scotland being pulled apart by a tragedy. I should be lending her my support, but I know we can't communicate.

What was it she said that day? Something about never attending family weddings and funerals? It's all true. What we have means I can only lend scant words, clichés and platitudes - and I can only do that if she relaxes her ban on calls and messages. I look at the last message she sent to me three days ago. I don't think we've ever gone that long without some sort of exchange. It says: 'I've arrived safe. It's terrible to have to say this, but we better not write or talk at all for the next few days. You understand, don't you? Xxx.'

Reading it now, I feel rejected.

'Yes, it was good to meet you too. And a great idea to go to Preston.'

The messaging app shows she is typing. It seems to be taking forever, but all that pops up on my phone screen is: 'Oh no... hmm.'

'What's up?'

'You've got me worried now that I've stepped over a line.'

'Why?'

'I kind of hoped that my message would engage you in something a little more than an exchange of gratitude. Should I back off?'

On balance, I should tell her to be more circumspect.

'I think there's no harm in us getting to know each other better. Yesterday evening was great. But I can't just switch someone else off and switch you on xx.'

'I'm not asking you to.'

'Are you sure about that?'

'Hmm. That's a leading question. Anyway, at least this time I get a x.' There's a cute smiley, and it makes me laugh.

'Make the most of it.' I add a laugh out loud emoji.

It's already gone past where I wanted this to go.

'Let's catch up again next weekend. But the boundary is still there. If that's a problem, then maybe we shouldn't meet.'

'When are you back from Sweden.'

'Either late Thursday or early Friday. Probably the latter.'

'Maybe we could grab lunch on Saturday?'

'Let's do that.'

'Meanwhile...'

'What?'

'Let's keep in touch?'

'Of course x.'

'xxx.'

As I see Victoria's status change to offline, I feel shameful and disloyal. I shouldn't be doing this.

By early evening my travel preparations for Stockholm are all complete and I'm online looking for places to stay in Shropshire. Everywhere seems expensive, more so than usual because of the holiday period. It leaves me thinking that I might as well have a blow out and stay somewhere very expensive, enjoy some luxury and pampering and treat Joe and Beth to the same. I warm to this plan and make a provisional booking and returnable deposit for three rooms at large country house hotel between Ludlow and Bridgenorth. Perfect; at least it should be. I'm sure they'll love it. Won't they? Unless something else falls off Amy's slowly unravelling world.

Then I swear out loud, profoundly and repeatedly.

It seems that no matter what I do, the end of my marriage seems to be never ending.

I've been up working since 0630, making up for the hours I will lose driving to Manchester airport later this afternoon. I take a break at around nine to get dressed and when I get back to my laptop there's a message from Annabel.

'Seen the news?'

'No.'

'We need to talk.'

Then I see the updates on my phone.

'Copenhagen's main airport locked down after attack. No news of fatalities.'

'Danish authorities playing down terror links.'

'Eyewitnesses talk of gun battle outside terminal building.'

213

And so, it all starts again. I call Annabel who is stoical.

'I've just heard from Peter and Pat White that all air travel on company business will be banned this morning. And that's regardless of reason for travel.'

'Right. That's a pain. So you're trapped over there?'

'Yes and no. I am scheduled to be here without a break until end of March.'

'Even so... if there's an emergency.'

'It is what it is but it's going to create some work for us to do, and quickly. Will you still go to Wood Street?'

'No idea. Possibly not.'

'Get your travel plans sorted then we need to get in a virtual room and come up with a way to deliver what you would have delivered here over next three days. It won't take long, but we need to make sure it's seamless in the client's eyes.'

We end up having a series of calls, reviewing PowerPoint documents and re-writing the scripts for our presentation. I love working with Annabel on stuff like this; she has a controlled intensity and focus that pulls me in and makes me inspired. We break every forty minutes or so, then rejoin with new ideas and with any barriers knocked down. It takes us until mid-afternoon to baseline what is needed.

Throughout these sessions, friends are in touch asking if I'm affected by events in Copenhagen. Beth calls five times even though I message her to say I'm all right and will call her later.

There's nothing from Jude. What can I do about her? Will she be thinking or worried about me? Then it occurs to me that I don't think I told her I would be in Sweden.

'Let's take a break from this now Ed. Do other things. Will you be free at around five your time?'

'I've nothing in my diary at all this afternoon; should have been travelling.'

'Of course. Well let's revisit the slides later. Prepare for a full dry run okay? Then we can fine tune anything lacking credibility or substance.'

I call Beth and reassure her that I'm safe and am no longer travelling. She tells me to stay at home and gets tearful when

I joke that I might have to go to Preston the next day. It's no laughing matter, she tells me.

Victoria messages me: 'I'm guessing you might not be going to Sweden now.'

'You guess right.'

'You staying at home or reverting to London?'

'Staying local, I think. Sorry Vicky - I need to go.'

'OK. But just FYI, I hate being called Vicky.'

By the middle of the afternoon the news from Copenhagen is baffling. Acting on intelligence, police and security services have shot and incapacitated an airside employee; he appeared to have been driving his pushback tractor at a vehicle refuelling a plane. He is now in custody. But the reporting has descended into a dispute about facts. Experts say that, while it was a frightening possibility, failsafe procedures mean fuel could not be ignited in such a collision. Opposing opinions are horrified about the potential for copycat attacks and claim that all expertise is deluded. So the experts stick to evidence; the machines and systems have cut-off routines. So the sceptics call it a viable attempt at mass murder and express scornful disquiet that anyone with evil intentions has held a high security job and evaded due diligence. The debate rages on. As if the threat isn't frightening enough, the ensuing, endless arguing seems simply to become its own form of terror.

I arrive at our Fulwood office early to avoid the risk of delay on the M6. The office is on a business park on the northern edge of Preston. It's a short drive, thirty minutes or so, at the right time of day but it can take much longer. This is the first time I've been here in almost twelve months. But I'm welcomed warmly.

The meeting with our Swedish client starts at nine and finishes early, more than twenty minutes before its scheduled end. It feels like it went well, but Annabel calls me within minutes and is ecstatic. I was, apparently, a massive hit with the client's team and they are expecting to see me there once our travel ban is lifted.

I enjoy an hour catching up with colleagues around the office; the warmth still feels sincere.

My whole day was supposed to have been spent in Stockholm, wooing a client and it means there's nothing in my diary until late in the afternoon. I check in with the project team leaders and they're all coping without me. Annabel is marked Do Not Disturb. It's a pleasant enough day so I jump in my car and take the long way home, up into the hills to the east of the M6. The lanes are too narrow and winding to really open up the S4, but I manage the occasional blast. It feels like fun and as I drop down into Caton and the Lune valley, I feel as if I've blown away some dust that had settled on my life.

I'm back home and working by mid-afternoon, and my adventure hasn't been noticed. The flurry of meetings I attend between four and seven are routine. I have a one-to-one with Oana who has been assigned as the project lead for Ganymede. It's nearly nine pm her time when the call ends, but she is positive and focused.

While I'm at the gym, my phone pops up that I've a notification on Chattabox. I finish my forty-five-minute session on the cross-trainer before I look. It's a direct message: 'You did the right thing. Now stay clear of things you don't understand.'

It's from *&bubblygummy* and, at first, I feel like I've been thrown off a building. Almost a week has passed since I felt any kind of need to engage in the fallout from my social media gaffe. I'd slowly weaned myself back into the fold on SocMed and Chattabox and even checked some profiles on *matchmates*. It felt safe again, and I was calmed by the lack of any new whispering in the wings. The need for me to be a competent, capable employee, and a parent, and to engage with friends old and new had pushed me forward and away from all that stupid paranoia.

But this time I'm soon thinking straight. I reply to the message with a simply worded acknowledgement, then screen shot the thread and save it to photos. Then I go to my Chattabox home and randomly Repeep something and place *&bubblygummy* in my comment. They're still there a few minutes later, so I log out of Chattabox, then back in again. *&bubblygummy* no longer exists and their message has gone from my inbox.

Back home, I start scrolling through the *White Lines - Won't*

Do It page on SocMed. I'm looking for clues about who is a regular in that camp. I want someone who seems to be more than just a local mouthpiece or a sheep bleating about their washing getting dirty from all the dust in the air. I suppose I mean an activist; someone who maybe has an engagement in many causes, not just the road building programme. It's like searching for the proverbial needle in a haystack so I switch to the main pro-road page, *No Overtaking - Roads Matter.* It soon feels as if what I seek can't be found.

I move away from my iMac and grab a beer. I shouldn't drink during the week, but I need something. I feel hemmed in by my lack of clarity. What characteristics am I looking for? I don't even know where to start. Are they good people saying bad things? Or the opposite?

By the time I'm halfway through a second bottle of beer, I've decided to look for someone who is unerringly kind, even if provoked with great vitriol and malice. I need to start with insults. The person I'm looking for will be the one that deflates the most appalling balloons with kind, carefully placed needles.

During this epiphany a text pops up from Arif.

'Parliament has passed the Brexit Bill.'

It's like he's goading me. Why would he do that? Again, I'm struck by how strange he is being. We disagreed about one specific thing. It should be history between us but he's still dismissing me with a contemptuous wave of his hand. I sense it fluttering virtually at me now.

When I don't reply, he sends a second text: 'Celebrate what we've achieved. The country is back on its feet.'

I don't know what to say to him. We belong to the same Party, joined by that bond. It isn't why we are friends, but it makes us comfortable in our feathered nests. Yet this issue divides us, and his taunts seem vehement and lacking in empathy.

There seems to be nothing I can say to him, and in the end I just type, 'I'm glad you're happy Arif.'

He doesn't reply.

I flick back through the posts on *No Overtaking - Roads Matter* looking for something truly nasty. It doesn't take long. In December, one of the companies aligned to the pro-camp posted an advert for its forthcoming Christmas Charity Ball; all holly and ivy with glittery sparkle; and a taunting rejoinder saying 'Here's something not one of those idiot protestors will ever understand or engage with; an event that does good and raises money for needy causes.'

Ouch.

I suppress the snigger that starts when I think about charity balls I've been to, at which the needy were far from everyone's thoughts. And rightly so; you don't dress up to the nines, spend a fortune on drink and drugs and network like fuck for the sake of faith, hope and charity.

The post is liked, loved and bolstered by many adherents who are quick to slap down any attempt to propose a view that the opposition is equally charitable. In the ensuing torrent I keep seeing a name crop up - Jennifer Juniper. This person, or entity, keeps replying to the most belligerent messages and posts with a calming tolerant kindness. Perhaps this is who I'm looking for; except I just don't believe that name.

The results of a quick online search make me even more sceptical. The top ten hits for Jennifer Juniper reveal that it's a song from before I was born by someone I've never heard of. I jump forward to the tenth page of search results on Google and there's nothing there that might link to this SocMed being.

On the *White Lines - Won't Do It* page, Jennifer Juniper is everywhere, with a constant stream of comments, posts and support. The posts are stuff about every conceivable reason why this road isn't needed, and how its genesis is a colossal administrative mistake by ministers and civil servants who've misinterpreted the socio-economic indicators and evidence about logistics. There's science, there's politics, there's association and above all there's a shining light of certainty and a kind of love in all these words. Her statements really are everywhere, but who is it? I'm both intrigued and deeply suspicious of yet another fake identity.

I don't know what to do, and I don't know where I'm going with all this, so I step away from all my machines, lie in the bath for nearly an hour and find that I can't help thinking about Jude.

21

My routine is in tatters when I wake up early that Wednesday, but I feel like I'm warming to the idea of being at home with my work schedule still blocked out in favour of meetings I won't attend. By eight I've cleared the small number of mails that dropped in overnight and accepted invitations to a series of meetings in the coming week. It soon feels like there's nothing else to do.

Instead of working, I go to messaging and write to Jennifer Juniper.

'Hi, I've seen your posts about the Tamworth Bypass. I think I have some things you should see.'

I pretend to work for another hour or so, time interspersed with squash fixture match ups, a few messages to and from Beth and Joe, and a significant amount of laughter at the Chancellor who has caved in spectacularly on the national insurance issue.

By lunch time my message to Jennifer Juniper hasn't been seen, and she hasn't accepted my link up, yet I know from an almost constant tracking of the activity on SocMed that she or he is online and resolutely on message. I start liking posts and comments emanating from Jennifer Juniper; not just the current stuff, but back in to time. When this support doesn't seem to make any difference in terms of a reply to my message, I try replying to one of Jennifer Juniper's posts, selected randomly, with my own thoughts. A few moments later, my post gets a like; from Jennifer Juniper. Then from others.

Then my phone lights up, and I feel a jolt of something physical - between pleasure and pain - because Jude is calling me.

'Hey honey. Can you talk?'

'Of course. Always.'

'Where are you?'

'At home. What's the latest with Lewis?'

'He died this morning. Peacefully.'

She starts to cry.

'I'm so sorry Jude. That's terribly sad.'

She can barely speak. 'I'm just outside the hospice now. Told everyone I needed to call my mum but called you first. This call really can't be long.'

'I understand.'

Joe has messaged me: 'Dad, can you talk?'

I reply: 'Give me 5.'

'Sure.'

'I wish I could hold you right now my Teddy. And I feel utterly appalled that I am standing less than fifty yards away from a dead man and his grieving family and saying that to you.'

'You need to go back to them. You know that.'

'Yes. I do. And...'

'What?'

'...and everything we have is torn apart by this. I always said we could never share things like family or friends. This just proves it. Totally... fucking... proves it.'

'Jude; don't think about me or us now.'

'I have to. You're all I want and need. My every single desire. Yet you can't fill the gaping hole in my life that today might bring. How can I cope with that? How can I want you in my arms, feeling your strength and love when that simply cannot happen?'

'You need to do what matters for your family. Let's stop talking. Call your mum. She needs to be told.'

'I know. And you didn't need to be told. But I had to tell you.'

She's sobbing quite uncontrollably now.

'Hey: wish I could hold you. But you and I don't matter right now. Do we?'

'We matter more than ever.'

'Go. Thanks for letting me know by calling rather than text. It's wonderful to hear your voice. We'll see each other soon.'

'Goodbye.'

A moment or two later, a message pops up from Jude; it's just a whole screen covered with the letter x.

'Dad, can you talk now?'

I call Joe. 'Sorry to keep you, I was on a call.'

'Oh right. Well I won't keep you long. I just want you to explain this whole redundancy thing. What's mum actually facing? She seems incapable of explaining it without losing the plot. I've tried to look online but don't know where to start.'

I explain the rules and the legislation as I understand and know it.

'She's saying the company just wants to get rid of her, and the process involving seven other people is a sham.'

'It might be.'

'What? Then what's the point of rules?'

'To protect workers, notionally. Has she ever mentioned consultation?'

Joe seems uncertain about this. He tells me Amy gets really emotional every time he speaks to her.

'Okay; I'll send you a couple of links about redundancy and how it has to be managed. Have a look so you understand them, then pass them on to Amy. You need to tell her to be very clear with her manager and company about how those rules are being applied. Okay?'

'Right. Yes.'

'But the bad news is that if her company really does want her out, they will go to these lengths to make it seem like it's an equitable process, even though she is the target.'

'That sucks Dad. It totally sucks shit.'

'I know.'

Joe says, 'So all this crap about the EU protecting British workers is a lie.'

'It is: just like the view that they are a terrible busy body stopping employers behaving badly. An opaque deception from both camps.'

'But you voted not to leave. So, were you fooled?'

'No-one was fooled by any of it. People got what they wanted. I've moved on.'

It's the early hours of Thursday morning that Jennifer Juniper replies. I've been unable to sleep so the message doesn't disturb me, unlike the conversation with Jude and the news about Amy.

My mind is addled by the phrase Jude used; that I can't fill the hole in her life - the gaping hole. Just the same as I couldn't fill, or even build a bridge over the chasm that eventually appeared in my marriage. Why is that? What do I lack?

'Hello. I'm not sure if I should be curious or concerned.'

'I'd say both.'

'Are you going to threaten me? Because I've been threatened by professionals, so you'll need to be good.'

'No threats. Just some images that need wider distribution.'

'And this relates to?'

I head to my office so I can type on a proper keyboard. In a series of messages, I tell Jennifer Juniper about the photos I took, and what they show, and the strange things they caused when I posted them on SocMed. It takes me around five minutes to compose and send these words.

She doesn't respond.

Late in the evening, I get a messenger wave from someone called Jenny Donovan. I'm not sure I should wave back.

'Easier if we chat using my real name.'

I shake my head. What has happened to create the need for all these aliases?

'But Teddy - I am hoping that is your real name - it's late. So perhaps also easier if we discuss what you've told me in the morning?'

'It is my real name. I don't need an alias.'

'That's fine. No need to be concerned. I'll explain tomorrow.'

'I'll be working. When are you thinking?'

'Will try you around ten. I'm good for an hour then.'

'Try me how? Messaging?'

'Yes. Safest on there, for now. Night.'

Safe how? Safe why? I don't understand.

And I barely sleep, other than a couple of hours after five in the morning when I've given up on it. It leaves me feeling worse than if I hadn't slept at all and it takes me ages to come to terms with the fact that I'm awake and need to work. I stumble through an hour of mails and admin, wondering why I'm not busy with calls and meetings. Then it clicks that I am still in that convenient zone where I was supposed to be elsewhere and had cleared out my schedule to be at a client's beck and call. It energises me to think I've nothing to do and I go and sing in the shower for twenty minutes. When I get back to the real virtual world there's a message from Jenny.

'Tell me why you want me to see these photos.'

I explain that I've been following the opposing SocMed pages related to the new road. That I found her name by looking for someone who seemed real and good - even though it turned out half of that equation was a lie.

'And what do you think I will do with them?'

'I don't really care. I just want to screw MarMap.'

'It's personal.'

'I suppose so. I think they are behind the threats I've received.'

'You want revenge.'

'I want justice.'

'Nothing I do or say with whatever you send me will help you.'

'Why?'

'Because I doubt you've got anything I don't already know.'

I decide to cut through this crap by sending her the two photos of Kriss Jarvis' email. Ten minutes later, she replies: 'I'll get back to you.'

I stare disinterested at my work laptop for a bit, then do some personal stuff; a walk planned for the weekend; a couple of notes to Jude, started then deleted; a call to the hospice to enquire after Mark Hodgson. I'm munching on some cereal when a tone announces the arrival of a message.

It's Victoria.

'Are you still in Lancaster?'

'I am. It's very strange.'

'Would it add to the strangeness to have a squash match this evening? 5.45? I've been jilted.'

'Jilted? At squash?'

'Hmm. It happens to me a lot.'

'Hmm.'

We transmit a few emojis.

'Is it a league match?'

'Was supposed to be, but you and I can just play a friendly.'

'No way.'

'Fighting talk.'

More emojis, then a hastily concluded agreement to meet and play. And maybe have dinner afterwards. There's a discourse in my head that links a second meeting with Victoria to Jude being in the bosom of her husband's family, and possibly reconciled with Craig. I want to know where she is, how she's thinking and what she wants. But all I have is a sobbed statement that I can't deliver.

When I throw my racquet and bag in the car, I've heard nothing from Jennifer Juniper, nor her doppelgänger and I've done nothing to chase it up. But I'm distracted by what's coming and there's a kind of tunnel vision in play. I don't ever want to think that someone is an easy option, yet Victoria seems to be giving signals, like a hashtag only I can see and use.

Our match two weeks ago was played out with her wearing a fairly standard squash outfit; an all-in-one dress; somewhat predictable; prim and proper. Now, as she walks on court she's dressed in black leggings under an electric blue skirt and an expensive looking hoody. There's a racquet carrier slung over her shoulder. She smiles, then tosses a ball to me and tells me to warm it up while she gets ready.

She takes out one of two racquets then drops the carrier in to the locker outside the court, along with her hoody. Her long-sleeved top is a matching electric blue.

Neither of us plays well. For my part, that's partially because I'm tired and drained. But I'm also distracted by Victoria's physique and the small noises she makes during long rallies. Her movement around the court seems effortless and efficient. She's coordinated and supple. Occasionally, when she plays overhead, her shirt lifts and I glimpse highly toned muscles on her stomach and obliques.

An hour or so later, we agree that dinner is needed, but nothing too grand. Victoria knows just the place. As we sit in the dimly lit bar waiting to be served, we're still talking about her narrow victory in the match.

'I'll beat you next time. I've got your game sussed.'

'We'll see. There might not be a next time though. I need competition and you seemed well off your game this evening. Why was that?'

'Oh, I haven't been sleeping too well and...'

She listens for a while, sipping occasionally from a glass of fizzy water, laden with ice. I don't get to finish my excuses.

'I'm not blind Teddy. I could tell you were looking at me rather than thinking about winning points.'

I'm stammering. 'Sorry; I shouldn't have... I wasn't... I'm not like...'

'I was distracted too. But I know how to be discreet.'

The food arrives but it barely covers up my concern that I've done something highly inappropriate. Victoria is unperturbed.

'Did you like what you saw? Any particularly interesting bits?'

'You first.'

She smiles and puts her veggie burger down, unbitten.

'Are you sure your involvement doesn't preclude me telling you your best bits?'

'Let's say it's acceptable.'

'No Teddy. It isn't. Let's eat.'

The bar claims to have the best burgers, regardless of ingredients, in Lancaster. After a couple of mouthfuls each, both of us are endorsing that claim. We've forgotten about our admiration for one another.

'I've got an early start tomorrow. Long drive to see a potential client in York which is a total pain in the arse on a Friday. So, with regret, I think I need to get home.'

'That's fine. It's probably best for me too.'

'Plans for the weekend?'

'A walk somewhere, as it's overdue. Plus some voluntary work that I do.'

'Well well. Hidden depths. Fancy a companion on your walk?'

'Let's say it's acceptable.'

225

Victoria reaches over and places a hand over mine.

'Like I said before; it really isn't. But since you seem malleable about this, I'll keep seeing how far your boundaries extend. I'm going to pay the bill. Call me tomorrow evening.'

After a more powerful squeeze on my hand, Victoria walks off to the bar and soon leaves. I'm thinking about chasing after her but can't decide why I would want to. I grab my kit bag and head off to collect my car and go home.

I still have no reply from Jenny Donovan and her messenger status shows she has been inactive for ten hours. I sent both of her entities the same message: 'What are you thinking? Will you be using my photos?'

Victoria messages me.

'I need to tell you something.'

'OK. Go on.'

'Your best bits: shoulders; quads; arse.'

'Hmm.'

'Yes. Hmm.'

'Next time I better wear leggings and a skirt.'

Nothing happens for a few minutes. Then she's typing for ages.

'I thought I should leave something to the imagination.'

'Well you certainly did that.'

'Save telling me about my best bits until you're less involved.'

Before I can think of a reply, Victoria's status shows she's inactive, where she remains for the rest of the night.

I have no idea what I should do or say next.

22

There's an increased level of notifications from SocMed about activity on the *White Lines - Won't Do It* page. And plenty more on Chattabox, where many of the people I've started to follow have begun a new keyboard war. I'm busy with work, so don't find the time to look at what's happened until late that morning and it takes me a few moments of scrolling to find the cause.

Jennifer Juniper has posted my photos of the Kriss Jarvis email with the words: 'We all knew that companies like MarMap are implicit in the threatening behaviour of police and security personnel. Those photos prove it - they make it explicit.'

She's copied the profile name of the local police force for good measure.

What follows is an increasingly barbaric level of invective, interspersed with predictably embittered exchanges about the veracity of the photographs. It's really so easy to just claim anything is fake news, or photo-shopped; you can make something a truth or a lie in the time it takes to sow the seeds of doubt. I know they're real, where I took them and what they've caused. I know that my system and devices stamped the photos with indelible proof about where and when I took them along with assorted metadata. A solid proportion of others are happy to deny me my knowledge. And the facts.

I'm so distracted by what I've seen, and so frustrated by Jennifer Juniper's decision to use my photos without warning, that I miss the start of a conference call and have to play catch up when I finally join. Then I'm straight into another call with Annabel. Over the course of an hour, we map out the series of meetings and messages I will attend and deliver as if I was in Stockholm.

'It's likely the travel ban will be lifted over this coming weekend.'

'That's quick. I thought it would be in place for longer.'

'Everyone did, but it seems a gaggle of seniors will be flying over next week for a Grand Tour of Duty in London and other European offices. I'm guessing they need their points and air miles more than they need an inconvenient travel ban.'

'Do I need to make new plans to come over to Sweden?'

'Hold back on that for now. I got a message from Peter the other day suggesting he wants me to return to London sooner than planned; potentially next week. No point you being here without me. Can we make next week's calls video?'

'Don't see why not. We can try video now if you like?'

'No. I'm in my hotel room.' She giggles. 'And inappropriately dressed. Let's try it on Monday when I'm back on their site.'

We chat for a while longer, and when it's clear we're gossiping and joking rather than working Annabel tells me to get on with some work. She, it seems, has the rest of the afternoon off and plans to spend it in a sauna.

Stewart Hatton sends me message. 'Hi boss. Just letting you know I've had a handover session with Stef ahead of my holiday next week.'

I am staring at those words for fully five minutes. Why didn't I know? Or had I just forgotten? I've lost my grip on the basics: it's unforgiveable.

In the end, my response is nothing more than a reflex: 'Ok mate. Thanks. Have a good break.'

By the middle of the afternoon, there's a very strange mix of claims being made about my photos. Jennifer Juniper is boldly sticking to her statement that it's no-one's business where she got them, and they're now a matter of public record. This is being met by two contradictory threads of thought: that the pictures are fake, and shame on the tree huggers for wasting everyone's time with fairy stories; or that the source of the photos is known and will be dealt with. The implied consequences are kind of funny, but more than a little frightening. I log off social media and tune back in at work in the knowledge that I don't need to see whatever is being lined up for me.

In the two days since her brother-in-law died, I've heard nothing from Jude. In fact, in the two weeks since we saw each other at the beer festival, we've been more or less incommunicado. I know we can't be in touch, but I feel a confused sense of loss, as if there is something coming along that prevents Jude and me from being together. She's been in my life for a year, and for half that time has been a constant, if intermittent good companion. But even though we've recently declared that we are in love, we both know it's incomplete. What she told me on the phone two days ago is right: the tragic death in her family is the end for us.

As I think about that, I find I'm chewing on the inside of my lips and cheeks.

I'm worried.

And, when I'm worried, I rely on Jude's help.

But she's missing, perhaps forever, and my mind is boggling.

Jude.

How can I get her back?

It's after seven when I go back onto SocMed and there's more of the same from earlier, although the reaction to the photos has largely died down and a whole new spurious argument has started; it's like two bald men arguing over a series of combs. I feel relief. But it's short lived, because when I go to the pro-road site, I find several posts in which the protest groups are being roundly abused and, en passant, I am being mentioned. For example, some mighty being has written: 'These fools are at it again, posting made up photos. The same made up photos we've seen before, from that Clayton bloke. Remember?'

Plenty do remember, it seems. Likes and Angry faces light up her post. That Clayton bloke is troublesome.

Before I can stop myself, I've replied, 'I suppose you mean me?'

Everything goes quiet. I look at the person's profile which has no privacy settings. It's a vague, unrepentantly ordinary set of words backed up by a few standard images; kids; dogs; cocktails; a hard-looking significant other. Lives in Burton-upon-Trent. 68 friends. Wears sunglasses that cover half her face in all her photos. Hasn't posted anything since November 2016; incognito for almost half a year, yet since lunch time today she's screeched out six posts about me and *those twats in their tents*.

As the evening progresses, I'm getting all kinds of abuse on Chattabox and SocMed. I keep a stuck record playing, responding that if my pictures aren't real then maybe I'm made up too. I'm told to be careful, to be worried, and I'm told to fuck off. I open a beer and keep going with my calm goading ripostes. It's fun, and I'm enjoying myself. This arm's length mudslinging is quite amiable; like a commons debate, it achieves nothing but makes the people doing it feel they are essential and powerful.

Even after a fourth beer I'm keeping a lid on my own abusive tendencies, sticking to simple honest responses and starting to feel a bit bored by it all. I tune out of the main contest and take a look on *matchmates*.

Since Mandygate the other week I've not done a great deal on the dating site, partially because I was concerned about more difficult things but mainly because I didn't feel the need for that particular source of flattery. When I get on to the site, it tells me my profile has been viewed 37 times since my last visit and I have been made a Favourite 19 times. I also have six messages in my inbox.

I open another beer.

The first message is standard stuff: someone putting down a marker; Jodi from Market Harborough; a shot in the dark; Love-Your-Profile-What-Do-You-Think-of-Mine? Then the next two messages are identical, word for word: 'Getting in touch with you Teddy, because your profile is all lies and I'm reporting you for harassment.'

Then two more like Jodi's.

The sixth message says: 'Teddy, you horrible man; it's Carla. Remember me? You should do because I've not forgotten you and how you treated me. You coward; you vile piece of shit. So here's how it's going to be: you crossed a line when you ditched me and it seems crossing lines is your forte.'

I drop out of the messaging platform and drop in to the profile. It isn't the Carla I was linked to in February. There's no photograph and the supporting words are a kind of template. Nothing about this seems real, but I go back to her message.

'Anyway, I'm going to tell the world that we met and you raped me then dumped me in the middle of nowhere and drove off. Police informed Teddy Clayton. You're going to burn.'

I screen shot the three messages, even though I can hear the clamour about fake photos if I ever publish them.

I'm supposed to be really scared about this, but I'm not. All the flimflam from earlier has given me a highly tuned sense of this being badly written fiction. I go to the main page and search *Carla*. It tells me I need to add more detail. Back in the messaging section I scroll through my deleted chats. The Carla correspondence is still there, but shaded out, presumably because I've blocked her. I click on her name but can't see her profile; she's blocked me; if she'd left the site our chats would have disappeared.

Has she become a new entity on the site in order to attack me with false accusations? As I'm running through the implications of that possibility, my phone bleeps a noise: it's a message from Victoria.

'Hey. How was your day?'

'Busy.'

'Hmm. Me too.'

'How was York?'

'Good for business - new client secured.'

'Brilliant.'

'Wish I could have seen more of the city.'

'Are you back home now.'

'Just. Decided to stay over there till the traffic died down. It still took four hours.'

I look at the clock on my screen; it's approaching ten fifteen. Victoria is writing.

'Still planning to walk tomorrow, and would it be ok if I join you?'

'Definitely. And definitely.'

She sends a smiley face, then 'Let's talk in the morning. I need a shower and my bed.'

Predictably, the messages from people who've made the wrong sort of pass at me have gone now I've read them. Three genuine ones, presumably, are still there awaiting my pleasure. Now I look at them again, I'm drawn to the possibility that none of the women involved is real. That a programme carefully designates me as in a group deserving of X, in turn giving me a series of *X-centric* options any one of which might be either a robot, a troll or a profile that hasn't been live for months but remains conveniently undeleted. When I go to the site's home page, I'm shown a deck of cards - my queens. *Are these your matches?* it asks. And before I can consider that challenge, a new set of six is unveiled and then moments later six more. Then I notice that *Matilda, 44 from Oxford* has the same photo as *Brione, 47 from Basingstoke*. But then a whole new face appears, also called *Brione, 47 from Basingstoke*. What a piss poor excuse for a real world this is. A carousel whose horses and riders change every revolution.

But I feel I have bigger things to fry than these catfish and sit back in my chair with a large intake of breath, then a karmic sigh. After the days I've spent reviewing the name calling and discourse on the road pages it feels easier not to be troubled by these latest threats. It's intimidation without substance. Except for *matchmates* and Carla; that makes me worried again.

Who knows that I linked up with someone called Carla? It can't be a coincidence; the reference to ditching her was right there. Someone knows I had that dalliance and that I ended it abruptly.

I go to bed but can't sleep. There's a cacophonous swirling in my head that only stops when I open my eyes, and it doesn't help that I've drunk beer. When I get up to relieve the second of those problems, I watch the stream of golden yellow gushing into the toilet water turning it the colour of camomile tea and it calms me down and helps me decide what to do. Moments later I'm back on my iMac and on the internet site for *matchmates*. Ignoring any other details – Views, Messages, Favourites - I go straight to the section about my profile and account. In five clicks, I've deleted them.

Jilted, the site flashes several messages up at me: I'll lose all my contacts; I won't get a refund for an unexpired subscription; my messages will be lost. The inevitable email is required, in which I have to affirm my intention to go.

Within a quarter of an hour, I'm back in bed and tumbling in to sleep. It's a good sleep.

23

Jude has sent me hundreds of messages, texts and voicemails. In a year of being lovers, she has filled our lives with brief correspondence; words without end; Amen. Overnight, she's sent me an email, and it seems like it could be a first and last.

'My Teddy, I've no idea why I'm using email for this. My head is all over the place. No need to reply, but maybe tell me you're OK?

It's Lewis' funeral on Monday and we're all unbearably sad. He was so young.

I'll be home on Wednesday evening it seems. Can't wait to see you.

Jxxxx'

I can't decide what to say in reply. In the end, all I send is a nine-word text: 'Jude, be strong. I'm thinking of you constantly. Ex'.

As I type this bland inadequacy, Arif sends me a message about Osborne being made editor of the London Evening Standard.

I don't want or need another Brexit lecture and reply: 'What's the latest with your suspension?'

'I should be back in the chair before the end of the month. Will Beth and Joe be with you over the coming holiday? We should all have lunch one day.'

I explain that our plans don't involve any family time in Lancaster. Arif replies with his commiserations, as if I'm in mourning, but his invitation isn't extended to me as a singleton.

I pick up Victoria and we head down the A6 to Scorton. It's relatively quiet up on the lanes near Nicky Nook and we're soon booted and ready to walk.

'Want to do the climb straightaway? Or shall we go around the roads for a bit?'

'You choose.'

'Let's amble.'

The lane heads north east from our parking spot and we soon pass the place where walkers are heading up to the beacon. It's a jumble of cars and people, some with dogs and children. Like a waiting room for some kind of procedure.

'Tell me about your new client.'

'It's a company that specialises in supply chain and contract management. Ambitious people, who already have global reach. They're looking for a supplier to do a re-branding process and yesterday was me pitching my proposal. And I won. They just awarded me the business there and then, even though their process was technically supposed to have several stages remaining.'

'Lucrative?'

'It won't make me rich, but it's a good win simply because of their client base. They do work for a lot of companies, so now I can tap into that.'

'Fantastic. Are they based in York? Will you be there a lot?'

'Most of what I do will be done from my office at home in Lancaster. But I'll also use my London base when I need time face to face. Two of the five people running the company live in York, including the CEO. But their head office is London.'

'You have a base in London?'

'I have use of an apartment there. In Camden. Don't look so puzzled.'

'I'm shocked, not puzzled.'

'It's the place my dad used before he retired. Nothing sinister.'

I've slowed my pace to a dawdle; Victoria ends up several metres ahead and turns to tell me to keep up.

'I can't keep up. We haven't known each other long but I thought you said you were wiped out by your divorce and now live just marginally above the bread line. Yet you have property in London.'

'I think that was selective listening.'

'Selective how?'

'Mainly because I didn't say anything of the sort. Alex took virtually everything, but the Camden apartment wasn't mine to lose.'

'And you told me that the guy you'd been seeing dropped you because you had no money.'

'I didn't have any money, so it was true. But money isn't why he dumped me. His wife found out about us and he went running home to her.'

'You could have told me that. Why did you need to pretend?'

'I'm sorry. I just wanted to make sure you knew I was single and available - free from ties.'

I look across at her, and she returns my gaze with strong lingering eye contact.

'Forgive me?'

'You should have just told me the truth. I've always been completely open with you.'

'But not with your involvement.'

'How do you know I've been anything other than open with her?'

She grabs my arm above the elbow and draws us to a halt.

'You're out walking with me. Not her. Does she know?'

'About you? No. Nor about me being out walking today.'

'And why would that be Teddy? Am I a dirty secret?'

'I suppose you are.'

'But so is she, from everything you've told me. Are you just accumulating a bevy of concealed women?'

She's giggling; this is amusement, apparently. I tell her some of why Jude is unavailable for me at the moment, and my fears that whatever we have might be over. Victoria laughs aloud.

'Oh, so I'm being lined up as replacement am I?'

'No one is being lined up here.'

'So am I wasting my time?'

I can't think of anything to say and she quickly fills the silence. 'You don't have to answer that. Just don't tell me we can only be friends until you make your mind up about your duplicity.'

Jude's laughter about cheating on adulterers is all I can hear.

We walk in silence for several minutes. Victoria apologises for being needy; I tell her I don't think she has been.

'No Teddy, I have. I must wait; play the long game. I've been on my own for three years, and in truth for most of the previous thirteen. Another few months won't hurt.'

'Alone? How come?'

'Because my husband and I stopped loving each other within just a few years of getting married. I could spend ages coming up with smart-arse theories about why that happened, but the simple truth is we were bored by each other. It drove me to have an affair, when what I should have done was end it with him first. Then the affair fizzled out in to nothing. It's left me lonely and guilty.'

'Guilty about what? Your affair?'

'No. About my failure as a partner. And my failure to keep the promises I made in a ceremony.'

We've reached the point where we can fork right and head up the hill or go left into the wooded surroundings of a small reservoir.

'Let's get our heart rates up. Come on.'

'Good change of subject there Mr C. I'll race you.'

I find it touching and funny that a relative stranger has called me Mr C; it feels like an affirmation that three decades of silliness with Luke truly has value.

Victoria has set off up the hillside path at something close to a jog and I have to run to get past her. We're laughing again and it slows our progress. Some kids, sitting on the top of a stone structure of some kind, laugh at us as we march past and we quicken our pace onwards and up to the beacon.

It's a small white obelisk with the red rose of Lancaster on its four pock-marked faces. It looks undermined; or as if it is trying to uproot itself and fly off to a less populace hilltop. Morecambe Bay lies over to the north west and, sweeping around in a 360 turn, I take in hills to the north and east, the vale of the River Ribble to the south and can just make out Blackpool Tower, like an upturned tack.

'Have you been here in the evening as the sun goes down?'

I confess that I haven't.

'We must come back here in the summer to see it.'

'Does this place hold special memories for you?'

Victoria looks at me, as if surprised I should ask, then turns away again and the breeze catches her hair.

'It's a place we came to as a family, for dog walks or picnics. I can still picture my mum and dad, sitting back to back on a blanket surrounded by Tupperware boxes full of stuff while we gambolled.'

'You have brothers and sisters?'

'A sister. Elizabeth. My dad has a penchant for the queens of England. I'm pretty sure if they'd had a third daughter, she'd have been called Elizabeth the Second.'

'Not Boudicca?'

'No Teddy, he wasn't a wanker about it.'

Now she stands with her back to the beacon, laughing so much that tears spring up in her eyes. I watch her and find her laughter infectious.

'Where's Elizabeth now?'

'Just up the road near Kirkby Lonsdale; married; three kids; two dogs; dreamily gorgeous hunk of a husband; happy; the daughter who delivered.'

'What about your parents?'

'They spend half their time in Portugal now Dad's retired. They've a nice place in the Douro valley. Otherwise, their home is a cottage up near Broughton in Furness.'

She's still got her back to the obelisk but has sunk to her haunches. The laughs have dissipated now.

'Stand up. Let's get a photo together to mark our inaugural walk.'

'No way. I look like a gurning duck in selfies.'

'All the more reason to mark the occasion.'

Laughter resumes and, in one take, we generate a smiling happy image; two people and a restless obelisk.

We've only been walking for about thirty minutes, so I suggest we turn around and head back down to the reservoir. The main path is well worn and has steps built into it. It's not precarious but there are places where a slip or stumble could involve quite a fall. We talk intermittently.

'Despite me wanting us to be more than friends, I don't want to cause the end of your involvement.'

'I think you probably do. But you won't. I'm not sure I'll be the cause of its end either. Like I said, the current situation is pretty fragile; bereavement and grief are in control. It's a terribly sad event for any family. She is bound to be drawn into that and away from me. She needs to be part of them, not us. I think it's made her feel that whatever she has with me can't be sustained. Because it has no value other than intimacy and secrecy. We've always said that one day our relationship would just end. She always tells me that if I find someone else, someone I want to be with, that we will part. Without rancour.'

'Okay then I hope maybe I can be the cause of the end of your involvement.'

'Hold that thought.'

'I will. And even though it doesn't seem like we've walked far I think we've earned tea and cake at the Barn.'

For the next 24 hours, I barely notice anything happening on my social media connections, good, bad or indifferent. After dropping her off late in the afternoon, Victoria begins a fusillade of messages and I'm powerless to stop myself from engaging. There's no single topic, and no sense that we are bonding. It's just nebulous get-to-know-you stuff: likes; dislikes; places; faces; histories; friends; families. As if a whole evening of this isn't enough, it starts all over again as I work through some personal admin and work planning that Sunday morning. We eventually agree to take a deep breath and do other things. I need the gym, and time with Joe and Beth.

It's Jennifer Juniper, in her real guise, that drags me back to the main event.

'Do you have some time to chat now?'

'I can't talk. But yes, we can chat on here.'

'I meant written, not verbal.'

'Right. Why didn't you tell me you were going to post my photos?'

'Why would that be a problem? Isn't it why you sent them to me?'

I sigh loudly; it's for her benefit but she doesn't know.

'It would have been helpful to prepare myself for the outcome.'

'Well that's your problem. I understood you wanted me to use your photos, so I did.'

'Right.'

'Have you had problems since Friday?'

I type a long summary of the scolds I've received from various sources. It takes me a while and by the end Jenny is inactive on messaging. When she returns, it seems she didn't read what I wrote.

'I've been looking at some of it. Tame stuff in the main. You're taking the right approach though - keep doing that. Keep it simple and factual. Many of these people are in it to cause and bolster as much offence as possible. They don't cope well with calm. Is it just on SocMed and Chattabox?'

'No. I was using an internet dating site. But I quit.'

'Extraordinary.'

'How do you mean?'

'I never thought I'd speak to someone who's used one of those.'

This time my sigh is complimented by a shaken head.

'I think I've been judged enough, don't you?'

'Touché. Will you quit social media?'

'Not sure.'

'OK. Perhaps stick with it but copy the worst of it on to the White Lines group pages and Chattabox feeds. It isn't nice but it's not serious. A game on almost every level.'

'When does it stop being a game?'

'When you get a security guard's fist smashed into your mouth while the police look on. But I'm guessing you won't be joining us at an actual protest.'

'Really? Why not?'

'Because you've made it clear that your motives are revenge and justice, and that the target may or may not be MarMap Logistics. You want to even the score. That's not about protest or about action. It's just a pissing match. One you can't win.'

'Thanks.'

'You're welcome. Anyway, I wanted to check something with you.'

'Go on.'

'Your photos were taken on a train between Lichfield TV and London, right?'

'Yes. On Feb 20th.'

'OK. Did you see Jarvis hit send on that email?'

'No. I stopped looking once I'd taken the pics.'

'Do you know who he is?'

'I found some stuff about him.'

'An interesting, and slightly dangerous man.'

'Why the alias? Do you know?'

'More game playing. That's MarMap's style. Why were you on the train?'

'I go to London every week for work.'

'OK. And out of interest did you see him doing anything else?'

'He got on at Lichfield. He did the work you've seen, and it wasn't long before he was asleep. For some of the time I was looking he was sexting with someone.'

'Did you get any photos of that?'

I'm not sure where she's going with this.

'That depends what you plan to do with them if I did.'

She ducks under the challenge. 'Did you get a name or clear image of his sext partner?'

'I'll send you the photo. You decide.'

About fifteen minutes after I've sent it, Jenny replies with: 'Thanks.'

Then much later she sends: 'Let's catch up in London some time. Not this coming week. I'll be in Tamworth.'

'Don't you live there? Or near there?'

'No, I live in London.'

'I just assumed you were local to the construction route.'

'You need to stop assuming things.'

I'm back on the train again and listening to Jude's voicemail for the fourth or fifth time. She'd called late the previous afternoon, but I couldn't answer and she left a message. When I called back later in the evening, it went straight to voicemail.

The brief words she spoke had an enforced calm, but there was a shake in her voice like I've never heard in any voice before.

'Teddy, my lovely Teddy. I wish you had answered but I guess you're working. I'm sorry. Well; the funeral has finished. I've got no time to talk but I had to hear your voice. It can wait till I'm back - Wednesday looks favourite. We should get together if you're around, let me know if you're in London. Message me. Today was so sad. I can't begin to describe it. There's something... I have to go.'

I should be working but keep listening to the voicemail.

Something what?

If I'm around?

The train is slowing into its approach to Warrington Bank Quay station, and I'm enjoying the space afforded by first class.

No queue of folks standing and waiting to leave. No concern that someone will get on and make me move my bag from the spare seat next to me. There is space all around. As the train draws to a halt, I look at the people standing three-deep on the platform waiting to find and squeeze into a seat.

At first, I don't know what is causing the pain.

Something hot is burning from my lower left cheek into my neck.

There's a smell of chocolate, sickly and almost burnt.

Then a commotion behind me; some shouts and cries of pain and concern.

The scalding has spread on to the top of my shoulder and down the front.

But as it spreads it dissipates.

The acute pain is on my jaw line, like I've been branded.

Then I'm surrounded by crew from the train. One of them has been hurt after being shoved out of the way by my attacker. She's getting support from other crew members. They've called emergency services. A first aid kit is retrieved, and I'm being helped out of my shirt. I feel pain from the scald. The train is still stationary, and I'm vaguely aware of an announcement telling people that departure is delayed so that British Transport Police can attend an incident. Voices come and go, some expressing concern about me, others thinking aloud about CCTV footage and how to retrieve it.

Am I okay?

Is there a lot of pain?

Have I got a spare shirt?

Do I have any painkillers with me?

They can't give me any pain relief without my consent.

My bag is retrieved from the stowage area and I shuffle around for a clean shirt. A dressing with a cooling gel has been found in the first aid kit, and someone applies it to my face and neck.

It helps.

I can hear quite powerful crying and I ask how their colleague is. They think she has a broken wrist.

There's a strange combination surrounding me. A genuine care for my injuries is being countered by the sense that they want to get the train moving. They keep looking at their watches. Then a new voice is heard, telling the crew that the attacker wasn't detained and escaped into Warrington. The local police have been informed and a first responder paramedic is coming. The voice is saying the train may be cancelled, terminated here and everyone asked to wait for the next London service in thirty minutes or so. Then there's a lowering of voices. Odd phrases flip out; it's a crime scene; witnesses need to be interviewed; can't it be done while the train is moving? No; it can't. This is a serious incident, involving assault and injury to a passenger and a staffer.

Other passengers are trying not to look, but I see some of them staring crossly at me. This delay is my fault. None offers me any comfort.

Soon a paramedic is next to me and tells me her name is Jules. She asks questions about the pain and my breathing. She says the dressing was the right thing to do. I tell her it's relieved the worst of the scald, but I still hurt. She offers me paracetamol via an IV, but I don't want it. I feel slightly stupid, sitting there topless but Jules tells me I should try to cope. I sniff at the shirt I was wearing; it smells of chocolate and there's a brown mess all over the collar, shoulder and down to the breast pocket. It's ruined.

Jules says I have to go to A&E so a doctor can properly assess my injury, but I say I prefer to get to London. No, she says; that's not going to happen. I ask if there's Wi-Fi at the hospital. Jules shakes her head, puzzled. I repeat that I don't want to go to hospital. But she insists; the scald is serious. I back down.

The police officer is working his way through the carriage asking for witnesses. It doesn't seem like anyone volunteers. I hear one or two people say they heard a shout, then a scream. The officer spends time taking names and addresses.

I feel sore now. Jules has gone to help the crew member. I look at my watch. The call with the Stockholm client is at 9.30am and I can't miss it.

242

A raised voice further along the carriage expresses anger and disgust that Traincom has caused her to miss a flight to Milan. A quieter voice says something, and the raised voice says it doesn't care how badly hurt anyone is. Another quiet response. It must be reassurance because the complaints stop.

The carriage is a little noisier. People are on their phones announcing a delayed arrival. One or two swear.

Jules is back and I tell her the pain has become more like a sting. When I touch the scalded area it hurts, but I feel it's time to put on a shirt. I tell her I need to make a phone call and she says it's fine but keep it brief. I call Annabel and tell her what's happened. She tells me to go hospital and then go home. She seems genuinely shocked when I tell her I want to do the client call. Her voice is vaguely affectionate when she tells me not to be ridiculous.

I call Beth and Joe too but get voicemails. I tell them I'm all right.

I don't know who else I should call. Work and family. Two calls. That can't be the sum total of those who might care. Should I put something on SocMed?

The police officer gets back and wants to interview me, but now the ambulance crew has arrived and want to get me off the train. I say I was looking out of the window and saw nothing, and I've no idea why someone would assault me. Dissatisfied, he says he'll see me later. Finally, he tells me he needs to keep my shirt.

Jules is back tending the crew member.

They put a shawl of some kind over me, then guide me from the train and through the concourse to a waiting ambulance. I sense eyes on me and whispers as I pass. As I climb in to the ambulance, another one pulls up.

It takes no time to reach Warrington Hospital and not much longer for me to be seen by a doctor. The scald is worse on my jaw line and down the line of my carotid artery. The doctor shakes her head a few times when I tell her what I recall about the incident. She tells me the scald isn't blistered so there's no risk of any scarring or long-term wound. I'm told to take pain relief and to avoid wearing anything with abrasive material and categorically no jewellery anywhere near the scald. Then a nurse comes in and applies some gel and a dressing then helps me to carefully pull on a fresh shirt and my jacket.

A taxi drops me at Warrington station where I meet the transport police officer and give my statement.

I eventually climb on to a train back to Lancaster and spend the whole journey staring, oblivious, from the window. When I alight the train, I'm in a bad way and some kind of autopilot makes me walk from the station to my apartment. When I get there, I stand at the communal door wondering how I get inside. I put my bag down and pat my pockets. I need keys, but don't seem to have any. Why aren't they in my pocket?

They're in my bag.

I'm soon inside the lobby, and then into my apartment. As I close the door, I realise I've forgotten something. What is it? I look around me and feel for my bag again. It isn't over my shoulder. I've left it outside.

Back inside, safe at last, I look around my hallway then conduct a meek, anxious search of each room. I find nothing. It really is a safe place.

Eventually I switch on my laptop and log in, then message Annabel to let her know the latest. She tells me off for being online, then calls me to tell me that in person. I tell her I'll be all right for tomorrow's calls, but she says she's on standby to cover me and will assume I won't attend. By mid-afternoon I'm sitting in my home office shaking with shock and apprehension.

I go to bed.

Beth is calling and messaging me constantly to ask if I'm okay. She doesn't seem convinced, even when I tell her I'm safe in my own bed.

I get a call the following morning from the police, telling me that the CCTV footage has provided evidence that my attacker joined the train at Wigan and was clearly carrying an insulated travel mug. He was on camera walking along my carriage and unscrewing the lid before hurling the contents at me. They have a clear image of his face, and an arrest warrant is in place.

By lunchtime I feel reasonably normal and the scalding has become nothing worse than a minor soreness. There's a visible patch of red though and when I pop out, to pick up some food and essentials from the shops, I wear a polo neck to hide it. That makes it hurt again.

Jude sends me a short message: 'Headed home now.' I want to tell her what's happened but realise it's not something with which I can burden her ahead of her long journey. The kids keep checking in on me, then I get a message from Luke saying I've made the local news and am I all right? Victoria calls me with the same news, and we talk at length about what happened. Unlike everyone else she seems most concerned about my welfare, rather than the attacker's motives and what I've done to cause the attack.

She's in York again, or she'd be round to nurse me. That feels warming yet sad.

For the rest of that day, I try to focus on bits and pieces of work and it's distracting to an extent. I really want some company but don't want to ask anyone for help.

I get up early the next day, intending to make it a fully productive one. I've a growing sense that I am and will be all right, but that relief is dissipated just after lunch when I hear keys at my front door. Jude is standing in my hallway with tears streaming down her face. She declines the offer of a hug. A small kiss on the cheek and a stroke of my hair are the only intimacy we share. When she comments on my discoloured face and neck, I have to tell her what happened and it makes her distressed and tearful again, but her care for me remains verbal. At her insistence, we remain in the hallway.

'I'm not going to stay here. Right up until Monday, I was looking forward to being in your arms, in your bed and feeling you near me. But something, I don't know what it is, has clicked inside me.'

'How do you mean?'

'It's like my disloyalty is suddenly a huge burden. Sitting in rooms and churches; standing beside graves; it's made me sense that, for all that I feel for you, I need to focus some care and maybe some love on my husband and our family.'

'I get that.'

'No Teddy. I don't think you do. It's not just a few days of contemplation and then back into your clutches. We need to cool off for a sensible period. Like weeks; months.'

'But why?'

'Because I can't keep wanting you and feeling great waves of guilt and sadness whenever I think of you. My husband needs me to give him some love and support.'

'He's always needed that Jude; and you decided not to give it.'

'I didn't know he needed it. He was all Business as Usual. I had no time with him. Not until we had these trips to Scotland.'

'So you're saying we're finished?'

'I'm saying we have to take a break. And learn whether or not we can cope with a break. I certainly can't cope with the distraction of you.'

'I don't want us to part. But if you need the time then take it.' I shrug.

At last she smiles. 'You don't know how much this hurts. I don't want Craig in me, holding me, kissing me. I need that to be you. But I have to be at his side, showing him that I'm there for him and his parents and his nephews and niece. And Freya.'

I take a step towards her, but she backs away.

'Teddy; don't. We can't. I will weaken if you touch me. I'm going to go.' She holds out a ring with two keys. 'Here; I shouldn't have these anymore.' When I don't take them from her, she places them on the hall table.

As she closes the door, I conclude that I might not see her again. She doesn't even message me with a parting shot.

All the corporate things I need to do become ignored. I take the occasional look at my emails and schedule of appointments and decide I can't be bothered. Annabel has mailed me, copied to a whole posse of others, expressing concern about my wellbeing and thanking me for going above and beyond at what must have been a difficult time. Her boss Peter has weighed in, telling me to take time out if I need it. I tell Annabel I'm going to sign off for the rest of the day but might work tomorrow. She tells me to take all the time I need.

Victoria messages me: 'Hey. Can I call?'

I call her.

'Are you okay?'

'I'm feeling a bit edgy but will be fine.'

'You sound a little weird.'

'Really? How?'

'Like someone who's had bad news. Wish I could come and give you some company.'

I don't tell her, but I really want that too. Instead I meekly suggest we catch up tomorrow.

'Will be stuck here until late again, sorry. Saturday could be good. But I think by then it will be too late. I think you need some TLC right now.'

I tell her I'm fine, have stopped work and intend to have another early night, accompanied by a sleeping pill. She tells me to be careful.

'It's only herbal.'

'Best not to. Are you working tomorrow?'

'My boss told me to take time off if I need it. But I'll probably work.'

'You should take their advice. But I suspect you don't like advice.'

I giggle and she giggles too.

'Thanks Victoria. It's good of you to check up on me. I'll be fine. Why don't we catch up tomorrow for a drink?'

'I already said I'm not around tomorrow. You're not all right, are you?'

'I meant Saturday. Sorry.'

We agree to talk in the morning and to meet for dinner on Saturday evening. I take one of my herbal sleeping pills then, a few moments later, a second. Two is safe and they do their job.

Luke calls me as I'm closing down for another week.

'Mr C. I'm outside in my car. Come and have an end of week pint or two with me. Not a late one.'

'I'm not decent.'

'I'll give you five minutes, then my offer ends.'

I don't want to drink, but I like the idea of some company and Luke's all I've got. When I get in his Range Rover, he smiles and strokes my shoulder.

'You okay?'

'I have been better Mr C.'

'Then we need proper beer. I know just the place.'

It was the pub where we drank as kids. Externally it isn't substantially different today than in 1990 when, as cocky underage drinkers, we started having the odd pint there.

Luke gets a round in. He says he'll risk a pint. Within a couple of sips, I realise I actually do want to drink and might end up having too much.

'Have you recovered from your ordeal?'

'I think so.'

'Any news from the police?'

'They've told me the guy they're after isn't known to them and no positive ID has been made. Seems he dashed from the train and out into the depths of Warrington, never to be seen again.'

'The local news said you were shaken but unhurt.'

'It hurt a lot.'

'It looks nasty Mr C.' He's staring at my wound. 'Is the official view that this was a random act?'

'The transport police told me they thought it was exactly that.'

'Aside from this assault on the train, is anything else wrong?'

He hasn't touched his pint. I've finished about two thirds of mine.

'I'm all right. And work really is busy.'

'You're always busy Mr C but it's never worried me before.'

'Why are you worried?'

Now he takes a mouthful of beer and keeps hold of his glass while he swallows it, as if planning a hasty follow-on slurp.

'Some of your posts on SocMed have been pretty edgy recently.'

'Edgy?'

'Maybe *downright weird* a better term.'

I finish my pint. We've been in the pub less than ten minutes. I stand to get another round, but Luke won't let me go.

'Stay here for a bit. You've unfriended a few people. Why is that?'

'How do you know that? Is it any of your business?'

'It is my business when a mutual friend is concerned and upset about why you've ditched them.'

I'd got really fed up with Will Peacock, another old school friend of ours now living in northern France. He just seemed to keep posting completely pointless things, mainly about items of news, and it all seemed so repetitive. Before that, I'd fallen into a pattern of becoming incensed by some of what friends were posting. So, irrational and subjective, I started unfollowing people to avoid seeing their bullshit. But when I lost it with Will and unfriended him, it felt like a hit; like something powerful and decisive. It led to me starting a cull.

'Is Will the only one?'

I try a smile as I reply, 'He had to go.'

'This isn't funny Ted. Some of your latest posts have been obtuse to the point of embarrassment. And a few people have told me you're the same on Chattabox. You've always been a bit full-on but just recently it's like you're not entirely in control.'

'Can we get another drink?'

He looks angry and stands up. 'I'm not having one. And if you can't cope with me challenging you like this maybe I'll just go.'

I tell him to sit down and wait while I get a drink. He still looks angry but does as I ask. I get us both a pint, even though I know he doesn't want a second. When I turn back to the table, he's sitting there stabbing fingers and thumbs onto his phone screen. He holds up a hand to indicate I shouldn't speak. I drink half my pint in two mouthfuls. When he finishes whatever he was typing, he slams his phone down on the table.

'Problem?'

'I've always got problems Mr C. And work is a constant niggle right now. I really will need to go soon. Sorry I lost it just now.'

'It's fine.'

'If you don't want to tell me whatever is wrong, that's also fine. But I am offering to listen to your woes and help if I can.'

'Well that's good of you. And there's nothing to worry about.'

'Are you lonely? Is it because you're single?'

'I've been lonely and single for four years Mr C and have developed numerous sensible coping strategies. Why would you suddenly express concern about it now?'

'Don't turn this around on to me Mr C. I'm trying to understand why your habitually benign and measured behaviour seems to have been replaced by something erratic and perverse.'

He isn't being brushed aside with denials and I don't know what to say to him to stop his inquiry. I appreciate his concern, but don't want to open the Pandora's Box of my recent experience. Then, just as I'm getting desperate about what I could deploy as a cause and effect, Luke's phone rings and he erupts in to smiles.

'It's Pippa. Hello you. Good day?'

I finish my second pint and make a start on the one I bought for Luke. He is oblivious. I sit through ten minutes of half a loved-up conversation, then he stands and says 'Yes, I'm leaving now hun. Need to drop Teddy back at home... hold on babe. Mr C - are you okay if I leave you to make your own way home? Pippa's expecting me.'

I raise my glass to him and without another word he walks out of the pub, his phone pressed between his ear and shoulder as he tries to get his jacket on.

On balance, being left to fend for myself is a good escape from Luke's interrogation. I have another pint to celebrate, then call a taxi. When I get home, it's only a little after eight but I switch off all my devices and switch on the television to gawp at its easy virtues.

It's not the first Friday night without Jude in my home, but it feels empty and sad when I go to bed alone. As I drift off to sleep, I compose a message to her in my head asking her what's changed. When I wake up, briefly, I've forgotten whatever words I'd used. Then later I'm awake again and concerned about Luke's lecture and my inability to simply tell him that I'm behaving oddly because I'm in an odd situation. Sleep returns and I'm dragged around some dreams that leave me bruised by their harshness. At four in the morning I wake again and after an hour of tossing and turning I decide I might as well get up and see what I've been missing in the big wide world.

There's a half dozen missed calls from Beth, who followed up with increasingly frantic written messages. There are also three missed calls from Victoria. I send Beth a reassuring text and say I just needed to zone out for an evening. Joe too has been in touch but mainly because Beth's been bugging him, and he wants me to get her to back off. I clear about thirty work emails either with answers or sidesteps. On SocMed there is nothing from friends, but I've become a punch ball in the road groups. Some of the abuse written to me and about me is extraordinary and after reading all that for ten minutes or so I can't take much more and drop out. It's even worse on Chattabox, where there are messages telling me I'm going to burn. One particularly chilling one says, '&tedgranclay where chocolate failed acid will deliver'. There's a constant reference to being burned. It's horrible, and as I read through this catalogue of intimidation and odium, I begin to feel that I can't stand it any longer.

I Peep: 'That's the end of this for me. I appreciate all your words.'

Then I log off.

Victoria sent me a single message, just before midnight: 'I've just got back. Been calling. Hmmm. Why aren't you picking up?'

It's still not six am. I make tea and head back to bed with my iPad, intending to watch something on Netflix that might lull me back to sleep. But instead the tea makes me alert and I start trying to draft the message I want to send to Jude.

'Hey, how come you're ignoring me?'

It's Victoria. She sent the final message of my yesterday, and first of my today.

'What are you doing awake at this time?'

'Back from running and just seen that you read my message.'

'Not ignoring you.'

'Are you recovered now from Tuesday?'

'I think so. Bit sore. I closed everything down last night and tried to just rest and sleep.'

'Decent plan. Still fancy catching up today?'

'Sure.'

'Talk later. We can arrange something then. I'm way too sweaty now. xx.'

24

When I get to the hospice late on Sunday afternoon, I'm struggling with a growing attraction for Victoria. We've met twice this weekend - dinner yesterday and earlier today for brunch. Neither was supposed to be a date, but both ended with kisses. Yesterday evening's was like an unstoppable force. From an initially tentative brush of cheeks, it seemed we both wanted to taste more. It went no further, and during a phone call this morning I felt that Victoria seemed reticent; as if she might be backing off.

But then she blurted out that she needed to see me and we ended up gazing at one another over neglected plates of food. When we left the pub she said we should meet again soon, but it won't be till Thursday. Something to look forward to, we agreed, and sealed it with a kiss.

This distraction leaves me oblivious to the sombre gloom and the lack of smiles as I'm greeted by one of the staff.

'Hello Teddy.' He seems on the verge of saying more but I interrupt with my own greeting. Then he continues.

'You'll be sad to hear that Mark Hodgson passed away in the early hours of Saturday. He was increasingly unwell and struggling to breathe all week, and on Friday he slipped into a coma.'

I am blinking and slack jawed. Why didn't they tell me?

'His son and daughter-in-law were with him at the end.'

'He was a lovely guy.'

As I stand in the small kitchen with a kettle boiling noisily beside me, I look through into the seating area and conservatory where I'd met Mark. We wouldn't have connected in any way if he hadn't been terminally ill, yet now that makes me feel that our encounter had more value than most. In this place; this oasis of peace and of incalculable humanity; where the rules and processes governing life and death are set aside; where the innate sadness is like faith; like succour; here, the briefest association with a dying man had seemed to have a kind of longevity. After I'd left my hand-written note that day, Mark got one of the staff to reply. It was succinct, with thanks; a request for another book to read; and that my tea was perfectly made so the last few drops of syrupy sweetness made the tannic bitterness of what preceded it more bearable.

Poor Mark. I find myself wondering if, in their final days and hours together, he found any kind of peace with his son; reconciliation; a bond.

The kettle's roar suddenly stops with a click and halts my reverie. I make a pot of tea and some instant coffee in a jug.

'Is there some tea available please?'

'Just made a pot. How do you take it?'

'White, no sugar please.'

The man seems unable to sustain eye contact, as if he can't show me whatever sadness he's feeling. I expect him to wander away when I hand him his tea, but he remains next to the large counter where tea and sympathy are dispensed.

'You okay?'

'My brother is here. For now. He has stomach cancer and doesn't have long.'

'I'm sorry. Do you want a snack or something? I've got biscuits?'

'No thanks.'

He remains there, grasping the mug between both hands with its handle facing me.

'What do you do here?'

'I'm a volunteer. I try to come in once a week and help. If I'm needed.'

'Once Charles is gone, I might do the same. I'd never been in a hospice before. There's almost a kind of hope here isn't there? Despite the fact that it's the end and you won't leave through the same door that you arrive. Sorry, I'm sure that's poor grammar or syntax or something.'

I offer him more tea, but he shakes his head.

'I better go and give my brother his dinner. Thanks for the brew. Good tea.'

He gives me a small smile, little more than a fleeting movement of his mouth. I don't have time to reflect on the man's words as, suddenly, there's a rush of requests for drinks and I need to distribute what I've already made, then make more.

'Why don't you get a fukin job you twat?'

It's started early this week. And it's still a mashup of polluted knowledge. The individuals spewing out their distaste for whatever I do or don't believe, or say and do, tend to pick and choose what I am depending on the time of day. Right now, I'm a protestor in a smock with a stalk of straw in my mouth. It won't be long before the theme changes to fit different facts.

'I do have a job.'

'Scrounging benefits isn't work.'

'I don't claim anything and never have, even when I was entitled to.'

'Your all the same. Stopping decent people from making money.'

'That's *You're all the same*. Which decent people?'

'All of us. Hard working families doing their best.'

'I work hard every day. For my family's sake.'

'But you'll be there at some point stopping progress. With your other flat earth wankers.'

'I'll be at work all today and all this week.'

'What do you do? Something really useful I bet. Like a fukin social worker or something.'

'Why do you misspell fucking but not wanker? What are you afraid of?'

There's a pause for several minutes so I get out of bed and make some tea and a bowl of porridge.

'How come you oppose this road but drive a car?'

'How do you know I drive a car?'

'Everyone drives a car.'

'I do have a great car. And I don't oppose the road.'

'Get a proper job and stop scrounging benefits you bastard.'

'My job pays me around eighty grand and I drive a really nice, really fast car. I live in a smart place worth a fortune.'

This causes some base insults and accusations of being a serial liar. Then the two people who've been sneering and snorting at me are joined by a new voice.

'Then you're a class traitor.'

'To which class?'

'US. The fukin working class. People who work and pay their taxes.'

'I'm not working class and I pay a lot of tax.'

'You're still a traitor, and traitors get hung.'

'Hanged.'

'Think your clever don't u? That smug smile will get wiped off your face soon.'

'I'm not smiling but yes I do think I'm clever. I went to university and got a degree.'

'Like all your other scummy socialist twat friends.'

'I vote Conservative. And always have. Don't you know anything about me?'

'I know plenty about you Teddy boy.'

And now they start talking amongst themselves, as if in a restroom and they don't realise I'm there on the toilet, behind a closed locked cubicle door.

'Tories don't vote against real things.'

'I know. He's lying. Anyone can make up shit about how they vote.'

'He is a liar, and he's a traitor to us all.'

'Yep. And he's going to get what's coming. To his flashy place in Lancaster and his kids in Bath and Leicester. And while he's on the streets in London.'

'If I see him at any of the sites, he's dead.'

Holy shit.

Jenny Donovan messages me as I'm working on an update for Annabel to present at the global team's month end meeting later in the week. It's also quarter- and year-end so there's more to gather and include. I'm working hard but have this sense of foreboding about some of the things those people wrote yesterday. My journey earlier this morning, especially in the crowded areas at Euston and in the underground, was deeply disturbing. I felt at risk; menaced; a target. I found myself staring around me like a fugitive. I'm guilty of nothing, yet those four hours in transit left me troubled by the sense that I am a criminal.

When I reached the office, I called Beth and Joe three or four times each, but neither answered. I left messages telling them to call me and to take care.

'Hi. Are you in London now?'

My sense of being in danger is heightened. I think about ignoring her. Is she really an ally? Someone I should trust and confide in?

'Hello. Yes, I'm here.'

'What is the nearest tube to your office?'

'Moorgate or St. Pauls.'

'Can we meet later?'

I look at my diary. I've time free between three and five. I could block it out.

'Do you mean this evening?'

'No, I mean mid-afternoon. After 2 before 4.'

'I could be somewhere from around 3.15.'

'Perfect. Meet me in the Paternoster. It's near St. Pauls tube.'

'I know it. Nice boozer. What time?'

'I'll be there from three. Any problems, let me know by 1.30 latest ok?'

'No problem. See you there.'

What if someone has hacked her and those messages are from someone who means me harm? I don't even know what she looks like. Her profile has a symbol, not a photograph.

The pub is busy and when I peer through the large glass windows, I don't see any unaccompanied women among the suits. But I don't know what I'm looking for. I have no compass about Jenny and what she might be. I think I should turn around and walk away. But as I move across the threshold, I don't feel dozens of pairs of eyes turning on me, so I push my way through to the bar where I order a shandy and some salted peanuts. As I'm taking delivery of the latter a voice says: 'Hello. I'll have whatever you're having.'

She's medium height and quite slight; mid-fifties with dark hair that sits just above her shoulders. It looks quite well-groomed. Her business suit and laptop bag blend well in this setting.

'Lager or bitter shandy?'

'Oh; bitter, I think. Young's as a preference please.'

The bartender nods and starts preparing this mix. Jenny stretches out a hand: 'Good to meet you. Thanks for agreeing to see me.'

'Nuts? Crisps?'

'No. Thank you. Let's find a table.'

'When we get there, I'd like some assurance that you're who you say you are please.'

'That makes sense and I'll give it. But please don't worry.'

It takes a few minutes but eventually I see a group leaving their seats which we grab in haste. Without saying a word, she holds up her phone and hits the button for her messaging app. She shows me the conversation we had earlier. Then she quits and goes to her settings page and there is her name and a photo of her, smiling and effusive.

'Is that enough? Are you satisfied it's me?'

'Yes, I guess so. How come you use the symbol on your SocMed and messaging profiles?'

'It's symbolic. Many more nasties being thrown at you yesterday.'

'It was difficult.'

'The stuff about where you live and your kids: it's easy for me to say this, but it's just bluffing.'

'It shocked me. I spent most of my trip down here feeling like some sort of renegade.'

She takes a long drink from her pint. 'As I said; try not to see these threats as having any substance. Those people aren't dangerous. The really dangerous ones are probably plotting to kill politicians or journalists; but I doubt you're on their list.' Jenny has an accent I can't place. She's not a Londoner, for sure. But nor is there a midland or northern timbre. It doesn't help that she speaks in a monotone.

'Some of those posts were almost too much. I tried to be calm, but it was hard. What do these people think they are achieving?'

'I doubt any of them ever thinks.' She smiles indulgently at me. 'Unlike you.'

'Yesterday left me thinking I'm really not up for this.'

She's still smiling. 'Up for what?'

I start to speak, then realise I can't answer.

'You don't have to respond to these posts you know. To any of it. You might have noticed that it's only when you prolong your participation that the sewage rises up and overflows. But let's not dwell on your impotent battles and how to handle them. I'm curious about you, and why you've suddenly appeared on the relief road scene. What are you hoping to achieve?'

I tell her we've covered this in our various messages, but she asks me to restate where I'm coming from, as if it's for the record. She maintains steady eye contact but behind their soft brown facade there is a harsh, condemnatory undertone; like I see on the faces at business meetings when things aren't going well. I sense that I'm going to be confronted with something. Blame, perhaps?

So I repeat what I've already told her; that I appeared on the scene because I want to get to the bottom of why I was threatened; that I want to try to find a way to stop power being abused; that I want to unmask all the craven faces creating fear and alarm from behind their disguises.

Jenny nods as I say this. 'That sounds like a politician's speech. Rehearsed and polished.'

'What? Why?'

'Above all because it sounds evasive.'

'It isn't. It's the truth.'

She nods some more, her lower lip sticking out.

'Well okay, sure; if you say so. It's the truth then: your approach to me and giving me those photos aren't about engagement in the issues. You just want to wring some necks. To right wrongs.'

It's time to defend myself. 'I am engaging in the issues.'

'No. You're not. Because you're wearing a mask too.'

I don't agree with her and want to haggle, but she's got me confused and hesitant, like I'm not really sure about what I want.

'You're part of the problem Teddy. May I call you Teddy? Another middle class, well-off prick who wants his tummy tickled for dabbling in things he can't understand, no matter how hard he tries. You'll never be part of any concerted opposition to anything because you're too embedded in the corporate self-interest that makes all these things possible. Like a tiny rabbit staring fearfully into the juggernaut's headlights, knowing it means harm but also knowing you are just about fast enough on your feet to dash away.'

'So you're saying I'm not allowed to care.'

'I'm saying you don't have what it takes to care. You're too unsafe in your outlook to understand protest. Your replies to some of the haters yesterday said it all. You couldn't resist listing your material gains and your well-paid job. You might as well have mentioned the thousands of pounds you pissed away on school fees too. It was like teenage bragging rights after a football derby.'

My desire to question how she knows I paid school fees is relegated down the leagues. I need to correct her view of me. 'I wanted to shut them up. They said I'm a jobless waster.'

'They did, but that's just standard rhetoric. They look at any protest and blame the jobless because they assume you've got no job if you aren't sitting at a desk all day being fed scraps by a benevolent employer, like they are. They probably spend a high proportion of their working day spewing out complaints amongst their co-workers about how vile their manager is. Or the company's owner. Or whatever. It's a safe place in this country. You love your soap operas.'

Her use of *co-worker* helps me place the accent. She isn't from anywhere in England or the British Isles. She's from the United States; or Canada.

'There's a long list of demons for them: jobless; the gays; pensioners; vegans; the god-squad. Immigrants - a given. And on and on; you name it. Basically, anyone who doesn't fit an identikit photo of the safe, everyday person in the office or factory or street.' She looks around the bar; 'Or pub. And as you discovered yesterday, there's a whole class argument too. A very, very strange class argument.'

'Yes. What's all that about? This thing about class treachery?'

'Another example of them using an extreme accusation to embellish an essentially schoolyard piece of abuse. It's funny really. You're being vilified as a traitor to something that doesn't exist: a brotherhood of workers. Thirty or more years after your Trades Unions were battered into non-existence, to the delight of millions, there now appears to be a body of people who thrive on being in a collective. So ironic.'

I blink as I try to absorb this statement. I can't, so I change the subject. 'How do they know so much about me?'

'Because you tell them.'

'What, because I use social media?'

'You do. And you don't guard your own back while you're using it.'

'That doesn't help anyone know where I live and where my kids are.'

'They don't know your address and post code Teddy. But your assorted profiles say *Lancaster* and *Kids at Uni* and *Here I am on the train again*. That's the beginning and end of all they know about you. It's not much, but in the hands of well-motivated bullies, it's a motherlode. Enough for someone to find you on a train.'

She watches me as I tip a few peanuts into my hand, then toss them into my mouth. It's the way my mum used to look at me before telling me how bad those are for me.

'The people you've encountered aren't the ones you should worry about.'

'Why? Because they speak up?'

'Yes. They are foot soldiers. And to protract the military metaphor awhile, they are sent in to battle without weapons by generals and majors you'll never hear from.'

'Like Marcus Mapplewick?'

Jenny looks at me and squints. 'He's more of a lance corporal. Stripes on his arm to set him above the troops who don't realise he hates them now he's risen above their kind. He's gathered around him an assortment of possessions and assumes everyone's looking when he displays them, like peacock feathers. But he's isolated by his own lack of real authority. Vaguely dangerous, but easy to control because of his ego. And because of his insecurity. The reaction to your photos was a massively apprehensive act, confirmation that the email was sent and received.'

'You seem to know him well.'

'I know him well enough. In fact, I've met him - a pleasure which I genuinely hope you never share. Why are you frowning?'

My confusion is turning to frustration with the growing list of things I can't explain. I change tack. 'You're not the only one that's curious. I'm struggling to understand why you wanted to meet me. I can't work out if I'm getting a warning or a medal.'

'Neither. I just need to know where you really sit in amongst all these demons. And I need to know if you're just another plant. And because you could say it's my job.'

'Whose demons? Your side's? Or theirs? Assuming your side sinks so low as to bestow demonhood.'

'Well that isn't a word. But I get your meaning and yes, bloody right we do.'

'Then it's just a... what was your phrase? Pissing match?'

'No. There's a chasm between the sides where demons are concerned. What you encounter each day is a small but well organised troupe, tip-tapping their contempt into a bucket. As a form of debate, it's broadly the equivalent of being a sperm donor. Pleasurable, but not really for your own good.'

I splutter and cough as a welling laugh meets a swallowed mouthful of nuts.

'What's so funny?'

It takes me a while to recover, helped by a few gulps of beer.

'That was funny; your debating analogy.'

'Thank you. Glad you got it.'

'Tell me why they aren't dangerous.'

'Because of their hypocrisy. For starters they will wear their Law-Abiding Citizen badges with great pride, while quietly ignoring laws that irritate them. They quite probably have unemployed friends, pensioner parents, a Sikh workmate, the odd dyke somewhere in the mix. A vegan kid. A disabled aunt. They like the demons in their camp and give them love and support. But the demons in the opposition camp are there to be despised, because these people just love the idea of having something to hate. They just oppose opposition.'

'Which is all you do. Isn't it?'

'Yes; and no.'

'You can't sit on the fence on that one, surely?'

'Well we have our foot soldiers - it's true - and they do their share of loathing and contempt.'

'It's an imperfect world.'

She hasn't smiled much for a while, but now she positively scowls. 'Don't spend time looking for honour and the milk of human kindness. You fight fire with fire.'

'So the chasm is?'

'Our demons have actual entities with a proven case to answer; we challenge them with facts and science, not insults; and with evidence, not liability. The name-callers and hissy-fit mob you've come up against just pick (or have picked for them) whatever group it suits them to blame; and blames it.'

'Like you blaming me for being a corporate monkey? Or the establishment for its complicity? Or for my belief in the power of wealth creation?'

'Yes. Why not?'

'Because you're no more right than they are.'

She lets out a small laugh. 'Right? This isn't about being right or wrong. There's no right and wrong anymore - for that matter there's no right and left either. There's just unreliable; and unimpeachable.'

I must look dumbfounded, because she asks: 'Perhaps I'm going too quickly for you? Look Teddy, take a step back: I'm here to prevent you making a complete and utter cunt of yourself.'

'Am I supposed to be shocked by that?'

'By me saying *cunt*?'

'Yes.'

'It's just a word. And if you're offended then you've given me a clue about some of what I need to know. While I go and get us both another shandy, have a think about why you agreed to meet me and what you intend to do next to dig yourself out of the hole you think you're in.'

While she's gone, I look around the Paternoster and its charming wood and leather décor. Our Father... mislead us not...

I look at the laptop bag hanging from the back of her chair. Its name tag is turned away from me and I wonder about looking at it to see if it tells me more; she won't be able to see me if I do it quickly.

'I got you more nuts since you seem to like them so much. Here's your pint. Did you learn anything from your sneaky peek at my case?'

'That your name really is Jenny Donovan.'

'The name on my bag tag is Jenny Donovan; true. Tell me why you really got in touch with me and agreed to meet me.'

I repeat it all: that I'd sought her out on SocMed; I saw her saying things that appeared to be balanced and factual; I felt she could explain the inexplicable and rectify some of the wrongs I'd been confronted by.

'I didn't think you were necessarily one of the good guys. But I thought you might be good enough to listen, then help me learn.'

As before, she's watching me closely during this soliloquy, eyes hardening then set.

'You're saying you wanted to give me the ammunition to fight something you yourself won't fight.'

'No. I wanted to show you something that I believe affirms my credentials as a potential ally.'

There's another squint.

'Well I suppose I can accept that. But... you're in the wrong place. You should back off. Go home and kill your SocMed and Chattabox accounts. You really don't know what you're doing or what you're trying to fight. That makes you a threat to yourself and others.'

'I left Chattabox over the weekend.'

'Good. Keep off it: it's a despicable wasp factory, and you know it. Give it a month or two, then rejoin SocMed and reconnect with the people who matter most. And for fuck's sake stay away from internet dating sites. I'd say you're better than that. Go back to what you desperately want: that veneer of respectability on your ever so slightly rebellious soul. Don't see it as a defeat, just a tactical withdrawal. Take a holiday or go ask your boss if you can work in another country for a bit. Invisible Idiot.'

'What?'

'Never heard that?'

'No.'

'Invisible Idiot. The response of an allegedly all-powerful computer, back in the day, when asked to define the phrase *Out of Sight, Out of Mind*.'

'Very good.'

'It's a very old joke. Destroy the photos you have from the train that day, and all your messages with me in which we discussed them. If your posse of haters can claim they're fake, then so can you. Walk away from it all. Don't reconnect with me. You're not in this to stop the road being built. And you don't actually care about it, do you?'

'Why should I care about it?'

'Exactly. What you've become involved in is nothing to do with the creation of an ecological disaster for wildlife and the environment. You're just lashing out at something peripheral, your own little cage rattle. It's touching in its way that you reached out to me and sought some solace. But that's all you wanted. Peace of mind. A binky.'

'A what?'

'A pacifier. A dummy - is what you call it over here. It's such a telling word.'

The pub is starting to fill up with a group of noisy celebrants who, from their happy sounds, seem to have won a deal of some kind. It would be irritating if Jenny and I were intimate, but it makes it easier to say what is brewing.

She asks, 'Tell me; do you know who Foxy is? From the pictures?'

'No. Do you?'

She nods. 'Keep it that way. You don't want to know.'

'Can you stop the road being completed? I don't see how you can. All you're holding up is the day to day lives of the people in and around the construction sites. With your protests, lying in the road, stopping transport and families getting to school and work. And your love-in singalongs; who cares?'

Jenny looks at me with another admonishing smile.

'I think you've been overexposed to the pro-roaders. You sound like one of them.'

'Maybe I am.'

'No. You're too charming and kind. And riddled with doubt.'

'Flattery will get you nowhere.'

'It wasn't flattery; I don't do flattery; it was actually the opposite. Like I said earlier: stop wanting some Olde Worlde Charm to matter. It doesn't. It probably never has but categorically hasn't for at least six decades. Your kind heart and vaguely cute, disarming style bear no relation to what these fuckers and their celebrity mouthpieces aspire to. This road isn't being built because any of them wants it.'

My phone is on silent, but I feel a vibration in my pocket.

'Well what do they want?' As I say that I take out my phone and see it's a withheld number, which means it isn't work so I don't have to answer.

'They want a history none of them lived in; the sweet harmonious world that existed for us all before all those pesky demons spoiled it for regular people. The Good Old Days; Happier Times; when everyone drove an Alvis, loved the discipline of rationing and believed that National Service was a good thing but only for other people. Let's get back there, they say, before drugs and satire and hippies and political correctness. It's what they say, but it isn't what they mean or want. What they want is a voice; to have their say, and to be heard. No matter what they say. They want their safe, closeted world with houses, cars, pay rises and a mass of things that join them for as long as it suits them to be joined. To stop needing to claim victimhood and a permanent state of being disenfranchised. To shout down the doubters. And they want to take back power, grab control, to doff their caps at the Establishment and respect the powers that be - as if back then everyone was empowered, and anyone listened to them. If they looked beyond the end of those needs and wants, they'd probably see that they would endure a different kind of victimhood. One without any Establishment and a different set of controls. Maybe that doesn't matter because at least they'd be happy. Demon free.'

Another buzz from my pocket, then two more in succession. Someone is desperate to sell me something I don't need.

'And you think I want that too?'

She shrugs. 'You should be like that, because of your politics and status and lifestyle. But I'm not sure you are, and I can't quite figure the reasons for that.'

'Why did you say I'm full of doubt?'

'Because you're here with me, instead of aligning yourself unequivocally with the other camp.'

'That doesn't mean I agree with you.'

'But it does mean you might have a problem agreeing with them. Doubts work like that.'

'I have no doubt your protests can't stop that road. It will happen, so why should I care about it?'

'You know what? It's fine that you don't care. The road is little more than a folly. A huge display of dick waving by the great and mighty to piss off the tree huggers.'

I'm getting weary of her riddles, and the sense I'm being lectured.

'It's time I got back to the office.'

'And I to my evil machinations. I'm glad we met. Do as I suggest okay? Walk away from me now, and from the madness when you get back online.'

'I'm not sure I'm glad we met.'

'Did you think it was a date?'

'You're not my type.'

She throws back her head and laughs. I'm smiling too. It's the first emotion she's shown that might be genuine.

'I'm sure your type is ready and waiting and isn't a pain in the ass, full of piss and wind; like me.'

'How do you cope with it all? How can you advise me to walk away and keep taking the punches?'

'They can't get to me. I have an inside track to the people at the top of the pro-roaders. We meet often, over tea and cake. And if you quit now, they won't get to you either because, despite all the invective, you don't matter.'

As I walk back to the office, I see that Jude has called, and all the buzzing was caused by a voicemail alert and some messages from her.

First: 'I left you a voicemail.'

Then: 'Don't reply.'

Her voice is shaking with worry.

'Teddy, I'm absolutely certain Craig knows I've been having an affair. He might also know it was with you. We cannot be in touch anymore. I'm sorry. I'm so sorry. Goodbye Teddy.'

The last two words are thick with emotion and what sounds like tears.

Part Three

Lines Blurred

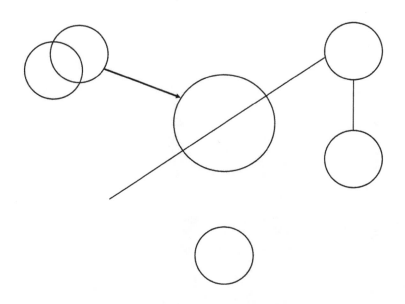

25

I feel like I've been disposed of again.

Jude and I knew it couldn't last forever, and there was always this certainty she would never leave her husband to be with me. But I still feel hurt and fractured and I frame an internal argument in which Jude has broken a code by making our end unilateral. I thought the idea was that, when it happened, it would be an understated, unanimous closure. We'd walk off in opposite directions, looking for a sunset or two.

And what about Victoria?

I can't decide if my gradual surrender to her should or would ever have happened if Jude hadn't begun to detach herself.

Despite the knowledge that we could never be a couple, I'd developed a state of mind in which Jude and I would be lovers forever with neither commitment nor complication. Yet, even though there was initially a hazily defined boundary and a degree of circumspection, I didn't ignore the chance presented by Victoria.

What a mess. Like a fuse with no bomb, my relationship with Jude was an entity lit at opposite ends to fizzle out with neither explosion nor damage.

We both broke the code.

I don't know who to tell about the end of a relationship that I couldn't share and should never have been in. I mull over the option to discuss it with Annabel but dismiss that on the grounds that it's a bad thing to share in a work environment: more tick boxes on the list of reasons that could get me kicked out; can't cope; unreliable; easily knocked off balance; dubious personal life.

I'm also desperate to talk to someone - anyone - about the descent into madness created by the street-fighting and rhetoric of my dalliance with what now seems like a potentially fake activism. This afternoon's meeting with Jenny Donovan has left me thinking that there was something counterfeit about her and much of what she said, although the advice about quitting SocMed was the best I've been given in months.

There's no abiding trauma from last week's assault. I'm not mentally scarred, perhaps because I can enclose the cause of it in a container marked *You Asked For It*. The police haven't updated me about their investigations. There is no pain on my face and neck. There's just a sense that it was a massive, incomprehensible overreaction. But to what?

And, as if that isn't enough, I need to find ways and strategies to help Beth and Joe cope with the implications of Amy being made redundant.

Once I'm back at my desk these problems are cords of preoccupation with which I must grapple to prevent them becoming knotted together into a noose. But, mainly, the mundane irrelevance of office life is the perfect distraction from distraction. There's not much of the day left, but my job keeps me busy well into the evening.

When I return to my hotel, the Work-Life-Balance pendulum swings back to red. I'm grateful, and always will be, that I don't ever drown my sorrows in alcohol. Otherwise it would be very tempting indeed to drink myself to a standstill and, in that dubiously contented state, inform the world of all my problems by packaging them in posts on SocMed or in messages. Instead, I order a simple meal from room service and try to engage with events on television. The overwhelmingly good news is that a new pound coin is now in use, its twelve sides apparently making it the most secure coin ever. I smile, then laugh, at the notion that money should need to be protected at a time when the security of life seems so equivocal.

Victoria is offline, but I decide to send a message. 'Hmmm. I've had better days.'

By the time I go to bed, just after midnight, she hasn't replied and remains offline, shown as *Active 7 hours ago.*

When I get up at six, Victoria's offline status has increased to thirteen hours. She uses SocMed but it's a minimalist thing; the odd post about day trips; photos of her nieces and nephew; the occasional news item, enveloped with disbelief or endorsement. Her last post was more than three weeks ago, just before we connected as friends.

But she uses messaging with alacrity, so I start to feel a needling worry that she hasn't been active for more than half a day.

It's the middle of the morning when her reply pops up on my lock screen.

'It can't have been any worse than mine.'

I'm in an interminable virtual mass meeting about the company's coming year-end. Listening to the country's leadership team as they declaim their PowerPoint slides, I've slipped through my habitual stages: committed attention; mild interest; sudden engagement; mild disinterest; committed diversion. Victoria's message finds me desperate for relief from the repetitious cajoling threats and bad news about finances.

'Hmmm. I don't want a fight about it.'

She sends a laugh out loud emoji and our conversation becomes littered with symbols and their ciphered subtext.

'If you'd been within spitting distance last night, I'd have been ready for a punch up. It would have been a proper release. What happened to you?'

I tell her to go first, but I kind of don't mean it.

'Aren't you at work?'

'Yes, but in what my company mysteriously calls a town hall.'

'I shudder to think what that means.'

'Tell me all your pain. <uses Frasier Crane voice> I'm listening.'

Victoria explains that she's been ditched by a client who won't explain why. She's done nothing wrong, but they aren't responding to questions.

'How much is the contract worth?'

'Best part of fuck all. It's utterly weird. And insulting.'

She keeps typing and whatever it is takes longer than the time it takes our finance lead to explain the content of a small graph showing how salaries have to remain flat until a few hundred more jobs are moved to countries with cheap labour. It will also mean redundancies.

'I'm really tempted to sue them for breach.'

'Can you cope with the lost revenue?'

'Easily. But they can't cope without my designs and ideas, which I still own.'

'How come?'

'Because I'm a shit-hot negotiator and because they've never read our contract properly. Are you still ok to chat?'

'Yes. Meeting has 40 mins to go.'

'Tell me about your bad day.'

'Easier face to face.'

The dancing dots do a hesitation waltz.

'Is this involvement related?'

'It might be.'

'Hmmm. When you home?'

'Tomorrow evening. About ten fifteen. PM.'

'Can you give me a hint?'

I know I need to tell her. 'Let's just say it's over.'

'Me or her?'

It doesn't feel like a time for frivolity. I don't reply and she soon goes back to inactive.

Once the meeting ends, the news about job cuts causes an outpouring of messages and mails; outrage and disbelief; resignation and foreboding. I should engage, take a responsible leadership stance and own the corporate hoopla. Instead, I slip quietly around it all and get on with the kind of task-based activity that isn't real work but keeps people thinking I'm productive. While I'm fiddling with spreadsheets and tools, directing traffic, tidying disorder, my mind is switched off from anything external and it does me good. But, whenever I breakaway from all that, I can't stop this thing welling up in my throat. I join meetings and talk normally, but in between times feel my eyes glazing over and my breath coming in gulps.

Annabel calls me and doesn't beat about the bush. 'Can you cope with regular trips overseas? I mean from a family perspective.'

She's been back from Sweden for a few days now, but I've not seen her at the office.

'You mean Stockholm?'

'No. Bucharest. Then Sofia.'

'How regular?'

'Weekly for four to six weeks. Stays of three nights max. Starting April seventeenth.'

When I pause, she quickly challenges me. 'What's up? Not like you to be tentative.'

'I'm just a bit surprised. The message I got from the town hall was that we are in a trough.'

'Are you in a private room?'

I tell her I'm in open plan. The call goes dead. She types, 'Find a private room and call me back.' It takes me less than five minutes.

'You heard or listened to the wrong message. But, regardless, I need you to get out there to recruit a team of up to ten people to replace the UK PM team.'

'Including me?'

'Of course not. Stop being obtuse. Change is coming and you will be running a new European Project Management org, with team leaders in both Romania and Bulgaria. The plan is to have both teams operational by May and you need to be in there from day one.'

She goes on to explain what this activity will save the company. It's an eye-watering amount of money but it means redundancy for people I have worked with for years.

'Is the wider business okay with this? Sometimes I pick up real animosity towards the Romania team.'

'Who cares? This is pure spreadsheet economics Ed. And it affects roles in almost every UK function. Ours is a relatively modest number.'

'How do we keep it quiet? Won't everyone guess I'm up to something?'

'No-one in Bucharest below VP knows what's happening yet. The UK team will be put at risk on April third; next Monday. All eight roles to be made redundant. I seriously don't think they'll notice you're not around. But anyone who kicks off will be side-lined and offered an enhanced package to shut up. None of that is your concern.'

I feel my throat swelling up again. None of my colleagues is a friend, not even a social acquaintance. But this is horrible.

'I know you were planning to be on holiday in the week after Easter, but can you work? Probably best if you travel out to Bucharest on the Tuesday afternoon and work there until the Friday.'

'It's the week before Easter I will be on holiday. It's Joe's birthday on Monday the tenth. I'm not letting him down.'

'I'm not asking you to. What are your plans?'

I outline the family weekend in Shropshire. 'But I can cancel the Tuesday to Thursday if it helps?'

'Yes please.'

'If everyone is being put at risk next Monday, why are we waiting a couple of weeks before I go to Romania?'

'Basically, to give HR and the local leadership time to continue trawling the local market and agencies for talent. Your job will be to lead the interviews and decision making about the shortlisted candidates. They'll all be good, we know that; you need to get us the very best and then shape them into a high-class operation.'

'Right.'

'I need to go. This is hugely confidential so keep it dark. Don't worry about the fallout when the At-Risk notices are sent. You've no part to play as a manager. And you will get an At-Risk notice too.'

'Probably just as well.'

'It is. Your role will be made redundant, but you will be the successful applicant for a new role as European Project Controller. You've got a lot of people in your corner Ed, so you'll be fine.'

'That sounds so dodgy. Is it legal?'

'A good barrister could drive a bus through it. But by the time everyone has accepted their packages, your new role won't even have been announced. You just need to hold your nerve, join in with the sob stories and make sure you one hundred per cent know what we need from whoever we recruit in Romania and Bulgaria.'

I'm logged out from SocMed and, with every second, I'm thankful for my decision to quit Chattabox. My finger keeps itching to touch that grey and orange button on my home screen, but I have enough courage left to avoid it, so I see no pain. Attempts to hit me with abuse by messaging are easily ignored, then curtailed by blocking, but no-one has tried in the last day or so. When I get to the hotel, I decide to just dump all my things in my room and head back down for a bar meal and a pint. I watch work emails skidding into my inbox, but none requires corrective steering.

Once I've had a pretty decent curry, I ask the bartender to bring me a coffee in about thirty minutes then take my second pint of lager to the sofas. By the time my coffee arrives, I've had quick calls with Joe and Beth. They were both busy, but I tell them I'd rather talk than message because they needed to know that my relationship with Jude is over. Although they'd never met her, they knew the bare essentials of what that relationship was.

Joe asks if I'm upset; I say that I've been better.

When I tell Beth that it's for the best, she ticks me off for an appalling cliché. But within a few minutes of our call finishing she sends me a message: 'I could hear in your voice how sad you are. You deserve to be happy, my lovely father. And now you can be.'

Then Joe sets up a group chat and writes: 'Hey old man Dad. Me and Beth will cheer you up when we see you at this posh hotel you've booked for us.'

Beth writes: 'Beth and I.'

All I can do is select smiley, then teary, then hearts for eyes emojis.

'You big soft bugger,' is Joe's response. Then he too tells me not to be sad. I finally find that I can type properly and tell them to stop worrying and go and have fun. Then it's kisses all round till they leave the group.

I order another coffee and ask for a slice of cheesecake.

Much later, Victoria sends me a message as I'm dozing off in bed with the television drip feeding me bits and pieces of nothing.

'You didn't answer my question.'

'And you didn't give me time. But I'm over it.'

'Why don't you come and have some supper at mine tomorrow? I'll get something simple ready and pick you up at the station.'

I send a thumbs up.

'You can't believe how much I've wanted some of your emojinal intelligence xxx'

'Very well played.'

'I've a busy day tomorrow so don't expect much contact. Phone or text when your train's left Preston. Are you working at home Friday?'

'Yes. But planning an early finish.'

'How come?'

'I've done no shopping or anything remotely domestic for ages. Need to fix that.'

'Are you all right?'

'I think so.'

'Tell me. Really. Come on.'

I want to talk to her face.

'I'll be all right. See you tomorrow. Hope you get some sleep.'

'Hmmm.'

A flurry of kisses and other signs ensue and those sustain me through the night and then another day at the office, where I find myself stuck in a rut.

The news Annabel spilled out yesterday has made me feel that I don't want to engage with my team, or at least with UK-based colleagues. But I can't completely ignore them, so it's a strain for me to retain equilibrium. I have to remind myself frequently that any burden I feel is nothing alongside what those people are about to face.

As an aside, messages start arriving from friends wondering why I've been so quiet on SocMed. I use a stock excuse that work is busy, and about to get busier; no need to worry. No-one digs deeper.

Work is low key all day, but busy, and I almost miss my habitual deadline to hit the streets and Moorgate tube. Somehow, I climb onto the train at Euston with time to spare. Work on some last gasp emails takes a few moments but the train is still stationary as I gaze out at the stark concrete grotto; it doesn't matter how many times I've seen it; it never changes; dismally grim; a place you want to leave.

I end up falling asleep in my cosy first class seat and miss all the free junk food and drinks. By the time the train departs Preston, I'm wide awake and catch up on some new incoming from work.

When I message Victoria, she replies: 'Come out onto Station Road. I'll be there.'

And she is.

As I stroll out with my bag, I see her leaning against an old Jaguar XKR. She smiles at me and as I get within a couple of metres, holds out an arm and drags me in to an embrace that I struggle to reciprocate. There's no kiss, and no whispered greeting. Just warm contact. It makes me purse my lips and blink a lot.

We disengage and say hello at last.

'We could have walked, couldn't we?'

'True. It's not far. I thought you'd be tired.'

'Thanks.'

'And I didn't fancy a walk in the dark.'

She starts the engine and it makes a growling accompaniment to our conversation. There's a reassuring smell of well-worn leather.

'I should have thought about that, shouldn't I?'

'Perhaps.'

In the deserted evening streets, it takes her less than five minutes to reach and pull into a driveway beside one of the townhouses on New Quay Road.

'You need to get out. The car only just fits in my garage.'

As soon as we walk in, I smell the food. Wondrous smells; like being on the sea front at Villefranche around lunch time.

'Are we having Bouillabaisse?'

'I really am that good, but not on a Thursday night. Similar flavours. Less work.'

She turns up the heat under a large ceramic skillet then takes off the lid. It's filled with vegetables and ochre liquid and, as it comes back to a simmer, she throws in some orzo. A plate with chunks of white fish, prawns and scallops, is ready to be added.

I'm still standing, holding my bag, a few feet behind her. She turns and laughs at me.

'You look like someone waiting for permission without knowing what will be authorised. Go back into the hall and leave your bag and that extraordinary jacket out there. Take your shoes off and come back in here.'

Working my way through these instructions, I hear her say: 'Actually Teddy, before you take your shoes off can you take this bin bag down to the wheelie bins? It's full of fishy bits and already stinks.'

When I get back, she's making last minute culinary embellishments but turns and walks to me. This time, I can fully engage in our hug.

'You okay?'

'I am. Thank you.'

She narrows her eyes and looks sidelong at me. 'I wish I was convinced by that statement. But I'm not. You will need to tell me more while we eat. Look in the fridge and you'll find a carafe with some iced tea. There are ice cubes in an old ice cream carton in the freezer - glasses there.' She points with her spatula at a face-high glass fronted cupboard. It doesn't seem to trouble her that flecks of goo from the spatula drip to the floor.

We're soon seated at a table near French windows that, in daylight, would offer a view over the Lune on its last stretch. Victoria spoons a helping of food into the large bowl in front of me then the same amount for herself. I pour drinks into the ice-laden tumblers.

'Hope you're all right with seafood and Provençal flavours. I'm a wannabe veggie and rarely eat meat. But I can't resist shellfish.'

I tell her I love them too.

'Then eat. It's amazing.'

'So's this drink. What is it?'

'It's earl grey tea with lemons and mint, and some honey to cut through all the acidity.'

We eat for a while in silence until I thank her for looking after me. She reaches a hand across and touches mine.

'I have a feeling you would do the same. But tell me what's happened. I'm a great listener.'

She already knows some of the basics, small shards of history about Jude's recent reticence and what caused it. But I wind back to the 2016 beer festival, and how we met that night. The febrile secrets that followed; an acquired target from both sides; courting by message; and a final meeting.

'This was your first meeting?'

'Yes; the only one in public. I suppose it was a date. But we'd been pretty full-on by text and the occasional phone call. We both knew where it was going.'

'Did you think it would have longevity?'

'I don't think I cared really.'

'So you were after sex?'

'I suppose that was a feature, yes. Then.'

She nods and moves food to her mouth, then chews. A raised eyebrow indicates I should continue.

'That night, we sat on my bed mapping out how we could remain lovers, safe from prying eyes and ears. I was away on business a lot, so was her husband; a useful starting point. We realised that we wouldn't and couldn't be full time or extensively involved. But there wasn't a great deal of difficulty in making things work. My place is in a discreet dead end; no-one goes down that road to get anywhere other than the house; it would be unlikely she could be seen in the neighbourhood by a passing acquaintance.'

I go on to explain how she used the excuse of travelling to friends, and how that eventually became embedded as our time together. Within three months of the beer festival initiation, we had a thriving, robust love affair.

'And that was enough for you?'

Victoria speaks with no inflection of blame or criticism. I look at her and see, behind her grey/green eyes set in their pools of subtly dark shadows and liners, that her curiosity is intense. And then I take in all the rest; her long, dark blonde hair, brushed back stiffly from her forehead to one side - not how it looked when we visited Preston, or at any meeting since. Her eyebrows are full but seem free from enhancement; two lines between them suggest she frowns too much. The brows arc into her nose which is straight, neither short nor long. Her mouth is wide, and her lips full; the frown lines above counteracted by the smile lines either side of her mouth. It's a wonderful face, more so for the smile she's giving me.

'Is the food all right?'

I nod, hoping that the previous question was rhetorical. But Victoria repeats it.

'It was plenty. It filled a void. I'd been alone for three years since the end of my marriage.'

'Surely you had something going on?'

'Nothing worthwhile. I tried to kick start things using dating apps.'

Victoria rolls her eyes, 'That's an experience to share another day. But you remained unattached?'

'Yes. I felt this intense need to get my children's lives to the front of the queue. To keep them happy and safe from any fallout from the divorce. I put myself down the pecking order.'

Victoria offers second helpings which I decline. The meal was utterly delicious, but it's late for too much food. We stay at the table for another half hour or so, have mugs of hot tea and then agree to go and sit together in the living room. She pats her hand on the sofa cushion next to her, and here we are; shoulder to shoulder.

'Jude made things simple for me.'

'Did you mean to tell me her name?'

'I didn't. But it's difficult to keep using *she* all the time.'

'Simple how?'

'Because there was no future. We always knew it, always said it, always believed it. And because she provided all the means necessary for me to be part of something.'

'Do you think your relationship with Jude was monogamous?

I mean in the sense that you weren't her only lover?'

I lean forward to pick up my mug from the coffee table. As I do, Victoria brushes her foot against my extended arm.

'Leave your tea and give me a kiss.'

It's a simple, short and quite purposeful moment. We've kissed before, but this feels much more like the real thing; tentative; exploratory; then decisive. She pushes me away and nods down at my tea.

'Drink - go on. I think it gives you courage.'

'If she had other lovers, she was both a stupendously good liar and a seriously good organiser. I'm sure it was just me, although she was completely fine that I might move on. She knew I was using dating sites.'

'Can I know her surname?'

'McNish.'

She nods and takes a sip from her own mug.

'Never heard of her. I think we should change the subject. Pass me that remote. Let's look at a film or something. What time do you start work in the morning?'

'Any time after six thirty.'

'It's nearly midnight. Something irrelevant instead then.'

The TV lights up showing some late-night talk show that remains an aside. She pulls me close and rests her head on my shoulder then takes my hand and squeezes it.

'Anything else I need to know about Jude?'

'Nothing. It was fun while it lasted. Just over twelve months of fun.'

'Do you love her?'

She turns her face up to look at me.

'In the last few weeks we both started to say that we loved each other. It didn't change a thing, and it can't have been true. Because it meant nothing when something much more serious got in the way.'

Victoria moves her head back to its resting place. 'I'd be amazed if she loved you Teddy.' Then she sighs noisily and deeply. 'What are your plans for the weekend?'

I don't hesitate to say, 'As much time as I can get with you.'

I feel her laughing.

'That's good. How about tomorrow evening at home? Here as a preference I'll be busy until late.'

'I could cope with that. And I'll cook for you.'

She laughs again then silence descends between us. It's calm in this place. We watch the talk show host losing control of one of his guests.

'You know something, Teddy? This is something I'd given up on.'

'What do you mean?'

'This. Sofa stuff. TV à deux. Candlelit dinners with smiles lit up by reflected cut-glass illumination. I like going out and I love to dance and drink in a bar. Day trips. Dinner parties. Weekends away. But when you've got someone to cuddle up to and share what is effectively nothing, it's... everything.'

I kiss the top of her head. 'Then let's do it often.'

Now she sits up and takes my head in both hands and kisses me passionately. 'Yes: let's.'

She pulls a quirky smile that fades to serious. 'Anything else I need to know about your involvement?'

'I've given you chapter and verse.'

'Good. Because I don't ever want to discuss it again.'

And, on that, we are agreed.

It's late when I set off for home. Victoria wants to call a taxi, but I prefer to walk and think. We kiss endlessly as we work our way from living room to front door via my shoes, coat and bag. In between these bursts of oral union, there are short speeches: about tomorrow; and Saturday; next week; plans to be executed.

The only thoughts I can muster during my fifteen minute march home are: that Victoria is a sensational kisser; that she delivers cuddles that have everything; and that each argument that pops in to my head about how improbably quickly this has happened is defeated by Beth's words; that I deserve to be happy.

When I get back, there's a goodnight message from Victoria: 'Let me know you got back ok.'

I reply that I am safe.

26

Despite that late finish, I'm in the supermarket just after it opens at seven and, once I return home, I make a start on some of this evening's meal. Pudding first, then a salad dressing and finally a herb and vegetable concoction. All the while, I've an eye on my laptop screen showing the slow gathering of my people for this Friday morning's endeavour. Just after eight fifteen, the whole team is shown Green for Available. We'll soon be in our regular end of week meeting.

'What are you cooking for me this evening?'

'Something to match the splendour of last night's meal.'

'Good boy. Pat on head.'

'I'm planning to be with you by about 5 latest. Is that ok?'

'Come whenever. Let me know when you're setting off.'

'K'

'But leave me alone now. I've a lot to do and want to finish in time to devote my entire evening to you.'

I send a blushing smiley.

Stewart Hatton messages me: 'Have you heard anything about redundancies in our team?'

'No. Why?'

'Can you talk?'

I can't refuse. He soon connects.

'I've been told that up to sixty jobs will go in the UK and around fifteen of those are in OS.'

Operational Support is the over-arching function that our team reports to.

'I've heard nothing. Who told you?'

'It's just the rumour mill Ed. But you'd know, right? As a manager?'

'I'm not a manager. I'm just controlling work.'

'Yeah but they'd tell you, wouldn't they?'

'I've no idea. I doubt it. I'm not focused on anything other than delivery.'

He tuts. 'All this self-interest Ed.'

I take mild offence. 'What? How am I self-interested?'

'Not you. The company. The bosses. The markets. So much utter self-interest makes anything possible.'

I repeat that I've heard nothing and divert his attention by asking about his projects and our call ends. He doesn't want to discuss real work. I feel a small tug of something related to what Stewart said. Perhaps we are good companions, underneath our taut professional interface.

But my real emotion is smug pleasure with myself; faced with a challenge, I've successfully danced on the lines between lies.

When my phone rings and I see Arif's face and number, I feel a compulsion to ignore it. As if guessing my reticence, the ring tone stops. Then he sends a message: 'Sorry. I guess you might be working. But I wanted to talk. I have good news. Call me soon.'

Later, when we speak, it sounds like he's in a pub. It's just after noon. He doesn't seem to have time to listen but peppers his broadcast with questions.

'How are you my friend? I think I told you all would be well, and the good news is that I return to work on Monday. Isn't that excellent? The internal investigation found nothing untoward. How are Beth and Joe?'

'Congratulations. You must be delighted.'

'I'm beyond delighted. And in other news, we have found a new school for Ali. She is going to a boarding school up in the Lakes.'

'Has the bullying continued?'

'We solved the problem. But there was a nasty taste and Ferzana and I knew change was needed. Shaqir will stay on there until he finishes his A levels in June.'

'Are you drinking?'

'No, but a few of us from work are in The Red Rose. Come and join us.'

'Better not. Got lots to finish off today.'

'Of course. But I thought I should share my news.'

'What happened to your accuser?'

'She was made an offer she couldn't refuse, and then withdrew her allegations. She will leave the company with immediate effect.'

I congratulate him again, then make an excuse that I need to join a call. It's another in the series of communications with him in which I've felt uneasy about Arif's manner. And, on this occasion, I also sense that something about his reprieve sounds pretty flaky, as if the facts weren't really established. I remember his outright denial that evening in the health club.

Yet it needed a payoff.

He wasn't proved to be innocent, and she wasn't proved to have lied. Strange thing for an investigation to conclude.

See you later, allegation....

I feel like I'm missing something.

When I park in front of Victoria's garage, I see her in running gear, smiling down at me from the first floor. She's on the phone and waves to indicate that the door isn't locked.

I need two journeys; one with bags full of ingredients; the other with boxes and bowls on a tray. I can hear her talking so get on with setting up what I've brought. Her kitchen looks like it's been subject to a Kaizen process; everything in a logical place and flow; food storage; chopping boards; knives; the hob and oven; pans and ovenware stored nearby. Within a few moments I'm able to start work without guidance or directions to the key tools and accessories.

'Well look at you with your calm efficiency in my kitchen.'

I'm busy with some slicing and dicing and feel her touch my neck then run her hand down my spine before pulling me round for a kiss.

'I know my place.'

'That's just as well. I've got a call in an hour with the MD of Smith and Co. The lot who sacked me. Says he needs to discuss something urgently. I made him wait till it suits me.'

'Well I can just crack on so leave me to it.'

'First of all, I'm going for a short run. No more than thirty minutes. See you in a bit.' She turns and goes after double checking I know where everything is. I tell her I don't but not to worry. Then I'm all alone, domesticated and working hard in a place I had never been until yesterday.

Victoria stays in her running gear to make the call. She starts it in the kitchen and, after some brisk salutations, goes quiet.

Headphones mean she can hold the handset at arm's length, and I see she's staring hard at its screen, listening and concentrating.

'Hasty in what way Darren?' She drifts out of the room, but her side of the discussion remains audible. Level and unemotional, she speaks in short bursts asking open questions or making simple observations. Victoria is calm, assertive and seemingly in control.

It isn't long before a message pops up on my phone: 'That was fun. I need to write down my notes about what he just said, then I need a shower. Make me a nice big drink, from anything you think suitable, in about 20 minutes'

She re-appears in a tee shirt and ripped jeans, winks at me, grabs the gin and tonic then wanders off again. She shouts: 'Of course, when I said *anything you think suitable*, I did mean a gin and tonic. Ooh, yummy, it's perfect; can you make me another one exactly to this specification?'

I confirm I can. And soon she's standing next to me watching me fill two more tumblers and chatting away in a review of the dinner menu and its accompanying drinks.

'No-one makes panna cotta Teddy. No-one.'

'Except me.'

'Clever boy.'

And so, interspersed with checks and balances on the hob, we set off on a detailed review of histories, emotions, families and senses. This is now possible; permitted. It wasn't before.

The meal is good, and the wines I bought match up nicely. It seems Victoria and I have an appreciation and enjoyment about food, cooking and eating. Somehow, in between all the other stuff, we keep coming back to those subjects like we've never discussed them with anyone before.

Without clearing anything away, we move from the table and sit facing one another from opposite ends of the sofa, the final few mouthfuls of red wine on the table beside us. There is an equality of challenge and compliment in our conversation, with a lot of laughter scattered through every topic.

And there are small notions of planning: Victoria wants an early repeat of our Preston outing, with no holds barred; I suggest we should head to the hills tomorrow for a decent long walk;

she suggests we supplement that with an evening in Lancaster for cocktails. We both want more squash; a stay over in York; walking is a firm favourite; and Victoria keeps emphasising how much she wants evenings at home as a couple. It seems we really have become a couple.

But these plans aren't obligations. We are tripping fantastic light switches and agree eventually that it might all be forgotten the next day. We can't possibly be a couple.

'It's still early. Why don't we watch something on TV? A film?'

'If you've got Netflix, why don't we pick a box set and embark on it?'

'Are we too drunk now? Or shall we have another glass of something?'

When I get back with two fresh gins, Victoria suggests we watch *Line of Duty*.

'The first three seasons were great. You'll love it.'

We watch the first two episodes in silence. But it is silence interspersed by a series of interactions that leave no doubt that we both deserve to be happy.

It's past two am when I start to make noises about heading home.

'You're not planning to drive, are you?'

'No.'

'Well you can't possibly walk. I won't let you.'

'And I shouldn't stay.'

Victoria nods. 'No, you shouldn't. But I want you to. You can sleep in the spare room. It's very comfortable.'

'Sounds good. But are you sure?'

'I'm sure it's right for us not to sleep together. But it's been too lovely an evening for us to part. Let's watch episode three and see what it brings.'

It's many, many months since I woke up with a hangover that is on the very cusp of incapacitation. After I've lain awake in bed for a few moments, I realise there's no noise in the house. I head down to the kitchen to find it is spotless. A sheet of plain paper sits next to the kettle. It has writing.

'Teddy, you shameless drunkard, have some proper coffee and drink a lot of water. If you need food, there's plenty. Help yourself. I've gone out running, back around 1030 but don't wait for me. Let yourself out and set the alarm - I've messaged you the code. You need to get your walking things so we can do that walk we planned last night. I'll drive, so leave directions to yours. I'll be there by 1230. Then this evening, we should do something sensible and cultural to make up for last night's overindulgence.

Oh, and just for the record, you're lovely.

Victoria. X'

Her writing is neat and flowing, but not flamboyant. I like it.

I pick up the pen and, on the reverse of her note, draw a map showing where my house is, then write very brief route details. Then I add a cartoon house with a flag flying from it and Casa Mia on the flag. That immediately feels stupid, but I shrug it off.

A few glasses of water are my only compliance with her orders. Before I leave, I add to what is now my side of the paper: 'Thanks for a wonderful evening. You're lovely too. xx'.

I get home and spend thirty minutes catching up on work, thankfully all the time I need. I have a mild bout of panic that I've lost my walking boots but eventually find them in my car. When I get back inside, there's a message from Victoria telling me to pack an overnight bag, a nightshirt and my favourite book at bedtime.

It takes a while to crawl through the city but Victoria drives with patient care.

'Are you a nervous passenger?'

'Not so far. Should I be?'

We're crawling along to the motorway and when I look online, I see it's because there's a long delay southbound.

She dismisses this with a shrug.

'Just as well we're headed north then.'

'I thought our plans were Clitheroe and environs?'

'They were. But this morning I found this walk centred on Dent, up near Sedbergh. We'll be there in no time. And while I was looking at the route, I also found a B&B in the village, with vacancies. So, sit back and relax.'

The XKR is quite old but it's still capable of delivering a mighty rush, if you like that sort of thing. Victoria floors it as she joins the M6 and even uphill out of the Lune valley she hits a hundred in no time.

'I'm still not nervous.'

She laughs loudly and backs off until we're cruising along at seventy.

'That meal you cooked last night was very good. Do you always make such an effort?'

'It hasn't been a major feature of my life for quite a while. It means that you got the works.'

I can see her broad smile. 'That's nice. But you didn't really answer my question.'

'I think making food to share is something you invest in.'

'How do you mean?'

'It's like giving a completely unique gift. You must work hard. Food made with love is always special, whether it's a corned beef and mustard sandwich or something like you and I did these last two evenings.'

'I agree. Although don't ever make me a corned beef anything; I could never love you for that. Does this mean you prefer entertaining to eating out?'

'Well that has its place I suppose, but I never feel I'm getting value for money.'

She puts on a Mrs Overall accent: 'It's all about the company.'

'Or about spending time with people you don't like enough to invite to your house.'

'Ouch Teddy. But you and I must try to find the right balance. Go roaming for good value and places that smell right.'

The rest of the journey, like long swathes of last night's conversation, is taken up by questions and answers about favoured food and recipes and ingredients. We love to cook, and we love to eat. It's a reassuringly calm harbour and our anchor remains dropped in its depths.

Victoria leaves me outside the B&B and tells me to get us checked in while she finds somewhere to park. It's a homely little place and after months and months of being greeted by a plethora of uniformed smiles and Have-A-Nice-Day cant, it's wonderfully reassuring to be received by a remote, slightly harassed but business-like woman. When I ask if the rooms are ready, she looks askance then confirms that the double room booked by Mrs Wright will be ready by four. I'm relieved of our bags and of the details of our planned walk.

She seems impressed and critical all at once. 'That will take a couple of hours if you're brisk. Some lovely views, although perhaps not today. It might be boggy along the riverside when you get back down into the dale. Enjoy your walk.'

Victoria is outside with my boots and a kiss.

Despite both of us being fit and active, the steep climb up from Dent leaves us both blowing hard and momentarily uncommunicative. There's a stream dashing down alongside the path and it's the only sound we hear during the ascent. Once we reach the summit and turn away to the north west, we recover our appetite for chat.

'I think this is the longest I've seen you go without looking at your phone.'

'No signal. It disappeared ages ago.'

'Even so, it's still helpful that you're not welded to all that intervention. You're a bit like a teenager; eyes and fingers zeroed in on all the starry spangly things elsewhere. At one point last night I nearly snatched it from you and threw it down the waste disposal. But I'm pretty sure even that wouldn't have stopped you.'

'Were you offended?'

'No, I wasn't. But I think you need to find the means to engage with the here and now, rather than the constant input from other people and places. Stop behaving as if being online is the only form of existence. Don't I have enough to retain your total attention?'

'You do. You really do. Just slap me in the face next time.'

'I will.'

She tells me I still look bleary-eyed, but I don't feel too bad.

'I'm astonished you were able to get up and run this morning. How far did you go?'

'About fifteen k. I never do less than five k in the mornings, hangover or not. Do you run?'

'I sometimes do, but my heart's not in it. I don't even use a treadmill at the gym.'

We're keeping up a quick pace, but Victoria stops frequently to drink water and makes me do the same. There's no-one else on the same paths and when we reach and cross a lane there's no traffic. The lady in the B&B was right; there's not much to see.

'Tell me about this stuff you've been engaged with on SocMed. Seems like it's been a crusade for you.'

'A crusade?'

'Yes. You're determined to impose something, but I can't work out what it might be. And determined to be the victor, but I'm not sure over what, or who. So tell me.'

'Have you been stalking me?'

'If that's how you want to think of my amorous curiosity about you, then yes. If you create a story, the way you have and do on SocMed, then it deserves to be noted, even if it's actually several stories.'

I want to side-track her with more questions, but she urges me to explain, so I work through the events of the last few weeks. Despite Victoria's occasional questions and requests for clarity, it only takes about fifteen minutes and it all feels like one long unpunctuated sentence. As we walk, I create a catalogue: two photographs; shared amusement; threats; a retreat; a rogue colleague; a married mistress; an investigation at work; my inquiries; marshalling of knowledge; a colleague's sacking; lighting of blue touch paper; abuse; assault; and strange encounters. It feels like it's all in the distant past, but it's only four days since my lecture from Jenny Donovan.

Victoria pays more attention to the characters than the action but asks me why I intertwined events at work with the social media stuff. I tell her that the two seem linked, like two creeping climbing plants snatching each other's space. She nods but there's no protracted analysis or challenge when I arrive at the current status. She just asks, 'And what have you achieved?'

She doesn't accept my response that I don't know.

'You can't doggedly pursue something the way you have without an objective. Come on: think. What have you achieved?'

We've stopped again for water and share an energy bar. The whole hillside, and possibly the whole of the Yorkshire Dales are ours. When I start to speak, she puts a finger up to my mouth and tells me not to talk while I'm eating. It's another of her icebreakers; affectionate and giving.

'All I've done is reveal to myself the extent to which I'm naïve.'

'About?'

'The ways in which people differentiate themselves.'

'That's a very big word. What does it mean?'

I tell her she knows what it means, but she reminds me about her dislike of American words and phrases. We're stationary, still.

'Okay. Let me say it another way. I learned that I wasn't aware of the extremes to which people will go to make a point; myself included.'

The route descends through fields, then a small hamlet and on to the Dee riverside. We take a selfie or two in the lea of the stone bridge and it's turning into a cool, rather gloomy late afternoon when we arrive back at Dent. Throughout the two-and-a-bit hours since we reached the summit above the village, there's been barely more than a few minutes in which we weren't talking. Latterly we've moved away from my life in the fog of social media and, as we stroll the last few hundred metres into the village, we are debating a thorny dilemma: tea and cake; or beer and crisps?

The B&B's small tearoom is busy, so we dump our boots and Victoria's rucksack before heading to the village store for sugary fizzy drinks and flapjacks. Then we find that the pub serves tea, but the beer is too tempting, so we sample it for a while. By seven it's obvious neither of us wants to admit we're too tired to carry on.

Back in our room, we undress and cuddle up in bed. Just as I start to nod off, I tell Victoria she has an amazing body.

She wakes me up in the dead of night: 'Yours is amazing too. Let's see what happens when we put them together.'

It's early when we make our way to the small dining room for breakfast but we're both starving and begin a leisurely graze through plates laden with cooked food.

'I might be a wannabe veggie, but I'm weak beyond words when confronted by this stuff.' She's speared a chunk of black pudding and is looking at it, dewy-eyed.

'I can't believe you got us in here at such short notice. There should be a queue back to Kendal for the chance to stay in such a palace.'

'I have mysterious and winning ways. As I hope you discovered during the night.'

'You definitely do. It was quite a journey. So much for our cultural, sensible evening.'

'I found some of your techniques highly cultured. Let's have a bit longer stuffing our faces, then get another short walk in before we go. Down by the river?' She looks at me with a smile, which fades suddenly. 'Or do you need to get back for your charity work.'

'I do, but not until late afternoon. Another walk is essential.'

It ends up that we have two.

After a leisurely muddy stroll along the riverbank it's still not eleven when we get back to the car.

'We'll take the scenic route and get some history under our belts.'

'History?'

'Specifically, our magnificent industrial heritage Teddy. Want to drive?'

I do, but I don't like the idea of bending Victoria's car on the narrow, winding lanes. She blasts out of the village, apparently unconcerned by those risks. It's a relief when we arrive at a T junction and she turns right towards Ingleton. It's a busier wider road, peppered with racing motorcyclists, so our pace is slower.

'It's lovely up here isn't it? I always think it's retained something wild and unkempt.' She looks across at me. 'Do you know where we are?'

'Yes. I do. I know this road well. Joe and I used to come over this way to find places to walk; to avoid the obvious options in the Lakes.'

'It's a good way to get over to the North East if you're not in a rush. And, ooh… we should add Richmond to our list of places in which to spend time. But the overwhelming benefit of coming along here is right there.'

In weak spring sunshine, the Ribblehead Viaduct looks like it always looks; solid; reliable; certain. A safe passage for travellers over a rift in England's green pleasantry. An unmissable part of the landscape.

Victoria has parked up. 'Come on. Let's go and take a closer look.'

It takes fifteen minutes to walk from the car to the far end of the viaduct. It's busy with people and their cameras; a forlorn ice cream van has been parked up. Victoria keeps stopping to look at the structure and whenever she does, I take photos on my phone. As we reach the point where the arches give way to embankment she just stops and stares.

'You look as if this place has significance for you.'

She takes my hand. 'No, not really. But it's one of those structures I feel drawn to. That I can't drive past.'

We walk under the last arch and she lets go of my hand to go and touch the stonework.

'People died to build this. Accidents, disease, violence. At a church somewhere down the road there's a memorial to the workforce. All around here were temporary camps where the workers and their families lived. Hundreds and hundreds of them. There was an industry attached to it, all around these fields.'

We start ambling back to the southern end of the viaduct. Victoria starts to giggle.

'You must think I'm a crazy bitch. I drag you to a small B&B at the arse end of Middle Earth to consummate our relationship then start giving you lectures about a monument.'

'I wasn't going to say anything.'

'Wise. But I'm not crazy. This structure, and the reasons for its creation, are symbols of something we can't shake off.'

I take a guess. 'Lost greatness? An empire that's slipped from our grasp?'

'No. The opposite of loss. These arches were built, around a hundred and fifty years ago, so one rail company could race a competitor to Scotland. An evolution, some believed. Railway vandalism, a fearful few called it.'

She's back touching the limestone masonry, her voice barely a murmur. 'And now we call it a listed building and the descendants of those fearful few protest vehemently if anyone threatens to shut the line.'

'How do you know all this?'

'I have a degree in History. Weren't you listening during that discussion?'

'I was listening. You got a first in History at Bristol. I'm guessing therefore that British History in the nineteenth century might have been in the mix?'

'With a long hard look at our industrial revolution. Mammon. Absurd idolaters.'

She looks at her watch.

'We better get moving. Or you'll miss your slot at the hospice.'

This time I accept the offer of the chance to drive. It's quite a car; very different from mine. Less gadgets and fewer telemetric reins; I need to think about each action and manoeuvre. Victoria lets me get on with it and seems to relish being a passenger, lounging in her seat, enjoying the ride with her feet up on the dash.

'What dating sites did you use?'

'Just *matchmates*.'

'I tried a few but settled on *Singularities*. It seemed to have the fewest married men posing as lost souls but was still a sad, sad experience. There are only so many dick pics I can stand. Did you ever do that?'

'Send a dick pic?'

'Yes. Isn't that what it's all about for men?'

'Not my style.'

'At first, once it was completely clear I'd made a terrible mess of my love life on two counts, I found the attention from those sites quite endearing. Some of the guys I encountered were nice enough. Did you meet many women? I mean really meet?'

'Four, one of whom got up and walked out after less than twenty minutes. Two ended up with us agreeing it was nice to have met, but...'

'... something isn't right?'

'Correct.'

'And the fourth?'

'We spent a really lovely evening together. Coffee became a drink or two; then dinner. We laughed a lot and I think there was something between us.'

'That dreaded chemistry. The times I heard and read that word. Did you meet again?'

'Nope. She wanted me to go back to her place and made it clear she wanted to have sex. When I politely declined, she told me to fuck off, stamped her foot and stormed off.'

'Why did you turn her down?'

'Not my style.'

Victoria strokes my leg. 'You did the right thing. That was a very dangerous offer on a first date with a total stranger. But tell me: what is your style?'

'Well the simple truth is I don't have one.'

It's only another fifty minutes or so before we pass under the M6 and arrive in Lancaster. I've already grown to like Victoria's way of moving on from potentially difficult or confrontational topics and finding newer happier things to discuss. On this occasion, her outrageously accurate imitation of the B&B owner as she checked us out and revealed her smouldering dislike of unmarried couples is an outright winner. I want to carry on laughing and smiling, so decide to give the hospice a miss. We head back to my place to listen to music and grab more time together.

'I like what you haven't done with the place Teddy.'

'In what sense?'

'Well I'm not one for frilly frivolity and cheesy chintz, but this really is minimalist.'

'It's a practical place for me not to be. My sense of material things having any value whatsoever took a dive when I moved from the family home. So now I just have what makes sense.'

'That sounds suspiciously like a stance.'

'No. It's not. But your viewpoint deserved clarity and context.'

Victoria nods. 'Don't worry. I'm not going to measure up for curtains.'

'That's good to know.'

'Shall we have a glass of wine? I know it's early, but....'

'Don't see why not. Take a look in the fridge if you want white or there's a couple of reds over there. I really could do with a shower.'

'Go then. I promise not to peek. I might rifle through your sock drawer.'

'Make yourself minimally at home. If you want a shower too then...'

'Are you saying I smell?'

'Yes.'

I'm back in the kitchen in around fifteen minutes. Victoria has opened one of the reds and it stands on the worktop with two glasses. One of them has a tiny terracotta pool in the bottom and smeared lip mark on its rim. I stream a playlist onto my speakers and rummage in the deep freeze for something to eat. There's nothing remotely classy in there. The fridge isn't much better.

I can hear that the shower has stopped so I call out, 'Are you hungry?'

'I might be, later.'

I'm still looking in the fridge at wilted greenery, blocks of cheese, a pack of salami, some smoked bacon, chicken thighs. Not great on the wannabe veggie front.

'How do I look?'

I turn and immediately collapse with shocked laughter. She's found and is wearing the rubber gloves I use for bathroom cleaning, and a hotel shower cap. And that's all. This outstanding vision is finished off by a rampant toilet brush, held aloft like a coronation sceptre.

My queen Victoria soon re-appears in the pyjamas she didn't wear last night, and we pour glasses of red, put more *Line of Duty* on in the background then ignore it in favour of cuddles, kisses and conversation. During a segment about Joe's birthday, I just fall further in and invite her to join me for the weekend; to come and meet Beth and Joe.

'I'd love to join you, but are you serious?'

'Yes.'

'Are Beth and Joe bringing their partners?'

'I didn't suggest it.'

'Why not?'

'Mainly because they will be going straight to see their mother and she may not want them all.'

'I think you should invite them now. Go on.'

She leans over and watches me contact Joe via messaging. 'Hey Joe. I know it's short notice but please invite Lulu to join us for your birthday weekend. I'd love to meet her again.'

Victoria is wiggling her wine glass at me for a top up. As I pour another glassful each, I see her grab my phone and smile. 'Joe says Lucy would love to come. He wants to know if Beth is bringing Matt.'

'That's handy.'

'How do you mean?'

'She was seeing Matt for most of last year but at Christmas she told me it was off and on a lot because she was so focused on her finals.'

It's not long before I've told Beth to invite Matt to join us next weekend and that it's time I met him.

Beth replies 'Are you sure?'

'I'm totally sure. Let me know. We can sort out lifts or whatever nearer the time.'

It's only an instant until Beth replies: 'Matt would love to meet you too. Thank you. What's brought this on?'

I tell her to wait and see and she sends an emoji with two heads and heart. I tell her to get on with some studying. Then I send her a winking emoji.

Victoria draws me in to an embrace. It's like she does it by nature. 'Are you totally, one hundred per cent sure you want me to be there?'

'Two hundred per cent.'

We finish the wine and, as the box set progresses on screen, she falls asleep on my shoulder, one arm around my waist. By ten I'm starting to doze too, and gently nudge Victoria who stirs sleepily and murmurs that I'll have to take her to bed. It's easy to lift her up, and, as I do, she pulls herself close to me as I carry her. She's not asleep, but not really awake.

As I walk, she moves her face closer and then whispers in my ear, 'Please, please make me happy.'

27

Victoria wakes me just after 05:45. She's in her running gear and says she's headed out running and then home. I tell her I'll drop her bag off later, but she tells me she doesn't need it urgently. We part with a kiss of such powerful warmth and tenderness that I almost cry. I don't get back to sleep and soon switch on some Gregorian chant and begin the process of getting up and ready for the working week. It's not long till Victoria sends, 'I am pinching myself about what's happened.'

'Me too.'

'Are we going too quickly?'

'No.'

A laugh out loud emoji pops up then she writes, 'Can I buy you dinner this evening?'

'I thought you'd never ask. Where you thinking?'

'Somewhere with pizza.'

It's less than ten minutes after I log in that Annabel calls me.

'Morning Ed. Good weekend?'

'The best.'

'Well there's a first. Are you planning to be in London tomorrow? I think you should stay away.'

'What's happened?'

'You will be getting your redundancy notice today, along with your colleagues. I think it makes sense to be remote.'

'I don't. I think staying away will suggest I had prior warning. I'm going to behave as if nothing has changed. I have my rail ticket and hotel booking and today's news won't change that.'

'I suppose that makes sense. But listen Ed; while this process works through to its conclusion, you and I need to remain at arm's length. I need to maintain that with everyone.'

'Yes, but we still need to retain our working relationship.'

'I just meant let's cut out any personal stuff.'

I'm not sure she's right, but we agree.

At just after ten I get the email informing me that my role is at risk of redundancy. It's very strange indeed to receive this and know that it's humbug.

Reading the regret-filled transcript, about consultation with staff representatives and necessary workforce reduction, I find myself beaming then laughing at how futile it is. Rules and laws about following due process take up weeks of time and energy simply to create a myth that equity exists. In my case, they've been used to create a kind of fairy tale and my smile soon fades; I can't decide if I'm the wolf or grandma.

There's around twenty minutes until my first call of the day and every second of that time becomes filled with the outpouring of fear and anger from my fellows. Some accuse me of being at the root of the company's action. Others call me, in tears, to ask what will become of them. There is a sanguine undertone in many messages that this has been coming. Everyone expresses surprise that I am in the mix and I tell everyone I'm too upset to discuss it.

Victoria messages me to suggest a squash match before we go out to eat. Our evening takes shape. She signs off the thread with a warning not to disturb her busy day, then a single closing sentence: 'I hope you feel as good as I feel xx'

My working day should be shattered and complicated but all I have to do is play out the masquerade that I am also a victim. And I flip up the sound bite that we have to keep working, remain professional and await the outcome with as positive a mindset as we can muster. I tell them it's business as usual, but I dare not speak what's in my heart; that our contribution, collectively and individually, is an irrelevance when the fingers point and the markets bay for blood.

Meetings come and go. I agree to meet three colleagues, including Stewart, tomorrow in London. Morning coffee talk. It will be a test, but all I can do is sit and take it.

When we leave the sports club, Arif is parking his car and hails us.

'Good evening you two. Another league match? Or is this a chance encounter?' His smile is wolfish and smug. He shakes Victoria's hand, then mine and I confirm it was a friendly.

Arif hasn't stopped looking at Victoria. 'I hope you gave him another good hiding. Our Teddy needs to be given these lessons and kept in his place.'

'It was close. But I won. Like I always win.'

'Indeed. Well it looks like you have places to go, and my opponent has already reminded me that I'm late. We must play soon. Enjoy your evening.'

I drive us back into the city and Victoria tells me she's added my pecs to her list of favourite bits, but that's nothing to do with our squash match. 'You never did tell me which bits you like best.'

'The whole package is perfect. If I single out anything specific it would be unfair on all the rest.'

She giggles and reaches across to stroke my neck. 'Are we sleeping together tonight?'

'I'd love that. Early start though; I'm on the red eye to Euston.'

Victoria shrugs. 'I'll drop you at the station, take your car back to yours then run back home. Stay with me at mine. You can give all my bits a detailed analysis.'

The bistro is busy and vibrant, and we test the staff's patience by failing to choose anything for more than twenty minutes. At the fourth visit to our table, the waiter more or less insists we choose some food, so we pick antipasti and a shared pizza. She seems massively offended that we don't order alcoholic drinks.

'Have you played Arif recently?'

'I thrashed him the same evening you and I first played.'

'He's an outstanding player. His remark earlier suggests you know each other away from the squash court.'

I tell her the history of family ties.

Victoria looks pensive. 'Has it survived now Joe and Beth are at uni?'

'Well in many ways it didn't really survive the divorce. But that isn't about Arif or Ferzana. It happened with almost all our mutual relationships.'

'People taking sides?'

'Some did. And then changed sides as the mood took them. But mainly I think it was just people not wanting a reminder that couples can become discrete singles. It was a nuisance to have that seat at the table with a vacancy opposite.'

'I was shunned.'

'Shunned! Now there's a word.'

'I know! Alex and I had an extensive network of friends from university, school, business, near, far. I crushed all that into a pulp with my slutty misdemeanours. He got the money and everyone's love. I got to be a new me.'

She pops an olive into her mouth.

'Were you slutty?'

Victoria smiles. 'Is that a leap to my defence?'

'Kind of. You had an affair because you didn't love your husband. Hardly the work of a slut.'

'In some eyes it was. But mine was a throwaway comment, so thank you. Your efforts to bolster my self-esteem will be rewarded.'

'I take it you were spared the matchmaking.'

'There was a time when I'd have given anything for someone to do that, but it didn't happen.'

'It happened to me once. Some friends lined me up with very a lovely woman. It was a kind thing to do but I behaved abominably and that was that.'

'You were the abominable no-man.' She sniggers. 'What did you do?'

'I just didn't behave like a grown up. I realised after meeting this woman that we had nothing at all in common and that I wasn't remotely attracted to her. And that made me wonder why our mutual friends would think we were a match. So, I just stopped communicating.'

'Well don't expect me to bolster your self-esteem on that one. Ghosting is very, very wrong and you shouldn't have done it.'

I feel like telling her there is no right and wrong any more.

'But let's look on the bright side Teddy. All of this means that we don't need to spend time massaging each other into any wider social life. We can make our own new, sparkling set of situations.'

We're interrupted by the arrival of our pizza whose quality keeps us quiet for a while.

'I should probably tell you that I used to use Lonsdale and Co as my accountants - for Maroon mainly, but they also did some financial advisory stuff on a personal basis. Arif did my books until I decided to take my business elsewhere.'

'What happened?'

'They messed up a VAT return. An avoidable mistake that cost me more money than I had in my budget. Lonsdale as a company, and Arif in particular, were less than stellar in resolving the problem. So, I quit. I also sued them for professional negligence. They settled quickly.'

I say nothing and after several seconds Victoria asks me why I've gone quiet. There's a massive conflict bouncing around in my head about whether to reveal Arif's recent problems. In amongst all the default get-to-know-you conversations, we've shared a great deal about each other's pain and torment, some of which breached long-standing confidences. Yet I'm still not sure about this one.

'Have I caused a problem mentioning this?'

'Not at all. Arif can be hard work. He was suspended on full pay recently.'

'I heard about that. There has been a lot of gossip about it in local business networks. Seems Lonsdale quickly settled that problem too.'

I decide it's safe to share what Arif told me about his suspension, and his determination to clear his name.

Victoria dismisses what I tell her with a shaken head. 'The word on the street is that the whole thing was much less complicated than he told you.'

'Really? In what way?'

'They were having an affair. Quite a long-standing affair, apparently.'

A piece of pizza falls from my mouth. Victoria picks it up and feeds it back to me then wipes my face with a serviette.

'Sorry Teddy, but I fear you've been fed a party line.'

'But this is hearsay? You called it gossip.'

'Yes, but it isn't speculative tit-for-tat on social media. The details are from people who know the personalities involved, including the MD at Lonsdale. Arif made the decision to end the relationship and his lover kicked off about it. Threatened to tell Arif's wife. Claimed they'd had business trips on the company that were nothing of the sort. The same old scene. He hasn't been suspended. He's on gardening leave.'

'How could he lie to me?'

'Like you said; he can be hard work.' She holds my gaze. 'I think perhaps you attract people like that.'

I sit back, bristling. 'How do you mean?'

'Never mind. Let's change the subject.'

As promised, Victoria picks up the bill and we drive back via my house so I can I pack my bags for London. It's only nine-thirty but we go straight to bed. It's the third consecutive night that we've slept together but it feels like the first in which we're making love. It's wonderful, sensual, and complete. But we need rest ahead of an early start and soon calm things down. Victoria likes to sleep close, but not entwined. As she moves alongside me she says, 'It's going to be strange without you close for the next few days. I feel so good around you.'

'I'm back Thursday, and we'll get plenty of time together. And we can be in touch. It's a small world thanks to technology.'

'It is, but do you know what I'd love? It would be amazing if we can just talk. No messaging or texting. Talking; perhaps video calls. It would be good for us. Especially since you're away so often. You've gone quiet. What's up?'

'I'm thinking about your dig earlier. About attracting people who are hard work.'

'It wasn't a criticism.'

'It felt like one.'

'You don't strike me as the sensitive kind. Maybe I've hit a nerve?'

'Yes. You did...'

She puts a finger to my lips and shushes me.

'Okay, so I need to work on being too blunt, and you need to be more openly self-aware. And all of that will definitely work best if we avoid endless messaging. We will pick up the phone and talk, right?'

'Bit difficult at work, or on the train.'

'Well one liners are fine. But let's make this work without all the anxiety and analysis of what a written message does or doesn't mean. Why are you smiling?'

'Because it's such a good idea. It's what I try to do with Joe and Beth.'

'That settles it then. Come here.' She embraces me and our bodies melt together again. 'See you bright and early. I'll make you tea and toast for 0430.'

Kisses; smiles; she turns away and is asleep in moments.

I switch on my phone as the train gathers speed out of Lancaster and there's a message from Arif. He sent it shortly after midnight. 'Are you and the dreamy Ms Wright an item?'

By the time I reach London I haven't been able to concoct a reply, so I stick with the new rules and call Victoria.

She speaks beautifully, both in timbre and diction. 'Good morning lover.' What a voice. As I walk from the train towards Euston's concourse, I tell her this. I also tell her about Arif's message. She tells me to ignore it; to answer him face to face next time we meet.

'But are we telling people about us? I'd like to, but we should agree shouldn't we?'

'That's sweet, but what's the rush? Let's wait until I've met Beth and Joe. And you've met Lizzie and Graham; perhaps Mum and Pops too. They should be first to know. The rest can wait. And I need to go. Got things to create. Call me later - after seven, okay? And don't forget that analysis you owe me.'

The journey to Moorgate is a heaving horror show, but it's nothing alongside the succession of messages and discussions and meetings I have about the redundancies. I keep trying to make a mental note of what I want to tell Victoria about her body. It's very wrong of me, alongside the shattered confidence of my colleagues, and my notes evaporate every time. The face-to-face meetings are actually easier than those conducted by phone or over email. In between all the pain and broken hearts,

I try to keep our projects and activities moving forward. It feels like I'm on my own, flying a plane where autopilot has failed, and I've forgotten what half the controls are for. It's a huge relief when Costin mails me to say I should lean on him and the rest of the Bucharest team.

It's well past seven when I find time to close down some routine tasks, clear some emails and give a short summary of latest activity to Annabel. She replies quickly with thanks and an instruction to leave the office and get some rest.

I've set a specific tone for Victoria's messages, and it chimes at me.

'Messages like this are allowed. I'm all done for the day but thinking of heading to the gym.'

'Go. I'm still at the office. How long do you need?'

We agree to talk after nine and exchange a single X each.

I've set myself two objectives for the evening: to comply with Victoria's request for my feelings about her body; and to extract myself from all social media, once and for all. It takes less than five minutes to open SocMed, then close it forever.

> My account
>
> Settings
>
> An endless scroll down to see Delete Account and Profile
>
> An array of passive/aggressive options is displayed
>
> Am I really sure?
>
> Why not take a break?
>
> You'll miss us, and all the jolly fun
>
> And you don't want to miss out on the messaging.

A rectangular box says *Delete Account*. I touch it; a few seconds elapse; I emit a final sobbing tear. Then I'm out.

All gone.

It feels like a defeat.

Then it feels like a release.

I open my calendar app and create an all-day event for today, April 4th, 2017. I call it *I am no longer on SocMed* and write *Everywhere* in the location field. Then I make it a recurring appointment to remind me every week.

By the time I pick up my phone to call Victoria, I've sent a few messages and called a few people. The words I use are varied and bespoke to their audience, but the core message is the same: I've quit social media; I'm never going back; I'm available by phone and text. Email too. I'm still me.

Joe tells me he hasn't used SocMed for years, so it makes no difference.

Beth tells me she's never taken any notice of my posts and hasn't missed me on Chattabox. She says she might miss some of my photos, but so what?

Annabel doesn't answer her phone, so I leave a short voicemail.

Luke replies: 'not before time'. That's it. Three words.

When I call Dave he tells me he's glad I might have got a life at last. But he's much more eager to discuss our planned lunch meeting tomorrow. He wants to discuss the message I sent him about things being over with Jude.

I've also been to the bar and, while consuming some food and a cup of tea, written a poem for Victoria.

> *I can write down all the things*
> *That I like about you.*
> *But don't ask me to.*
>
> *I want your smile*
> *Reassuring and wide*
> *And those eyes*
> *Free from lies.*
>
> *Caresses, comforting*
> *Words, reassuring*
> *Enduring affection.*
>
> *And that is all*
> *Keep breaking my fall.*

'Hello Victoria. Good workout?'

'Hi, yes it was. Weights and some cardio. Nothing too excessive but enough to make me feel sane.'

'Were you insane?'

'Raving mad pal. How was today? Did you soothe any brows and wipe away tears?'

I summarise my day in a few sentences, and Victoria digs in with some questions about my face to face meetings.

'I've never had to deal with that. You must be unbelievably tough to sustain the pretence that's been created. I understand why she did it, but I think your boss has put you in a dreadful position. I suppose it does mean that she must really trust you.'

'It's more than ten years since I saw anyone behave with integrity or honour at work. That doesn't excuse the sham, but it does make it easier to keep up the facade.'

She tells me how it went with her client, whose position has softened and she's no longer on notice of termination. But her problem now is a total lack of trust, even though they've invited a proposal from her to outline a better way of working together.

I tell her that's an opportunity.

'But I have other news. I took your advice.'

'Does that mean my list is on its way?'

'No. You're getting something much better than a list - more of that in a moment. I've quit SocMed. I no longer use any social media, including the grown-up business end.'

'Bravo. Pat on head with supplementary tickle of tummy.'

I hit send on the mail I'd created with her poem. The only other text in the mail tells her that I can't think of a title.

I tell her, 'You've got mail.'

'What? When? Oh, what's this?'

'Read it.'

It's several moments before anything happens.

'I don't know what to say Teddy. No one has ever written a poem to me before.'

'It's a first for me too.'

'Read it to me now, over the phone.'

It takes me less than thirty seconds.

'I've always, always loved your voice on the phone. But it's an even bigger turn on when you're reading my first ever poem to me. Again please.'

By the time I've spoken it three times, I don't need to read it.

'I'm in a considerable state of arousal now but we are not doing phone sex. I'm going to have to go and have another shower.'

'I didn't write it to turn you on and I categorically do not want phone sex, now or ever. The poem is because I've already shown you that every inch of your body is perfect and that every touch of it makes me feel a kind of privilege.'

'Is this really Ted Clayton? I think you're an imposter.'

'Stop it.'

She turns silent so I keep talking. 'Instead of writing down some tame inventory of cold words telling you how amazing your body is, I preferred to let you know that I care about the things in that poem much more.'

After a short pause, Victoria says: 'And this proposal I need to write to Smith and Co. Should I do it by email or post?'

We both laugh but she takes longer to stop than I. When she's finished, I tell her the poem is now the first and last.

'I deserve that. Ignore my silly games. I will treasure this forever. For ever.'

I lie awake after our call ends and as the night becomes morning, I send Victoria another email. Once more, it contains the poem, and I've added the title: *Forever*.

28

Dave travels to meet me in the City and we have lunch at a café near St. Paul's Cathedral. It's the first time we've met since Ella and he were in Brussels. I prompt him to discuss the experience, which he does willingly but it's clear he is still affected by it.

'It was pretty grim, and even though we were some distance from the epicentre of all the killings, it felt like we were in the thick of it. It was hard to retain any level of calm, such was the depth of fear. And, my god Ted - the sirens.'

He takes a long pull on his pint. 'We were well looked after at the hotel, but some of the staff were weeping, disconsolate with worry about friends and family. And several of them said they felt great shame that this had happened to us, guests in their city and country. Some of our fellow residents were hysterical, screaming about safety. I didn't think we'd get out of the city or out of Belgium for days. It was as if we'd been imprisoned.'

'Maybe you had been?'

He looks up sharply. 'What do you mean?'

'It just feels to me that we're all incarcerated by these atrocities.'

He reaches over with his empty pint glass and pings it against mine. 'Are you allowed another? Or maybe I shouldn't tempt you?'

I tell him I'd love another beer. Sitting in silence while Dave fetches the drinks, I realise I haven't looked at my phone once since we arrived and, on his return, Dave tells me he noticed too.

'What you said about how the mass killings imprison us is spot on Ted. But we can't be incarcerated by this. There is no guilt, even though some want us to accept this view that, somehow, history makes us culpable for the terror.'

The arrival of food prompts a suggestion that we change the subject and we turn to less fraught topics. After more than an hour, I announce that I have to get back to work. As I pay the bill Dave says, 'I was going to ask - face to face and eye to eye - if you're coping all right since you lost Jude the Unsure. But I don't think I need to.'

'How do you mean?' The waiter thanks me for a generous tip; his smile is endearing, and I almost add more.

'It's in your eyes Ted; something I haven't seen since Birmingham.'

It isn't a long walk back to the office, and it's in completely the wrong direction for Dave, but he joins me so I can tell him everything. Not about Jude, and the end of the affair: but about Victoria.

When we part at Aldermanbury Square, his hug is protracted and accompanied by giant slaps on my back.

I'm unproductive at work, but this seems to be excused in the current environment. The atmosphere is shocking, made worse by many people behaving as if nothing has happened. There's rarely any compassion or empathy in the company, but the lack of common decency is palpable. Those unaffected by the redundancy programme appear to have dug in on the line that blames those waiting to be ejected: for being sub-standard; for being weak.

Annabel isn't around though Peter Dixon is highly visible. Perhaps it's because he is being saddled with blame for the redundancies in our team and wants to right that wrong. Usually the senior-most are scarce when these programmes are announced, but his presence looks like defiance. Despite being the embodiment of the maniacal slash and burn activities all around us, he is here with us, like a soothing ointment for the team to apply to its wounds.

Since Monday's announcements about job cuts, the office has been busier than I've seen it for months. It's like a force has united people: to see and speak to one another; to be there in the faces of the bastard managers and directors who are never affected; to cause a change of heart. As if the heart has any part in this darkness.

I can't summon the strength needed to conceal my duplicity and before four pm I slip quietly away from the office to go and finish work at the hotel. I listen to some chant as I walk and muse on the notion that I should form a plan to stop coming to London once the team has been washed away. I can manage the offshore teams from anywhere. Annabel doesn't need me in London anymore. Seems Paul Wilson was right: it is a waste of time and money.

Victoria calls and we smile then laugh through a short conversation about how today has been. It's uncomplicated and relieving but we're both against a deadline to do other things.

'Before we finish, I need to confess something. I told someone about you today.'

'Anyone I know?'

'You know her relationship to me, although I may not have told you that I sometimes call her Lizzie Beth.'

'What did she say?'

'Not much. I'm summoned to Kirkby Lonsdale this evening and will get a grilling. Am I allowed to show her pictures?'

'Pictures, but not poems.'

'Which reminds me, you lovely man. That title was a cute addition. Am I allowed to propose an alternative?'

'Go on.'

'Well, I don't have one. I just wondered if *Forever* is set in stone.'

'Like coal.'

'That's a rubbish title.'

'I'm sticking with *Forever* but am willing to negotiate.'

'Ha. Just you wait. How was lunch with Dave?'

'It was good to see him, and I'm afraid I told him about you.'

'Afraid?'

'It means we are already slipping away from Beth and Joe being first to know.'

'How did Dave react?'

'I got hugged and slapped.'

'That's sweet. Speak soon.'

Shortly after my next meeting starts, Victoria sends me the winking, kissing heart emoji. I tell her I don't actually know what it stands for, so she sends a further ten of them. The emoji trail ends with a series of short messages: 'It doesn't matter what it means. It's just a nice way to show what I feel. A smile, a kiss and a lovey-dovey heart. So, we're common knowledge now. How wonderful xxx. I'll call you this evening. Might be late.'

Annabel messages me early the next morning to say she is already in the office, so I ditch my nascent plan to skulk at the hotel all day. I'm with her for most of the morning in a cold, detached review of current projects. Neither of us seems willing to state the bleeding obvious. Then Peter joins us for fifteen minutes and asks me about the mood in the camp. My short response causes nods and tuts and a seemingly reluctant comment that I should hang in there. I nod but decide against any tutting. Annabel briefs him about a project that shows signs of being out of control and it makes us happy to clutch this straw: a discussion about how to halt the decline then steer things back to safety; we are efficient and calm; detached from the nasty business of people's feelings; of sackings; and of their impact. When Peter leaves, he fires a parting shot about whether I'm all right following the train attack. I tell him it's history. This time, he shakes his head and tuts, but recovers some gravitas to tell me he's grateful that I'm keeping the plane flying.

At Annabel's suggestion, I set off on my journey home much earlier than usual. By the time I sit down on the train at Euston I feel scarred by the additional bustle on the streets and underground. The train is packed and all around me are the voices of endeavour, remotely asserting what has happened and what is needed. The people who aren't talking are frantically massaging their phone screens, sometimes interrupted by snorts of laughter, sometimes by scowls of outrage. Everyone is engaged by something out there; above; beyond.

The seat opposite me has a reserved tag, but as the train glides into London's northern suburbs it remains unclaimed, so I dump my bag in the seat and get my iPad out and open Safari. I run a series of searches to see whether *Teddy Clayton* and all its variations still collars me anywhere online. I search again using my old log in names. Page after page of search results suggest I have no presence on Earth. I know it's all still there somewhere and a skilled bloodhound would easily find me, trace me, track me. But any casual glance won't clock me.

I do no work, graze through the first-class food and drink and recline my seat for a snooze, a plainsong lullaby murmuring in my headphones.

Dozens of people leave the train at Lancaster and I dawdle up the platform to let them dissipate. Victoria is there, sitting on a bench, reading a book that must have engrossed her because she doesn't notice when I sit down next to her. She glances sideways as I cough gently to announce my arrival.

'What time do you call this?'

'I call it the earliest time I've ever got back from that London.'

She takes my hand. 'It's wonderful to see you. I missed you. Mine or yours?'

Before I can speak, she pulls me to my feet and gives me a great squeeze of welcome then a long, searching kiss.

'I really don't mind where we stay.'

She looks pensive. 'I need to finish a piece of work. Come over to my place and I'll give you the privilege of finishing off dinner while I do that.'

We walk hand in hand towards the river, discussing the book she was reading. She tells me it passed the time nicely and took her mind from the work she needs to finish - a rebranding concept for her new client. When we get to her house, she immediately shows me the work on her iMac, and it looks fantastic. She's shown me her work before, but never something new or in development. It looks great; uncomplicated; easy to understand.

'But I need an hour to finish it so come with me to the kitchen so I can show you something.'

There's a potful of something bubbling on the hob and vegetables to prepare and cook. Victoria gives me quite precise instructions, but I tell her to go and work.

'Okay chef, but what I really wanted to show you is this.' She opens a drawer and takes out a folded towel or garment of some kind; it quickly unfolds to reveal an apron. Victoria slips the strap over my head then pulls me in to another clinch and, while kissing me and whispering reminders about the recipe, ties the bow behind my back.

'Now then. You need to get on with our meal, and I need to get on with my livelihood. No interruptions, you hear?'

I look down at the apron to find it has *Sex & Drugs & Sausage Roll* imprinted in white on the front. It makes me giggle, then laugh. She calls out, 'I said no interruptions.'

I laugh louder. But it's not as loud as the laughter that envelopes her when she returns to the kitchen to find me putting finish touches to dinner wearing nothing but my sexy new apron.

I make breakfast too and, while we eat it, we chat away about the day to come and what good will look like. She tells me not to fret about the pretence that's been thrust on me.

'You're a long way from the storm so just shut down the extraneous noise.'

'That's pretty much what I intend to do. When are you presenting your stuff to Page Gordon?

'Ten thirty. Doing a dry run as soon as you've gone.'

'I wish I could stay and watch you in action.'

'Another time. Thank you for making and sharing two meals with me. It was such a special treat to meet you from your train and know that we were together the moment you got home.'

'It was lovely.'

'So was your arse peeking out from that apron. I prefer it unclad.'

'Unclad is best. And before this conversation breaks in on time we don't have, I'm going to go.'

Shortly after midday Victoria calls with news. 'They loved it. And as a result, they've asked me to do an additional piece of work we hadn't previously discussed. I am officially a star.'

'Of course, you are. Tell me what they said.'

She outlines the feedback from her client and their new brief.

'Then we must celebrate.'

'Yes, but not this evening. I have a cunning plan. Hmmm. It's more of a cunning suggestion actually. Let's go to the cinema. We can walk down if it's dry.'

'Okay. What do you want to see?'

'I've nothing in mind. Why don't you choose? Let me know the arrangements later.'

I'm interrupted by a phone call from Annabel. I decline it once, then twice so I can carry on with Victoria. But when a third call lights up and a message appears on my laptop screen saying, 'Please pick up your fucking phone', I tell Victoria I have to go, but will augment her suggestion until it's a plan.

Annabel is in a panic bordering on meltdown.

'I'm sorry for swearing Ed, but every single piece of work I've done has disappeared. Have you done anything to my folders?'

'No. Why would I?'

She goes off at a tangent about what might have happened, and what will happen if she can't retrieve them.

'What's the folder called?'

'AJGustafsonAB. All in one string.'

The folder's there. I ask which files she's worried about.

'All of them. They've all gone.'

'No. They're here.' I scroll down. 'There must be at least fifty files.'

'Then why can't I see them?'

I tell her to try turning her computer off and on again, but she doesn't appreciate the levity. When I open a video call and share my screen she thanks me and closes the call. A few moments pass till she sends me a message that she's losing the plot and doesn't know what she'd do without me.

I don't reply and spend the rest of the day coaching and guiding anyone who'll listen, then log off shortly after five, do a few errands around the house before a shower. When I arrive at Victoria's I'm relieved that my arrangements are well received.

'I'd like to admit that I've read reviews of the film you've chosen but I haven't. The overwhelming plus point is that you picked one with Hugh Bonneville in it.'

We're walking along the last few hundred metres into the city. 'He's dreamy. But I'm guessing you didn't pick it just because of my mid-life crush on an actor.'

'I didn't, no. I picked it because of my longstanding crush on Gillian Anderson.'

'Well isn't that just perfect?'

'Because?'

'It shows how fabulously conventional we are. I was dreading the possibility you'd pick some highbrow film that I couldn't cope with after a week chasing numbers.'

'Well it might not be highbrow, but I think it is a tough subject.'

'My Hugh can make any subject adorable and cuddly. Tell me about your crush on Gillian.'

I explain how the X-Files had been like a parallel world during my final year at university and how Agent Scully always left me speechless. She'd never seemed unduly painted as a stereotypical star might seem. An older woman, but not too old. Her demeanour was never weak, but always slightly bemused and endearingly uptight. A sceptical civil servant, ticking boxes, doubting anything she felt was off-process or -regulation.

'Tell me the truth Edward; you masturbated thinking of her, didn't you?'

A couple walking towards us, ready to wish us a hale and hearty evening, do a cartoon double-take; Victoria rushes us forward, arm-in-arm to get away from their outraged surprise.

'No, I did not. I've never masturbated thinking about anyone I haven't met.'

'Not even in front of the telly, watching Dana Scully offing some sinister invader?'

'Not even then.'

We're chuckling, as we always do.

'But what of you and Hugh?'

'My prince! My king of hearts. Even at his stuffiest aristocratic best, Hugh has mischief in his eyes and querulous doubt in his smile. Gentle and genteel, yet strong. Sexy, in a pipe and slippers kind of way. Why are you laughing?'

'I'm considering a reprise of your mastur...'

'Stop right there Mr C. Don't even go there.'

She skips ahead then turns to face me, walking backwards with her eyebrows raised and a wicked smile. 'You're all I need to think of when I don't have the real Teddy. And, if you're a very good boy, one day I'll give you a demonstration of what that looks and sounds like.'

When we take our seats, Victoria empties her pockets and bag to generate a small stockpile of sweet snacks: chocolate; fudge; biscuits; some of those pre-brewed packaged café latte drinks. It seems neither of us can allow Hugh and Gillian to be submerged beneath popcorn and gallons of cola. But then conversation is obliterated by the sonic barrage of advertising and instructions about how to behave. A competing salvo - chirping phones, rustling wrappers, slurp and munch - is part of the ambience. It used to be so much more romantic having a date at the cinema.

But the seats are comfortable and, reclined almost horizontal, we hold hands all through the film. Victoria strokes my leg a couple of times but nothing naughty interrupts our focus on the screen; we're in the premium seats, after all.

It's dark when we set off for her house and the streets are noisily busy. We stop at the Riverside Arms for a drink and a summary review of the film. We both liked it and enjoyed the performances from our heroes but wanted more of them and less of the love story downstairs in the Viceroy's household.

We're also not massively clear about whatever party politics were in play in 1947 but conclude that, just for a change, the nation was tearing itself apart about something. A couple of drinks later and we don't really care; it's time for us to reacquaint ourselves with our bodies.

Outside the pub, we barely walk more than twenty paces before we stop to kiss. Some lads on the other side of the road start up a ribald chorus, then one of them yells 'Fook 'er.'

Victoria breaks off. 'He will, and incredibly well - because he's not a wanker.'

I don't like the look of their reaction to this, and one of them makes a move to cross the road. But his mates don't back him up and, when he trips and falls, their amusement at his misfortune makes them forget any confrontation.

'Take it easy. That's the kind of thing that ends up with a trip to A&E. Or worse.'

'They were pussies.'

'There were six of them.'

'We could have taken them.'

'I'm serious Victoria. Don't confront people like that.'

She looks closely at me. 'What's up?'

'What have I been through?'

'Oh, shit Teddy. I'm so sorry. Come here.' She links arms. 'I won't do it again.'

'Please don't.'

We're so closely entwined that our pace is slow, made worse by the fact that my legs are shaking like I've been in an accident.

'Is shouting stuff at gangs of lads a regular feature of your nights out?'

'Of course it is. I believe in free speech.'

My sudden laughter makes me feel doubly wobbly.

'Well I doubt that lot share your view.'

We walk in silence. Then I'm worried that she's too worried about me so I pose a view that we probably could have had them.

'Probably. But change the subject. What's the plan for tomorrow?'

We begin a conversation that accompanies the remainder of our walk, a couple of beers at Victoria's house and some of the time needed for kisses and caresses. But the subject doesn't survive once we undress.

29

There's a long lie-in, uninterrupted by any morning running. Instead we have one of those long discussions in which the words become relegated beneath assorted exchanges, by hand and mouth. Our legs are intertwined under the covers. It's almost as if we begrudge the need to get up.

But we do, eventually, and set off for the motorway just after lunch, Victoria's car laden with bags.

'Only a week Mr C, and we're a couple going off on holiday. Looks like you got me.'

'A holiday? In Shropshire? I don't think so.'

Victoria reaches over and strokes my head and neck and traces around the fading pinkness of the scald on my jaw line.

'I can't work out if I'll miss you on SocMed. In my stalking phase, I looked back through some of your history. You can be quite funny. And poignant.'

'I do my best.'

'But sometimes you were a total twat.'

'Hang on; stalking phase? I thought you said you were not and have not been stalking me?'

'Actually, I said that if you chose to describe my curiosity as stalking, then that's your choice.'

'You did say that. True.'

'But you are a stalker's paradise Ted.'

'Hence all the threats.'

'Yes. Sorry; I shouldn't belittle what happened. Do you think the attack on the train was connected to your interaction with the road groups?'

'Who knows? The police are still sticking to the view that it was a completely random incident.'

'I suppose they have evidence that it happens frequently. Nutters get on trains with super-heated drinks and select a victim based on...?'

'I don't know. Put like that it does seem unlikely.'

'Well I was being sarcastic.'

'I know. The easy thing to do is assume a simple motive and what could be simpler than an arbitrary selection by the perpetrator?'

'Did the police not dig deeper into the stuff you were doing on SocMed? Surely that was a line of enquiry?'

'They didn't ask, and I didn't offer it as a likely cause.'

'Why not?'

'Partially because I just assumed they would call it a dead end. But mainly it was because I felt ashamed.'

'Ashamed about what?'

'About everything I've ever said and done on SocMed and Chattabox.'

Victoria becomes silent, staring out of her window at the bland landscape to the east. The motorway isn't busy but it's impossible to maintain a steady speed and it's a snail's pace past Preston.

'I'm not sure it's a cause for shame. Who is judging you?'

'Probably no-one. But I think I use social media - used social media - a great deal more than most of my friends and associates, almost in spite of the knowledge that it wasn't good for me. So, I'm easily defeated by any criticism that all social media are essentially bad and that my excesses were appalling.'

'I hope you've learned by now that I don't judge people, especially you, but let me turn what you've just said back on you. It's ridiculous for you to be someone who deserves criticism based purely on an assumption. If you cared about the impact of what you said and did on SocMed, or wherever you existed, then probably you'd have done and said things differently.'

Before I can say anything, Victoria continues. 'The thing you got sucked into wasn't about you. It was like some weird pantomime full of grotesque, half-real people. Quite possibly some of the ones screaming their hatred at you weren't real at all.'

'Well the train attacker was real.'

'And that's why you should have told the police. And told them about that superannuated DelBoy Trotter with his trucks and his fake news fixer.'

I'm laughing.

'It's really not that funny. I meant what I said about how you seem to attract weirdos. Your boss, who sounds like a control freak who can't control anything. The nut job on the train, who luckily was just armed with hot chocolate. There's DelBoy and his poodle. An affair with someone who dropped you the instant she had to face the responsibilities of grief and family. A small-time crook, screwing the company and a possibly unwilling moll. A whole busload of crazies fighting the good fight about road building. Fuck knows how many serial victims on your dating site. And best of all, maybe it's worst of all, the obliquely named Protester in Chief.'

'You're not supposed to be judging me.'

'I'm judging them Teddy. And let's not get started on Arif.'

'Let's not.'

'Tell me how many people you know who've exposed themselves to that kind of stuff.'

I shake my head. 'Nobody. It's perverse but if I try to explain it you could really get judgemental.'

With another stroke of my neck and shoulder, Victoria suggests I should still try.

So I tell her that life was too easy. A marriage built on the confidence that grew from being teenage-sweethearts-forever. Careers growing, with a kind of ease. Houses, cars and holidays with more and more in them to show the world all that success. Kids, happy and healthy.

'When all that was guillotined, I couldn't tell if I was the head or the body.'

'That's quite an alarming metaphor.'

'Is it a metaphor? Or a simile? I'm never really sure of the difference.'

'Well whichever it is, it's definitely alarming.'

'No. It's not. Because I was still both things, but everything was disconnected; disembowelled. My body kept doing the stuff it always did. Work. Play. House. Retained belonging. Meanwhile my head was screwed. It had me clinging to things I didn't need but that seemed essential. Things to make me wanted and needed. Things to make me keep going and link me to what mattered.'

'Like what?'

'My friends and acquaintances via SocMed. A platoon of people I've always known but never see. A whole world of romantic potential via *matchmates*. Virtual dreams, faceless flirting. And Chattabox - all that credulous narcissism - made me feel like I was roaming the streets, alive, protesting, hitting the high notes. It was all like a stage onto which I could walk and be a new me.'

Victoria sighs. It sounds cross, but I'm concentrating on speeding so can't be sure. Her voice sounds calm. 'I tried Chattabox once. It was unnerving. All those random, unconnected connections that go nowhere. Or lead to a place that sucks you in to an onslaught of thinking; no empathy or reassurance. Just lunges of harm.'

Now I look across at her. 'Did you stay long?'

'A few months. It was all I could stand. The unyielding disharmony wore me out. Causes; principles; opinions; unresolved conflict. Fight the good fight.'

'Put downs without knock downs.'

She laughs aloud. 'Yes Teddy! Brilliant. That's exactly what it is.'

'Except sometimes it's not funny at all. And sometimes people really are knocked down by the spitting, snarling acrimony. Hate masquerading as debate. Little Brother at work: mostly harmless; yet terrifying if you can't find the off switch.'

Victoria pulls a bottle from her bag and offers it to me. The water is cold, with a slight tang of metal.

'What did you mean about being a new you? Did you become something new? Or was it more of an amended version.'

'New and amended.'

'You're saying you channelled your difficulties into completely the wrong outlets?'

'They seemed right to me. Until I stepped off the nice, cute, smiley stuff and peeked into the broken world I didn't know existed.'

'And is that all behind you now? No more doubts or anxieties?'

'How can anyone have no doubts or anxieties? Wherever you stand, the world is imperfect and can't be fixed. I shouldn't speak for you, but in our brief time together I think I've learned that we share the same basic view; that we are effectively disenfranchised by a political system in which no party really speaks for us. But for my part, I stick with the narrow plateau on which I am safe from harm, unthreatened by the potential for loss.'

'You can speak for me Teddy, it's rather honourable of you. But I haven't voted for years, much to Daddy's chagrin. I refuse to give the conservatives my mandate; especially their ministers; all those creepy middle-aged men from snob schools. None of them ever portrays any sense of service and they aren't in touch with real people, even their own followers. They just serve themselves and their money, and their *we know best, do as we say not as we do* mantra. I'm a sole trader, their dream voter, but they speak a different language to me. I need new things. I refuse to consider the mainstream alternatives, both of which are so obsessed by arguing about what fair and good look like that they're paralysed. And, the final clot in the artery, the whole lot are so riven by factions that they have no credibility at all when they talk of unity.'

'They do have credibility: in the hearts and minds of people who have all the answers.'

She's absorbed once more by the scenes to her left.

'Huh. Imagine that written on the side of a bus: *Herein lies the answer to every question.*'

Silence descends on us.

'On the plus side, I'm increasingly of a mind that you, Edward Clayton, answer a large number of questions that I've always had. And best of all, you don't ask where we're going.'

A few days later she drops me near Birmingham New Street station and watching her drive off is like losing everything. I call her before the Jag is out of sight and when she answers, we're both in tears.

But she doesn't reverse back to me, and I don't stop walking for my train.

It's a very much Newer Street than the one I recall from my days at the city's university. I wonder if Elrond will be there, guiding people to the right platform, such is the glistening beauty of the station's transformation. But the likeness to

Rivendell is soon a memory and the forbidding tunnels and scenes as my train pulls away to the east aren't so different. I feel more at home as we trundle out under the Lawley Middleway, past Garrison Lane Park then over the canal and on to the airport and Coventry.

My laptop is on the table and I'm tip tapping my way through some work, but my mind is in a myriad places.

In a hotel bedroom, pulsing with sensual joy as Victoria and I made love on arrival then again after a visit to the spa. Face down on a table, looking across at her as we were massaged with great vigour, wishing we could do more than just stare. Being bumped around, laughing, on the train from Ludlow to Shrewsbury then finding the town quite beautiful and grand where a relaxing meal was easy to find and enjoy. More four poster antics into the night and early hours. A drive down to Hereford for breakfast and a stroll along the river before a racing, maniacal flight back up the A49 to be at the hotel in time to greet Joe, Lulu, Beth and Matt.

The nervous panic I felt when I introduced Victoria and the calming joy when she was just so cool and simpatico with my kids. Laughter and irreverence as we all shared a ludicrously priced afternoon tea before the kids and their partners went off to spend the evening doing their own thing in Ludlow.

And Beth messaging me to tell me how happy I look, and Victoria telling me how Joe is a chip off the old block. And sitting in the hotel's bar sharing a bottle of wine with Victoria and telling her how my kids are such stars and hearing her telling me how much they love me.

It was the first time I'd been with Joe on the morning of his birthday for two years. We celebrated with a crack of dawn walk into Ludlow, then along the Teme, before looping back around the racecourse to the hotel in time for breakfast.

We all made a huge fuss of Joe. Beth had sorted a cake and we spent ninety minutes indulging our birthday boy. There were gifts and cards which seemed at one point to have overwhelmed him and he hugged us all to mask his tears. We played croquet, or at least a made-up version of it; Victoria and Matt claimed a made-up victory.

Lulu had bought Joe a pampering session, so they went off to the spa before lunch. Victoria also took a break and went to the gym, then Beth needed time on revision, so I had time together with Matt. He was gentle and kind, softly spoken and full of humour. He knew more about me than I about him, but we slowly corrected that imbalance. Best of all, there was not one second of the judgemental hesitancy that might exist between a young woman's boyfriend and father.

When we all reconvened for lunch it was precious and sublime. Informally, yet somehow underpinned by good manners and etiquette, we ate and drank like a family would. Beth chose the wine; Lulu proposed a toast and Joe demanded no speeches. I kept looking around the table and smiling. Every time my eyes rested on someone, they returned my smile as if we'd always been in this place.

But the wine and time ran out; by just after three there was an undignified scurrying to collect bags and boxes of gifts. Our goodbyes and hugs were happy ones, then a taxi whisked them back to Much Wenlock and a week or two with Amy.

It was our last evening and night together for a few days, so Victoria and I shared a quiet meal in our room and fell asleep after a contented discussion about the coming Easter weekend.

I can't focus on work with all that in my mind. I call Joe, but it goes to voicemail: 'Joe, it's Dad. I hope you enjoyed the second half of your birthday as much as I enjoyed the first half. It was wonderful to share yesterday with you. Call me later if you can.'

Over the course of the journey, messages pop up on my phone from numbers I don't recognise: Matt and Lulu, each thanking me for my kindness and a wonderful celebration of Joe's birthday. Then Beth tells me that she and Joe have just dropped off their partners at Telford station and will be out for the rest of the day with Amy. When I ask for news about Amy's work situation, Beth tells me that everything seems less troublesome.

My train is fast and seems to take no time at all to reach Buckinghamshire. As I hurtle down the last seventy or so miles into London, Victoria has stopped for tea at a service station and sends a message telling me that she hates the M6. It seems her journey has been awful, with no obvious sign of relief. When I reply with an apology and regret, she calls me to say every hour lost on the motorway is worth it for what we shared over the weekend.

The office is quiet, and I wonder why I agreed to work when I was supposed to be on holiday. Calls and emails remain riddled with the tension of looming loss, but it seems some of my colleagues have found a sense of hope and opportunity. Phrases like *it's time to do new things*, and *this is the kick up the arse I needed*, and *there's demand for people like me out there* have started to surface. I maintain my front and, when challenged about my plans, say I'm thinking of becoming a contractor. Meanwhile, I log in to the company travel booking tool and start arranging flights to and hotels in Bucharest.

Annabel arrives mid-morning, in a filthy mood about the trains from Ascot. I take her a coffee, but her smile and words of thanks don't appear to be sincere. It's well past lunch when she asks me to join her.

'Ed, how are things? I'm sorry about my demeanour earlier. There are days when I seriously question how a country that can't deliver something simple like a rail service ever manages to get anything done. How was Joe's birthday?'

'It was marvellous. We had a great couple of days.'

Her smile still seems to lack charm. 'Good. We need to do some work together to ensure your trip to Romania next week is productive. Can we do that this afternoon please? I'm good any time after three.'

We meet later and create the package that will generate the strong sense of renewal needed in the souls replacing today's team. It's mainly my work and it kind of hurts to do it, but Annabel demands a result. Whoever we end up recruiting over there will be in no doubt about how important they are to the company's continuing growth and power.

Thinking about these activities, about creating replacements, drags me down; so much so that during my short walk to the hotel I end up thinking about Jude. It's taken two weeks, but she has become yesterday. Should I care about how she's feeling? Worry about her state of mind and any grieving she faces? I don't reach any conclusions, so I head straight to the bar.

'You look like someone with troubles.'

A name badge tells me it's Jake talking to me. He must see hundreds of faces every day, with countless expressions to fathom. Yet he's on the money about mine.

'Maybe a glass of wine will help?'

'Maybe, although I'm thinking I'd prefer a beer. What's in the fridges?'

I settle on a bottle of weissbier and watch Jake pouring it with great care into a branded glass.

'How's your friend sir? He was with you for dinner a few weeks ago. He knew his wine.'

It takes me several seconds to realise he means Dave, and now my respect for Jake is almost off the scale. I end up telling him the story about Dave and Ella being in Brussels during the recent attack. It happens in segments, while Jake serves other customers, but he keeps coming back to hear more then asks me loads of questions about it and how it made me feel. I have another Erdinger and we chat contentedly for ages.

'How would you have felt if your friend had been one of the casualties?'

'I honestly don't know. And I don't want to know what that would feel like.'

Jake looks at me as if he expected a different response. And now I'm worried he has lost someone close in a similar event.

'I know what you mean sir. But I'm sure there are plenty out there who, if something that dreadful happened to me, would tell me what to do and say and think and feel. To take hold of my grief and shape it to their agenda.'

'I'm sure you're right. But you seem like someone who wouldn't let that happen?'

'I think perhaps grief makes you weak. And you're easily led.'

He has to go to serve another drinker and then another. He looks across at me after several moments and shrugs. I raise my glass to him. Our discussion can wait until tomorrow.

When I get back to my room, I haven't answered my questions about Jude. I should have, and probably do have, no hatred for her and what she decided to do. In the end, for sure, it was all about her; but I wasn't hurt; I didn't fall; maybe I stumbled a bit, but Victoria was there to catch me.

I call her. 'Hello Victoria Wright.'

'Hey lover.' She sounds tired. Her journey home just kept getting worse.

'Should I have called sooner? I've been drinking beer. And I haven't eaten.'

'You can call me any time. You know that. But I need to sleep soon. Let's not talk long?'

She doesn't see me pout.

'After I dropped you at the station today, I cried for ages. I needed wipers for my eyes.'

'I cried too.'

'That's good.'

'Crying is good?'

'Always. But especially about leaving someone who you don't ever want to leave.'

'Are you all right? Did your bad journey cause any work problems?'

'Not really. But I had plenty of thinking time.'

'What did you think about?'

'You. Me. Our somewhat incredible romance.'

'Still think we are moving too quickly?'

'I can't think that after the time we just spent together. And I can't wait for our second consecutive extra-long weekend. Are you okay?'

I tell her I'm lonely in my hotel room. She tells me to go back to the bar, to eat and mingle. It's probably a good idea, but when we end our call a few moments later, I order rubbish from room service. I'm tired too but it doesn't stop my mind from rambling off into troubled places.

Am I in love with Victoria?

It's not terribly long since I felt I was in love with Jude and told her that I loved her.

Was I in love with Jude? Or just with the certainty of all the intimacy? With the easy contentment that came from having nothing to go home to, nothing to project, nothing to have and hold - yet still to have something.

And it's not much longer since the day that I stood in a church and avowed my eternal love for Amy. With an audience of several dozen family and friends as witness, none of whom raised a just cause.

Was I in love with Amy? Or just with the stable strength of a relationship that survived our youthful growth pangs and emotional curiosity. And, eventually, with the creation of hearth, home, offspring, careers, success, the cut of material things. The joys of parenthood. Stability.

If you've been in love with the wrong people, how can you ever spot the right one? I can make mental or actual notes about all the things Victoria has done that make me feel huge affection for her; feel leaps and bounds in my heart when I watch her moving lithely through any scenario or smiling at me as we share a meal; feel strength from the way she never judges me or shows scorn for my mistakes; feel a depth of mature simplicity in every conversation we have; feel constant laughing recall for her jokes and craziness; and feel the need to say her name aloud, as an impulse. And I can put all that in a container with *Love* stamped on the sides, top and bottom.

It's a reality that, at this time, the friendship and affection between Victoria and me means I am not alone. And I am probably falling in love with her. But I can't shake the feeling it's too soon.

As I clear away my room service detritus into the corridor, to join multiple other trays of barely enjoyed insufficiency, my phone pings a calendar reminder. Life has just ticked over into Wednesday and it's the anniversary of me quitting SocMed.

One whole week, and I'd barely noticed. But I'd be surprised if anyone has.

Two more days at work. Busy days, starting early and in the case of Wednesday finishing after nine. Beth has set up a messaging group with Joe and me. They're on a road trip with Amy, currently in Aberystwyth and, from the photos they send, it looks like they're having fun. Coastal scenes, snacks and happiness. Both of them look so full of joy and I find myself wishing they'd send a photo of them together with Amy, so I can gauge her happiness too.

By the time Thursday arrives, I just do not want to be in London. The brittle atmosphere in the office has made work seem broken and pointless. Meetings are cold, filled with giant pauses followed by monotone dialogue. I rarely leave the office for lunch but decide to get out and go and eat something bad for me. When I tell Victoria I've eaten a dodgyburger and fries, with onion rings and sauces from bottles with congealed goo around the spouts, she is less than impressed. And so is Dave when I meet him for a couple of beers at the Euston Tap; it seems my breath is malodorous. But it's an early end to the working week and our party has started.

Interregnum

Marcus Mapplewick walked through the right hand of the double doors of his home to be greeted by the sound of things being smashed. There was swearing too; Tracy swore occasionally, but this was profound cursing in a voice Marcus recognised as her street-fighting contralto. In between all the crashes of crockery were small squeaks of French; pleas for mercy.

He frowned.

It could be a poorly risen soufflé.

But Tracy sounded like she had an inside track.

Benjamin Mapplewick appeared on the mezzanine above his father and made a noise that attracted attention.

'Hello Benj...'

He didn't get to finish his son's name.

'You're a disgrace, you revolting old man.'

Instantly angered, Marcus made a couple of steps towards the stairs, with every intention of ascending to give his son the kind of beating he'd suffered from his own father, provoked or otherwise. But Tracy appeared from the kitchen.

'Hello darling. Good day at the orifice?'

Marcus did a small double take. He felt threatened.

'Fucking the maid, Marcus. How quaintly Victorian. You turd. You utter prick.'

Marcus was used to difficulties in business discussions and negotiations and had stored up any number of retorts to attacks by his inferiors, perceived and actual. But his wife was a different matter; especially with an orange cast iron casserole lid in her hand. Behind her, Sylvie was visible, clutching her shoulder. She looked terrified.

Marcus had used up his allotted ten seconds of conversation control time and all he had come up with was: 'What's going on?'

Tracy raised her eyebrows, so they arched into almost perfect inverted V shapes.

'What's going on? Well I tell you what Mister Mapplewick...'

Marcus winced at the uncanny way she mimicked his tone.

'... let's start with the local paper, shall we?'

The cast iron discus was set aside while she walked to a fake Hepplewhite console table over in the shadowy depths of the atrium. Marcus glanced up at his son who was looking down with a grimacing contempt. Then he looked towards the doorway where Sylvie no longer stood.

'Where are we?' Tracy held the local rag and pulled, almost ripped at it to reach a page. 'Here you go. Page seven. Dear me, Mister Mapplewick; you don't even warrant the front page.'

Marcus walked towards her, but before he'd taken two steps Tracy hurled the paper at him, yelling the headline at him: 'Local Business Leader in Lurid Film Exposé.'

Marcus was trying to pull himself together. What the fuck had happened? Film?

The Mercury was all over the floor. Tracy stood over it like a Colossus, except she was more stylishly dressed and bejewelled. Marcus looked down at the detritus of news and soon spotted the headline she'd relayed.

All was quiet as he knelt to pick up the paper. The headline was tame compared to what he read below it:

'The Mercury has been sent copies of a film in which managing director and owner of Staffordshire company MarMap Logistics, Marcus Mapplewick, is shown having sex with an unnamed woman allegedly at his home near Whittington. The Mercury can exclusively report that the footage has appeared on several social media sites including the anti-bypass group *White Lines - Won't Do It* as well as on You Tube...'

Marcus sucked through his teeth. What the fuck was going on? He played golf with the Mercury's editor. How was this news? How had he been shat on like this? That little cockney cunt was toast.

Tracy was ahead of him. 'Interesting reading isn't it? Your little puppet paper not so under control as you thought? Benjy? Can you come down and show Daddy the film you found online please?'

Marcus stood in silence as his son descended the right hand of the two staircases with his iPad Pro.

'All right Tracy. Let's take this offline without involving the children. Please; come into my study.'

'I think there's been enough coming in there, Mister Mapplewick.'

Marcus snorted impatiently. His son was next to him: 'Here you go Father.'

There it was; Sylvie bent over the Chesterfield whelping as he himself banged her from behind. Marcus swallowed hard. He couldn't dispute this. All he could do was get angry.

To his son: 'Get away from me you worthless ponce. I'll deal with you later.'

And to his wife: 'This isn't evidence of anything.'

But he was no longer master of all he surveyed. Tracy was staring at him.

'How dare you call our son a ponce? Tell me Marcus: how did someone as ridiculous as you ever become a captain of industry?'

Now she was just roaming the hallway, acting out a soliloquy to an invisible audience of empathy. 'And how did you ever get me? How many more lies did you construct into all our vows and guarantees? Is this French whore the first? And is it just women or does my solicitor need to know that actually you're the ponce here? You certainly seem to enjoy it from behind.'

Marcus took a step towards his wife, but his son stepped between them. And then Clarice appeared, and Marcus' heart sank. His daughter was the apple of his eye but here she was, descending the other flank of stairs like a contestant in a deity game show; Hebe; a paragon of youthful innocence.

Then he just lost it. 'Why the fuck should I be held to account by any of you? I'm a proper fucking rich powerful businessman - I own things; I do things; I am things. This video is a construct. It's not me. It's not her. She's never been in my study. She's the fucking maid.'

Tracy looked at him evenly. 'I'd recognise that tiny excuse for a cock anywhere Mister Mapplewick. Or dare I call you MM? Whole millimetres of pleasure? You pig. You utter fucking pig.'

Marcus stared around his home, or at least around the tiny fraction of it in which this soap opera was being washed out. Now Sylvie was standing in the doorway leading to the kitchen and beyond - sad and ready to run; Tracy had grasped the casserole pot lid and looked terrifying with it; his children were sneering at him. Who had done this? Who knew? It was either the French tart herself or... Or who?

Now he wanted to see the film again. What was the camera angle? He couldn't remember. Was there a date on the footage? Again, he drew up reserves of proud self-defence.

'This is a piece of propaganda and it's exactly what the fucking peasant socialist scum wanted. To turn people against me.'

'People, Marcus? People? You're saying that your wife and children are just commodities who can be made to hate you because of something you don't agree with? Something political?'

'No. Yes.'

Marcus felt a kind of courtroom tension in the air. Like in a television drama. Like all his dramas.

'Which is it then? Yes or no?' It was beautiful Clarry who questioned him now. How could she hate him?

Marcus stood in isolation; condemned; bang to rights. But he didn't lose by admitting guilt, no matter who accused him. He won by crushing opponents and killing their arguments.

'That French whore has done this. It's not me in the film. I can prove it. You can't judge me on something in the papers or online. It's full of lies.'

'Really Dad? Like your *No Overtaking - Roads Matter* site?'

Marcus did it again; another step towards one of his children, intentions unfettered by chivalry.

'You know something Marcus? This is your problem and not ours. So, let's keep it simple.'

Tracy sounded level-headed and confident.

'The children and I are leaving. We are going to move to somewhere rented; it's already sorted, and you won't know where it is. We will be unavailable for comment when the media comes knocking. Nothing you say or do will change the inevitable: divorce and destruction.'

Marcus stared maniacally around the hallway. How could this woman be so boldly challenging his right to this home and castle?

'We won't be back to this nonsense of a house, other than to return with a removals truck to take away the children's and my belongings. Get in the way of that, you tiny-cocked nobody, and you will regret it forever.'

Marcus had never had anyone refer to his cock like that, especially in front of his children. All his years of being that big business bruiser, the man who could, had never prepared him for this. All he had was being sucked out of him.

'Tracy. This is all a con. I have not had sexual relations with our maid.'

She looked at him with a huge smile.

'Really Marcus? Is that a Clinton denial? Or just another lie?'

Before he could say anything, Sylvie arrived in the hall, sheepish and defeated.

'I'm sorry Tracy. I don't know why I did it. But I did it. And if you need me to support your case in court or whatever, I will. He made me do it. He fucked me lots. And often very badly indeed.'

Tracy looked from her servant to her master and grinned evilly.

Marcus snarled. But no-one was taking any notice. Benjy and Clarry were heading back up the stairs, instructed by their mother to bring the bags they'd already packed for up to five nights away from home. Sylvie was dragging a small case towards the front door. Tracy stood, smiling at Marcus, her head tilted to one side. It incensed him and he snarled again, then shouted: 'Do I get any fucking say in any of this?'

'What would you like to say Mister Mapplewick?'

It took Marcus all his reserves of restraint to stop himself punching his wife in the face. How dare she exert control over him in his own house? How dare she stand there grinning like an ape when he'd given her everything? Paid for everything she had? The bitch.

'Thinking about all the money Marcus?'

'What? No.'

'Me neither.'

Marcus shook his head and blinked. 'What do you mean? You're not getting a penny from me. You're the one walking out.'

'It doesn't matter Marcus. After all this, you won't have a pot to piss in. I know your business model and I can cope outside of whatever you are obliged to pay me in a settlement. In a week, possibly less, your silly company won't be able to survive.'

'MarMap is not a silly company. I'm about to expand into new markets...'

'No Marcus. You're not. And I'm not staying here any longer. Goodbye. Get a solicitor who knows how to lose divorce cases. That's all you're going to need in the next couple of months.'

Clarice and Benjamin Mapplewick stood either side of their mother. Marcus stared at them belligerently, with no hint of loss. As they turned and walked out of the house to Tracy's Porsche Cayenne, he remained rooted to the spot until he heard the car's engine disappear down the driveway. Then he walked to the doors and closed them.

Intervention

The old-style mobile in her coat pocket only rang when there was work on. It would be that voice, the harsh one with the accent that was vaguely Midlands. Not full-on like the gangsters in Peaky Blinders. Maybe the man put on the rasping breathless tone to conceal something? After all, this was all about a concealment; instructions in a code they both understood.

Her phone showed *Unknown Caller* but she pressed the green key and held the handset to her ear.

'It's a go code.'

She nodded, spuriously.

The voice kept talking: 'You need to help with some removals.'

'What is the pick-up point?'

'Midlands, possibly North. Could be either urban or rural.'

'When will I know?'

'You'll get a signal. Usual notice.'

'Okay. Any specific mode of transport?'

'Something basic, not flash.'

'Will the fare be together or is it two jobs?'

'Two jobs. They don't travel together.'

'Any chance they will be close to each other geographically?'

'That's TBC; but different pick up points assured.'

She mentally ticked off the basics. It could be a single driver.

The man was still talking. 'Usual fee: two up front; two more on confirmation; final two on delivery.'

'That's all fine.'

'The two fares cannot be linked.'

'Explain what you mean.'

The voice didn't change. She hadn't rattled his patience.

'Two destinations. One fare.'

'I understand. Timing?'

'Booking and exact details will be confirmed soon. These jobs need finishing early-mid May. Photos available.'

She folded all this information away in a mental envelope. 'Received and accepted. Will await final details.'

The line went dead.

Interred

Craig McNish alighted from his executive taxi at Edinburgh airport staring at his smartphone's screen. It had been a difficult call that started before his trip from Colinton and ended as the car turned off the A8 on to the airport approach. His sister-in-law's recent plummet into binge drinking had become a pain in the arse, and her bickering phone call, filled with accusations of his neglect, had left him seething with suppressed anger that almost boiled over when he saw the news that his flight was delayed.

He didn't need this; any of it. What he wanted right now was the sublime distraction of the grinding monotony of airport processing. He wanted to close down all that was in his head; all he felt about his brother's death and funeral; all he felt about the care and support his parents needed; all he felt about Freya's contempt for him that was slowly poisoning their relationships; and, especially, all he felt about the thing concealed in his briefcase. He tore the headphones from his ears.

But now the monitors showed the Schiphol flight was expected to leave more than eighty minutes late. After cursing with great restraint, he wound his way to the check-in plinths then on into the security labyrinth. Thirty minutes later he sat in one of the executive lounges with a mug of tea and plateful of petit fours. Around him were assorted clowns necking the free booze and indulging in their pointless banter: like the Uruk Hai at Helms Deep, they roared themselves onwards and upwards to life's most fruitless, irrelevant defeat - the loss of decency and restraint.

Craig despised people who drank heavily before or during flights. He'd happily sign up to a law that required the ban of all drinking on all flights sine die. Once, on a trip to India, he'd had a man next to him in Business Class who sucked his way through three glasses of champagne, the same of Californian white, two glasses of Burgundy with his meal, then two cognacs as a digestif; all within the first two hours of the flight. The drinking was bad enough, but the guy proceeded to snore and fart his way through the skies over the Black Sea, eastern Turkey and Iran, waking with a snort of surprise that it was dark outside and the descent into New Delhi had started.

Turning his back on the fuckwit few, he opened his laptop at one of the workstations and checked in with work; mails; share price; revenue. His business brain logged all he saw, and he dispatched actions and messages to his team. But his lonely heart wasn't in it, and soon he unzipped the centre compartment of his Italian leather briefcase. A white envelope, bearing his name and office location at the Edinburgh site, was torn at the side where he'd opened it in haste yesterday. His frustration at being sent hard copy of anything was soon overcome by the sickening stomach cramps caused by the lines of text he read.

'My Teddy, I've no idea why I'm using email for this. My head is all over the place. No need to reply... Can't wait to see you. Jxxxx'

He'd asked his executive assistant to get copies of his and Jude's company phone bills for the last three months. There was nothing untoward. She'd called him occasionally, her mother daily and her charity office several times a week. It logged calls to and from their social set at home and further afield. A few to the Porsche dealership up in Kendal. When he tried some of the numbers he didn't recognise, he got through to shops and service providers. In the pages and pages of detail, what damned her wasn't the numbers she'd called; her guilt lay in the absence of any calls to numbers in Ulverston.

Craig stared around the lounge and his eyes rested on new arrivals ordering prosecco at the bar.

Jude didn't do prosecco.

She never had.

When he first saw her that night in Newcastle she'd been quietly sipping from a glass of white wine, surrounded by fellow students with more predictable beverages. Just recently turned thirty, Craig McNish didn't think of business trips the way his peers did. He wanted to work, then work some more. He had no ties and no reason to do anything other than drive himself towards bigger, better jobs and rewards. His colleagues, all married men, treated their time away as an escape; a time to drink too much and shag people; to create the kind of myths men crave. The decision to trawl the pubs and bars where students might be in need of some attention left Craig desperate to head back to the hotel without his workmates; but they played the team-building card.

In the end, no-one pulled. But as they were leaving, Craig felt a tug on his arm and found himself looking at a pretty face arched by a shock of white hair with pink streaks through it.

'Don't look so bored,' she'd said. 'Your friends are the boring ones. Will you still be in the City tomorrow?'

He was.

Craig met Jude for a lunch time drink at a pub in Jesmond; they had a bite to eat too; and then they fell in love. At the end of that trip he returned to his home on the coast near Aberdeen and she continued her studies, eventually graduating with a degree in Business Management. They met often in Newcastle and, outside term time, at Jude's mother's home near Morecambe. There were visits to Edinburgh too, where Jude met Craig's parents and his brother Lewis.

As Craig's career took off in leaps and bounds, Jude was often left without him as he travelled the globe on business. So, she started a small company in Lancaster providing counselling and support services for young offenders and victims of abuse.

When they married in 1999, Craig's parents were bitterly disappointed that they made their home near Galgate just south of Lancaster. They had no truck with the multiple logic for the decision to live in North-West England: that Jude needed to be near her widowed mother; that his transformation from financial *enfant terrible* in to corporate *eminence gris* meant he could live and be anywhere; that Craig himself felt happy living in Lancashire. And the parental displeasure was redoubled when, after several years trying, Jude hadn't delivered any grandchildren; something that would have been assured in Scotland. They didn't lighten up even when it was clear that Craig was infertile as a result of Celiac Disease. His switch to a gluten free diet didn't help but even if it had, they were a couple too far past the point where children would have been a blessing.

To compensate, Craig showered Jude with the things he believed she needed. He'd carried on believing that she needed those things right up until a few days ago, for Jude had never once turned down or been dismayed by these material pleasures.

But now, the one thing he could be sure of was that all she had ever needed were a secret phone and a lover; a man she owned so entirely that she called him *My Teddy*.

Craig knew he was in the prime of his life, with unbridled wealth and success to revel in. Head-hunters and women pursued him but he was loyal and faithful. He was feted in the markets and industry as having the golden touch. Until Lewis' illness and death, Craig had never known turmoil or disorder because he deployed control and power to ensure stability.

Jude had gone out of control and abused his power.

But he still had power.

Interrogation

'How was our woman's meeting the other day with Mr C?'

'He seemed to swallow some of what he was fed and didn't realise what or who La Donovan might be, despite taking a quick peek at her briefcase.'

'Can we discount him? He's gone quiet.'

'Then perhaps he has listened to good advice.'

'Well that's reassuring but not quite the point. The objective was to establish whether or not his sudden appearance in the soup of this protest is part of any worrying domestic or external agenda.'

'Based on the transcript, it isn't. He's not. In fact, he's so centre ground it's frightening.'

'Frightening how?'

'He lacks the pervasive certainty of a true political thinker yet draws great strength from all the doubts he has. I don't think he agreed with, or even acknowledged a single word she said in support of the Left. Yet he signalled no real empathy with views he really should support, given his background.'

'A chameleon then. Follows any flag.'

'He blends in, but he doesn't seem to follow anything. He's too conventional, too determinedly ordinary. But Jennifer believes he has some rough, and rather endearing edges. Not many people engage an investigator to trail an errant spouse. Is there any news on the train attacker?'

'The local police have no clue. We think it's a paid thug who will never commit thuggery again. Was it wise for her to leave her briefcase where he could see?'

'It helped him to confirm the pseudonym and make himself content that he searched for, and found, a nice person called Jenny Donovan.'

'What if he'd found he was being recorded?'

'He didn't.'

'Does he need to be warded off?'

'Not on the basis of that meeting.'

'Bad answer. Let me hear the recording and I need your report. I want to decide today whether or not Mr C needs a less sociable encounter.'

Interface

When she started her break, she found a direct message on Postpix.

'Check latest post for passenger details. Photos 4&9. Middle man on pic 4. On pic 9, cherchez la femme. Call me to confirm. More intel when we talk.'

She waved her cigarette packet at a colleague who nodded in understanding. Out in the smoking shelter she lit up. After hitting the green and grey icon, she scrolled down to look at the post by *babycakes*. She was the profile's only follower. There was no hashtag and a meaningless caption about *a great wedding*.

She swiped past three photos. The fourth showed three men beaming at the camera and she captured the screen then saved the image. Four more shots were pushed left so she saw the ninth; a man and woman captured in discussion and without pose; she was resplendently shapely in a silvery frock, her smile wide and affectionate.

Another screen captured.

She stood for a while enhancing and cropping the two photos. It took another cigarette to get the two faces in crystal clarity and then her smart phone was closed down and returned to her trouser pocket.

She pressed and held 2 on the other phone.

'Yes?'

'Details logged.'

'Be ready to go in less than a month. Seems both passengers will be looking for drop off by May 10th latest.'

'Any news on pick up point?'

'Nothing concrete. On homeland. North from you.'

The connection dropped.

She scrolled through the names on her contact list then pressed the call button to reach *Smetana*. A smooth voice answered, 'Yeah?'

'Get drivers ready for jobs in coming 4/5 weeks.'

'How many cars?'

'Two max. Line them up today but could be a single fare so make sure they know. ID on site by end of today.'

Another dropped connection. She strolled back into the store and a final two hours stacking shelves. As her shift and the constant flirting from the guys doing fruit and veg ended, she set off for home. The bus was less than a quarter full.

On a SocMed group named *Great Romantic Composers 1800-1950*, she posted the two photographs. Within a few moments, the post was Liked by another group member called Joe Lyons. She deleted the photos from her phone and from the SocMed group; then she left the group and unfollowed *babycakes* on Postpix. Finally, she discreetly removed the sim card from the old mobile, slipped it into an empty cigarette packet and when she left bus dropped it and several other items of litter into a waste bin.

Interconnection

As the plane carrying Craig McNish to Amsterdam rolled back from its airbridge, he looked again at the piece of A4 paper and Jude's message to Her Teddy. She wouldn't have known, because he never told her, that his company laptop had tracking software on it that recorded any dubious activity. This was above and beyond the usual spyware deployed against employees. Craig's position as Chief Finance Officer meant that his activity online was constantly monitored for potential intrusions and irregularities. That day in Colinton, Jude had used his laptop to do some online shopping and those sites were reported to Craig for him to confirm he had been the user. The email she sent to this Clayton bloke must have been an aside; a confused, last minute decision. Her email proved that point; she had no idea why she sent it. The tracking tool recording that a mail was sent from an unknown Gmail account to a potential spam account. As owner of the laptop, Craig was required to validate the circumstances and he confirmed the email was a legitimate personal communication.

The 737 started to taxi and just as the final request was made for phones to be switched off, Craig fired off a message to his executive assistant.

'Get hold of Piet Magielse in Security please and find a time later today when he and I can meet in person for 15 mins. I'll let him know too. See you at around 4 local.'

Then, 'Piet - need your help and support with something. Beatrijs will be setting something up. Need you to prioritise please. Proost - CM.'

Intercession

Jack Fenton finished his shift on patrol at the outlet mall just after eleven. He reported in to control that he'd seen nothing suspicious on his last circuit, then signed off. It was a short walk to Bicester Village station; his train showed as on time. He set off at a brisk pace to shake the lethargy he felt from an evening on guard. It was three days until his next shift.

Standing, early and alert, on the station platform Jack looked left and right then took out his smartphone. A text from his mum told him there was something in the oven for him and to make sure he ate it after such a long day. A message from Andi wished him goodnight, and she missed him. Countless junk emails, selling him things he didn't want, sat above and below the only one that he needed to read.

It was from *It's Training Men* and requested that he create a training plan for delivery at a course during the week leading up to Easter.

'We'd like you to provide a plan that delivers strategies to help our students confront and pacify unarmed individuals. Please go to the attached link to acknowledge you can perform this work and to see details of the required timings for the course, its location and attendees. You will receive your usual fee once you deliver the plan.'

He touched the link knowing that it would contain codified names, addresses, car registration numbers and links to social media profiles. It took him five minutes to unscramble the details.

He hit the Accept button and added a note: 'First draft drop 0730, usual place.' Then he started to piece together a way to deal with the problem. Once he was seated on the train, he pulled out a small notebook and wrote some initial headings:

> Track – immediately
>
> Access – keys best
>
> Collect
>
> Transport – where?
>
> Action – tools/method
>
> Withdraw

It was an easy brief. He added more notes in amongst his headlines then, as the train pulled into Oxford station, put away his notebook.

Jack smiled at the thought that a few hundred extra quid would go down well with Andi and he sent her a loving goodnight message.

By just before 5am, he had covered two sheets of A4 paper with handwritten notes that methodically developed his initial headlines into a plan to meet his client's objectives. He folded the sheets in half and slid them into separate envelopes which he sealed before writing his own name and address on the front of each.

Back at Oxford station, Jack boarded the first available London train. He got off at Reading and walked out on to Caversham Road. When he reached the petrol station, he saw the rental car and its occupants.

Jack threw his jacket on to the back seat then sat behind the wheel and drove off over the bridge. No one spoke, but the guy in the back soon took out the two envelopes from his jacket and handed one to the front seat passenger. Jack drove carefully out of the town then cross country to the M40. The passengers swapped their pieces of paper and were soon instructed to put them away and describe the plan without reference to what was written. Once they were both able to narrate the plan aloud, Jack told them to stop and turned on some music, as loud as he could make it. When he switched it off, he asked them to describe the plan again, then again, and one last time.

He left the motorway at Banbury and parked the car at a supermarket where the front passenger got out and went into the store. A few moments later Jack also got out, grabbed his jacket, checked the paperwork was back in his inside pocket and walked off to the station.

Back at home he set the A4 paper and envelopes alight and flushed their ashes down the toilet. Jack's final action was on the *It's Training Men* link, where he sent coded instructions for some items to be dropped in a left luggage locker at Paddington station.

Interference

Marcus Mapplewick stopped answering the phone when he realised that its constant ringing was a clamour of media prurience. Instead he prowled around his house yelling abuse at the empty rooms. It was a comprehensive set of swear words and phrases, some of which he made up on the spot. It was pointless and indulgent, but it didn't solve any problems. He'd lost his temper and in the time-honoured fashion of anger mismanagement, he'd already lost every argument.

His efforts to claim innocence in front of Tracy and the kids had been dumb. Of course he'd fucked Sylvie and without needing the blue pills he'd needed, for years, to get it up for Tracy. And Sylvie played along with every moment. She loved it. She even sang that dirty sixties French pop song and all its coming and going.

The answer, he concluded, lay in his study. He needed to find the camera that filmed it all and work backwards from there. But first he needed an ally. He pulled out his phone and told Siri to call Jarvis.

Kriss had been expecting the call from MM since earlier in the day when he saw the report in the local press. It had made him look at the extent of the news coverage; it wasn't widespread and Kriss made a decision not to be proactive. The stuff on You Tube had spread to Chattabox and the anti-road crazies were loving every minute of every Repeep and share and shout out.

'I could do with your help Christopher. Can you get over here asap?'

'Of course Marcus. I need to finish some odds and ends here. Shall we say forty-five minutes?'

Marcus instantly cracked into a rage. 'Whatever you're doing it's a total and utter irrelevance alongside what I need from you. You're supposed to be my fixer so get over here and fix all this shite.'

When Kriss didn't immediately agree, his boss lost it even more comprehensively.

'You know what Krissy Pissy Jarvis? Forget it. I don't need you or anything you can offer. You're fired. Just fuck off and don't expect any kind of pay off. Are you listening?'

'I'm listening Marcus.'

'Good. Fuck off. I've had enough of your cocky deceit. Don't think I haven't noticed the way you sneer at me. You elitist university-educated cunt. Fuck off. You're fired.'

'I can be there in twenty minutes.'

'Too late. Get out of my company and leave all your MarMap property in my office. I'll be checking your laptop and phone for evidence of all your scheming.'

Kriss counted to ten. 'Marcus, we can manage these accusations. Please let me come to the house and talk it through.'

'Don't expect any of my champagne you little wanker. If you're not here in fifteen minutes, you can collect your P45 tomorrow.'

Kriss knew it was impossible to drive legally to his boss's house in less than twenty minutes. He'd already assumed that the reaction of Tracy Mapplewick would be prejudicial in the extreme and that MarMap might well be history within a matter of weeks. Marcus was so obsessed by his attention to the wrong details that he was disconnected from the grim realities of MarMap's financial fragility.

Listening to MM now, on the edge and broken, Kriss decided that he had enough to walk away and start again somewhere else. He'd had an offer to stay with friends near Penrith; they were starting a new business and had trickled down the notion that he could be useful to them.

He took a deep breath. 'You'll have my resignation in fifteen minutes. My company phone and laptop will be in the safe here at the office. I hope you find a way to resolve this latest crisis.'

Marcus exploded into a frenzy of invective.

'Goodbye Marcus. It's been a blast.'

Marcus whisked himself to new heights of rage but soon realised that his fixer had gone. This last act, this betrayal, was proof of Kriss' culpability in the covert filming. But he wasn't going to let that, or anything, destroy the Mighty Marcus Mapplewick and all he'd worked for. He fired off a text to Kriss' number: 'You're fired. Don't bother resigning. Screw with me and I'll see you in court.'

The study was quietly calm, like it always was. Marcus touched some paperwork on his desk, then sat to switch on his computer. When it booted up, he went to Outlook and fired off an email to MarMap's finance director asking her to provide a current statement of the company's fiscal situation by nine the following morning. After he hit send, he sent her a second mail asking for a statement of each company director's shareholding. Finally, he typed a third email telling his FD to freeze the company's accounts and assets until further notice.

He gyrated his swivel chair through 180 degrees to examine the room's layout. Like a rugby union kicker, he focused on the back of the Chesterfield imagining Sylvie was there with him behind her. Then his eyes followed a line up and away from the sofa, back and forth until he was ready to start his run up. Looking at the wall and ceiling where any concealed camera might be, Marcus felt suddenly bereft. He'd just sacked the person who would have been able to get some covert scan of the room and investigate who had instigated the filming and leaks. He himself didn't know where to start. From his habit of making enemies at every juncture, Marcus Mapplewick now had no friends to call on.

30

As I open the door there is no beep from the alarm and then no tonal countdown. But there is post lying on the floor as well as in a pile on the table. I tut, and I feel a bit angry with Victoria: it means my home has been unprotected since she dropped off my case and suit carrier two days ago.

I drop my Gladstone bag on the bed and kick off my shoes. I feel my anger drain away then smile at the memory of such blissful times shared with Victoria in the last few days and weeks. It's happened so quickly, yet feels perfectly, happily real; and permanent. I turn on some Gregorian chant and head to the shower to wash away the coating of smells and disgust from the train and its contents. The crashing power and intense heat of the water is like a balm that soothes and enriches me. I stay in the cubicle far too long, and it's nearly eleven when I pull on my pyjamas and pad into the study to dump my work laptop and fire up my iMac. Everything seems fine online; I leave all the machines to synchronise my life and go to make some tea.

The man sitting in one of my armchairs looks quite appallingly evil. His eyes are dark, almost black, under arched eyebrows. He has jet black hair, short at the sides with a great sweep back over his head. There's a tattoo down the left side of his neck; letters; symbols. He's dressed in skinny jeans, a baggy shirt over a plain tee shirt. Trainers. He looks lean and fit. His face is blank and impassive, but he raises his left hand and I see the gun.

Whenever Ian Fleming wrote scenes like this, James Bond would note the steely eye of the pistol and calmly see past its gaze to the face of his true enemy beyond. All was not lost. Something would come up. A laser beam in his tie pin, or a watch that puffed deadly knock-out gas. With a measured objective cool, 007 would assess the situation knowing he had strength and lethal violence on his side.

I pissed myself.

If I hadn't just had a dump, I'd have shat myself too.

'Good evening Tedwood.'

I can't speak. My head is spinning. I'm only just able to see and can't work out what has stopped me from blacking out. There's a dark veil over my eyesight, pulsing and flapping like a curtain.

'Sit down Tedwood, before you fall down.'

He waves his gun towards another chair and I follow its arc and sit down. His hand looks strange; smooth and false. Is it a glove? Why is he wearing gloves? My pyjama shorts are still piss-warm, and it feels vaguely comforting. But it's soon cooling and then I feel the acidic burn on my inner thighs.

'The cat has your tongue Tedwood. Say something.'

I didn't think I would be able to form words, but I manage three.

'Who are you?'

He is looking round the room nodding his head as if my question was expected but of no consequence and unworthy of a response.

'Wait and see. Wait and see.'

'How did you get in?'

I'm on a roll now, words tumbling into my brain to be processed before skipping out of my mouth. Questions. Curiosity. Emboldened that I'm still alive, in spite of the gun aimed at my chest, I feel I can risk a conversation.

'People are careless.' He takes out keys on a small fob and waves them, with a tinkling noise. 'Easier to steal this from a bag than to break in. Easier too when there's no alarm.'

He has an accent. It's like Costin's and Georgi's. Somewhere in Eastern Europe. Except: sometimes it sounds as if his accent is over-embellished.

'Where are you from? What's your name? Who sent you here?'

He looks at me darkly.

'I am from Newark. I live there.' Suddenly he erupts with laughter. 'Funny joke Eduardo, no? And perhaps it's untrue. Because I know you don't care about where I live. You ask to find out the country of my birth, perhaps to help you place me in some hierarchy of immigrants: the English love this so they understand what job I might steal. But don't worry Tedwood: I have a nice generous employer and I don't want your job. Or your woman.'

He has a joyous look on his face. This is entertainment. I feel a heightened sense of threat.

'And yes, I know big English words like hierarchy; recompense; orthodontic records. My home before I came here was in a small town called Vulcan. Like the bomber Tedwood. Like the bomber. But I am from the country you call Macedonia.'

I want to ask him to use my real name. Or maybe he's just being offensive, above and beyond any insult I might feel from having a gun pointed at me. And I want to ask why it is that his accent seems to waver away from the timbre and vowel sounds of central or eastern Europe, yet he has an elaborate back story about living in the Balkans.

'My name you don't need to know. Who sent me? I don't know Eduardo. I get a call. That voice belongs to someone I never met. Beyond him, or maybe her, more calls and anonymous voices create this activity. I take the action I am given, like in one of your projects. I tick boxes, then go back to Newark, or wherever it might be, and put on my overalls to work hard in the factory.'

'Can you call me Teddy or Edward please?'

'Why, Tedwood? We don't need first names or real names. I call you this and it keeps me from pretending you are personality.'

I close my eyes. This sounds terrifying. He is going to kill me.

'What are you going to do with me?'

He looks calmly at his gun and gives a small shrug.

'I'm going to help to create your death. The voices on the phones, they need that.'

I nearly blackout again. All the small talk, laughter and chummy revelations of his home and work were a false flag. And it's burning. I'm really going to be killed.

'Let me tell you what happens now. Please go to your bedroom and wash yourself; pull on some clothes; pack a small bag with things you would use if you go away with your girlfriend. To the Midlands perhaps. Or Scotland.'

'Wait. I need to know.' I'm gibbering now, shaking with terror. I'm only just able to say these things. 'Is this because of my post on SocMed; because of MarMap? The protests?'

He looks at me with the benign empty gaze that the Well-To-Do might give a tramp in a shopping mall. Then he performs a giant shrug.

'I don't know what you mean Tedwood. These things are nothing to me. Remember? I am voice-activated, like your Bluetooth phone in a car.'

The numbness creeping up from my knees is paralysing. I can't do what he says. Can't stand up for falling down.

'Let me help you Tedwood. I see you are scared and that is how it is meant to be. Bravery has no place here. Will you suddenly try to attack me? No. Will you scream out so your neighbours will do rescue? No Eduardo. No. They are used to your girlfriend's screams, I think. It won't seem like there is anything new. Just pleasure and pain like when you come together as in porn films.'

I swallow hard thinking about Victoria. I will never see her again. Never hold her again.

'Let's go. I will watch you carefully while you get ready, and then we will quickly create a view that you left with a purpose. Places and people to see.' The accent slips away again.

He is guiding me along the hallway. As we pass the study, I hear my phone ping: it's the first noise I've been conscious of hearing since I walked into my living room. For the first time ever, I am faced with a reality in which a message sent to my phone has no possible outcome: whatever it says, whoever caused it, whenever I eventually get to see it - it is an end game.

'We will deal with your messages soon. Now: please change.'

He stands watching from the bedroom door as I take off my pyjamas. It's me who laughs as I put them in the dirty linen chest.

'This is funny? Good Tedwood. I like to hear you laugh. Now, take a shower.'

He walks across the room behind me and stands holding the bathroom door open while I wash myself again.

'Terrible smell of shit in here Eduardo. You ate something bad for you at lunch, I think. And maybe you had some of that horrible warm English beer in London.' He nods. 'At the Euston Tap probably.'

This shower is as hot and crushing as the previous one, but I feel like it's eroding me; erasing me. He knows I had a beer with Dave at Euston. He knows I ate that fucking cheeseburger and chips for lunch. He can't smell it on the shit-laden air in my en-suite bathroom. This is intelligence. Fucking shitting hell: I've been followed or tracked. How long has someone been doing this?

I step from the shower and pick up the towel I'd discarded on to the floor earlier. It doesn't really dry me. He is gazing at me impassively, still holding his firearm so it's pointed at my solar plexus. I feel my cock and balls shrivelling like they used to after sport at school; the judgement of the changing room.

'Put on simple clothes, like you would wear for a journey. Trainers, joggers, tee shirt. A hoody. You have them?'

I nod.

'Good Tedwood, then get them on now.' He points at my Gladstone bag. 'What is in there?'

'Clothes and stuff from the last few days.'

'A phone? Laptop?'

I tell him they're in the study and he seems satisfied.

'Okay Teduardo. We will take this bag as if you are spending a day or two away.'

With a wave of his gun he beckons me out into the hallway.

'Leave the bag there. Now we go to your toys, then we send some messages.' He sees me frown. 'It's no mystery. We have to tell the world you've got some place to go to spend your day off tomorrow.'

We're in the study now.

'Why do you have two phones Eduardo?'

'It's complicated.'

'It's excessive. But now you switch off this phone.' He points at the company Samsung. I feel like I want to start making reasons not to obey his orders. Make up a strange warning about how I never switch off my company phone, and if I do it will trigger an emergency message to someone who will immediately call the police and require that a SWAT team raids my house.

These are such futile thoughts, as if a dull project manager from Lancaster would have such a contingency plan.

'Next we must see who has been sending you messages. Hold up your iPhone where I can see it Tedwood. Ah-Haaaa, you have nice latest iPhone. Much better. And I see you have a missed call and four messages: let me see them.'

One is from Beth, the others from Victoria who had also tried to call me about twenty minutes ago.

Beth.

Oh no; Beth. I can't stop myself from sobbing aloud.

'Calm please Tedwood. Stay calm. Who is Beth and who is Victoria?'

I whisper my reply. Then wonder why he doesn't know.

'Your girlfriend is Victoria. I see. Show me what Victoria said.'

I scroll to her name and press it. Three bubbles are there.

First; 'Tried to call but guess you're in a train dead zone.'

Then; 'Please don't be mad at me. I don't think I can make tomorrow. My folks asked me over for dinner and I've never been able to turn them down.'

Finally; 'It's late now. Let me know you got back ok. We can talk in the morning. Night night. Love you xxx'

'You had plans to see her this weekend?'

I nod in affirmation. He is making calculations.

'Will she expect you to call her?'

'No.'

'If you send messages, will she answer?'

I tell him she usually puts her phone on Do Not Disturb.

'Good. Send her something. Tell her not to worry about tomorrow as you will go to see a friend. Small emergency of some kind and you decided to leave this evening as the roads will be quiet and your friend needs company. You will try to call her tomorrow.'

I type my own version of what he's said.

'Show me. Good. This friend, Sam, is real? She knows him?'

I nod.

'So the scene is set Tedwood. Any other messages other than from Beth? Emails? Show me your messages.'

I feel rage boiling up in me. That he should say my daughter's name again. That he is going to kill me and has no thought for my children. My children. For fuck's sake. I will never see my children again because of this bastard. And because of the voices in his phone, and the phones of countless others up the line to some supreme being that wants me dead.

Beth.

Joe.

My rage turns to tears.

'Please don't cry.'

'Make me.'

'At last Tedwood, a little bravado. But bravado is always foolish when you are so utterly weak. I can't stop you from crying. You must do it yourself. And don't be petulant.'

But I'm still crying and almost unable to breathe. I wonder if it will make him do something out of character: something weak; some hole in the defences.

'You still need to send more messages, so stop these tears. Say goodnight to your kids. Tell them you love them. Give them short version of your message to your woman. About going away. And please add that your phone never works properly in that place, so don't worry if no communication.'

I write these messages shuddering with sadness, and a kind of grief. Neither Beth nor Joe replies.

'And so, we are ready Tedwood. You need your car key. And you need to switch off your iPhone and give it to me.'

I seriously doubt that I will be able to drive. Aside from the shaking in my hands and legs, there is still a kind of darkness phasing across my eyes. I fumble with the off switch on my phone and it takes me three attempts to successfully operate the virtual slider on its screen.

He makes me pick up my bag and open the front door. He holds up the gun, showing me that it still represents a clear and present threat to my existence. That gesture glistens with the unspoken demand for me to be silent, or else. His dark eyes stare at me, insistently reinforcing his needs.

He pulls my front door, so it shuts on to its latch with barely a click of sound. For once I need my neighbours to be milling around in the lobby or out in the communal space for our cars. Instead, as we walk towards my Audi, a small uncaring cat pads its way across our path. My gaoler sniggers but doesn't speak. He points at the car door and mimes an *open it* gesture. I look around for options to make a run for it; I'm fit and fast; I reckon I could make it to the gateposts before he could react and shoot. Except I'm also shaking so much I doubt my legs could carry me. And my hands are full; keys; bag.

I keep obeying his gestures; hand me the bag, one says; get in the driver's side, another says; this is a gun, and if you try to raise any alarm, I will use it, the last one says. I slide the keys into my hoody pocket and open the driver's door but before I've properly sat down, he jams my case between me and the steering wheel. I'm trapped. And it's still dark. That's not right.

He throws something on to the back seat, then gently closes the door and as he does so he waves at me, almost affectionately, and walks briskly away towards the rear of the house.

'Put the bag on the passenger seat and start her up Teddy. We're headed to one of your favourite haunts.'

I feel something cold and metallic touching the base of my skull. When I do nothing, it is pressed harder.

'Do it. Drive towards the motorway. Northbound.'

No foreign accent now. This is a calm English voice. Harsh, southern, clipped.

'Nice motor, by the way.'

Again, I'm thinking about escape routes. I could smash the car into something or someone and attract attention. Or sound my horn continuously. Or drive round to Victoria's place and scream for help. What are the chances of this new attacker actually executing me while the car's in motion? He'd die too. Win-Win. Kind of.

The voice comes from my left now, and lower down. He's lying across the rear seat and as I try to glance over my shoulder he says: 'Eyes front. Stick to the speed limit. Let's get out of town quickly. And if you're thinking of trying some heroic escape or raising the alarm, forget it. Let's not drag anyone else into this.'

My valour slips away in the face of the implied threat to family or friends or innocent bystanders. I cruise up past the station, into the city then out to Junction 34 where I accelerate on to the almost deserted motorway.

'Arnside please driver. No need to stick to seventy, but don't go over eighty.'

We get there in no time and he directs me, monosyllabically, through residential streets above the promenade. There's barely any street lighting and, at a fork in the road, we join a lane with no lighting at all.

'Slow down and don't over-rev the engine.'

Driving the car has given me a focus on something vital, and it's almost made me forget there's a gun pointed at me. It's only a matter of yards before the road climbs quite steeply past the bulky shapes of houses to the right. My headlights, even dipped, seem incredibly bright.

'Switch to sidelights please.'

The sudden change of luminosity is bewildering, and I brake sharply.

'Take it easy. Up ahead on the left; that lay-by. Pull in there and switch off.' He's sitting up now and in my rear-view mirror I can see that he is alert, conducting a recce of our surroundings. I guide the car past closed gates and draw to a halt alongside a high wall. A brief sense of rebellion rises up in me; if I rev the engine now - really rev it - there would be a sound like a screaming banshee. There's quite a large building away to the right, perhaps fifty metres away behind a fence or wall of some sort. Occasional squares of light pepper its surface. Someone would wonder; would check; would raise an alarm.

'Come on Teddy boy, switch off and let's get moving. Once we're out of the car, don't speak unless I tell you to.'

As I switch off the engine the usual automated aurora of interior lighting fails to swell; it's why there was darkness at the house; he must have switched them off. How long has all this been planned?

He tells me to put my bag in the passenger footwell and while I do this he gets out and pulls open my door. With a sideways nod of his head, I'm instructed to join him on the lane. He has a bag with a strap over his left shoulder so it hangs down by his right hip.

His voice is just a murmur, yet crystal clear. 'Close your door quietly, and don't lock it with the remote.'

There's a covering of trees, and their bare branches form a web over our heads. It's dark and my eyes haven't adjusted yet.

'Give me the keys. Good. Let's walk. Slowly. If we meet anyone, let me do the talking.'

We're soon clear of the trees and, after a steady climb for fifty metres or so, he tells me to stop next to a small gateway on the left. There's a signpost pointing over the fence and gate, but I can't read whatever it says.

'Wait here until our night vision improves some more. Then we climb.'

The night air is chilly on my face and neck so I'm glad of the warm clothing. I look around: the lane disappears into the darkness; I can make out a featureless hillside; opposite the gate are fields; below us, the line of trees we left a few moments ago and the rectangular block of that building, now with no more than two or three lit squares on its facia.

After ten minutes standing still, with the man staring at me, he waves his gun at the gateway.

'Go through there and wait on the other side. Move.'

There's no moonlight, but now my eyes have adjusted to the darkness it's possible to make out the lie of the land. I feel grass underfoot; we're standing in a field that slopes down to the left; a couple of trees are nearby - ghostly shadows; the skyline is visible above the hill that I now realise is Arnside Knott, where I'd stood staring at the grey yonder just a few weeks ago.

He's pointing up at the two trees. 'That way. Watch your footing.'

How perverse that he should give health and safety advice.

We climb for around a minute and I hear a whispered 'Stop'. We've climbed up about thirty feet. Dots of lights in clusters are visible below us and further afield. There's virtually no sound at all other than an occasional screech or howl or bark. We're no more than half a mile from people, in houses, with kids and dogs and cars and lives, but this hillside feels isolated and remote. I vaguely have a sense of direction and compass, but I have no sense whatsoever about what is to come; what will create my death. If he shoots me, the noise will be heard won't it? Someone in one of those houses just down the hill will hear it and raise the alarm. Won't they?

'Looks like we're all alone Teddy boy.' He's still talking quietly. 'Go that way.'

I follow his instruction and we move along the hill, rather than up it. But he soon tells me to bear right for another climb. When we arrive on a small plateau, perhaps one hundred metres from, and perhaps fifty feet above the gate we used, I'm told to stop and wait.

The gun has switched hands and the man is opening up his shoulder bag with his right hand. He takes out what looks like a bottle.

It is a bottle.

It looks to be clear glass with a dark screw cap and a large dark label.

I think it might be vodka.

'You'll be found, some time - it could be a long time - lying somewhere on the slope away from here, down maybe fifty feet or so. Perhaps you'll have a broken neck or limb from the fall. But no other signs of violence. It's all self-inflicted. Why would you climb to this place and drink a potentially fatal amount of vodka? Something made you do it. Some inner sadness or worry. Things not so good at work? Money? Your love life? The people around you will care and be sad, but you'll be just another discredited loser in the eyes of most: not coping is not an option; shame on you for not being a man.'

While saying all this, he's been deftly unscrewing the metal cap one handed. He sniffs the neck of the bottle then hands it to me.

'Start drinking. Down in one. All of it.'

I take the bottle and put it to my lips. I see him raise his gun so it's pointing at my throat. Almost as soon as I taste it I know it's not neat. It isn't harsh on the throat like neat vodka would be, especially the cheap stuff from the bottom shelf. There's vodka in it, quite a large proportion, but it's weakened or diluted in some way. My mind starts revolving through options. This is my last chance to fight. I stop tipping the bottle in to my mouth.

'Don't stop drinking you cunt. Neck it. Come on. This is what kills you.'

I've drunk about a quarter of the contents. I'm trying to do that thing I did when I was a kid and got given things to eat or drink that I didn't like. Tea. Parsnips. Medicine. Strange mushrooms with daft names. The motions of consumption without swallowing.

'Swallow it. Stop fucking about.'

Now I decide to take counter-offensive action. With the bottle still in my mouth, I lurch forwards and then try to smash it downwards at his gun hand. Before I get close, he takes two paces towards me, kicks me hard in the balls then lashes a forearm across the top of my nose. I tumble forwards still clutching the bottle and feel wetness on my hand and wrist as I crash to the ground. I see some of the liquid running from the bottle where I've dropped it. The fact that the bottle didn't smash feels like a decisive, crushing defeat.

Still pointing the gun at me, he picks up the bottle.

'Get up you prick. Don't think you can take me on.'

As I scramble up onto all fours he tells me to stay on my knees as if in prayer. I'm told, in a hoarse whisper, to take the bottle from him and keep drinking. The pain in my bollocks and across my face is intense. I raise the bottle again and gulp down two mouthfuls, then I feel something washing over me, and coursing through me. I drink another mouthful.

I lower the bottle and see he is smiling at me, like a victory has been won. The pains in head and groin start to fade. I hear him say: 'Vodka is such a mug's game. Stand up and keep drinking.'

I put down the bottle and get to my feet, swaying like a sapling on a breezy day. Once on my feet I can barely stand.

'Pick up the vodka.'

I bend down then crash forwards before I can touch the bottle. On my knees again, I hear an other-worldly voice telling me to take and drink all of this. I reach for the bottle and clutch its neck and tip more of its contents into my mouth and swallow it. As I lower the bottle, I'm almost senseless but feel something on my chest. This thing makes a forceful movement, rigid and fast, pushing me away. I'm tumbling sideways and backwards, into a roll then over and sideways, round and round, like a barrel. I can't feel much despite the sense of hitting things, like a bouncing bomb. All I can sense is that half my world is charcoal, and the other half is blank with a vaguely slippy, wet thing going on. I don't know which stops first: the rolling and bouncing; or my sight.

I wake up dead.

31

There's a chilly, silvery hint of dawn away to my left. I'm laid diagonally at the bottom of a small slope with my feet slightly above me. I'm cold, stiff and hurting. There is soreness everywhere: shoulders; hips; wrists; nose; neck; jaw; abdomen. Some of that is outright pain. I am nauseous and wracked by palpitations.

I feel the need to move and small cross checks reveal that no pain or soreness is increased by a lifted arm, a turned ankle, a clenched fist or a bent knee. I roll on to my front, then push up on to my hands and knees. When I lift myself, so I'm sitting on my haunches, I can feel my heart pounding in my chest. Something makes me pull my hood up over my head, then put my hands in my kangaroo pocket. I wait like this for a few moments.

When I eventually try to stand, the combination of dizziness and an adverse camber makes me tumble forwards. I wait longer, a few moments, before trying again.

It's lighter now and I realise I don't know where I am. Further down the hill are small signs of habitation but none that I recognise immediately. Is this my home?

To my left and right the slope of the hillside has no obvious clues. A short distance below me, perhaps fifty metres or so, there's a stone wall with quite dense tree growth beyond it. Above and past that landscape I can see the bulk of some hills.

Why am I here, wherever it is? I try to stand again. It takes many seconds, but I finally get to my feet. I shuffle slowly forwards, then hear a metallic noise near one of my trainers. I look down; it's a bunch of keys; they are mine; I know that and I pick them up.

I put my hands back in my hoodie pocket but it's empty. I have a sense that there should be something in there. This makes me even more confused. I'm focused on the wrong things: about something lost; not about why I'm apparently cast adrift on a deserted hillside. I begin a frantic search around me, with no idea what I need to find. The turns I make cause another spell of disorientated staggering, and I crash back to the grass.

I lie still. It's a bit lighter now and I'm desperate to renew my search. On my hands and knees, I move in slowly increasing circles.

And then I see a rectangular shape and I know it's my phone. I rise stiffly to my feet and stumble a few paces to where it's lying. The screen is blank, and the stick-on protector has a couple of cracks in it. This is easy; I know what to do. I press the side button, hoping there's no internal damage despite its battered appearance. The black apple's background suddenly dazzles me, so I look away, which makes small cascades of liquid drop from my nostrils. When I use my sleeve to wipe away the rest, it sends a stab of pain up my nose. This rush of discomfort doesn't completely eradicate the sense that I can smell alcohol.

Start drinking. Down in one.

My thumb print doesn't work and even though I know the PIN it takes me three attempts to get it right. A colourful life-saving mosaic is revealed. I hit the maps button and it shows me I'm near a road called Knott Lane which leads, eventually into Arnside.

Arnside please driver.

My phone warns me there is 20% battery life left and asks a subsequent question. I wonder if there's a limit on my own life now, although most of the pain has dissipated. Except for my nose. I'm able to stand, steadily, so I do small footsteps on the spot.

I type something into the search box, and the map centres on Arnside station. I touch the *directions* button then the *walk* option; it tells me it's *1.3 mi* and will take *28 mins* via Red Hills Road. I assume *mi* means miles and *mins* means minutes. But I'm not wholly certain.

I move slowly towards where the blue line begins and there's a kissing gate between the field I'm in and the road.

There's a wooden sign pointing the way I've just come; it's worn and in the early morning light I need to get up close, really close, to see that it indicates a Public Footpath; Red Hills; High Knott Road.

Then we climb.

I'm walking slowly, stiffly under a rapidly dawning sky. The movement seems to punch small slivers of data into my head. Knowledge. Revision. I have been to Arnside before. I turn around and look up at the hillside. I walked here.

And there are people I know; names bounce up; and some stick in my head.

My phone battery has dropped rapidly to 12% so I switch off the automated verbal directions and revert to simple map reading, holding the phone up in front of me as if it holds the source of all knowledge. I'm so focused on the screen that I walk past my car before I realise it's there. For a moment or two I just stand there, staring at its shape, disbelieving that the Audi is parked here in a sheltered lay-by near an impressive double gateway.

So; I drove here. Why did I come here?

Nice motor by the way.

I take out my car remote and look at the symbols and buttons. When I press Unlock there's a faint click from the car and the indicators flash. It's a sudden, brief, disorienting shock of light. I open the door and climb behind the steering wheel. Priorities merge into chaos: what do I do next? This space is homely and familiar, but it has so many switches and buttons. I have a glimpse of something to suggest that this should be safe ground.

Somewhere that puts me back in control and confident. Yet it feels impenetrable, blank, a gaol.

But I put my phone in a slot and a tiny tone accompanies a changed screen with the image of a battery, partially filled with green. Then I grip the wheel and press a button to start the car. Somehow this is all understood; I know this machine and all the processes in my head and limbs that will make the car move. I reach to the heating dial and turn it so the number 28 appears.

From a place, perhaps long-forgotten research for cold-weather walking, a fragment of knowledge surfaces about hypothermia. It's bad to warm up too quickly. Is that right? I'm already warmer from walking, but perhaps I should just sit here for a while to get my core temperature to a safe level? What is my core temperature? Is there an app for that? I turn the dial back towards 20.

I decide to drive and call someone.

It will be Victoria; another name I have absorbed.

She'll be back from running. Victoria does running.

I manoeuvre the car into a U turn which is done in one take. The lane drops down for a bit and I realise I've been here before. But now I have recovered enough about the processes involved with this environment to realise that my driving efforts are shaky. After just a couple of minutes at the wheel it's clear I can't safely drive for any distance. Yet I have no choice.

I pull over and press a button. The sat nav screen shows me that I'm very close to the Promenade where I parked that day in February. Yes, February: that's when I walked down this lane. With the car's guidance, I set off again and crawl along Red Hills Road to a T-junction then left until I reach a pub called Albion and the line of car parking spaces that face the estuary.

When I pull to a halt in one of the spaces, the engine cuts out. This is good. An idling engine is wasteful, harmful and noisy. The idea of attracting attention troubles me, but I'm not clear why. My phone is still charging.

I'm wondering what has caused me to be here; why did I wake up in pain on a hillside? How come my car was parked on a quiet roadside? Where was I going with the overnight bag stuffed into the passenger foot well? What can I be sure of? What is the last thing I can remember with certainty?

I work forwards from the point at which I left the office.

Goodbyes to the few left ahead of a long weekend.

Underground so busy I was able to feel people's breath on my face and neck.

Euston station horrendous, Euston Tap magical. Dave in great form. Double rounds; four pints before heading for the half seven train.

First class busier than I've ever known it. Even after Warrington where it usually thins.

Needed to piss a lot on the train. Drank water to rehydrate.

Walked to house, let myself in.

No alarm.

Something clicks now. The man and his gun. The bladder opening terror. Another man in my car, and the drive to Arnside. In the darkness, a stroll on a hillside. A bottle?

My phone shows 25% now and it's enough to call Victoria. She doesn't answer until she messages, 'Give me five mins please? Just getting dressed.'

'K'

No, it's not k. I change my mind. 'I really need to talk. Something bad has happened.'

She calls me.

'Hey. What's up? Is it Sam?'

I explain that my message about a sick friend was made up, then I explain why I sent it. I explain everything that I know has happened, without omission, and some of what I think might have happened. When I say it all out loud it seems clearer. Yet there is still no real recollection of what happened.

It takes me about five minutes to summarise the events. Victoria is calm, but I can hear some semblance of trembling in her voice.

'Where are you now?'

'Sitting in my car on Arnside promenade.'

'Okay. You mustn't drive. I'll come and get you. Do I need to get anything from your place?'

'No, it's fine. I'm warm in the car.' I look down at my joggers.

There are muddy lines and the areas around both knees are wet.

'Wait while I check train times.'

She keeps talking while she searches, and I reassure her that I haven't broken anything and don't feel any of the symptoms of shock or hypothermia that she reels off.

'It's not looking good Teddy. Trains on Good Friday appear to be non-existent. I'll get a taxi.'

I am too tired, and increasingly upset, to argue that it will cost a fortune.

'Keep warm in your car but get a warm drink if you can. Try to stay awake. I'll let you know once I'm in the taxi. Need to go to phone them. Will you be all right?'

I can't answer because now I'm in paroxysms of anguish with tears running down my face.

'Teddy. Hold on to the thought that I'll be there soon. Just keep thinking of me. Of us.'

It isn't long before a message arrives telling me Victoria is on her way. I reply with details of where I'm parked. Then I tell her to get dropped off at the pub, not near my parking space. There's a paranoia ticking away now. I don't want anyone to see where I am. I even think about deserting my car.

When I see her, I get out of the car and hold the door open for her. But she doesn't get in. I'm looking around, like a fugitive.

'Calm down Teddy. It's okay.'

'I just want to get away from here.'

'I'm sure. But let me look at you.'

She looks into my eyes, and I hold her gaze. She recoils slightly.

'Teddy, you reek of alcohol. How far have you driven like this?'

I shake my head, incapable of speech now she's with me. She takes my head in her hands and repeats several questions about how I am, how I feel, where there is pain. I jerk my head free and it seems to upset her.

She breaks a short silence. 'Is there anything I need to know about you or what's happened that I should treat as a fiction?'

'No. I've been completely honest with you, always.'

'Okay. Have you ever had any kind of assault on you, of any kind, before these last few weeks?'

'No. Absolutely not.'

She spends ages staring into my eyes.

'Are you unhappy or hiding anything from me? Or from anyone?'

'Until these last few hours, I've never been happier. Nothing is hidden. And that's because of you.'

She squints and I want her to smile, but she seems sceptical. 'Okay Ted. Let's go. Here. Drink some of this, slowly.' Victoria takes out a thermos.

Our journey back to her house is filled with talking and questions. She makes me work through what happened again, and then a second time with a dissection of specific segments. Saying it all out loud seems to have dissipated the fog in my head. I can recall things. Most things.

What train were you on? The usual, into Lancaster just after ten pm.

Any sense you were being followed or watched? None, though I'd had four pints and was far from observant. But the guy in the house knew about my Thursday lunch and beers with Dave.

Did he mention Dave? No.

Did he mention anyone else by name? Only when he saw your and Beth's names on my phone.

How had the first man got in and over-ridden the alarm? With keys; he said people are careless. So I guess he somehow got copies. He said the alarm hadn't been set.

And he had a real gun? It looked real to me.

It must have been terrifying. I literally wet my pants.

Victoria looks across at me and her face portrays a sheer, unadulterated concern for me. Like a mother's love and fears for a child who's been hurt.

Why did you send the message to me about being away? He told me to; to create an external view that I was leaving but there was nothing to be worried about.

What made you say you were going to Sam's? He kind of prompted it. Told me to say I'd be somewhere remote; it just made sense because my phone has never worked over there and everyone knows it.

So, it really was just a spur of the moment story? Yes. It was.

Who else did he make you contact? He told me to say goodnight to Joe and Beth.

Have you told either of them what's happened? No. I don't know what I would say to them.

Could you describe the man at your house? Yes. In great detail, including how he talked.

We've reached Junction 34, but Victoria keeps heading south and for a change I have a question. 'Why didn't you drive into the city?'

'I want to get my head around what's happened to you before we decide what to do next.'

I can't tell if she's curious, incredulous or angry.

Did you consider attacking the guy, to disarm him? No. I believed he meant to kill me. He said that was his intention.

How could the second man have got into your car? They must have found my spare remote, then taken it from the apartment and kept it in the car to stop the alarm going off.

The guy in the car was also armed? Yes.

Is there any CCTV at your house? No.

Did you hear the two men exchange any comments or acknowledge each other? I expected the first guy to get in the car with me. It was a complete surprise when he ran off and I was handed over to a second assailant. Any communication between them was non-verbal.

Same question as before: could you describe the man in the car? Not until we got out at Arnside. And it was dark so it's a bit vague. He was slightly shorter than me; well built. Nondescript clothes. He wore a hat. Was definitely wearing those gloves, like surgical ones. In fact, both men were. His accent suggested south east England, but his diction was well educated. And he was a fighter.

How do you mean? When I tried to stop him, the speed and agility of his response were decisive and measured. Trained into him.

How much did you drink from the bottle? I don't know. After I tried to fight him, it's like things get hazy. Less than half, I think. But that could have been in ten seconds or ten minutes for all I know.

Did you think about just spitting it out? Yes. But I thought he would shoot me if I didn't do what he said. He kept pointing his gun at my throat.

What was the liquid? He said it was vodka, and I think it had vodka in it. But I don't think it was neat. I don't remember it burning the way neat vodka would.

Could you taste anything else? No. Nothing.

How did you feel after you started drinking? I can't remember.

Did he definitely push you down the hill? I can't remember.

What happened to the bottle? I've no idea. I'm guessing it's still somewhere between where we started and where I landed.

Did either of the men say anything about why they were doing it? The first one said he'd had an instruction by phone. The second one said he was staging something that was either an accident or suicide. Neither of them mentioned any kind of owner for their actions.

Staging something? He described what was intended. For me to be found dead with an excess of alcohol in my system.

So you're in danger? It seems so.

We've reached and passed Junction 33 and as we approach Forton Services I give an involuntary shudder, prompting Victoria to ask if I want the toilet. I realise I haven't urinated since I wet myself more than ten hours ago, yet don't need to do so now. I tell Victoria I just want to go somewhere and get changed and warm.

Do you think this attack is linked to the one on the train? I think it has to be.

Why do you think this is happening to you?

Before I can answer, I am overwhelmed by tears. Victoria reaches over and strokes me; my leg; my arm; my shoulder and neck.

'Okay Teddy let's get you home. Come to my place and we'll work out what to do together. Sit back and try to relax. It will take about half an hour.'

The calm certainty of her voice, and her apparent lack of any fear don't help me. I am still crying and shaking when we arrive back at her house. The sense that everything is in slow motion starts to grip me and I try to tell Victoria this, but I'm talking in slow motion too. She takes my hand, then feels my pulse.

'Your heart's racing Teddy. I know it's not what you might want to do, but perhaps we should go to A&E.'

I have a massive palpitation, like I remember getting the first time I had Turkish coffee.

'If we go to A&E, we will need to explain why I'm in shock and have so much alcohol in my system. That might mean the police get involved.'

I'm still talking incredibly slowly.

'We can say you fell while walking. We don't need to mention the attack. You were stupid, walking off the effects of a long drinking session.'

I tell her that isn't plausible.

'Why don't you want to tell the police?'

'Because it alerts whoever did this to the fact that I survived. I think I just need to get cleaned up, get some rest and sleep.'

She looks at me with great scepticism. 'Okay. You do that, I'll make you some more tea. Are you hungry?'

I tell her I'm not and mention another bit of dredged-up, dubious first aid - that you shouldn't consume food or drink if you're in shock. I have a small glass of water, take a lukewarm shower and lie down in the spare room. Victoria joins me for a while, whispering comforts and holding my hand until I fall asleep.

When I wake up in the early afternoon, Victoria tells me she's upset her parents because she's told them she can't visit them after all.

'I can't leave you Teddy. But I simply hate letting them down. How do you feel?'

'Better. A bit hungry.'

'I made you some pasta and salmon. It's in the oven keeping warm. Would you like some?'

My nod isn't convincing.

Victoria says she thinks I should switch off and not use my personal phone; and that it's sensible to only use my work phone for the foreseeable future. She also tells me she's put my car in her garage and that she thinks we need to go to my house.

'Why do you want to do that?'

'I just think we should see if there's anything that reveals why this has happened.' Her voice has a tiny shake in it.

I have another palpitation and tell her I really don't feel up to going there. But she's right: we might learn something; she should go.

'But I don't want to leave you Teddy. I can't leave you.'

'I know. And I don't want to be alone. But it's only thirty minutes. Forty-five tops.'

We discuss and test a hasty plan. Victoria can walk to my house. She can let herself in. She can film the rooms on her phone and show me. Reconnaissance. Reassurance. What if there's someone there? We agree there probably won't be. But she can't go alone.

'I'll be fine. And maybe I can bring back some things for our journey tomorrow?'

I'm shaking my head. 'You can't do this alone. I'll have to come.'

'I'm sure I'll be okay. The other flats will be occupied, won't they? I can get help if the worst happens.'

'No. I will have to come with you.'

Our plan had always been to travel to London early on Easter Saturday morning, spend the weekend sight-seeing, dining and dancing and for Victoria to see me off to Heathrow and Bucharest before heading back to Lancaster during the following Tuesday. This plan also included my acclimatisation at her London apartment.

'You can't walk and bring back all that I need. It would need several trips and will take too long. We will have to drive round. Fuck. This is so scary.' I'm crying again. She wraps her arms around my head.

'It is scary, but we need to go. We must still go to London tomorrow. It will be much safer there. Won't it?'

Our hasty plan is augmented. We will drive round in her car and she will let herself in; this won't seem strange if any of my neighbours see her. If everything seems okay, I'll go in too. If not...

'Everything will be okay Teddy. Let's be positive.'

We agree to go while it's still light and to be in and out as quickly as possible. To avoid any dithering, we make a list of all that I need for the coming week. Ideas keep popping up, as if this requirement for the basics of admin are somehow a shield against the unspoken fear of what might be happening.

'Would you usually let your neighbours know you're away?'

'No.'

'You won't be back for a while. And your car won't be there. I think we should let them know. Explain that you're away on business, overseas and more or less permanently until further notice. Your car is garaged with a friend who will be coming and going to keep an eye on things.'

We review if this is sensible. What if my attackers come back and check in with the neighbours? It could be a signal I survived. We decide it's less risky than Amber suddenly getting curious and calling the police.

We type and print three copies of a chatty message. I sign them.

Victoria takes a long detour, into and through the city before heading back to the house. I pull my hoody up over my head as she drives and leave it up when she pulls up in the parking area outside the apartments. I sink right down into my seat.

We wonder why there are no other cars. Perhaps everyone is away for a long weekend? I don't voice my sudden horror that they might all have been murdered.

Victoria says she will try all the apartments first and post the letters if no one answers.

I spend the next few minutes staring out from the car with a kind of terror welling up in me. My vision has curved edges, so it feels like I'm looking through a fish-eye lens, making the familiar scenes around me warped; distorted. From this periphery, I see Victoria appear at the main entrance and beckon to me. I dash across the several metres of tarmac to the haven of familiarity, just around fifteen hours after the chilling events that saw me leave it under duress.

Everything appears no different than it's ever been.

Nondescript.

Neat.

Nothing to indicate any alien presence at any time.

Victoria takes my hand, leads me to the kitchen and points to some keys on the kitchen worktop. It looks like the same ring and keys that the first guy waved at me yesterday.

'Best not to touch them Teddy.'

'Maybe we shouldn't touch anything.'

'I don't know.'

We're looking at each other with mounting dread, and then have another broken conversation in which we conclude that we are evading the sensible option to call the police. I'm staring at the keys. Up close I can see that they are not originals; cheap cuts that could have been done anywhere but definitely not by me. And from which originals? My head is pounding with questions; and none of them has answers I could give to a police officer.

I don't need much time to pack clothes for the weekend, and then my trip to Bucharest plus the usual work machinery. While she takes these bags to her car, I pack an additional case with more clothes for Victoria to bring next weekend.

'I took a look around the outside of the house. I can't see anything suspicious. I took a picture of the road too. And now I don't know why I did that.'

Her face is pale, and her eyes seem close to tears. Her voice is wobbling as she says, 'How do you feel Teddy? Will you be all right not being here for a bit? It's your home after all.'

'It's never felt like home. Just the place where I've been living.'

'That's so sad.'

'It's realistic. And now it's essential we're not here. Come on.'

The food she's made is comforting but it's cold now and I eat less than half of it. We sit together on the sofa and find we aren't saying much about anything. A numbed silence descends. It's not much after five in the afternoon and Victoria has her head on my shoulder, an arm around my middle and her legs curled up underneath her body. She falls into a deep sleep and I am left deep in thought.

There can be no doubt that her question about me being in danger is a valid one and I'm troubled by where the source of that danger lies, and what events and circumstances lend weight to it being real.

The incident on the train was clearly not a random attack; I have to assume the two are connected, but probably with different executors. Which means the most likely root cause is the SocMed post showing the Jarvis email and then on into the fun filled world of MarMap. Any other conflict I can think of from recent weeks is small, pale and insignificant. Why would Paul Wilson get involved in conspiracy to murder? Or Carla; and anyone else I might have offended on *matchmates*? Or Amy?

All the abuse on SocMed and Chattabox might hold the key somewhere, but those links just form a chain ending with MarMap. Except for Jennifer Juniper, and she didn't seek me out. It was me who chased after her to establish some sort of empathy with her side of the road protests.

But then it was her that wanted the meeting. I replay as much as I can about that encounter in the Paternoster. She wasn't quite what I expected and some of what she said didn't seem like a default protest-or-die rhetoric. She focused on the differences between the groups more than their arguments; as if she needed to draw out some hidden standpoint. To place me in a periodic table of political colours. And what was all that about knowing Marcus Mapplewick? Why would they have met? If she isn't the super eco-warrior in her posts, what is she? And more to the point what possible reason would she have to authorise an attempt on my life? Her message to me was essentially a kind one, if robustly delivered: step away from what you don't understand.

I don't see how it can be her.

And that leaves Jude.

I'm absolutely certain Craig knows I'm having an affair. He might also know it's with you.

Assuming she was right, it might have led him to take some sort of punitive action. Would a director, his company's senior-most financial officer, be that dumb? Take such a risk? Exert such executive power, like a game? But would that just be against me? Wouldn't he have something in store for Jude too?

Is she safe?

If you dare go near her, I will never talk to you again and I might get my husband to have you killed.

By the time Victoria wakes up, I've pulled myself into little pieces with a kind of distress that I can't quantify or rationalise. I'm so convinced that I'm in real danger, mortal danger, that I begin firing these fears at her as soon as she opens her eyes. I was supposed to die; someone wants to kill me; and even if there's a grace period in which my death isn't discovered or reported, the next murder attempt will follow soon. They might even be watching me now.

It makes no difference when she takes my head in her hands to comfort me. I'm gibbering with terror when she rocks me like a babe in arms, humming a made-up melody.

32

Neither of us sleeps soundly but we manage some bits and pieces of rest and recuperation. In the morning, there's a sense of hope; that we had a collective, inter-connected nightmare, and it's ended with nothing more troublesome than a morning shiver of recollection.

By the time we have readjusted to the grim, dawning realisation that something terrible has happened, it's time to get up and get moving.

The taxi arrives and we load our luggage then head to the station. We're in plenty of time for the quick train at around 9:40 and, like the southbound platform, it's more or less deserted on board. The journey seems to flash past in almost total silence. Like fugitives, we sit staring at anyone we can see; at each stop we become alert and frightened about potential threats from new passengers dawdling in a search for their seats.

At Euston we jump in another taxi and in less than twenty minutes we're hauling our bags into Victoria's apartment near Camden Square. It's on the top floor of an old terraced house, cosy and comfortable and immediately feels safe, protected and calm. We confess how fragile we felt on the journeys we've just made. As I look around and Victoria makes drinks, she explains how her father, like many people in the City, had made a lot of money in the late seventies and on into the nineties. Sick of living in hotels and in rented flats, he'd decided to take the plunge and buy a modest London home, meaning he could live there Sunday night to Thursday, then return north to be with the family.

Sitting opposite one another, coffee cups between us on a table, stumbling through bland chit-chat from cake-filled mouths, Victoria suddenly switches subject.

'I've been thinking this over. Either the attack on you was a serious attempt on your life and you were supposed to die; so, it failed; or it was a very well-planned frightener intended to scare you into submission about something. It wasn't supposed to kill you, but it wouldn't have been a problem if it had.'

'Why do you think it could be a frightener?'

'Because all that happened was incredibly well organised and executed. Why do all that and leave you alive?'

I sip some coffee and squint at her. 'How do you know they left me alive? What if it was just luck that I survived?'

'All right then, I'll say it differently: why do all that and not make absolutely sure you're dead?'

'Perhaps they just believed what had happened was enough? That unconsciousness and exposure would do the job without any further intervention. So, like I said: I got lucky.'

'It doesn't feel to me like luck has any part of this. And I just think your car is critical. If they meant to kill you, they wouldn't have left your car there. Its presence miles from home would eventually get someone to ask why it's there and set hares running. Whereas if they brought it back and left it at your house it wouldn't attract attention. Neighbours would assume you're away on business, like you often are. And will be. Then you could have lain on that hillside for days without being found.'

Now she's frowning. 'And that's another thing; it's quite busy up there isn't it. So why did they choose somewhere so commonly used? If you were supposed to die, they would have found somewhere much more remote with fewer dog walkers, hikers and pedestrians. Somewhere you might never have been found.'

I suppose she's right. 'But if they only meant to frighten me, why make it so elaborate?'

'Like I said, to make it credible. And actually, to make it incredible too. It's why there's probably no point going to the police.'

'How do you mean?'

Victoria pauses, calculating something, before she explains her view that everything this plot set out to do was to show no third party was involved. I drove my own car off to Arnside in the dead of night. I drank a load of alcohol while walking in the dark on a hillside. I fell and tumbled. I've got injuries attributable to a fall. I've had a tough time lately. Work pressures, including imminent redundancy. The end of an affair. The attack at Warrington station. The crazy behaviour on SocMed, which friends had noted with concern. Worries about an ex-wife's problems and how they affect my children. More than enough reasons for something to flip and make me do something stupid. Or to want to kill myself.

'They've made it plausible that you intended to harm yourself Ted. Take the actual scenario to the police and you'd get nowhere. There's no CCTV of someone in your car with you. The one thing that might support your story – a discarded bottle with traces of whatever drug they used – is no use.'

'What do you mean by the *actual scenario*? Are you saying you don't believe me?'

'I believe everything you've told me Teddy. Why would you lie to me?'

She endorses these words with lingering eye contact, but I feel a heightened sense that no-one will ever believe that what happened is real.

'But their DNA would be all over my house and car and that bag. Fingerprints on the keys.'

She reels off a list of counter arguments. Surgical gloves prevent fingerprints. There'd be no detailed investigation and no DNA checks. Even if there was, the perps probably have no known trace – like the train attacker. If reported, this story would be viewed through sceptical eyes right from the start.

'If you insisted on an investigation, they might send plod over to the hillside who might find a bottle with your fingerprints. But probably some concerned citizen will have found and binned it. And what other evidence is there? They might do some door knocking to see if anyone saw you being led from the car or was wondering why a strange car was parked overnight. There's no provable crime. It's all circumstantial. They've bigger fish to fry. Proper crimes to solve.'

She's really been thinking about this. All I've done is stare into the distance.

'The alarm is weird though. If I hadn't forgotten to set it on Tuesday, what would they have done?'

'I dread to think.'

She gasps. 'It means I caused this. Jesus Teddy. If only I'd...'

I'm shaking my head and reach across the table to touch her hand. 'None of this is your doing Victoria. These people.... it's like you said; this is so well planned that they probably had a way to find the code or disable the alarm.'

She stares at me, unblinking. 'But that could have involved attacking me to get it. It's the same with the keys. Have they somehow made copies from mine? Or Beth's or Joe's?'

'Or mine.'

'But when and how? Have they been following us all to pick a moment to steal and copy the keys? Who else has a key? What about Jude.'

'No. She returned hers to me the other week.'

'But they still could have been taken and copied without her knowing.'

My mind is reeling. 'If that is the case, then this whole thing has been planned for weeks. And I really don't want to think how much threat there might be to Beth and Joe; or to you.' I can't prevent a tremor rippling through my voice as I say that.

There are many minutes of shocked silence and it calms us.

'Whatever was intended, one thing is clear - to a greater or lesser extent, your life is in danger. We need a plan, and one that covers both sides of their intentions and keeps you safe from harm.'

'What do you mean: both sides of their intentions?'

'If it was a frightener then we take steps to make any more frighteners difficult but work on the assumption there'll be no more. So, be watchful but not paranoid, and perhaps keep a low profile. If they really meant to kill you then you need to be somewhere else.'

Invisible idiot.

'And right now, I'd say being here in London for a few days and then your trip to Romania probably covers both bases.'

She stands and takes my hand to show me around the apartment, all the places where everything is kept, how to use all the apparatus in the kitchen. There's an alarm, and serious locks on the doors and windows and she hands over the keys I need to keep it all safe. And it really does feel very safe indeed when Victoria halts any further review of the property by luring me to bed and seducing me. We stay there for the rest of the afternoon, all evening and night. The only interruption is for glasses and wine, then a pizza ordered for delivery. It's past midnight when we appear to have run out of steam and call a truce on our battling libidos. Victoria curls up next to me, with a background of something inane on television. She's murmuring in my ear.

'Wowser Teddy boy. Thought you'd be a bit useless after what's happened. But that was bravura.'

My giggles are infectious. Not even the fleeting shadow of doubt that I have no right to feel happy and safe, just forty-eight hours after an attempt on my life, can stop me from feeling a huge surge of adoration for Victoria. Not to put too fine a point on it, it feels like she might have saved my life.

She goes out running the next morning, so I acclimatise a bit by getting online and making sure I can connect to my work's network on this new Wi-Fi. Then I get on to messaging and the group Beth, Joe and I use to chat together and let them know that I'm in London with Victoria.

Just about the only thing discussed on yesterday's train journey was a review of the risks of using my personal phone; Victoria convinced me that there was more sense in using it than making up a potentially incredible story about why I can't. We also agreed that I had to get in touch with Beth and Joe but should avoid discussing the attack.

'Hi pops.'

'What is this new madness? When have you ever called me pops?'

She posts a laugh out loud emoji.

'Just felt like being American for some reason. So many reasons to love and copy them right now.'

Now it's my turn to send a smiley.

'Where's Joe?'

'He's gone to church for the Easter services with mum.'

'You're joking.'

'Yes, I'm joking. He's in bed. Mum is out somewhere.'

'How is she doing?'

'She's ok. How is London?'

'V has a really nice place.'

'She told me about it. When are you off to Romania?'

'Tuesday. But we will talk before then.'

'And how is Sam?'

'False alarm.'

A rolling eyes emoji comes next, then: 'V is lovely. Well done pops.'

A smile cracks my face, then I start crying and can barely type.

'You cannot believe how much it means to me that you've said that.'

'Awww. But I need to make use of this peace and quiet to get some revision done. Why don't I get Joe to join me on a call later?'

'K'

'Any time to avoid?'

'Message me first.'

Victoria and I have no plans to do anything other than settle into this new domesticity. I don't feel like going out at all and she's patient about that. By mid-afternoon, it feels warm enough to sit outside on the small roof terrace.

'Your nose still looks sore.'

'It was doing fine until you hit your head against it during last night's love-making.'

'Was it love-making?'

'I thought so.'

'Some of it was just banging though, right?'

'Maybe you could point out the difference next time.'

She sips her iced tea and raises an eyebrow as she lowers her cup. 'Ignorance might be best on that particular topic. I'd hate to make you think it matters.'

'And I'd hate you to say anything remotely nice while we're fucking.'

Victoria laughs so violently and falls from her chair so quickly that she kicks over the small table with our cups sending most of their contents over my legs and shorts.

I go and change, and she pours more drinks.

'How are you feeling now. We've not spoken about what happened for more than a day and you shouldn't avoid the subject.'

'I haven't been, don't worry. Getting here, and being here, and... last night... were all good distractions. Are you absolutely sure it's all right for me to be here, more or less permanently?'

'Of course. Why not?'

'I'm worried it creates a problem for you with your parents or your sister?'

'It doesn't. So just live here, work here, be here. Invite Joe and Beth. If you want to get to Wood Street it's about a ten-minute walk to Camden Town tube and Moorgate is five stops; make sure you get the right train, via Kings Cross.'

'Not sure I'll be in the office much at all. These trips to Romania will take up most of my working weeks for the rest of April and May. After that, I'm not sure.'

'Once you feel settled, it probably makes sense to go in occasionally.'

'And what about Lancaster? I can't just leave it permanently vacated.'

'No, I agree. Let's get some food ordered and talk about that. We also need to talk about how you are going to keep fit without access to squash, gym and footie. I can't have you getting out of shape.'

We get some Indian food delivered and have some cheap sparkling rosé with it. The food is amazing, and I comment that with curries this good I'll be out of shape in no time.

Victoria laughs bitterly. 'Then you'll end up useless at banging, love-making and fucking. And that won't do. Get your iPad out and search for Camden gyms. There's loads and I don't care which one you join. Just make sure you do join one. What will you do out in Bucharest?'

'The hotel we use has basic gym facilities.'

'Have you packed some kit?'

'Some basics. But not enough for anything frequent. Didn't even occur to me.'

'Then let's get you out of here tomorrow and find you some stuff. I'll bring more next weekend.'

Our discussion about my apartment is less conclusive. We dismiss out of hand the notion that I could be sneaked in under cover of darkness every other weekend. There's also agreement that I can't sell it and leave myself nowhere to live. That leads to a detour discussion about our future and how we need to be grown up about it. It feels good, and we have become something special very quickly. But it's too early for a life plan and co-dependency. The arrangements that form are broadly along the lines that in the short term, six to ten weeks, I have a genuine reason not to be in Lancaster because work is taking me abroad. After that, Beth and Joe will be at the end of their respective university years and will need the comfort of a base with me. As it feels like we've reached a result, I wonder aloud if I could let my apartment, but Victoria tells me it's a very bad idea especially for Beth and Joe's sakes.

There's a normality in play, even though what we're discussing is effectively about some aspects of my life being rubbed out and pencilled in on a new page. By the end of Easter Sunday, I feel safe and I thank Victoria for taking charge. She looks at me askance and tells me nothing has changed. There is still quite possibly a threat to my life or safety; or both. But the fact that, for nearly seventy-two hours, nothing has escalated means I should keep taking small, vigilant steps away from what happened on Thursday night and Friday morning.

As Victoria and I settle down in bed, with no specific activities in mind, my phone alerts me to a message. It's Beth, complaining that Joe has disappeared out somewhere despite her telling him repeatedly to find time to join us in a group chat and call. I tell her not to worry and not to be angry.

And I fall asleep thinking that the small steps Victoria mentioned have already begun; back to that particular normality; I am still a father with children who can fight each other for fun.

We spend Easter Monday strolling around Camden, picking up food and ideas. I buy additional sports gear and we look in on the local gyms that are open. There isn't one with a squash court, so I just choose the nearest to Victoria's apartment and handover the jaw-dropping membership fee.

I don't feel so scared, or so watchful, as I did previously. No-one is staring at me or glaring. I don't feel observed. But then I didn't feel anyone was watching me at the Euston Tap on Thursday evening. All around me is a mass of life, fulfilling whatever tasks and activities are needed. There may be bad people all around me, with evil intent. Yet nothing happens to cause me harm. And no one else is being harmed or hated or hurt. The mass of life doesn't exist to improve or negate me. I am among it, if I want to be, or I can step outside it. I can pick at the things I like and find contempt for what displeases me. I can grab the opportunities or push them away. And I can be myself; or be someone else's me; or invent a me that fits whatever the mass decrees.

'Where on earth have you gone?'

Victoria has disengaged her arm from mine and stopped us walking further with a tug. 'I've been speaking to you; whole sentences of things needing your engagement. You seemed to be somewhere I'm not.'

'No, I wasn't. We were linked arm in arm, and I was still in love with you.'

'In love with me? Teddy, those bangs to the head on Friday morning must have been worse than you're admitting.'

I take a deep breath. It was the truth, but premature - emboldened by the retreat from fear she has caused. This is love, and now I can't deny it.

'Whatever injuries I suffered tumbling down that hillside didn't make me mad or delusional. I felt this before.'

'You felt that you loved me?'

We're standing in the middle of Camden Market surrounded by the smiles and joy of a retailing fix.

'Yes, I did. But I wasn't sure. Right up until the moment you asked *why would you lie to me*? On Saturday.'

She turns me to face her and, for the umpteenth time since she picked me up at Arnside, I see a combination of concern and reserved happiness.

'You're saying you love me just because I believe in you?'

'Because you chose to believe when you could have walked away or dismissed what I told you. Or worse; you could have judged me.'

'Judged you how?'

'As a fantasist, with a story intended to suck you in and control you.'

'Fuck Teddy. Where has all this come from? Why would I think that? Are you feeding me a story here? That you made it all up to get me?'

She continues to stare into my eyes and the happiness has gone. She looks frightened, as if I'm suddenly dangerous. There are still people all around us, browsing the bargains; wondering which street food is best; sharing this ideal.

And then her face softens again. It's me that breaks the silence.

'I've never been more scared than I was on Friday morning. And I've never been more certain that what you did, all that you did from the moment I called you until just now when you pulled me to a halt in the here and now; you did all that out of love.'

Victoria's face registers something I can't describe. The smile looks good, and the grin that follows is perfect. And her eyes are sparkling. And the hand she raises to brush back my hair is soft and tender. And the way her mouth has dropped open, like there's never been a surprise like this in her whole life, is the most endearing and captivating thing I've ever seen. There's no noise around us, no rushing haggling stream of consumerism. The stares that lock us together are unbroken.

'You said something to me once; you said *please make me happy*. I've never asked why you said that.'

Her blinks break the bond and push a tear to one side. She seems unable to speak but recovers.

'When did I say that?'

'The night you stayed at my place, after we got back from Dent. You fell asleep, cuddled up to me watching the telly. I picked you up to carry you to bed. And you said *please, please make me happy.*'

Now she's crying properly. Her eyes just fill up and overflow, then send rivulets down her face. The mass of life now has little segments looking in on us. Maybe I'm causing the tears and should be stopped. Maybe intercession has to happen. But Victoria's sudden joyousness, a smile like a thousand suns and a controlled, exasperated sigh, then an unrestrained laugh divert any concerns. Bargains for the masses are back on the menu.

'I think we need a drink.'

'I think you're right.'

'Walk with me.'

And she leads me to the best pub I've ever been in and we ignore the food and the cocktails and all that jazz. We stand in the middle of the bar, clink our pints together and say *I Love You.*

33

Victoria wakes me up, straddled on my stomach with her face up close to mine.

'It's six am Mr C and my train from Euston is too soon. Make me something to eat? Eggs? Toast? Coffee.'

'That's a wrap. I'm on it.'

But she won't let me out of this grip she has, physical and ocular. 'I don't want to go, and I don't want you to go. What if I go home and you go to Bucharest and we never see each other again?'

'We will see each other when you get here on Friday evening.'

I've learned that Victoria squints to express a question and/or to calibrate her understanding. Then she stops squinting.

'Make love to me. It can be quick. In fact, it has to be quick, so just do it.'

I don't get a choice and it can't be prefaced with foreplay. But it's all we will have until Friday.

Breakfast is as ordered. She comes to the table with wet hair and a towel wrapped under her armpits and devours it quickly.

She's rushing but still manages to look perfect in jeans, a top and a jacket.

'No sad goodbyes Teddy. No prolonged unbearable leaving. Kiss me then call me constantly between now and forever.'

Our tears have all flown. Now there are just smiles and a perfect exchange of hands and lips and looks. Thirty minutes later, she calls me from her taxi.

'Get your arse down the gym.'

'I'm just on my way.'

'Pat on head. I'll call when I'm home.'

'Be safe.'

'We will.'

When I set out to Camden Town tube with my trolley case, I know Victoria is home and she still loves me. In spite of a deep foreboding as she arrived there, she's been to my place and found nothing troublesome. She also met Amber briefly and they exchanged numbers just in case.

I need to get to Heathrow, and I feel jolts of fear. The streets are low on pedestrians but crazy with traffic. I should have caught a taxi and for a moment I stand on the roadside watching them zipping in straight lines across my path like black worker ants.

The underground is tolerable except at Kings Cross where that madness never stops. But then I'm on the blue line to Heathrow and I rest my bum on the end-of-carriage cushions where I can see whatever happens at every stop and start. When I have a signal, I message Victoria with small snippets of love and get no reply until, 'Teddy, I need to work sweetheart. Let's talk once you're sorted at the airport ok?'

It makes me smile that she called me sweetheart. In writing.

As I get to the terminal and start scanning the screens for my flight, I overhear people discussing the news that a snap election has been called. I grind to a halt and open the news apps I've been ignoring on my phone.

For nearly a week, perhaps longer, it's all meant nothing: headlines; current affairs; cut and thrust; other news. I'm staring at my phone trying to get my head back in gear. It doesn't compute. While these fools play their power games, I'm part of a plot to move jobs offshore. The rest will be automated.

As I crawl through check-in and security, I can't shake the sense that we are in the throes of a plummeting political free-fall. I feel suddenly marginalised: failed by my party; failed by company and colleagues; imprisoned by the knowledge that jobs and people and ideas will continue to flood from this country. To keep the money flooding in.

And the biggest and ultimate failure is me.

When I land at Bucharest's airport, it's late, dark and quiet. I don't want to be here. Victoria and I talk for ages once I'm in my hotel room.

'Were you all right on the underground and in the airport?'

'I did what you said: walked slowly; kept my head up; waited for queues to die down before getting processed.'

'Did anything really make you worry about being followed or threatened?'

'No. There was nothing to indicate either. Apart from the decision to call this election. I can't believe they've done it.'

'I need to check something with you about what happened last week. We should have discussed this, but anyway: have you told anyone else about being in Romania? Aside from me, Beth and Joe and your boss?'

'No. Nobody.'

'Why?'

'I'm here under cover. So far as colleagues are concerned, I'm working at home in Lancaster.'

'Then I feel I can relax.'

'What do you mean?'

'If the only people outside of work who know you're in another country are me and your kids, then you'll be safe while you're there.' She seems relieved. There is confidence in her words.

'Unless I'm being tracked.'

'Oh god Teddy. Please don't say that.'

We finish the call after nearly an hour, at least half of which is taken up with a review of what happened to me, and how we should stop being paranoid about it. Within a few minutes,

Victoria contacts me by Vidicall. 'I wanted to see your face. And your smile.'

'Both are here. And all yours.'

She pouts and looks away.

'Let's try not to be worried. It won't solve anything.'

'You're right.'

We smile across the airwaves.

'Call me in the morning Teddy. How far are you ahead? An hour?'

'It's two hours. So, it might be very early.'

'I'll stay in bed to greet you with something special.'

The twin essentials of family and work reset my head for the rest of the week. My need to spend time in the virtual arms of Victoria also drives that reset. I have long, adoring discussions with her in between the entangled strands of building a new team in a foreign place. Meanwhile, Beth and Joe sit above it all, dropping their wisdom and humour into the brew. When I finish the week's final briefing at eleven am that Friday, all I can think of is getting home. It doesn't matter that I have no home and that everything I might want to call home is in tatters. I just need to be there.

Before I board the plane, I send a last message to Victoria: 'Flight leaving on time. In to LHR about 1745. Back to Camden by... seven...? eight...?'

The plane is half empty. The various trolley excursions take no time at all and a kind of peace settles in for the second half of the journey. The descent into London is bumpy but not alarming and when I get online there are numerous messages from work about a successful first week of planning and team building. Annabel and above are pleased, but everyone is making warning sounds about this being confidential. Annabel has left me a detached-sounding voice message telling me to take down time on Monday morning. She also tells me she's set up a short meeting for Monday afternoon to review next week's Bucharest activities.

Joe and Beth have left messages hoping I'm home safe and Victoria has left a more troubling *Call Me X.*

'Hey honey. Good trip?'

'Hi. It was trouble free in every sense. What's up?'

'I can't get down to London this evening. These two short weeks have played havoc with my workload and I need to stay productive until late today.'

A shiver grips me. I'm walking away from baggage reclaim towards customs.

'When will you be here?'

'I'll be into Euston eight fifteen.'

I relax somewhat. I'm sure I'll cope for one night, and I tell her not to fret.

'That's a load off my mind. Thank you.'

'I'll meet you at Euston if you like. We can have breakfast somewhere?'

'No. Have a lie in. I'll join you there for four days' worth of cuddles.'

'I'll be into the underground soon. Better go.'

'And I need to get on. Love you. Be safe. Keep alert.'

'Love you too.'

I'm back at the apartment just after eight fifteen and lock myself in.

And so it goes. This first weekend is another in which I attune myself to being on loan in London. Victoria and I do happy couple things at home, in shops, at a restaurant. We map out what weekends will look like up to the end of May and agree that at some point I need to be in Lancaster. We have a long discussion about the Arnside attack and I increasingly agree that it was a warning; a massively over-stated warning; but nothing more. I tell her the memory of what happened still troubles me, and I had one sleepless night in Bucharest because of it.

Victoria says I need to avoid any kind of routine and be mindful about strangers accosting me or seeing the same faces in the same places. But, as we sit sipping tea that Sunday morning, the easy thing to focus on is that it's nine days since I was left for dead. But I'm alive.

She leaves early on the Monday morning and we've barely slept. Watching her go hurts like hell and I send her a long message telling her I find it impossible to cope for ages after she leaves. Her reply is a single huge heart.

I go to the gym at nine and open my laptop just after eleven, and the whole pattern resumes; except this week I'll fly and return at different times on different days. I've replaced Lancaster with London and London with Bucharest; otherwise work is still me doing and delivering my best.

The following weekend is a long one, thanks to the early May Bank-Holiday. During Friday, I call Dave and tell him Victoria and I are in town for a few days and without hesitation he suggests we meet for a late lunch on the Saturday afternoon. It's a wonderful few hours in and around Covent Garden. London is heaving with visitors drawn by the warm spring sunshine and an extra day for frolics, but it doesn't spoil our fun. We explain that I'm in London more or less full time for a few weeks - we don't say why - so Ella extends an invitation to join them in Wimbledon for dinner during the next long weekend.

Back in Camden it seems even busier as Victoria and I seek some space to enjoy a few intimate drinks. When we eventually stumble happily home, just around midnight, my phone announces a call from Joe. He wants to come and stay with us. After arriving back in Leicester ahead of the coming term, he's bored and wants to share food somewhere new. Victoria nods a smiling approval and mouths *With Lulu?* But Joe says it's just him.

We all meet at St Pancras, go sightseeing and eat sushi. When we get back to the apartment, Victoria goes out running so Joe and I sit chatting over beers on the terrace. He asks me if I'm living permanently in London now and I almost tell him that I've run and hidden. But I sense an underlying agenda, and it turns out he's thinking of staying on in Leicester for the summer and getting a job. Lulu's family lives nearby, in Oakham, and Joe says he wants to spend as much time as he can with her. So, I tell him that my work schedule means I'll be in London more than Lancaster until at least the end of May. Weekends will be with Victoria, but she needs to be back at base during the week. However, none of that changes whatever he might want to do. When I ask if he's spoken to his mum about it, he says he's told her and she seemed not to mind. He's got a job lined up and a place to stay and when I suggest that all he's doing is asking me to endorse the inevitable, he bursts out laughing and says that's all I've ever done. We have another amazing curry and Joe actually does pay - but I send him the money by internet banking. He leaves early the next morning.

Victoria and I spend May Day afternoon lounging in the sun before she jumps on the last train to Lancaster. As she leaves, she asks me to consider returning there next weekend. When I start to discuss it and create details, she puts a finger up to my lips and shushes me. It's something to consider and decide.

In the days after the bank holiday, it's formally announced that the UK Project Management team has been disbanded and its members have left the business. They are wished well and thanked for their contribution. Shortly, Peter Dixon sends a second mail to confirm details of the new Project Management organisation which, after a thorough selection process, I will lead. He proceeds with a lengthy eulogy about my abilities and how much I've done for the company. Then he offers his assurances that the new structure will deliver massive improvements in both the quality and quantity of project management outputs.

While I'm in Bucharest, I get a mail from Annabel with details of my new post. There are two attachments, and I learn that I've really been promoted: a small pay rise; a bigger, better bonus scheme; all the travel goodies I was granted during my pretend promotion a few months back are now permanently mine. The second attachment contains an award: commendation for the work I did in leading the team while she was away doing new things. The document reveals I have a series of vouchers I can spend at a variety of places; they have a total value of £1,500. Annabel signs off this message with *I'm really sorry it can't be more. You're a real asset and I value all you do.*

With a wry expression on my face, I look at those words. After all the troubles I felt about her and what she saw in me, I realise our bond is stronger than ever. She isn't remote, as I feared. Annabel is reliable. Her word can be trusted – it always could - and this citation feels like we've renewed our vows.

I nearly threw it all away.

I call Victoria and tell her I agree it's time for me to check on my property and reduce her overheads travelling to London. She tells me that wasn't her point but finesses the notion with news that she's proposing we should meet up with her family for

Sunday lunch. I get the company travel provider to find a way for me to fly back to Manchester instead of London but there's nothing direct that Friday. Victoria tells me to stay in Camden on the Friday and catch the first train out of London the following morning.

She meets me at Lancaster station and my car is parked outside. We drive to my apartment and I reacquaint myself with the odds and ends of a life that someone may have tried to end. She's making something in the kitchen, and when I join her our small embrace turns in to a concentrated, unstoppable fuck and ruined muffins.

We play squash late in the afternoon and Victoria wins best of five, but I win a sixth game and call it a draw. Then we drive back to her place where she finishes some work and I make dinner.

Sunday lunch means a drive out to Milnthorpe and a meeting with Victoria's family. A last-minute crisis with their children means that Elizabeth travels alone and arrives late. It also means there's a hiatus at the Cross Keys hotel, in which I am interrogated by Mrs Wright while Victoria's father chuckles benignly at my discomfort. It's a relief when Elizabeth arrives and makes a huge fuss of me. The meal ends up being great fun and, for Victoria and her father, quite drunken.

So, I revert to a discarded schedule, working from home on a Monday then catching the early train to London on Tuesday morning. Victoria checks in with me often during my time alone at the house and visits me for lunch, bearing salads and fruit.

I call Luke and Arif but get voicemail and no return call.

Early in the evening we have another squash match and this time I win 3-0. It's the first time I've beaten her, and Victoria is a very bad loser. But not for long because there is too little time for us to be sore about anything. We have a simple meal and quite complicated sex. Then sleep and another red eye to London.

When I arrive at Euston I take an unaccustomed direction, change at Leicester Square and jostle myself and my case to a place where I can pass the time along to Heathrow. I'm still watching and waiting, but no threat surfaces on the Piccadilly Line. Nor in the concourse at Heathrow's Terminal 5 where there are so many armed militia it's mandatory to feel safe.

There's hardly any time to wait but I message Beth asking if she's too busy to meet up next weekend. It's very close to finals and we agreed on Joe's birthday that she might need space to just get through all that is needed. She hasn't replied by the time I board and, when I switch off my phone, the message remains unread.

Her reply is the first item that greets me when I land in Bucharest. She tells me she needs all the time she can get but why don't we catch up in Bath next Saturday. The break will be welcome, and she'd love to see me and Victoria if that works. I check this with my partner; my partner Victoria; and my partner confirms that of course it works.

The week drags by, but we've recruited all the right people and I've spent hours with the team leaders working through how we will operate once the team is able to function at full speed. We agree to operate a buddy system in which the existing local team will mentor and guide the newcomers. Everyone loves this idea and, when I leave for the airport that Friday, it feels like all this upheaval is actually worth it.

Victoria is already at the apartment when I get there and the place smells of a divine meal to come. We've an early start, so we don't drink alcohol. There's a starry sky, so we eat kedgeree on the roof and talk way past a sensible time. But we make it to Paddington for the earliest Bath train.

Beth looks tired, strained, worried. Finals are close, a matter of days away. She hugs me like she used to as a child: unconditional yet needy. We head to a café, and once we start talking it's clear she is well prepared and knows what she needs to do: she's in a good place. It's also clear that Victoria and I are intruding on her time. We cut short any notion of lunch and tell Beth to get back to work. We will have plenty of time together in less than three weeks. I tell her I'll book time off work and she can join me in London, or Lancaster, or anywhere for a well-earned rest.

Victoria and I meander around Bath until early evening, have dinner, then head back to London and twenty-four hours together. Love, in all its forms, has become what we are. Our lazy Sunday, coffee and pastries at a nearby café then lunch at the pub and an afternoon on loungers, staring at the sky and planning the coming week, is the very essence of what we are together. We have an early night, with sleep if we need it.

As dawn breaks, Victoria offers the enticement of more to come when we are reunited next week, then heads to Euston and Lancaster. An hour after she leaves, I'm in my gym kit and ready for my Monday workout. It's a pleasant morning.

Here I am then, walking the streets of London. And I've fallen in love, but that's not a changing scene. It's not with buildings or industry; not with transport or traffic; not with a cavalcade of unattainable women. Just with one. One of them made herself attainable. And thanks to her, I probably am at the centre of things in this overwhelming capital; the mother of all cities.

Yes. Here I am, easily concealed in this setting. Hiding; unsought. Ready or not.

The gym isn't far, and I'm set for a big session. Victoria has got me hooked into the idea that I need to keep fit and be healthy. So, this Monday morning, I'm also in love with being close to a place where I can work out while I can still smell Victoria's aura on my skin and hair.

There are a lot of sirens. That's not rare but whatever has happened must be bad, because the sirens are so many that their two tones are merged in to a single two-note chord. And then there's some screams nearby and the noise of an engine being revved hard. I'm still walking. More screams, nearer now, and I turn around to see why.

There's a big van - one of those ones that is really too big to be a van and should be called a truck - bouncing on and off the pavement. Every one of its lurches off the street is accompanied by screams, and the sight of people being cannoned into gardens, walls or each other, like pins in a bowling alley. There are people running in all directions, and very loud sirens now.

The van is back on the road again and accelerating; escaping. But as I watch all this, it veers left and keeps accelerating straight at where I'm rooted to the spot. And as it hurtles across the kerb and paving stones, what I see through the windscreen simply doesn't make sense.

I hear a voice shouting something about armed police.

Breaking

May 5th 2017
Midlands TV News

'Staffordshire police continue to investigate the murder of Kathryn Tasker and are eager to interview this man - Christopher Jarvis – in connection with her death. Mrs Tasker, wife of Lichfield entrepreneur Jeff Tasker, was found dead near Tamworth last week with serious head injuries. Mr Jarvis, unemployed, was last seen on May 3rd at Manchester Piccadilly station.

The region is preparing today for a royal visit...'

May 10th 2017
North West Tonight – TV News

'In the last few minutes, Cumbria police have made a statement that the badly burned body found on the shore of the River Kent estuary near Arnside is Christopher Jarvis, from Lichfield in Staffordshire. Mr Jarvis had been sought by Staffordshire police in connection with a murder enquiry. We will bring you more about this news later in the programme.'

May 15th 2017
London TV - Morning News Bulletin

'The death toll in today's terror attack in Camden has reached nineteen. At least twice that number have been admitted to hospital, some with life-threatening injuries. No group has yet claimed responsibility for the attack but before returning to a COBRA meeting earlier this morning, the Prime Minister stated nothing has been ruled out at this time.

Reports emerged of a vehicle being driven at pedestrians just after seven forty-five. The driver appears to have taken a route from Holloway, down the A503 then into some residential streets near Camden Square. The worst of the carnage was on Murray Street, affecting local residents heading towards central Camden and its stations.

The driver of the Mercedes van, as yet unidentified, was shot dead by police marksmen. A second attacker escaped. Police are investigating some eyewitness reports that the second perpetrator was a Caucasian male, armed with a handgun.

More from the scene after sports reports..."

Scottish Border News, Evening Edition

'And in other news, the A7 near Langholm has re-opened this morning following the multi-vehicle, multi-fatality accident early this afternoon. A BMW X6 driven by Mrs Judith McNish from Lancaster, England, veered out of control on the approach to the single-carriage bridge north of the town, ploughing into a queue of cars waiting at the red light. Mrs McNish was among the fatalities, as were two as yet un-named occupants of a car driving in the opposite direction towards Hawick. Mrs McNish's family has expressed profound shock at the news, and her father-in-law Hugh McNish made this brief statement to Border News earlier this morning. *'We are all devastated by Jude's death. She knew that road well. At a time when we are still coming to terms with the death of our son Lewis, this is another terrible piece of bad news in such a short space of time.'* Meanwhile, traffic police are seeking any witnesses who can corroborate statements that, on several occasions, Mrs McNish's car was weaving dangerously across the A7's carriageway.'

Exitlude

Sent: May 18th, 2017

Subject: Ed Clayton

From: James, Annabel

To: All UK OS; All EMEA ProjMan

CC: Farmer, Kate; Dixon, Peter; Niesmann, Josh; White, Pat; Lal, Kalvinder

It is with intense sadness, personal as well as professional, that I write these words.

Our wonderful friend and colleague Ed Clayton was killed during Monday's attack in London. The evidence is that he died instantly and without pain. But that is a small mercy and his passing leaves a gaping hole in our lives, both as employees and as people.

My thoughts are with his children, Beth and Joe; I cannot begin to imagine how this affects them. They were a source of endless joy for Ed. I will make arrangements soon to send an expression of condolence, from us all, to them.

Ed joined us in 1996 from the Met Office and worked in the surveying team based out of our Fulwood site. When he joined Project Management in 2010, it was quickly clear we had gained a major talent: and so it proved. Ed was a formidable asset and all of us that worked with him learned from, and grown because of, his way of working. I had come to rely on his judgement, experience, ability to see solutions and unerring loyalty. But also on his humour, generosity, kindness and confidence.

This afternoon at 4pm UK time we will have a minute's silence in his honour.

As you read this you may be feeling (as I feel writing it) that this news is unbearable. Don't hesitate to take some time away from work today if you feel overwhelmed; and don't hesitate to call me if you need someone to talk to about Ed. We need to share whatever we feel.

Late last year Ed delivered one of his peerless presentations about how we can all work smarter and better together. He put up a slide with a quotation from Nietzsche: 'They muddy the water to make it seem deep.'

And he told us there are three choices when our path is blocked by muddy water: wait for it to clear; move upstream and find a safe place to cross; or jump in and hope. He said the best teams, working together, pick the right option to move on; but a team isn't united if it leaves someone to jump in alone, with nothing more than hope.

In his honour, we will continue to be the best kind of team, making the right choices together. It is what Ed would be doing.

Annabel

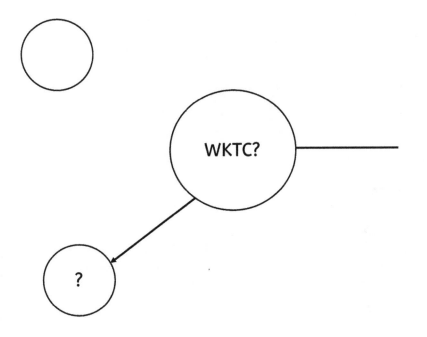

About the Author

Nigel Stewart was born in Corbridge, Northumberland, in 1959 and lives in Kirkham, Lancashire. The Lines Between Lies is his second novel. His first, Colouring In, was published in August 2019. A third novel, as yet untitled, is almost complete.